RAWHIDE AND LAC...

When Erin Scott left Tyson... Ranch, she vowed she'd never return. But now ... needed her back—without her, jobs would be lost. Erin cared deeply for the devoted staff of the ranch, but could she face the man she most hated—the man with a heart of stone and a will as tough as rawhide?

UNLIKELY LOVER...

Mari Raymond's matchmaking aunt had pulled a fast one. She'd tricked oilman Ward Jessup into inviting her young niece to his ranch—and persuaded Mari to accept the invitation and help the *elderly* rancher write his memoirs. But quickly they discovered that Ward was anything but old and sickly... and Mari was hardly a helpless little girl. Though they knew they had been tricked, could either of them fight the power of Cupid's arrow?

DIANA PALMER

COLLECTION

RAWHIDE & LACE

UNLIKELY LOVER

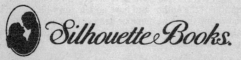

Silhouette Books.

Published by Silhouette Books New York

America's Publisher of Contemporary Romance

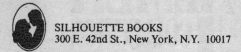

SILHOUETTE BOOKS
300 E. 42nd St., New York, N.Y. 10017

DIANA PALMER COLLECTION

Copyright © 1992 Harlequin Enterprises B.V.

RAWHIDE AND LACE
Copyright © 1986 by Diana Palmer
First published as a Silhouette Desire

UNLIKELY LOVER
Copyright © 1986 by Diana Palmer
First published as a Silhouette Romance

ISBN: 0-373-48242-6

First Silhouette Books printing August 1992

Printed in the U.S.A.

CONTENTS

Dear Readers,

I am so glad to see this reissue of two of my favorite books, *Rawhide and Lace* and its sequel, *Unlikely Lover.*

Back when I wrote *Rawhide and Lace,* I had planned to make it a very long book and go into great detail about the tragedy in Erin's life and Ty's harsh childhood. Though it wound up a bit shorter than I'd first envisioned, I am very pleased with the way it turned out, because these are two of my favorite characters. I only wish I could have made it longer; it was hard to say goodbye to it.

Unlikely Lover, on the other hand, was a joy to produce. I had been fascinated with Ward Jessup ever since he turned up, very unexpectedly I might add, in *Rawhide and Lace.* He sounded like just the kind of scoundrel who needed a good woman to save him from himself. By the end of the book, I was delighted with him. And to this day, every time I think of water, I think of Ward Jessup landing in it!

I hope you enjoy reading these as much as I enjoyed writing them. I am privileged to do a job I love for people who have to be the kindest, most loyal people on earth. I mean you, of course, my readers.

You have kept me going through bad times and sad times. You have made a difference in my life and in my faith in humanity. I hope that all of you know how much I appreciate you, and how dear you are to me. God bless you all, and may life grant you as much happiness and kindness as it has given me because of you.

Love,

Diana Palmer

RAWHIDE AND LACE

Chapter One

The hospital emergency room was full of people, but the tall man never saw the crying children and listless adults who covered the waiting area. He was disheveled, because he'd dragged on jeans and the first shirt that had come to hand and hadn't taken time to shave or even comb his thick, straight black hair.

He stopped at the clerk's desk, his expression enough to get her immediate attention. He looked rough and not in the mood for red tape—his face cold and hard, and very nearly homely.

"Yes, sir?" she asked politely.

"The sheriff's office said my brother was brought here. His name is Bruce Wade," he said, with barely controlled impatience, his voice deep and cutting, his silver eyes piercing and level.

"He was taken to surgery," the clerk said after a minute. "Dr. Lawson admitted him. Just a moment, please."

She picked up the phone, pressed a button and mumbled something.

Tyson Wade paced the small corridor restlessly, his shepherd's coat making him look even taller than he was, the creamy softness of his Stetson a direct contrast to a face that looked like leather and sharp rock. Things had been so normal just minutes before. He'd been working on the books, thinking about selling off some culls from among his purebred Santa Gertrudis breeding herd, when the phone had rung. And all of a sudden, his life had changed. Bruce had to be all right. Ty had waited too long to make peace with the younger brother he hardly knew, but surely there was still time. There had to be time!

A green-uniformed man walked into the waiting area, removing his mask and cap as he walked toward the taller man.

"Mr. Wade?" he asked politely.

Ty moved forward quickly. "How's my brother?" he asked brusquely.

The doctor started to speak. Then he turned, drawing Ty down the white corridor and into a small unoccupied examination room.

"I'm sorry," the doctor said then, gently. "There was too much internal damage. We lost him."

Ty didn't flinch. He'd had years of practice at hiding pain, at keeping his deeper feelings under control. A man who looked like he did couldn't afford the luxury of letting them show. He just stood there, unmoving, studying the doctor's round face while he tried to cope with the knowledge that he'd never see his brother again; that he was totally alone now. He had no one. "Was it quick?" he asked finally.

The doctor nodded. "He was unconscious when he was admitted. He never came out of it."

"There was another car involved," Ty said, almost as an afterthought. "Was anyone else badly hurt?"

Dr. Lawson smiled with faint irony. "No. The other car was one of those old gas-guzzlers. It was hardly dented. Your brother was driving a small sports car, a convertible. When it rolled, he didn't have a chance."

Ty had tried to talk Bruce out of that car, but to no avail. Any kind of advice was unwelcome if it came from big brother. That was one of the by-products of their parents' divorce. Bruce had been raised by their mother, Ty by their father. And the difference in the upbringings was striking, even to outsiders.

The doctor had paused long enough to produce Bruce's personal effects. The soiled clothing was there, along with a handful of change, some keys, and a clip of hundred-dollar bills. Ty looked at them blankly before stuffing them back into the sack.

"What a hell of a waste," Ty said quietly. "He was twenty-eight."

"I'm sorry we couldn't save him," Dr. Lawson repeated softly, sincerely.

Ty nodded, lost in bitter memories and regret. "He couldn't even save himself. Fast cars, fast women, alcohol... They said he wasn't legally drunk." His silver-gray eyes met and held the doctor's in a level gaze.

Dr. Lawson nodded.

"He usually drank far too much," Ty said, staring at the sack. "I tried so damned hard to talk him out of that convertible." He sighed heavily. "I talked until I was blue."

"If you're a religious man, Mr. Wade, I can tell you that I still believe in acts of God. This was one."

Ty searched the other man's eyes. After a minute, he nodded. "Thanks."

It was misting rain outside, cold for Texas in November, but he hardly felt it. All that rushing around, he thought blankly, and for what? To get there too late. All his life, where Bruce was concerned, he'd been too late.

It seemed so unreal to think of Bruce as dead. He and Bruce had been a lot alike in looks, at least. Both were dark and light-eyed, except that Bruce's eyes had been more blue than gray. He'd been six years younger than Ty and shorter, more adventurous, more petted. Bruce had been spoiled with easy living and an abundance of attention from their mother. Ty had been raised by their rancher father, a cold, practical, no-nonsense man who looked upon women as a weakness and brought Ty up to feel the same way. Ironically, it was Erin who'd finally separated Bruce from Ty and the ranch.

Erin. His eyes closed briefly as he pictured her, laughing, running to him, her hair long and black and straight, her elfin face bright with joy, her green eyes twinkling, laughing, as her full, soft lips smiled up at him. He groaned.

He leaned his tall, elegant body against the Lincoln as he lit a cigarette. The flare of the match accentuated his high cheekbones, his aquiline nose, the jut of his chin. There was nothing in his face that a woman would find attractive, and he knew it. He had no illusions about his looks. Perhaps that was why he'd attacked Erin on sight, he reflected. She'd been a model when Bruce met her in nearby San Antonio and brought her home for a weekend visit. Young but already well-known, Erin was destined for greater things. That first day, she'd walked into the Wade house with her elfin face excited and friendly, and Ty had stood like stone in the long hallway and glared at her until the vividness of her expression had faded into uncertainty and, then, disappointment.

She'd been so beautiful. A living illusion. All his secret dreams of perfection rolled into one flawless, willowy body and exquisitely sculpted face. Then Bruce had put his arm around her and looked at her with unashamed worship, and Ty had felt himself growing cold inside. She'd been Bruce's from the very beginning, a prize he'd brought home to big brother, to fling in his arrogant face.

He took a long draw from the cigarette and stared at its amber tip in the misting rain. How long ago it all seemed! But all of it had taken place in just a year's time. The first meeting, the long weekends when Erin came to the ranch and slept in the guest room in order to observe "the proprieties." Conchita, the house-keeper, had taken to Erin immediately, fussing and bustling over her like a mother hen. And Erin had loved it. Her father was dead, her mother constantly flying off to somewhere in Europe. In many ways, Ty thought, her life had been as unloving and cold as his own.

He took another draw from his cigarette and blew out a thick cloud of smoke, his silvery eyes narrowing with memory as he stared sightlessly at the deserted parking lot. He'd antagonized Erin from the start, picking at her, deliberately making her as uncomfort-able as possible. She'd taken that smoldering dislike at face value until one dark, cold night when Bruce had been called out on urgent business. Erin and Ty had been alone in the house, and he'd antagonized her one time too many.

He vividly remembered the look in her green eyes when, after she'd slapped him, he'd jerked her into his hard arms and kissed the breath out of her. Her lips had been like red berries, soft and slightly swollen, her eyes wide and soft and dazed. And to his astonishment, instead of slapping him again, she'd reached up to him, her mouth ardent and sweet, her body clinging like ivy to the strength of his.

It had been like a dream sequence. Her mouth, dark, soft wine under his hard lips; her body, welcoming. Soft cushions on the floor in front of the fireplace, her hushed, ragged breathing as he'd bared her breasts and touched them, her shocked cry as he'd touched her intimately and begun to undress her. But she hadn't stopped him; she hadn't even tried. He remembered her voice in his ear, whispering endearments, her hands tenderly caressing his nape as he'd moved her under him.

He ground his teeth together. He hadn't known, hadn't guessed, that she was a virgin. He'd never forget the tormented sound of her voice, the wide-eyed fear that had met his puzzled downward glance. He'd tried to stop, so shocked that he wasn't even thinking...but she'd held him. No, she'd whispered, it was too late to stop now, the damage was already done. And he'd gone on. He'd been so careful then, so careful not to hurt her any more than he already had. But he'd given her no pleasure. He knew, even though she'd tried not to let him see her disappointment. And before he could try again, could even begin to show her any real tenderness, they'd heard Bruce's car coming up the long driveway. Then, with reality, had come all the doubts, all the hidden fears. And he'd laughed, taunting her with her easy surrender. Get out, he'd said coldly, or Bruce was going to get an earful. He'd watched her dragging her clothing around her, white-faced, shaking. He'd watched her leave the room with tears streaming from her eyes. Like a nightmare, the pain had only gotten worse. But he'd had too much pride to back down, to apologize, to explain what he'd felt and why he'd lied to her about his motives. And early the next morning, she'd left.

Bruce had hated him for that. He'd guessed what had happened, and he'd followed Erin to wring the truth from her. A day later he'd moved out, to live with a friend in San Antonio. Erin had gone on to a career in New York; her face had haunted him from the covers of slick magazines for several weeks.

That night haunted him, too. It had been all of heaven to have her. And then, all at once, he'd realized that she might see his lack of control for what it was; that she might realize he was vulnerable with her and take advantage of it. God forgive him, he'd even thought she might have planned it that way. And she was so beautiful; too beautiful to care about an ugly man, a man so inexperienced at making love. His father's lectures returned with a vengeance, and he'd convinced himself in a space of seconds that he'd been had. She was Bruce's, not his. He could never have her. So it was just as well that he'd let her go out of his life. . . .

Bruce had gotten even, just before he'd left the house for good. He'd told Ty that Erin had hated what Ty had done to her, that his "fumbling attempts at lovemaking" had sickened her. Then he'd walked out triumphantly, leaving Ty so sick and humiliated that he'd finished off a bottle of tequila and spent two days in a stupor.

Erin had come back to the ranch two months later, and it had been Ty she'd wanted to talk to, not Bruce. He'd been coming out of the stables leading a brood mare, and she'd driven up in a little sports car, much like the one Bruce would die in almost six months later....

"I have to talk to you," she said in her soft, clear voice. Her eyes were soft, too; full of secrets.

"What do we have to talk about?" Ty replied, his own tone uncompromising, careless.

"If you'll just listen..." she said, looking at him with an odd kind of pleading in her green eyes.

Against his will, he was drawn to her as she poised there in a green print dress that clung lovingly to every soft line of her high-breasted body, the wind whipping her long black hair around her like a shawl. He forced himself to speak coldly, mockingly.

"Aren't you a vision, baby doll?" His eyes traveled pointedly over her body. "How many men have you had since you left here?"

She flinched. "No...no one," she faltered, as if she hadn't expected the attack. "There hasn't been anyone except you."

He threw back his head and laughed, his eyes as cold as silver in a face like stone. "That's a good one. Just don't set your sights on Bruce," he warned softly. "Maybe my plan backfired, but I can still stop him from marrying you. I don't want someone like you in my family. My God, you've got a mother who makes a professional streetwalker look like a virgin, and your father was little more than a con man who died in prison! It'd make me sick to have to introduce you into our circle of friends."

Her face paled, her eyes lost their softness. "I can't help what my people were," she said quietly. "But you've got to listen to me! That night..."

"What about it?" he demanded, his voice faintly bored. "I'd planned to seduce you and then tell Bruce, but you left without forcing my hand. So, no harm done." To avoid looking at her, he bent his head to light a cigarette. Then he glanced up, his eyes narrowed and ugly. "You were just a one-night stand, honey. And one night was enough."

That brought her to tears, and he felt a pain like a knife going into his gut despite the fact that he was justified in that lie. She'd told it all to Bruce, hadn't she? "What a sacrifice it must have been for you," she whispered in anguish. "I must have been a terrible disappointment."

"I'll amen that," he told her. "You were a total failure, weren't you? Why did you come down here, anyway? Bruce doesn't come here anymore, and don't pretend you don't know it."

"I'm not looking for Bruce," she burst out. "Oh, Ty, I haven't seen him since I left here! It's you I came to see. There's something I've got to tell you...!"

"I've got livestock to look after," he said indifferently, dismissing her. "Get out of here. Go model a gown or something."

Her eyes grew dull then; something died in them. She looked at him for a long, quiet moment, almost said something else; then, as if defeated, turned away.

"Just a minute," he called after her.

She'd turned, an expression of hope on her face. "Yes?"

He smiled down at her mockingly, forcing himself not to weaken, not to let her get the best of him. "If you came to see me because you wanted another roll in the hay, I'll let the cattle wait for a few minutes," he offered. "Maybe you've improved since the last time."

Her eyes closed, her face contorted as if in pain. "How could you, Tyson?" she whispered, then opened her eyes to reveal an anguish so profound that Ty was forced to look away. But the agony in her voice pierced his soul. "How could you? Oh, God, you don't know how much I...!"

Almost. He almost abandoned his lacerated pride and went to her. His feet even started to move. But suddenly, she whirled and ran to her car, gunned it to life and raced frantically down the long drive, sending the small convertible sliding on the gravel as she shot it out onto the paved road. He watched the car until it was out of sight, feeling empty and cold and lonely....

That was the last time he'd seen Erin Scott. And now Bruce was dead. He wondered if she'd still been seeing his brother. Bruce hadn't mentioned her. Of course, he'd hardly spoken to Ty in all those months. That had hurt, too. Lately, just about everything did.

He crushed out the cigarette. There were funeral arrangements to make. He thought about the roommate Bruce had moved in with and wondered if he knew. He got into the car and went directly to the apartment. It might help to talk to someone who knew Bruce, who could tell him if Bruce had ever forgiven him for driving Erin away. It was very nearly a need for absolution, but Tyson Wade would never have admitted it. Not even to himself.

Chapter Two

Bruce's roommate was a rather shy accountant, a nice man without complexities and as pleasant as Bruce had always been. He was drinking heavily when Ty entered the apartment.

"I'm so sorry," Sam Harris said with genuine feeling, raking back his sandy-blond hair. "I heard it on television just a few minutes ago. God, I'm so sorry. He was a great guy."

"Yes," Ty said quietly. He stuck his hands in his pockets and looked around the small apartment. There was nothing to indicate that Bruce had ever lived there except a large photograph of Erin in a swimsuit pose beside one of the twin beds. Ty felt himself stiffening at the sight of it.

"Poor old guy," Sam said wearily, sinking down onto the sofa with a shot glass in his hands. "He worshiped that girl, but she never even let him get close." He nodded toward the bed. "There's a whole box of letters she sent back last week under there."

Ty's heart froze. "Letters?"

"Sure." Sam pulled them out. There were dozens, all from Bruce, all addressed to Erin. All unopened. And there was one letter, from her, to Bruce. It was very recent. And opened.

"He went crazy when he read that last one," Sam told him. "Just hog wild. I never had the nerve to sneak a look at it. And he changed after that. Raged about you, Mr. Wade," he added apologetically. "He changed his will, made all kinds of threats.... I almost called you, but I figured it really wasn't any of my business. And you know how Bruce got when he thought someone had sold him out. He was my pal, after all."

Ty stared at the letters in his hand, feeling sick all over.

"There are some things of his in the drawers, too." Sam gestured aimlessly, then sat down again. "I keep looking for him, you know," he murmured absently. "I keep thinking, any minute he'll open the door and walk in."

"If you'll pack his things, when you get a chance," Ty said quietly, "I'll send for them."

"Sure, I'll be glad to. I'd like to come to the funeral," he added.

Ty nodded. "You can serve as a pallbearer if you like," he said. "It'll be at the First Presbyterian Church, day after tomorrow. There aren't any living relatives, except me."

"God, I'm sorry," Sam repeated hollowly.

Ty hesitated, then shrugged his broad shoulders. "So am I. Good night."

Just like that. He walked out, clutching the box of letters in his hands, more apprehensive than he'd ever been in his life. Part of him was afraid of what might be in them.

Two hours later, he was sitting in his pine-paneled den at Staghorn with a half-empty bottle of whiskey in one hand and a much used glass in the other. His eyes were cold and bitter, and he was numb with the pain of discovery.

The letters Bruce had written to Erin were full of unrequited love, brimming with passion and proposals of marriage and plans that all included her. Each was more ardent than the one before. And in every one was at least one sentence about Ty and how much he hated her.

Those were bad enough. But the letter Erin had sent to Bruce tore at his heart.

"Dearest Bruce," she'd written in a fine, delicate, hand, "I am returning all your letters, in hopes that they will make you realize that I can't give you what you want from me. You're a fine man, and any woman would be lucky to marry you. But I can't love you, Bruce. I never have, and I never can. Even if things were different between us, any sort of relationship would be impossible because of your brother." His heart leaped and then froze as he read on: "Even though the fault was partially mine, I can't forget or forgive what's happened to me. I've been through two surgeries now, one to put a steel rod in my crushed pelvis, the other to remove it. I walk with a cane, and I'm scarred. Perhaps the emotional scars are even worse, since I lost the baby in the wreck, too...."

The baby! Ty's eyes closed and his body shook with anguish. He couldn't finish the letter. She'd left Staghorn hell-bent for leather, and she'd wrecked the car. Her pelvis had been crushed. She'd lost the baby she was carrying, she'd been hospitalized, she'd even lost her career. All because of him. Because Bruce had told him a lie, and he'd believed it. And now Bruce was dead, and Erin was crippled and bitter, hating him. Blaming him. And he blamed himself, too. He hurt as he'd never hurt in his life.

And now he knew why she'd come to see him. She'd been carrying his child. She was going to tell him. But he hadn't let her. He'd humiliated her into leaving. And because of him, she'd lost everything.

The baby would haunt him all his life, he knew. He'd never had anyone of his own, anything to love or protect or take care of. Except Bruce. And Bruce had been too old for that kind of babying. Ty had wanted someone to spoil, someone to give things to and look after. And he'd tried to make Bruce into the child he himself would never have. But there had been a child. And obviously Erin had planned to keep it. His child. He remembered now, too late, the hopeful look in her eyes, the softness of her expression when she'd said, "I have something to tell you. . . ."

His hand opened, letting the letter drop to the floor. He poured out another measure of whiskey and downed some of it quickly, feeling a tightness in his chest that would not, he knew, be eased by liquor.

He stared helplessly at the whiskey bottle for a long time. Then he got slowly to his feet, still staring at it, his face contorted with grief and rage. And he flung it at the fireplace with the full strength of his long, muscular arm, watched as it shattered against the bricks, watched the flames hit the alcohol and shoot up into the blackened chimney.

"Erin," he whispered brokenly. "Oh, God, Erin, forgive me!"

The sudden opening of the door startled him. He didn't turn, mindful of the glaze over his eyes, the fixed rigidity of his face.

"Yes?" he demanded coldly.

"Señor Ty, are you all right?" Conchita asked gently.

His shoulders shifted. "Yes."

"Can I bring you something to eat?"

He shook his head. "Tell José I need five pallbearers," he said. "Bruce's roommate asked to be one already."

"*Si, señor.* You have talked with the minister?"

"I did that when I came home."

"Are you sure that I cannot bring you something?" the middle-aged Spanish woman asked softly.

"Absolution," he said, his voice ghostly, haunted. "Only that."

It was three days before Ty began to surface from his emotional torment. The funeral was held in the cold rain, with only the men and Bruce's roommate to mourn him. Ty had thought about contacting Erin, but if she'd just been released from the hospital, she wouldn't be in any condition to come to a funeral. He wanted to call her, to talk with her. But he didn't want to hurt her anymore. His voice would bring back too many memories, open too many wounds. She'd never believe how much he regretted what he'd done. She probably wouldn't even listen. So what was the use of upsetting her?

He went into town after the funeral to see Ed Johnson, the family's attorney. With the strain between himself and his brother, Ty expected that Bruce had tried to keep him from inheriting his share of Staghorn—an assumption that proved to be all too true.

Ed was pushing fifty and balding, with a warm personality and a keen wit. He rose as Ty entered his office and held out his hand.

"I saw you at the funeral," he said solemnly, "but I didn't want to intrude. I figured you'd be in to see me."

Ty took off his cream-colored Stetson and sat down, crossing his long legs. He looked elegant in his blue pinstriped suit, every inch the cattle king. His silver eyes pinned the attorney as he waited silently for the older man to speak.

"Bruce has changed his will three times in the past year," Ed began. "Once, he tried to borrow money on the estate for some get-rich-quick scheme. He was so changeable. And after last week, I feared for his sanity."

Last week. Just after he'd received Erin's letter. Poor boy, Ty thought. He closed his eyes and sighed. "He cut me out of his will, obviously," he said matter-of-factly.

"Got it in one," Ed replied. "He left everything he had to a woman with a New York address. I think it's that model he was dating a few months back," he mumbled, missing Ty's shocked expression. "Yes, here it is. Miss Erin Scott. His entire holdings. With the provision," he added, lifting his eyes to Ty's white face, "that she come and live on the ranch. If she doesn't meet that condition, every penny of his holdings goes to Ward Jessup."

Ward Jessup! Ty's breath caught in his throat. He and Ward Jessup were long-standing enemies. Jessup's ranch, which adjoined Staghorn, was littered with oil rigs, and the man made no secret of the fact that he wanted to extend his oil search to the portion of Staghorn closest to his land. Although Ty had been adamant about not selling, Jessup had made several attempts to persuade Bruce to sell to him. And now, if Erin refused to come, he'd have his way—he'd have half of Staghorn. What a priceless piece of revenge, Ty thought absently. Because Bruce knew how much Erin hated Ty—that she'd rather die than share a roof with Tyson Wade—he'd made sure big brother would never inherit.

"That's the end of it, I guess," Ty said gently.

"I don't understand." Ed stared at him over his glasses.

"Bruce had a letter from her last week," the younger man said, his voice level, quiet. "She was in a wreck some time ago. She's been crippled, and she lost the child she was carrying. I'm responsible."

"Was it Bruce's child?"

Ty met the curious stare levelly. "No. It was mine."

Ed cleared his throat. "Oh. I'm sorry."

"Not half as sorry as I am," he said, and got up. "Thanks for your time, Ed."

"Wait a minute," the attorney said. "You aren't just giving up half your ranch, for God's sake? Not after you've worked most of your life to build it into what it is?''

Ty stared at him. "Erin hates me. I can't imagine that she'd be charitable enough to want to help me, not after the way I've treated her. She has more reason than Bruce to want revenge. And I don't have much heart for a fight, not even to save Staghorn. One way or another, it's been a hell of a week." He jammed his Stetson down over his hair, his eyes lifeless. "If she wants to cut my throat, I'm going to let her. My God, that's the least I owe her!"

Ed watched him leave, frowning. That didn't sound like the Tyson Wade he knew. Something had changed him, perhaps losing his brother. The old Ty would have fought with his last breath to save the homestead. Ed shook his head and picked up the phone.

"Jennie, get me Erin Scott in New York," he told his secretary, and gave her the number. Seconds later a pleasant, ladylike voice came on the line.

"Yes?"

"Miss Scott?" he asked.

"I'm Erin Scott."

"I'm Edward Johnson in Ravine, Texas ... the attorney for the Wade family," he clarified.

"I haven't asked for restitution—"

"It's about a totally different matter, Miss Scott," he interrupted. "You knew my client, Bruce Wade?"

There was a long pause. "Bruce ... has something happened to him?"

"He was in an automobile accident three days ago, Miss Scott. I'm sorry to have to tell you that it was fatal."

"Oh." She sighed. "Oh. I'm very sorry, Mr. . . . ?"

"Johnson. Ed Johnson. I'm calling to inform you that he named you his beneficiary."

"Beneficiary?"

She sounded stunned. He supposed she was. "Miss Scott, you inherit a substantial amount of cash in the bequest, as well as part ownership of the Staghorn ranch."

"I can't believe he did that," she murmured. "I can't believe it! What about his brother?"

"I don't quite understand the situation, I admit, but the will is ironclad. You inherit. With a small proviso, that is," he added reluctantly.

"What proviso?"

"That you live on the ranch."

"Never!" she spat.

So Ty was right. He leaned back in his chair. "I expected that reaction," he told her. "But you'd better hear the rest of it. . . . Miss Scott?"

"I'm still here." Her voice was shaking.

"If you don't meet that provision," he said, his voice steady, even a little impatient, "your half of the ranch will go to Ward Jessup."

There was a long silence. "That's Ty's . . . Mr. Wade's . . . neighbor," she recalled.

"That's right. And, I might add, something of an adversary. He only wants the oil rights to Staghorn, you know. He'd sell off the stock. The ranch couldn't survive with what would be left. There are several families whose sole support is Staghorn—a blacksmith, several cowhands, a veterinarian, a storekeeper, a mechanic—"

"I... know how big the place is," Erin said quietly. "Some of those people have worked for the Wades for three generations."

"That's correct." He was amazed that she knew so much about Staghorn.

"I need time to think," she said after a pause. "I've just come out of the hospital, Mr. Johnson. It's very difficult for me to walk at all. A trip of that kind would be extremely hard on me."

"Mr. Wade has a private plane," he reminded her.

"I don't know..."

"The terms of the will are very explicit," he said. "And they require immediate action. I'm sorry. I need an answer today."

There was another long pause. "Tell Mr. Wade... I'll come."

Ed had to force himself not to grin.

"There's just one thing," she said hesitantly. "How long must I stay there?"

"No particular length of time was specified," he told her. "That leaves it to the interpretation of the people involved. And believe me, Mr. Jessup will interpret it to mean until you die.''

"I've heard that he's quite ruthless." She sighed. "I guess I'll cross that bridge when I come to it. I can be ready tomorrow afternoon, Mr. Johnson."

She sounded tired, and in pain. He felt guilty for pressing her, but he knew it couldn't have waited.

"I'll pass that information along. Meanwhile, Miss Scott, I'll get the necessary paperwork done. You're quite a wealthy young woman now."

"Quite wealthy," she repeated dully, and hung up.

She was sitting on a sofa that swayed almost to the floor, in a ground-floor apartment in Queens. The water was mostly cold, the heating worked only occasionally. She was wrapped in a thick old coat to keep warm, and no one who'd known her six months ago would recognize her.

Why had she agreed to go? she wondered miserably. She was in pain already, and all she'd done today was go back and forth to the bathroom. Her leg was giving her hell. They'd showed her the exercises, stressing that she must do them twice a day, religiously, or she'd never lose her limp. A limping model was not exactly employable, she reminded herself. But there seemed so little point in it all now. She'd lost everything. She had no future to look forward to, nothing to live for. Nothing except revenge. And even that left a bad taste in her mouth.

She couldn't see those people out of work, she thought. Not in winter, which November practically was. She couldn't stand by and leave them homeless and jobless because of her.

She stretched out her leg, grimacing as the muscles protested. Exercises indeed! It was hard enough to walk, let alone do lifts and such. Her eyes were drawn to the window. Outside, it was raining. She wondered if it was raining in Ravine, Texas, and what Tyson Wade was doing right now. Would he be cursing her for all he was worth? Probably. He'd been sure that she'd never set foot on Staghorn again, after the things he'd said to her. He wouldn't know about the accident, of course, or the baby. She felt her eyes go cold. If only she could hurt him as badly as he'd hurt her. If only!

She could stay here, of course. She could change her mind, refuse the conditions of the inheritance. Sure. And she could fly, too. All those people, some of them with children, all out in the cold....

She lay back down on the sofa and closed her eyes. There would be time enough to worry about it later. Now, she only wanted to sleep and forget.

Ty. She was running toward him, her arms outstretched, and he was laughing, waiting for her. He lifted her up against him and kissed her with aching tenderness. He stared down at her, his eyes filled with love. She was pregnant, very pregnant, and he was touching the mound of her belly, his hands possessive, his eyes adoring. . . .

She awoke with tears in her eyes. Always it was the same dream, with the same ending. Always she woke crying. She got up and washed her face, looking at the clock. Bedtime already. She'd slept for hours. She pulled on a cotton gown and went to bed, taking a sleeping pill before she lay down. Perhaps this time, she wouldn't dream.

By early the next afternoon, she was packed and waiting for whomever Tyson sent to get her. Her once elegant suitcase was sitting by the door, filled with her meager wardrobe. She was wearing a simple beige knit suit that would have fit her six months ago. Now it hung on her, making her look almost skeletal. Her lusterless hair was tied in a bun, her face devoid of makeup. In her right hand was a heavy cane, dangling beside the leg that still refused to support her.

At two o'clock precisely, there came a knock on the door. "Come in," she called from the sofa, only vaguely curious about which poor soul Ty would have sacrificed to come and fly her down to Texas.

She got the shock of her life when the door opened to admit Tyson Wade himself.

He stopped dead in the doorway and stared at her as she got unsteadily to her feet, leaning heavily on the cane. The impact of his handiwork was damning.

He remembered a laughing young girl. Here was an old, tired woman with green eyes that held no life at all, no gaiety... only a resigned kind of pain. She was pitifully thin, and her face was pale and drawn. She stared at him as if he were a stranger, and perhaps he was. Perhaps he always had been, because he'd never really let her get close enough to know him in any way but one.

"Hello, Erin," he said quietly.

She inclined her head. "Hello, Tyson," she said.

He looked around him with obvious distaste, his silver eyes reflecting his feelings about her surroundings.

"I haven't been able to work for several months," she informed him. "I've been drawing a disability pension and eating thanks to food stamps."

His eyes closed briefly; when they opened, they were vaguely haunted. "You won't have to live on food stamps now," he said, his voice rough.

"Obviously not, according to your family attorney." She smiled faintly. "I imagined you screaming at the top of your lungs for an hour, trying to find a way to break the will."

He studied her wan, sad little face. "Are you ready to go?" he asked.

She shrugged. "Lead on. You'll have to allow for my leg. I don't move so quickly these days."

He watched her come toward him, every movement careful and obviously painful.

"Oh, my God," he said tightly.

Her eyes flared at him. "Don't pity me," she hissed. "Don't you dare!"

His chin lifted as he took a long, slow breath. "How bad is it?" he asked.

She stopped just in front of him. "I'll make it," she said coldly.

He only nodded. He turned to open the door, holding it as she brushed against him. She smelled of roses, and as he caught the scent in his nostrils, he struggled to suppress memories that were scarcely bearable.

"Erin," he said huskily as she went past him.

But she didn't answer him, she didn't look at him. She moved painfully down the hall and out the open door to the street. She didn't even look back.

After a minute, he picked up her suitcase, locked the door, and followed her.

Chapter Three

It was all Ty could do to keep silent as he and Erin rode to the airport. There were so many things he wanted to say to her, to explain, to discuss. He wanted to apologize, but that was impossible for him. Odd, he thought, how much heartache pride had caused him over the years. He'd never learned to bend. His father had taught him that a man never could, and still call himself a man.

He lit a cigarette and smoked it silently, only half aware of Erin's quiet scrutiny as he weaved easily through the frantic city traffic. His nerve never wavered. Texas or New York, he was at home in a car even in the roughest traffic.

"Nothing bothers you, does it?" she asked carelessly.

"Don't you believe it," he replied. He glanced at her, his eyes steady and curious as he waited at a traffic light.

"Six months," she murmured, her voice as devoid of feeling as the green eyes that seemed to look right through him. "So much can happen in just six months."

Ty averted his eyes. "Yes." He studied the traffic light intently. It was easier than seeing that closed, unfeeling look on her face, and knowing that he was responsible for it. Once, she'd have run toward him laughing....

She turned the cane in her hands, feeling its coolness. Ty seemed different somehow. Less arrogant, less callous. Perhaps his brother's death had caused that change, although he and Bruce had never been close. She wondered if he blamed her for his estrangement from Bruce, if he knew how insanely jealous Bruce had been of her, and without any cause at all.

He watched her toying with the cane as he pulled back into the flow of traffic and crossed the bridge that would take them to the airport. "How long will you have to use that thing?" he asked conversationally.

"I don't know." She did know. They'd told her. If she didn't do the exercises religiously, she'd be using it for the rest of her life. But what did that matter now? She could never go back to modeling. And nothing else seemed to be worth the effort.

"I didn't expect you to agree to the stipulation in Bruce's will," he said suddenly.

"No, I don't imagine you did." She glared at him. "What's the matter, cattle baron, did you expect that I'd sit on my pride and let your whole crew lose their jobs on my account?"

So that was why. It had nothing to do with any remaining feeling for him; it was to help someone less fortunate. He should have known.

"You look surprised," she observed.

"Not really." He pulled into the rental car lot at the airport and stopped the car, then turned toward her. "You were always generous—" his silver eyes held hers relentlessly "—in every way."

Her face colored, and she jerked her eyes away. She couldn't bear to remember... that!

"It wasn't an insult," he said quickly. "Don't... don't make it personal."

She laughed through stinging tears, a young animal at bay, glaring at him from the corner of her seat. "Personal! Don't make it personal? Look at me, damn you!" she cried.

His hand reached toward her, or seemed to, and suddenly retracted, along with any show of emotion that might have softened the hard lines of his face. He stared at his smoking cigarette, took a last draw with damnably steady fingers, and put it out carefully in the ashtray.

"I've been looking," he said quietly, lifting his eyes. "Every second since I've been with you. Would you like to know what I see?"

"How about a burned-out shell; does that cover it?" she said defiantly.

"You've given up, haven't you?" he said. "You've stopped living, you've stopped working, you've stopped caring."

"I have a right!"

"You have every right," he agreed shortly. "I'd be the first to agree with that. But for God's sake, woman, look what you're doing to yourself! Do you want to end up a cripple?"

"I *am* a cripple!"

"Only in your mind," he replied, his voice deliberately sharp. "You've convinced yourself that your life is over; that you can come down to Staghorn and draw into some kind of shell and just exist while everyone else prospers. But you're wrong, lady. Because that's something you'll never do. I'm going to make you start living again. You're going to pick up the pieces and start over. I'll see to it."

"Like hell you will, Tyson Almighty Wade!"

"If you come back with me, you can count on it," he replied. He put a long hard arm over the back of the seat, and his silver eyes glittered at her, challenging, taunting. "Come on, Erin. Tell me to take my money and go to hell. Tell me to give Ward Jessup your half of the spread and put all those workers on unemployment.''

She wanted to. Oh, how she wanted to! But it was more than her conscience could bear. She glared at him out of a white face in its frame of soft dark hair, her green eyes alive now, burning in anger. "I hate you!" she cried.

"I know," he replied. His eyes narrowed. "I don't blame you for that. You have the right. I'd never have asked you to come back."

"No, not you." She smiled coldly. "But if I hadn't, you'd probably have come rushing up here to kidnap me and take me back by force."

He shook his head. "Not now. Not after what's happened." He let his eyes wander slowly over her frail body.

She eyed him warily. "Mr. Johnson told you about the wreck, I suppose?"

He looked down at the cane. "I read your last letter to Bruce," he said in a voice that was deep and quiet . . . and frankly haunted.

Her spirit broke at his tone. She could take anything from him except tenderness. Guilt. His. Hers. Bruce's. And none of it any use. A tortured sob burst from her throat. She tried to stifle it but couldn't.

His eyes lifted, holding hers. "I wish I could tell you how I felt when I knew," he said hesitantly. "The things I said to you that day . . .''

She swallowed, slowly gaining control of herself. "You . . . you meant them," she replied. "Reliving them isn't going to do any good now. You saved Bruce from me. That's all you cared about."

"No!" he said huskily. "No, that's wrong."

He started to reach toward her, and she backed away until the door stopped her.

"Don't you touch me," she said in a high, strangled voice. "Don't you ever touch me again. If you do, I'll walk out the door, and you and your outfit can all go to hell!"

His face closed up. It was the first time he'd ever reached out toward her, and her rejection hurt. But he struggled against familiar feelings of wounded pride, struggled to understand things from her side. He'd hurt her brutally. It was going to take time, a lot of it, before she'd begin to trust him. Well, he had time. Right now, that and the hope that she might someday stop hating him were all he had.

"Okay," he said, his voice steady, almost tender. "Want something to eat before we get on the plane?"

She shifted restlessly, staring at him, eyes huge in her thin face. "I . . . didn't have lunch," she faltered.

"We'll get a sandwich, then." He got out and went around to open her door. But he didn't offer to help her. He watched her put the cane down and lean on it heavily. "How long has it been since they took out the rod?" he asked.

Her eyes widened. She hadn't realized he knew so much about her condition. "A couple of weeks," she told him.

"Were you taking physical therapy?"

She avoided his probing look. "I could use some coffee."

"Therapy," he persisted, "is the only way you'll ever walk without a cane. Did they tell you that?"

"You've got a lot of nerve...!" She glared up at him.

"I busted my hip on the rodeo circuit when I was twenty-four," he told her flatly. "It was months before I stopped limping, and physical therapy was the only thing that saved me from a stiff leg. I remember the exercises to this day, and how they're done, and how long for each day. So I'll help you get into the routine."

"I'll help you into the hospital if you try it," she threatened.

"Spunky," he approved, nodding. He even smiled a little. "You always were. I liked that about you, from the very beginning."

"You liked nothing about me," she reminded him. "You hated me on sight, and from there it was all downhill."

"Are you sure?" he asked, watching her curiously. "I thought women had instincts about men and their reactions."

"As you found out the hard way, I knew very little about men. Then."

He didn't look away. "And as you found out, the hard way, I knew very little about women."

She flinched, just a little, then searched that gray fog in his eyes, wondering what he meant. It sounded like a confession of sorts, but it just didn't jibe with the picture Bruce had painted of him—a womanizer with a reputation as long as her arm.

"Pull the other one," she said finally. "You've probably forgotten more about women than I'll ever know. Bruce said you had."

His jaw tensed. "Bruce said one hell of a lot, didn't he? I heard what you thought of my 'fumbling,' too."

She stiffened and froze. "What?"

"He said you thought I was a clumsy, fumbling fool. That you described it all to him, and laughed together about it...."

Her lips parted, and her face went stark white. "He told you... he said that... to you?"

"Erin!" He leaped forward just in time to catch her as she collapsed. He lifted her, feeling the pitiful weight of her in his arms, feeling alive for the first time in months. He held her close, bending his head over hers, drowning in the bittersweet anguish of holding her while all around them traffic moved routinely and tourists milled indifferently on the sidewalks.

"Baby," he whispered softly, cradling her in his hard arms as he dropped into the passenger seat of the car and looked down at her. He smoothed the hair from her face, caressing her pale cheek with a trembling hand. "Erin."

Her eyes opened a minute later. She blinked, and for an instant—for one staggering second—her eyes were unguarded and full of memories. And then it was like watching a curtain come down. The instant she recognized him, all the life went out of her face.

"You fainted," he said gently.

She stared up at him dizzily, feeling his warmth and strength, catching the scent of leather that clung to him like the spicy after-shave he favored.

"Ty," she whispered.

His heart stopped and then raced, and his body made a sudden and shocking statement about its immediate needs. He shifted her quickly, careful not to let her know how vulnerable he was.

"Are you all right?" he asked.

She leaned her forehead against his shoulder. "I feel a little shaky, that's all."

He touched her hair, on fire with the sweetness of her being near, loving the smell of roses that clung to her, the warmth of her soft body against his.

"Bruce didn't say that to you—" she shook her head "—he couldn't have!" There were tears in her eyes.

"I shouldn't have said anything," he mumbled. "I didn't mean to. Here, are you all right now?"

She sighed heavily. It was a lie. A lie. She'd never said any such thing to Bruce. She looked up into watchful gray eyes and tried to speak, but she was lost in the sudden electricity that arced between them.

"Your eyes always reminded me of green velvet," he said absently, searching them. "Soft and rippling in the light, full of hidden softness and warmth."

Her breath was trapped somewhere, and she couldn't seem to free it. Her eyes wandered over his homely face, seeing the new lines, the angles and craggy roughness, the strength.

"You won't find beauty even if you look hard," he said in a tone that was almost but not quite amused.

"You were so different from Bruce," she whispered. "Always so different. Remote and alone and invulnerable."

"Except for one long night," he agreed, watching the color return to her cheeks. "Will you at least believe that I regret what I did to you? That if I could take it all back, I would?"

"Looking back won't change anything," she said wearily, and closed her eyes. "Oh, Ty, it won't change anything at all."

"I'm sorry...about the baby we made," he said hesitantly, his voice husky with emotion.

She looked up at him, startled by his tone. She saw something there, something elusive. "You would have wanted it," she said with sudden insight.

He nodded. "If I'd known, I'd never have let you go."

It was the way he said it, with such aching feeling. She realized that he meant it. Perhaps he'd wanted a family of his own, perhaps there had been a woman he'd wanted and couldn't have. Maybe he'd thought about having children of his own and taking care of them. He wasn't anything to look at; that was a fact. But he might have been vulnerable once. He might have been capable of love and tenderness and warmth. A hundred years ago, judging by the walls he'd raised around himself.

She looked away and struggled to get up. He let her go instantly, helping her to her feet, steadying her with hands that were unexpectedly gentle. Guilt, she thought, glancing at him. He was capable of that, at least. But guilt was one thing she didn't want from him. Or pity.

"I'm all right now," she said, easing away from him. The closeness of his body had affected her in ways she didn't want to remember. She'd given herself to him that night with such eager abandon. With joy. Because she'd loved him desperately, and she'd thought that he loved her. But it had only been a lie, a trick. Could she ever forget that?

"It's all right," he said gently, oblivious to the curious stares of passersby, who found it oddly evocative to see the thin, crippled young woman being comforted by the tall, strong man.

"I'm so tired," she whispered wearily. "So tired."

He could see that. Thinking about all she'd been through made him feel curiously protective. He touched her hair in a hesitant gesture. "You'll be all right," he said quietly. "I'll take care of you. I'll take care of everything now." He straightened. "Come on. Let's go home."

It wasn't home, but she was too exhausted to struggle with him. She only wanted a place to rest and a little peace. So much had happened to her that she felt like a victim of delayed shock. She couldn't cope just yet with the memories or the future. She wanted to close her eyes and forget that either even existed.

Ty took her arm to lead her toward the tarmac, and she followed him without protest.

That simple action hit him so hard that his face would have shocked her, had she been able to see it. Erin had always been a fighter, a little firecracker. He'd admired her spirit even as he'd searched for ways to beat it out of her. And now, to see her this way, to know that she was defeated . . . was profoundly disturbing. She'd been crippled, had lost the baby he'd given her, and he knew that she could never forgive him. He wondered if he could forgive himself. He only knew that he was going to see to it that she left Staghorn whole again, no matter what it took. He was going to give her life back to her, regardless of the cost. He was going to make her well enough to walk away from him.

And he hadn't realized until that moment that it was going to hurt like hell.

The plane was a big twin-engine Cessna, a pretty bird built for comfort and speed. There was more than enough room for Erin to sit or stretch out in the passenger space, but she wanted to see where she was going.

"Could I sit up front with you?" she asked.

It was the first bit of enthusiasm she'd shown since he'd found her at the apartment. "Of course," he replied. He ushered her into the seat beside his and helped her with the seat belt and the earphones.

She watched, fascinated, as he readied the big plane for takeoff and called the tower for permission to taxi. She'd never flown in his private plane before, although Bruce had invited her once. Ty had objected at the time, finding some reason why she couldn't go with them. He'd never wanted her along. He'd never wanted her near him at all.

He flew with a minimum of conversation, intent on the controls and instrument readings. He asked her once if she was comfortable enough, and that was the only thing he said all the way back to Staghorn.

The ranch was just as Erin remembered it—big and sprawling and like a small town unto itself. The house was a creamy yellow Spanish stucco with a red roof, graceful arches and cacti landscaping all around it. Nearby were the ultramodern stables and corrals and

an embryo transplant center second to none in the
area. Ty's genius for keeping up with new techniques,
his willingness to entertain new methods of produc-
tion, were responsible for the ranch's amazing climb
from a small holding to an empire. It wasn't really
surprising that he was so good with figures, though.
He was geared to business, to making money. He was
good at it because it was his life. He enjoyed the challenge of business in ways he'd never been able to enjoy anything else. Especially personal relationships.

Erin was fascinated by how little the ranch had
changed since she'd seen it last. In her world, people
came and went. But in Ty's there was consistency. Se-
curity. At Staghorn, very little changed. The house-
hold staff, of course, was the same. Conchita and her
husband, José, were still looking after the *señor*,
keeping everything in exquisite order both inside and
out. They were middle-aged, and their parents had
worked for *el grande señor*, Ty's father, Norman.

Conchita was tall and elegant, very thin, with snap-
ping dark eyes that held the most mischievous twin-
kle despite the gray that salted her thick black hair.
José was just her height, with the same elegant darkness, but his hair had already gone silver. Rumor had
it that Señor Norman himself had turned it silver with
his temper. José was unfailingly good-natured, and
such a good hand with horses that Ty frequently let
him work with the horse wrangler.

The house had two stories, but it was on the ground floor that Erin's room was located. Only two doors away from Ty's. That was vaguely disquieting, but Erin was sure that he'd only put her on the ground floor because of her hip.

"If you need anything, there's a pull rope by the bed." Ty showed it to her. "Conchita will hear you, night or day. Or I will."

She sat down gingerly in a wing chair by the lacy curtains of the window and closed her eyes with a sigh. "Thank you."

He didn't leave. He perched himself on the spotless white coverlet of the bed and stared at her for a long moment.

"You're not well," he said at last.

"You try going through two major surgeries in six months and see how well you are," she returned without opening her eyes.

"I want you to see my family doctor. Let him prescribe some exercises for that hip."

Her eyes opened, accusing. "Now look here. It's my hip, and my life, and I'll decide—"

"Not while you're on Staghorn, you won't." He stood up. "Your color isn't good. I want you seen to."

"I'm not your responsibility...."

Arguing did no good. He simply ignored whatever she said. "I'll make an appointment for you," he said, studying her. "Maybe he can give you some vitamins, too. You're awfully damned thin."

"Ty..."

"Lie down and rest for a while. I'll have Conchita make you some hot chocolate. That should warm you up and put you to sleep as well. The thermostat's over here, if it gets too cold for you." He indicated the dial on the wall near the door.

"Will you stop ordering me around!" she burst out, exasperated.

He studied her face, seeing the sudden color in it, the missing vitality. "That's better." He nodded. "Now you look halfway human again."

Her eyes sparked at him. "I don't know why I came here!"

"Sure you do. You've saving my people from bankruptcy." He opened the door. "Ring if you want anything."

"I want..." She lowered her voice. "I'd like to go and see Bruce's grave."

His face didn't change, but it seemed almost to soften. "I'll take you out there later. When you've had time to rest."

She studied his face, musing that nothing ever showed on that hard countenance. If he had emotions, they were deeply hidden.

"Do you miss him?" she asked curiously.

He turned. "I'll have José bring your suitcase in later."

He closed the door behind him. Yes, he thought bitterly as he moved off down the hall. He missed his brother. But he missed what he'd lost even more: he missed the life he could have had with Erin. Christmas was only a month away, and he was tormented by images of how he might have been celebrating it if Bruce hadn't poisoned his mind. It seemed such a short time ago that Erin had come running toward him, laughing, her black hair like silk around an elfin face. And he'd melted inside just at the sight of her, gone breathless like a boy with his first real date. It still felt like that, despite her scars, her limp. In his heart, he carried a portrait of her that would withstand all the long, aging years, that would leave her young and unscarred for as long as he lived. Erin. How beautiful life might have been, if only...

He made a rough sound in his throat and went quickly out the front door.

Bruce was buried in a quiet country cemetery just ten minutes' drive from Staghorn. Erin stood over his grave while Ty sat in his big Lincoln smoking a cigarette and watching her.

It was sad, Erin thought, the way Bruce had ended his life. He'd never seemed reckless. At least not until he'd started dating her. Once she'd realized that he was expecting more than she could give, she'd eased away from him. She hadn't known how competitive he was with Ty, or that he'd only been using her as a tool of revenge against the elder brother who dominated him. She'd been his crowning glory, his mark of achievement. Look, he'd said without words, showing her proudly to Ty, look what a beauty I brought home. And she's all mine.

She smiled wistfully. She'd been blissfully unaware of the fact that Ty's father and mother had separated years ago and that each had taken one of the boys. Norman Wade had raised Ty, without the weakness of love to make him vulnerable. Ty's mother had raised Bruce, making sure that he was protected from life. The outcome in both cases had been predictable—but not to the parents.

She glanced at the other graves in the plot where Bruce was buried. His parents were there. Norman and Camilla Harding Wade. Side by side in death, as they'd been unable to remain in life. Oddly enough, despite all their differences, they'd shared a deep and lasting love. Neither of them had ever dated after their separation. And it was the last request of each that they be buried together. Erin felt tears burn her eyes as she stared at the single tombstone that marked both their graves. Love like that had to be a rare thing. She wondered why it had all gone wrong for them.

Ty, sensing the questions, got leisurely out of the car and came toward her. He was back in his familiar denims, with high leather boots and the beaten-up tan Stetson he'd worn ever since she'd known him.

"Why couldn't they live together?" she asked him, curious.

He shrugged. "He was a cold man, she was a hot woman," he said succinctly. "That says everything."

She flushed as the meaning penetrated, and averted her eyes.

"What brought that on?" he murmured, and actually started to smile. "I only meant he never showed his feelings, and she wore hers on her sleeve. I don't know how they were in bed. I never asked."

The blush deepened. "Will you stop that?" she muttered.

"And I thought I was old-fashioned," he said. He took a draw from his cigarette and sighed heavily as he stared at the three graves. "I'm the last one, now," he mused. "Funny, I thought Bruce would outlive me by twenty years. He was the one who loved life."

"And you don't?" she asked, lifting her eyes.

"You work yourself to death trying to make a living, and then you die. In between, you worry about floods, droughts, taxes and capital outlay. That's about it."

"I've never known a man more cynical than you," she told him. "Not even in New York."

"I'm a realist," he corrected. "I don't expect miracles."

"Maybe that's why none ever happen for you," she said. She leaned on the cane a little and stared down at Bruce's grave. "Bruce was a dreamer. He was always looking for surprises, for the unexpected. He was a happy man most of the time, except when he re-

membered that he was always going to be second best.
You're a hard act to follow. He never felt that he could
measure up to you. He said that even your mother
talked about you more than she did about him."

He raised an eyebrow. "I didn't know that. She
seemed to hold me in contempt most of the time. We
never understood each other."

Her quiet eyes searched his face, the hard lines
around his mouth. The iron man, she mused. "I don't
think anyone will ever understand you," she said quietly. "You give nothing of yourself."

His jaw tautened and his pale eyes kindled through
the cloud of smoke that left his pursed lips. "Now
that's an interesting statement, coming from you."

It was the emphasis he put on it. She saw with sudden clarity a picture of herself lying in his arms by the
firelight, moaning as he touched her breasts. . . .

"I didn't mean . . . that kind of giving," she said
uneasily, and dropped her eyes to his broad chest. It
strained against the denim, rippling muscles and thick
dark hair that covered him from his collarbone down.

He took another draw from the cigarette. "You said
before that you never had anything going with Bruce.
Was that true?"

"Yes," she said simply. She searched his pale eyes.
"I'm sorry there were hard feelings between you because of me. I didn't volunteer anything, you know,
but he asked a lot of questions, and I was pretty upset. I don't even remember what I said to him. But I

didn't tell him about... what happened. He guessed. Maybe I looked like a fallen woman or something." She laughed bitterly.

"You aren't a fallen woman," he said. "I came up on your blind side, that's all. I should have realized when you didn't put up a fight that you were too naive to know what was happening. You thought I'd stop in time."

She shook her head. "I trusted you, it's true. But you didn't rape me. It was never that."

He sighed heavily and reached out a tentative hand to brush at the loose hair around her collar, pushing it away from her throat, from the scar on her cheek. She shivered a little at letting him see.

"Was it very painful?" he asked tenderly.

Her lips trembled as she formed words, and around them the wind blew cold and the sun gave barely any warmth, and death was in the trees as well as the graveyard.

"Yes," she whispered. She turned away, trying not to let the feelings overwhelm her a second time. All she seemed to do lately was cry. Impatiently, she brushed away her tears.

Ty shifted awkwardly. He wasn't used to women crying. He wasn't used to women, period. He didn't know how to handle this situation.

She straightened. "I'm embarrassing you," she murmured.

He'd forgotten how honest she was; she never pulled her punches. Just like himself. His broad shoulders rose and fell. "I'm not used to women," he told her.

She searched his eyes. "Why did Bruce tell me you were a womanizer?"

"Don't you know?" he asked quietly.

"You weren't, though, were you?" she persisted.

He reached for another cigarette and lit it. "What a hell of a question," he said shortly.

"Never mind, don't answer me; I don't care," she shot back. She moved away from the grave, putting more weight on the cane than was necessary in her anger and frustration. "I ought to go back to New York and let Ward Jessup move in with you!"

"We'd never get on," he said imperturbably, falling into step beside her. "He's a nonsmoker."

She didn't believe she'd actually heard him right. Dry humor—from Tyson Wade? She kept walking. "Bruce had moved out, hadn't he?"

"Bruce is dead," he said shortly, stopping to stare down at her. "What he did or didn't do, or said or didn't say, has nothing more to do with either of us."

"I'm sorry he's gone."

"So am I. But all the mourning in the world won't bring him back." He stared back at the grave, and for an instant there was a deep, dark hurt in his eyes. Then he erased it and turned a bland face back to Erin. "Right now, you're my top priority. I'm going to get you back on your feet again."

"I won't let you take over my life," she told him.

"Sure you will," he replied drily. "You're nothing but a little walking rain cloud right now. You don't have enough spunk to fight me."

"Want to bet?" she said angrily.

"I don't gamble. Look out, you'll break that cane if you aren't careful."

"Then you'd just have to carry me home, wouldn't you?" she taunted. All the same, she lightened up on the cane. "How long do I have to stay here?"

"Until you turn sixty-five, if I know Jessup." He sighed. He glanced at her as they walked. "Put a little more weight on that leg, honey, you need to exercise it."

"Listen, cowboy...!" she snapped.

"I'm not a boy," he said.

"Will you listen to me?"

"Sure. When you say something I want to hear. Get in. I've got work to do. Winter isn't quite as hectic as the rest of the year, but I keep busy. I hope you like reading. You'll die of boredom without something to keep your mind occupied."

"I can watch television," she muttered as he helped her into the car and got in beside her.

"I don't own a television," he told her.

Her jaw fell open.

"I don't like television," he persisted, starting the car.

"What do you do in the evenings?" she asked.

"I read."

She rested her head against the seat. What a wonderful time she was going to have. In between pain pills and being forced to exercise her leg, she could sit and watch him read books. It looked as if Staghorn was going to be a great rest camp—the next best place to hell. Oh, Bruce! she thought miserably, mourning quietly for her old friend, why did you have to die and leave me in this awful mess?

Chapter Four

Erin had vowed that she wouldn't go to the doctor, but Ty simply put her in the car and drove her there. To make matters worse, he raised eyebrows in the crowded waiting room by insisting on going in with her to talk to the doctor.

Her face flushed wildly as they followed the nurse down the hall.

"This will be all over town in no time," she groaned. "How could you do that to me?"

"Everybody knows you're living out at the ranch anyway," he said reasonably.

He was right, but that didn't make her feel any more comfortable about it. She hated being the object of idle gossip. People probably already knew that she was getting half of Staghorn, and she could just imagine what they figured she'd done to earn it.

"Will you stop torturing yourself?" he grumbled, glancing down at her as they stepped into the examination room. "What the hell does it matter if people talk?"

"Well, it won't be your reputation that gets ruined, will it?" she returned.

"Miss Scott? I'm Dr. Alex Brodie." The elderly, white-coated man entered right behind them and shook hands with Erin and then with Ty. He sat down and went over the details of her surgery with her. Apparently Ty had given him her doctor's name and he'd had a conversation with the man, because he knew exactly what had been done as well as the exercises that had been prescribed.

"Have you been doing the physical therapy?" he asked.

She colored delicately and averted her eyes. "There didn't seem much point," she began.

"Miss Scott, may I be blunt?" he asked, and proceeded to be so. "Surgery can help only to a certain point. You can walk again, but unless you do the exercises, exactly as prescribed, that leg will be stiff for the rest of your life, and you'll always limp. I understand that you were a professional model. That makes it even more important for you to exercise—if, that is, you have any idea of going back to work in the future."

She stared at her hands, clenched in her lap. How could Ty do this to her?

"We can, of course, have you drive to the hospital each day, and a physical therapist can instruct you and work with you."

She looked up, her eyes disturbed. "Oh, no. Please," she asked gently. "I couldn't bear that...."

"Suppose I work with her at the ranch," Ty suggested. He was sitting cross-legged in a chair, hat on one knee, looking impossibly arrogant. "I had a busted hip once, remember?"

The doctor cleared his throat. "Oh, how I remember!" he said. "One of my best nurses quit, two physical therapists retired..."

Ty just grinned, and Erin gaped at him, unbelieving. She'd hardly ever seen him smile like that.

"I could give you a list of the exercises," the doctor murmured. "But she'll have to do them twice a day, every day, thirty minutes at a stretch."

"She'll do them," Ty promised before Erin could open her mouth.

"I'd like to examine that hip now," he added, calling his nurse into the room.

Erin glared at Ty. "Unless you're planning to do a consultation, *Dr.* Wade, would you mind leaving?"

He cocked an eyebrow as he rose. "Testy little thing, aren't you?" He moved past her. "Watch out," he told the doctor. "She bites."

"Be sure your tetanus jabs are current," she whispered as he left the room.

It was amazing, the ease of that repartee, when once she'd been too tongue-tied to talk to him. In spite of everything that had happened between them, she was still drawn to him. Ty was stronger than any other human being she'd ever known. Just for a little while, she needed to lean on someone. And who better than the man who was partially responsible for her condition?

Dr. Brodie looked at the stitches, had an X ray made, and pronounced her well on the way to recovery. He prescribed some additional pain pills, in case she needed them, and gave her a preprinted sheet of exercises with special ones circled.

She stared at them all the way back to Staghorn, dreading the ordeal they represented.

"I don't want to start this," she muttered. "All that pain and cramping, and for what? I'll always limp!"

"Not if you want to walk," he returned impassively. "But you have to be willing to do the work. I'll help, but I can't do it for you."

"Why should you want to help?" she asked, turning in the seat to fix him with a cold, level stare.

He was smoking. He took a draw from the cigarette before he answered, and he didn't look at her. "Because I did that to you, as surely as if I'd pushed you in front of another car."

She stared at him uncomprehendingly. "Surely you don't think that you caused me to have the wreck?"

"Didn't I?" He laughed mirthlessly. "You were half hysterical when you left here."

"Yes, I was. And I pulled off the road and got myself together before I ever left the ranch!" she told him. "I'm not suicidal, and I'm not homicidal. I never drive when I'm not fit emotionally. By the time the wreck happened, I was at least levelheaded. Even the state patrol said it was unavoidable. I was hit by a drunk driver who took a curve too wide and came at me in my lane. He was killed outright."

Ty's face paled, and his hands clenched the steering wheel tightly. "Lucky man," he said under his breath. Erin knew what he meant without asking for explanations.

"So if you're on some guilt trip, let me reassure you," she continued quietly. "The only thing you did was try to save your brother from me. And you succeeded."

"Beyond my wildest dreams," he said coldly, lifting the cigarette to his lips. "I ruined both your lives."

She could hardly believe what she was hearing. He sounded bitter, anguished. "What could you have done that would have changed anything?" she asked calmly. "I would never have married Bruce. I didn't love him, and he knew it."

He glanced at her. "Maybe if I hadn't made a dead set at you, he'd have had a chance."

She shook her head firmly. "Not that way."

His eyes held hers for an instant before they returned to the road. "Didn't you ever want him?"

"Not physically. He was good fun; a nice, undemanding companion. I didn't want affairs, like some of the girls did. The fact that he had money never made him any more special to me. I like making my own way." She leaned her head against the seat and studied his uneven features quietly. "At least you never suspected me of being a gold-digger."

"I knew better," he said with a faint smile. "I tried to buy you off at first, if you remember. You took the check straight to Bruce and handed it to him in front of me. That cured me."

"And surprised you, I guess."

He nodded. "I'd thought I had you pegged. And I never really knew you at all." He turned onto the long ranch road that led back to Staghorn, down a driveway that boasted rough wood fenceposts, electrified fencing and mesquite groves everywhere among bare, leafless trees. "I thought you'd been to bed with half-a-dozen men. I got the shock of my life that night."

She felt her face growing warm. They shared such intimate memories, for two old enemies.

"Erin, why did you give in to me?" he asked unexpectedly. "You must have suspected what I was doing."

She looked at him, admiring the play of muscles in his arms as he manipulated the car along the dirt road. "Yes," she replied after a moment. "I suspected it."

"Then why give in? Were you really so trusting that you didn't realize what I had in mind?"

"I was too far gone to care," she said quietly, avoiding his suddenly piercing gaze. "I'd never felt like that with a man. I didn't want you to stop. By the time I was fully aware of what I was doing, it was much too late to say no."

"I would have stopped if you'd asked me, all the same," he said, jerking the wheel as he turned up toward the house.

"You couldn't have."

He pulled up at the front steps and turned to her. "I could have," he said firmly. "I wasn't that far gone until the last few seconds."

Her face went beet red as he looked at her, because she remembered those last few seconds with shocking clarity.

"You pulled me down to you," he said in a tone that was husky and deep, and unfamiliar. "I knew that your body was rejecting me, and why, and I was just starting to pull back. And you reached up to my hips and dug those long, exquisite nails into me, and I was lost."

Her breath caught in her throat. She tried to reply and failed, and he touched her lips with the very tip of his finger, probing them delicately apart so he could see the pearly whiteness of her teeth.

"I didn't even give you pleasure," he continued roughly. "I took you, used you, and you should have hated me for it. But you didn't. Your eyes were like velvet—so soft that I got lost in them. And I wanted to do it again, to try and make it right. But I started thinking about Bruce, and some things he'd said...and I was afraid to trust you. So I fed you a lot of bull about ruining you with Bruce and ran you off."

Her eyes widened, darkened. "You...really wanted me, didn't you?" she asked gently.

"Until you were an obsession," he replied, his voice low and slightly harsh. "You were so beautiful, Erin. Any man would have died to have you."

Then, perhaps, she thought. But not now, not with her scars and her limp and her lack of confidence. She averted her eyes. "Those days are over now," she said dully. "I'm not the same person."

"Aren't you? You could be, if you wanted to."

"With my scars?" Her voice broke, and she jerked away from him, wounded. Her eyes sparked at his puzzled face. "You wanted me when I was beautiful; you wanted me because Bruce did. But now I'm crippled and hurt, and you feel sorry for me. That's the only reason you're even tolerating me, Ty! You were my enemy from the first day we met. Even then, you looked at me as if you hated me!"

Of course he had, he mused, searching her cold face. He'd wanted her. Needed her. It had all been a defense against being hurt himself. He'd fought her because he wanted her so much, and he knew in his heart that she'd never want someone like him. But he couldn't tell her that. He couldn't let her know how vulnerable he'd been.

"So you're crippled," he said easily, brutally. "And apparently you like being that way, and feeling sorry for yourself, because you're not making any effort to change it. I guess you want to live under my roof and depend on me for every crumb you eat for the rest of your life, is that right?"

It was a calculated risk—it might send her into spasms of weeping, for which he'd hate himself. But he was betting it would have the opposite effect.

It did. Her eyes began to blaze. Her face went white with pent-up fury. She swung at him immediately, and he caught her wrist with her hand just a fraction of an inch from his jaw.

He jerked, pulling her across the wide seat and into his hard arms, and held her against him relentlessly.

"You . . . !" She struggled frantically until her own sharp movements brought pain. Then she stiffened, feeling the knifelike stab in her hip, and gasped.

"See what you get?" he chided. He held her with one arm while his lean hand massaged the throbbing hip through the thick corduroy of her dark slacks. "Does that help?"

"Stop it," she muttered, spitting out a strand of hair that had worked its way between her lips. "Oh, I do hate you, Tyson Radley Wade!"

His pale eyes kindled. "I didn't know you knew my middle name."

She shifted, grimacing as his kneading freed the tense muscles from their cramp. "I saw...your birth certificate...with Bruce's when we were looking at the family album one night."

His hand was less therapeutic now than blatantly caressing. He moved it slowly over her hip, watching her face curiously. "Odd that you'd remember something like that, seeing how much you hate me," he murmured.

"Ty..."

"That's how you said my name," he breathed, bending, "when I touched you for the first time. You moaned it, just like that, and the blood rushed into my head like fire."

"I didn't...moan it," she whispered. His mouth was almost against hers, and she stared at its hard, thin curve as if hypnotized. She didn't want him to kiss her. It was too soon; there had been too much pain....

But he was already doing it. His hard mouth caught hers roughly and took it, possessed it. He groaned, jerking her breasts close against his chest, crushing her mouth feverishly under the hardness of his.

She pushed against him, feeling the steely warmth of his muscular chest through his shirt, the powerful beat of his heart beneath her fingers. He wasn't giving her room to respond, even if she'd been able to. He was taking. Just taking.

At last, her lack of response seemed to get through to him. He lifted his mouth and stared into her eyes.

"What am I doing wrong?" he whispered huskily. "Show me."

She wondered at his choice of words, but only for a moment. It had been months, and the feel of him was making her weak. She reached up without thinking, curving her slender fingers against his cheek, and pulled him closer. She nibbled at his mouth, her lips barely touching his, probing gently, brushing so that he could feel their very texture.

"Like this?" he murmured, and followed her lead.

The soft brushing movements of his warm mouth made her tingle. She smiled against his lips and moved her breasts gently over his chest so that he could feel them. He stiffened, and his arms contracted with bruising force.

"Ty!" she whispered reprovingly. "Not so hard, please!"

He was breathing roughly. He let her move away, watching her hand go to her sore breasts, and his eyes traced them curiously. "You're delicate there," he said. "I didn't think. Did I hurt them?" He moved his hand over hers, lightly touching her, as if a woman's body were a new and mysterious phenomenon.

"I'm all right," she said breathlessly.

His fingers eased between hers, so that they were warm on the curve of her breast. His eyes locked with hers, and she could see the pupils dilating.

His lips parted as he found the hard tip of her breast with one long finger and began to rub it gently through the fabric of her blouse. She jerked helplessly and gasped, and he did it a little harder. He watched her bite her lip and realized that she was biting back a moan, because her expression was one of pleasure, not pain.

"God, that excites me," he breathed roughly. "Watching you like this drives me crazy!"

She could feel that; he'd turned her so that her belly was lying against his, and she knew that he was fully aroused.

He nuzzled his cheek against hers, hiding his glittering eyes. His hand gently moved hers aside and covered her breast, savoring its soft firmness, tracing its contours as if he'd never touched a woman like that before.

She was scarcely breathing at all, the pain forgotten, the memories forgotten. There was only *now*, and the silence of the closed car, the rasp of Ty's breathing at her ear, the furious throbbing of his heart. There was the sound of his hand smoothing the cotton print of her blouse, the whispery gasps she couldn't stifle, and the feel of his hard arms as she gripped him for support.

He kissed her cheek, her ear, his lips tender, urgent. His hand fumbled with buttons, and he muttered something under his breath as he found her bra and couldn't figure out how to get it open. Finally, he settled for sliding his hand roughly underneath, lifting her free of the lacy cup, and he groaned again as he felt the softness fill his hand, felt the hardness grinding into his damp palm.

"Ty..." Her voice sounded oddly high-pitched, helpless. She turned in his arms and buried her face in his chest, clinging to him.

He went over the edge at the unexpected vulnerability. He nuzzled her cheek with his lips; then, finding her mouth, he kissed it hungrily with a rough kind of tenderness. His hand cupped her breast warmly, insistently, and it was a long time before he lifted his head and looked down.

His skin was dark against hers, dark against the telltale paleness of flesh shielded from the harsh light of the sun. And the sight of his hand there, possessing her, made her flush feverishly.

He caught her eyes. "Have you had anyone since me?" he whispered huskily.

"No," she replied honestly.

"I haven't had anyone since you." His eyes traveled down to the softness in his hand. "Oh, God, Erin, you're so beautiful."

Her lips parted on a rush of exhaled breath. What was she letting him do? Where was her pride? He hadn't caused the wreck, but if he'd listened to her, it might have been prevented. She'd lost her baby, she was crippled....

She pulled away from him, crumpling her blouse together as she avoided his eyes. She was breathing hard, but so was he.

"I guess I shouldn't have done that," he said hesitantly.

"I shouldn't have let you," she had the grace to admit.

He took a steadying breath and removed his dress Stetson to smooth his damp hair. "We'd better go inside," he said, aware of his surroundings for the first time. He was grateful that it was José and Conchita's afternoon off, and that the hands were all busy in the equipment barn. Thank God for tinted windows and large shade trees and the privacy of a big car. He straightened, feeling sore all over from frustrated desire. He could hardly believe that she'd given him such license, after all that had happened. Perhaps, he thought, there was a little hope left.

"Are you all right?" she asked softly.

He stared at her, his face hard but his eyes kindling with a new emotion. "I just hurt a little," he said honestly. "Nothing to bother about. How's your hip?"

She swallowed. "I...uh...hadn't noticed." She touched it gingerly. "I don't enjoy being a cripple," she added, belatedly remembering the source of the argument. "And I'll be glad to do the exercises if it will convince you that I don't want to 'live off you.'"

"Good," he said with the hint of a smile. "I don't want to live off you, either. So suppose we start those exercises tonight? I think I could learn to like massaging that hip for you."

"You weren't massaging it."

"What was I doing, then?" he asked innocently.

She glared at him and got out of the car. And was so flustered that she walked firmly on her damaged side for the first time since the surgery.

Chapter Five

That was the first night Ty didn't withdraw into his study immediately after supper to work on his books. He had all kinds of equipment in there, including a state of the art computer with a vast memory in which he kept records of all his cattle. It was, Erin later learned, only a terminal, which was connected to the mainframe in his office. And he had two offices: one on the ranch itself, and another that he shared with several partners in some sweeping cattle-investment corporation. He had his finger in several pies—which accounted for his wealth.

"It takes a lot of figuring to keep up with it all," he told her as they went into the living room for their after-dinner coffee. "I have accountants, but I don't trust my books completely to anyone. I've seen out-fits ruined just because the man on top didn't want to be bothered with paperwork and made his people sec-ond-guess what he wanted done."

"You don't really trust anyone, do you?" she asked, curious. She sat down in a big armchair across from the sofa, careful not to look toward the fire-place. This was the room where Ty had seduced her, and the memories were disturbing.

"Oh, I don't know," he murmured, watching her. "I guess I'm learning to trust you a little."

"You didn't have much choice, with Bruce's will left the way it was," she replied. She toyed with the skirt of her pale-green jersey dress. "I guess you were pretty upset when you found out what he'd done."

"Ward Jessup and I go back a long way," he said dryly. "I wouldn't have jumped for joy at the pros-pect of oil rigs mingling with my purebred Santa Ger-trudis."

"I imagine not." She looked up. "But how did you know I wouldn't deliberately stay away just to make sure that happened?"

"I didn't," he confessed. He lit a cigarette and leaned back, his dark slacks and light shirt straining against the powerful muscles of an utterly masculine body. His hair was immaculately groomed, thick and black and straight, his face clean-shaven. He always looked neat, even when he was working cattle. Despite his lack of conventional good looks, he was more of a man than anyone Erin had ever known.

"I thought about it," she admitted with a faint smile. "And then I thought about how many people would be out of work because of my stiff pride."

"Softhearted liberal," he chided gently. "Wouldn't it have been worth it to see me brought to my knees after what I did to you?"

Her eyes searched his, and she felt the electricity that had never completely faded between them. "All I really could blame you for was listening to Bruce's lies and refusing to listen to me."

"Think so?" He got up and poured himself a brandy. She noticed that he didn't offer her one and remembered that she'd always refused liquor in the past. He didn't forget much.

"Anyway, it's over and done now," she murmured.

He turned, the brandy glass in one lean hand, staring at her intently. "Do you think it's that easy for me?"

She stared at him, bewildered. "I don't understand."

"You were carrying my child," he said in a tone that went straight to her heart. He looked down into the brandy snifter, sloshing the liquid around as if its color fascinated him. "You can't imagine how I felt when I read that letter, when I knew what I'd done."

Somehow breath had suspended itself in her throat. She felt as if she were drowning in the depths of his pale eyes, held there by something new and strange and vulnerable. He'd always seemed incapable of emotion, yet for one moment, one heart-stopping eternity, his expression had held such pain—such agonized loss—that now she was powerless to move, to speak, even to think.

He lifted his head and stared at the painting above the mantel. It was a scene of Texas that had been done by someone in his family almost a century ago, of longhorn cattle in a storm with a ranch house and windmill in the background.

"Erin..." He paused as if searching for words, his back straight and rigid. "I didn't plan what happened that night. I told you I had, but it wasn't the truth...."

Her hands fiddled with her skirt as she stared at him in wonder. He'd never talked to her like this. She waited silently for him to continue.

"I thought if I goaded you, I might make you mad enough to strike out at me," he said, lifting his eyes to the painting. "When you did, it gave me an excuse to touch you. I'd wanted that. You obsessed me, haunted me. I dreamed about how it would be, touching you that way." He shrugged wearily. "You kissed me back, and I went crazy. To this day, I don't half remember how it happened. I didn't even think about taking precautions. I assumed that you were already doing it, that you were experienced."

The confession fascinated her. She studied the hard muscles of his legs, his narrow hips, remembering how they'd felt under her exploring hands. She flushed a little at the memory. "I thought it was to get me out of Bruce's life."

He turned, pinning her with quiet, steady eyes. "I lied," he said. "Bruce was the last thing on my mind. I wanted you."

She felt like a trapped animal. He was doing it again, trying to take her over, own her. She clenched her hands tightly in her lap. "You let me go," she whispered.

"I had to, damn it!" he cried. "You were his, for all practical purposes. I'd betrayed him; so had you. I couldn't live with it. I had to get you out of here before I . . ."

"Before what, iron man?" she asked him. "Before you lost your head again? Is it so hard to admit that you're human enough to feel desire?"

"Yes!"

He slammed the brandy snifter into the fire, watching it splinter amid the explosion of blazing liquor. Erin jumped at the impact, but he didn't even flinch. He brushed back a lock of unruly hair and reached automatically into his pocket for a cigarette. He lit it and took a long draw while Erin sat nervously watching him.

He moved away from the fireplace restlessly. "My father's idea of marriage was warped. He saw it as a business merger. Sex, he always told me, was a weakness that a man with any backbone should be able to overcome." He paused in front of her and looked down, his silvery eyes cold and unfeeling. "Erin, I had my first woman when I was twenty-one, and it took weeks to get over the guilt. I gave in to a desire I couldn't control, and I hated it. And her." He lifted his shoulders. "Maybe I hated my father, too, for forcing his principles onto me. My mother couldn't live with him. She was normal. A warm, loving woman. He couldn't even touch her at the last."

He moved back to the fireplace and stared into the flames while Erin sat quietly and thrilled to the wonder of hearing these intimate things—things, she knew, that he'd never shared with another living soul.

"I'm more like him every day," he said dully, studying the flames. "I can't change. Walls work both ways. They keep people out . . . but they keep people in, too."

Her heart ached for him. Her own problems seemed to diminish a little as she realized what he was saying.

"You're lonely," she said gently.

He turned and looked at her, and for the first time his expression wasn't hidden. He seemed older, worn; and there was pain in every line of his hard face. "Honey, I've been lonely all my life," he said, his voice deep and quiet, the endearment curiously exciting to Erin because it was so unlike him. "My up-bringing and my looks have been two strikes against me with women ever since I can remember."

She blinked. "Your looks?"

"Don't be coy," he muttered. "I know I'm no prize."

"If you think looks make any difference, you're no prize mentally, and that's for sure," she said slowly, deliberately. "I've never known anyone who was more a man than you are."

His eyes widened, as if the compliment had shocked him. He stared at her, the cigarette forgotten. "I hurt you...."

"I was a virgin," she said softly. "Sometimes it's difficult for women the first time. You couldn't have helped that."

His jaw tensed. "Coals of fire, Erin."

She remembered the quotation from the Bible, about heaping coals of fire on an enemy's head by being kind to him. "It isn't flattery," she told him. "I don't like you enough to flatter you."

He actually laughed. "Aiding and abetting the enemy, then?"

She shrugged. "The enemy's managed to bring me back to life. I think I owe you a compliment or two."

"You won't think so when I start on that hip," he assured her. He lifted his chin imperiously and smiled. "Drill instructors will look like pussycats when I get through with you."

"You were a marine, weren't you?" she shot back. "'Once a marine, always a marine'—isn't that what they say? Well, you won't break me, mister. I'm tough!"

He liked her spirit. He always had. But the woman he'd found in that New York apartment hadn't shown any. It had taken this trip and a lot of goading, but he'd managed to shake her out of all that self-pitying apathy. And he was pleased with the result.

"You're pretty like that," he remarked, noting the color in her cheeks, the emerald depths of her eyes, the provocative disorder of all that black hair curling around her elfin face. "Scars and all. In no time at all, you'll never know where the cuts were."

"My hip will never look the same without skin grafts," she muttered, brought back to painful reality. "And I don't really want to go through any more surgery."

"Once a man got you undressed, a scar on your hip would be the last thing he'd be staring at," he said bluntly.

She'd forgotten that he'd seen her by the firelight without her clothing. She remembered that frank appraisal, as if he'd never seen a nude woman before and wanted to memorize every soft line and curve. Her breasts had fascinated him. He'd touched them so gently, caressed them, whispered how beautiful they were. Without warning, her face went scarlet.

"Yes, you remember too, don't you?" he asked, his voice low and sensuous. "It was right where I'm standing, and I looked at you until I got drunk on the sight. And you let me. You lay there all soft and sweetly moving, and you let me."

"It was new," she said defensively, lowering her eyes to her dress.

"It was heaven," he corrected. "The closest I ever expect to get in my lifetime. If it hadn't been for Bruce..." He turned and threw his cigarette into the fire, closing his eyes against the pain. "Oh, God, I'll never forgive him!"

His tone of voice disturbed her. It was bitter, yet filled with the anguish of loss...profound loss. She got up, unconsciously walking without the cane, limping a little as she paused beside him.

He was so tall. Towering. She had to look up to see his dark face, and the warmth and strength of him drew her like a magnet. It had been so sweet that afternoon to lie in his arms again and feel his mouth; and those memories were her undoing.

"It doesn't matter anymore," she said gently. "He's dead. Let him rest in peace. He had so little of it in life, Ty."

"How much do you think I have?" he demanded, staring down at her with tormented eyes. "It's eating me alive!"

She held him by the arms and actually shook him. "The car came at me around a curve, head on," she said, frustrated into telling him the truth about the wreck. "Nobody could have avoided it, upset or not!"

He watched her without speaking for a long moment. "Is that the truth?"

"Yes! And it was in New York State, just minutes from home, Ty. I could have been driving out of the city to an assignment and had it happen." She held his eyes with her own, adding slowly, "You didn't cause it."

He shook his head and smiled grimly. "Didn't I?" He took a slow breath and seemed to notice her hands for the first time. "Would you have had the baby?"

"Of course," she said without thinking.

He reached out and touched her cheek where the hairline scar ran just beside her ear. "Someone would have told me, eventually," he said quietly. "I'd have come to you. I'd have married you."

"What kind of life would that have been?" she asked sadly, searching the hard lines of his face. "You'd never have accepted what I did for a living, or even the way I was. You didn't want a butterfly—you even said so. And modeling was my whole life. I loved it; I loved the bright lights and the people and the delight of showing off pretty clothes." The smile that had animated her face faded as she remembered the wreck. "I lost all that. I can't go back to it, not like this. I can learn another kind of work, but nothing will ever replace modeling." *Except you,* she wanted to say. But she couldn't. She couldn't lower her pride enough to tell him that living with him and being loved by him would have been more than enough recompense for the career she'd lost.

She turned back toward the sofa, stumbling a little.

"Oh, damn this leg!" she burst out, near tears.

"If you don't like it, suppose you fix it," he said. "Exercise it, like the doctor told you. If you want your career back, earn it!"

She couldn't know that her remark about her career had caught him on the raw, that he was hurting because she'd as much as told him that he didn't matter. He deserved it, he knew he did, but it cut all the same.

"Okay," she told him defiantly. "I will!"

He smiled. "Good. Now go get on something you can exercise in and I'll coach you. We can have coffee later."

She hobbled down the hall to her room without a backward glance. And she told herself she hated him more than ever.

The first session was more painful than she'd anticipated. She did the exercises described on the sheet, with Ty looming over her, demanding more than she thought she was capable of.

"You can push harder than that, for God's sake," he said when she slackened.

"I'm not a man!"

He looked pointedly at her firm, full breasts under the revealing fabric of her body leotard, and a faint smile touched his mouth. "I'll drink to that."

"Stop looking at me there," she told him haughtily.

"Wear a bra next time," he countered, watching her from his armchair as she stretched on the carpet. "I can't help it if I get disturbed by hard nipples."

She gasped, flushed, and sat up in one sharp movement. "Tyson!" she burst out.

His eyebrows arched, and he looked as hopelessly the dominant male as any movie sex symbol. "Why the red-rose blush, honey?" he asked innocently. "Or don't you remember that you had sex with me on this very carpet?"

"Oh, I hate you!" she cried, eyes flaring, cheeks flaming, hair disordered and wild around her oval face. The leotard emphasized her thinness, but it also lovingly outlined a body so exquisite that lingerie companies had bid for her services as a model.

"No you don't; you just hate sex," he replied. "And that's my fault. But one of these days, I may change your mind about that."

"Hold your breath," she challenged.

"Daring me, Erin?" he asked, and his smile held shades of meaning as his silver eyes glittered over her body.

Watching those eyes, she began to tingle from head to toe. Her hip was throbbing, but she felt reckless all the same. She wanted to wipe that arrogant smile off his face. She wanted to make him vulnerable, wanted to watch the walls come down.

She arched her back, just a little, just enough to make the hard tips of her breasts blatantly visible. "Maybe I am," she whispered huskily. "So what are you going to do about it, cattle king?"

He was smoking a cigarette, but at her words he deliberately crushed it out in the ashtray. "I hope your hip's up to some additional exercise," he drawled.

And with a movement so fast it blurred, he slid down over her body and pinned her there, arching above her with one lean, muscular leg thrown heavily over both of hers.

"Okay, honey, now what do we do?" he said softly. "Is this what you had in mind?" And looking down, he blatantly slid one lean hand directly over a full breast, cupping it.

She felt her breath catch. Watching him earlier—and now—a lot of things were becoming clear to her. The way he'd been in the car, hungry but not practised; the way he was cupping her now, blatantly, without any preliminaries: she had a deep hunch that he knew less about women than he was pretending to. Male pride obviously ran deep. Well, two could play at this game. She didn't know a lot, either, but she'd heard women talk....

"Not like that," she whispered, lifting his hand. "Like . . . this."

She showed him how to trace the softness, to tease the tip until her body stiffened and trembled with the need to be touched. She drew his fingers against her until he understood and began to do it without coaching.

"You like it that way?" he asked under his breath, searching her eyes for an instant before they went back to the softness of her body under his hand.

"Yes," she whispered shakily. "It arouses me."

His breath shuddered out of him. He could hardly believe it, that she was willing to show him what she liked, that she wasn't complaining about his lack of finesse or laughing at him. All at once he wondered if Bruce had been lying after all, about that. She didn't seem the kind of woman to laugh at inexperience...especially now.

"What else do you like?" he asked huskily.

It was like drinking wine. She felt drunk on him. Her hip was forgotten, every other thought drained away. She was woman enticing man. She was a siren trapping a sailor, giddy with her own power.

Her hands eased up to the shoulders of the leotard, and, holding his fascinated gaze, she drew it down and bared her taut breasts.

"Oh, God..." He shuddered as he saw their creamy fullness, the dark mauve points lifting gracefully toward him. "Oh, God, you're beautiful, baby...!"

She felt beautiful. She felt achingly hungry as well. She reached up with trembling hands to take his hard face and draw it toward her body.

"What do you want?" he whispered, frowning.

"I want you to put your lips...here." She touched her breasts lightly, caressing their swollen peaks.

He stopped breathing. "On your breasts?" he asked hesitantly. "I won't hurt them?"

She felt the smile in her eyes as she shook her head. "Oh, no," she promised. "You won't hurt them."

He eased his hands under her bare back to lift her, bending over her in spite of his reservations. But her body had a scent like roses, and when he touched his mouth to the curve of her soft breast, she stiffened and began to tremble like a rain-tossed leaf.

More confident now, he began to draw his lips around the very tip of her breast. And when that made her moan softly, he opened his mouth and took the nipple inside, warming it with his tongue. She cried out then, and just as he thought he'd hurt her and tried to move away, her hands dug into the nape of his neck and she arched her soft body up to him with a tiny whimpered plea.

He groaned himself at the surge of pleasure it gave him to know that she was enjoying it, too. His hands smoothed down her rib cage, savoring her warm, silky skin while his mouth fed on the unexpected sweetness of her breasts.

When he lifted his head, her expression shocked and delighted him. Her eyes were half closed, watching him, her lips parted over pearly teeth. Her face was alive with color, her hands caressing the hard muscle of his chest.

"Could you take off your shirt?" she asked drowsily.

He couldn't take it off fast enough, in fact. His hands fumbled because he was aroused—as he hadn't been since that night with her. But that night was nothing like this. He was on fire. Burning up.

He ripped off the shirt and shuddered a little with pride as her eyes ran over him with blatant appreciation. She reached up hesitantly, smoothing over the thick mat of hair that covered the warm, bronzed muscles, and at her touch he felt his heart running wild.

She lifted herself up gracefully and kneeled in front of him. Her eyes traced his torso, and she seemed to sway toward him. She dug her nails into his muscular arms and leaned a little against him, drawing the very tips of her breasts softly, abrasively, against the hardness of his chest.

He shuddered violently. "Erin!" he gasped.

"Oh, Ty..." It was as much a moan as a whisper. She put her mouth on his and kissed him hungrily, feeling his arms come around her, crushing her, trembling as they fit her exquisitely to the contours of his chest. The hair was cushy and thick, and she liked the feel of it against her soft breasts. She could feel his heartbeat shaking both of them. It was so sweet. So sweet...

The sudden intrusion of a knock on the front door made her almost sick with mingled frustration and shock.

She jerked back. He looked as dazed as she felt. He looked at her one last time and cursed under his breath as he helped her back into the leotard.

He got to his feet gracefully and was just shouldering into his shirt when they heard footsteps echoing down the hall. Erin looked toward the door—and realized they'd both forgotten to close it!

"I used to be levelheaded before you came along," Ty muttered, glaring at her as he fastened buttons. "My God, with the door standing wide open...! You little siren," he breathed, his eyes warm with memories as they held hers. "God, that was sweet!"

"Well, you're helping me get back on my feet," she murmured demurely. "I thought the least I could do was divert you a little."

"That was more seduction than diversion," he replied. He reached down a hand to help her up. But instead of letting her go, he held her just in front of him. "Erin, we've got to do something about this," he said solemnly. "You knock me off balance pretty bad. I could lose control, now more than ever. I...don't want to make you pregnant by accident." The thought seemed to torture him; his face hardened into grim lines, his eyes grew dark.

"I'm sorry," Erin said quietly. "I won't do it again. I don't know what got into me, Ty..."

"No," he whispered, touching her mouth with his forefinger. "No, don't apologize for it. You made me feel like a man again, like a whole man...." He hesitated uncharacteristically. "I want you." He said it in a whisper, as if it were some terrible secret.

She drew in a slow breath. "I know." She dropped her eyes to his chest. She could have said the same thing, but she was afraid to give him that kind of power over her. His hands gripped her arms painfully hard just as José came to the door.

"*Señor*, it is the foreman, Señor Grandy. A wild dog has brought down a calf. He says it is the same dog as before, that of Señor Jessup."

"Damn," Ty muttered. Instantly he was the powerful cattle baron again, cold, relentless, indomitable; a formidable adversary. And a stranger. "Get my .30-.30 and bring me a box of ammunition," he ordered José. "And tell Grandy to wait for me. Call Ed Johnson while I'm gone and tell him the situation. I may have a court suit over this."

"*Sí, señor,*" José said graciously, and left them.

"It's Mr. Jessup's dog?" she asked Ty, watching him reach into the closet for his sheepskin jacket and the familiar old Stetson he wore when he was working.

"That's about the size of it. Part shepherd, part wolf. I've told him about that dog, but he won't pen it up. I've lost my last calf to it."

"But what if he sues you?" she asked.

"Let him. I like a good fight." He buttoned the coat and studied her in the tight leotard. "Get a good night's sleep. Tomorrow, you and I have to talk."

He came close then, framing her face in his lean hands. "I may be late. Don't wait up."

He bent and put his mouth softly against hers, with a new tenderness. She smiled against his lips and bit at the lower one.

He jerked back, frowning. And then he repeated the tiny caress on her own lip, smiling slowly at the reaction.

"How do you know so much about kissing?" he murmured.

"Because up until you came along, that was all I ever did with boys," she replied, and searched his eyes. "Be careful out there."

"Worried about the enemy?" he asked mockingly.

She touched his cheek. "Who would I fight with if something happened to you?" she asked noncommittally.

He brushed his finger against her mouth, brooding. "Erin... No. I can't talk about it now. Good night."

He left her without a backward glance, taking his rifle and ammunition from José on his way through the hall. She heard the front door slam behind him, and felt chilled to the bone.

What, she wondered, had he been about to say to her?

Chapter Six

Erin felt haunted that night. She couldn't help remembering Bruce and Ty and the way things had been. She recalled vividly one particular day, when she and Bruce were going for a ride in the chill of the early morning.

Ty had been working with one of his horses that day, and he'd stopped just long enough to tell Bruce which horse to saddle for Erin...

Bruce had bowed low, then glared up at him, all boyish and defiant. "I do know how to pick a horse," he'd drawled sarcastically. "I won't let her get hurt, either. After all," he'd added pointedly, "she is my girl, not yours."

Ty hadn't said a word. But he'd looked at Erin, and his silver eyes had been faintly hungry, possessive. Even in memory, the intensity of his gaze made her tingle. Up until that moment, Ty had been openly hostile, taunting her at every opportunity, picking at her, mocking her. But on that cold morning, there had been something in his eyes that had excited her, attracted her.

He'd held her gaze until she'd wondered if her heart could stand it. It had been like holding a live wire in wet hands. Her lips had parted, and his narrowed eyes had gone to them hungrily. If Bruce hadn't chosen that moment to reappear with Erin's mount, anything might have happened.

She'd relived that look all through the ride. When they'd returned, Bruce had been sidetracked by one of the stable boys.

Erin had spotted Ty, standing all alone by the corral, staring into the distance. And for some reason that she still didn't completely understand, she'd run to him.

Even now, she could see the expression on his hard, homely face, shock mingling with pure pleasure as she'd come toward him, her long black hair flaring behind her, her eyes alive with the joy of living. She'd darted up onto the lowest rail of the corral fence, beside him, and talked enthusiastically about the ride and the ranch and how much she was enjoying her visit.

Surprisingly, he hadn't been sarcastic or ridiculing. He'd smoked his cigarette calmly and answered all her curious questions, even seemed to enjoy them. But there still had been that hunger in his eyes when he'd looked at her. And it hadn't been very much later that Bruce had gone out on business and Ty had made one cutting remark too many.

She could still remember the feel of his hard cheek under her flashing hand, the shocked amusement in his face as he'd reached out arrogantly and jerked her against his hard-muscled body.

She'd thrilled to the unfamiliar contact...and all the arguments had suddenly made sense as the very real, explosive passion between them had been unleashed at last.

"At last," he'd whispered roughly, bending to her mouth. "Oh, God, at last..."

She hadn't questioned that strange wording, and when his lips had come crashing down against hers, she'd forgotten everything in the magic of being touched by him. For a long time, she'd forbidden her mind to relive that ecstatic night, but now she wanted to remember. She savored again the shocked gasp that had burst from his throat as she'd reached toward him instead of pushing him away, the pulsating hardness of his body as he'd smoothed her against its every rippling muscle and deepened the warm, rough kiss.

He hadn't been experienced. She'd known he was no virgin, but in retrospect, she realized that every movement had been spontaneous, unpremeditated. He'd wanted her desperately, and she'd wanted him. The nearness of him, the warmth of his mouth, the strength of his body—she'd wanted it all, without realizing what her desire meant to an aroused man. Her experience was even less than his . . . so that what happened had been inevitable. Inevitable . . . like the wreck . . .

She touched her flat stomach with gentle hands and felt the sting of tears in her eyes. The hardest thing of all had been losing the baby. She remembered how she'd cried when they'd told her about the miscarriage, about her crushed pelvis. The world had gone dark with Ty's stubborn refusal to listen, with his harsh renunciation. The wreck, the miscarriage, the terrible ordeal of surgery . . . it had been nightmarish. . . .

And now, because of the horror, she was here, close to Ty, beginning a relationship that was new and a little frightening. Did he only feel pity for her? And what did she feel? At first she'd wanted revenge; she'd hated him. But in time, she'd stopped being so terribly bitter and had drifted into a kind of numb apathy. Now she was back to stinging life again—and all because of Ty.

She rolled over onto her back with a troubled sigh. She felt desire; that much was sadly evident. Every time he touched her, her willpower vanished. She was his. And he had to know that. But he seemed hesitant, too.

His father had warped him, she realized. His ideas of intimacy and marriage were distorted. He didn't seem to know a great deal about women or closeness or giving. There was still a side of him that was guarded, buried, hidden from the world. Hidden from her. She wondered if anyone had ever seen that side of him. Perhaps no one ever would.

That made her sit up, eyes wide and troubled.

If he wanted her only because he felt guilty, responsible for what had happened to her, she'd have to try to resist him—after all, he might feel guilty now, but once she was whole again, his guilt would surely vanish, and his desire with it. There was something else to consider, too: right now, he needed her to keep Ward Jessup at bay. But if things ever straightened out, he'd have no need of her... and perhaps no desire for her. It would be wise not to get too close to him emotionally. She knew from hard experience that he didn't have a lot of sentiment, even though the loss of his brother had obviously affected him.

Hearing about the baby had affected him, too; Erin didn't doubt that. He was the kind of man who would want children. But when and with whom were questions she couldn't answer. She believed that he'd never completely forgotten what she was like before the wreck. He'd never liked her when she was a model; her beauty had repelled him, antagonized him. But now that she was scarred and crippled, she seemed to appeal to him much more. Why? she wondered. *Why?*

A car door slammed, breaking into the silence, and she tensed, listening. She was wearing a low-cut nightgown with a slit down the side of her scarred hip, and she couldn't bear to have Ty see the way she looked there. But surely he wouldn't come in...would he?

Just as the thought occurred to her, she heard the sound of heavy footsteps coming down the hall. The next instant, the door swung open.

Ty stripped off his gloves as he walked into the room, leaving the door open. "My, my," he murmured, studying the picture she made. "And I thought men only saw mirages in the desert."

"It's more a nightmare than a mirage under the gown," she muttered, scrambling for the covers. "The scar bothers me sometimes, and it stings when fabric rubs against it. The stitches haven't been out long. My hip doesn't like exercise," she couldn't help adding.

"Does it like being dressed in see-through gowns?" he asked, cocking an eyebrow to where she'd pulled up the covers. "That could get it into big trouble. I'd have a talk with it if I were you. While you're about it, you might tell it we're going to exercise it every day, so it might as well stop grumbling."

That didn't sound like the Ty she'd known months before. His humor was droll these days—not mocking and sarcastic—and he actually seemed to be making an effort to thaw her out. She stared up at him curiously. "Did you get the dog?" she asked.

"No. The damned thing got to the woods and hid, but Jessup's going to pay for that calf all the same." He moved closer to the bed, gripping his gloves in one hand as he walked toward her. He was still wearing the shepherd's coat, although he'd unbuttoned it, and his hat was tilted at an arrogant angle over his face. He stared down at her with narrowed, mocking eyes.

"Something on your mind?" she challenged.

"Yes, and you know what, don't you?" He slapped the gloves against his palm, letting his eyes run over the covers she was huddled under. "Why did you do that?"

She blinked. "Do what?"

"Rush under the blankets like that, the minute I walked in? You haven't got anything I haven't already seen."

She averted her eyes to the blue coverlet. "Maybe not. But you haven't seen it in its present condition, and you're not going to."

"Like hell I'm not."

Even as he said it, he was stripping away the covers. He pinned her to the bed simply by clamping one firm, hard hand down on her waist, and when he sat down beside her, he cut off her last chance at escape.

"No!" she cried as he stripped the gown up to her waist with his free hand, exposing the scarred hip.

It wasn't a pretty sight, despite the fact that it had healed since the wreck. The subsequent surgeries had left more scars, and only a skin graft would restore its former soft smoothness. But the scars didn't bother him—only her attitude toward them.

She closed her eyes because she couldn't bear to see his disgust. "Now are you satisfied?" she asked huskily.

"Not by a long shot, honey." He bent and put his mouth against the scar tissue, felt her stiffen and tremble, heard the involuntary sound that escaped her lips.

"Ty, you mustn't!" she protested, pushing at his head.

He looked up into her wide, frightened green eyes and smiled—actually smiled, although it was mocking and faint and didn't soften the hard face one bit.

"Frightened?" he chided. "Of what? You were terrified that I'd see you like this, so now you know. I'm not disgusted, or horrified, or repulsed. Any more questions?"

She backed up on the pillows and stared at him, heart pounding. "It's gruesome," she said under her breath. "I can't bear to look at it."

"But then you're a cream puff, honey," he said. "I've lived on a ranch all my life. I've seen things and done things that would turn your pretty hair white. By comparison, a few little hairline scars aren't much."

"They are to me!"

"Considering how you came by them, I guess so," he replied, his tone quiet, almost sympathetic. He touched the newest scar gently, where it was still tender. Erin saw his face grow pale, watched his jaw tense as if he were remembering things he didn't want to face.

"Were you in the hospital a long time?" he asked after a moment.

"After the wreck, yes," she confessed, and he flinched. "Ty—"

"It must have been damned painful," he said under his breath, still staring at the scars. "And with no one to look after you, care about you. God!"

He jerked up from the bed and turned away, his hands rammed into his pockets, the gloves forgotten on the coverlet. His back was ramrod stiff, and there was something disturbing in his stance.

She was just beginning to understand him. It wasn't that he didn't feel anything. He'd just grown adept at hiding his feelings. She remembered what he'd told her about having two strikes against him with women, and she imagined he'd been taunted all his life about his lack of looks. She grimaced at the pain she felt emanating from him.

It was just too much. Her own pain forgotten, she got out of bed and went to him. Talking wouldn't help, she knew that instinctively. So she went in front of him and slid her arms around his hard waist and pressed against him inside his coat.

He shuddered wildly for an instant. His hands caught her shoulders roughly and hesitated, as if he were thinking about pushing her away. And then the feel of her got through to him, the soft warmth pressed so close to his heart, the scent of her rising into his nostrils.

His hands flattened on her shoulder blades, savoring the feel of her. And he let her come close, let her hold him. His head bent over hers, his cheek finally resting against her hair with a long, aching sigh.

"You're very human after all, aren't you?" she asked softly, her eyes closed as she held him. "You lock it all up inside you and keep people from seeing, but things hurt you just as much as they hurt me. I know you feel bad about what happened, Ty. I'm not bitter anymore. I've stopped hating you for it. Does that help?"

He touched her hair lightly, and his grip didn't slacken one bit. "You see too deeply," he whispered roughly.

"It's like looking in a mirror," she said. "I've done the same thing all my life, too. Locked away the hurts, so no one could see. My father died and my mother started playing the field. One man after another was in and out of her life, and the other kids tormented me with it. You see, their own fathers weren't immune to her. She had affairs with at least two of them."

His hands tightened around her. "I guess it was pretty tough."

"Pure hell." She smiled ruefully. "I grew up near Dallas, remember; I was a small-town Texas girl before I started modeling. Small-town people are the salt of the earth, but they have old-fashioned ideas about morality, and they tend to condemn people who ignore the rules." She nuzzled her cheek against the soft cotton of his shirt, feeling the hard muscle and heartbeat underneath. "I guess that's one reason I never ran around."

He tugged gently on a strand of her hair. "At least not until I came along. I guess your conscience gave you hell about that."

"It did."

"Oddly enough," he said, "I had some problems with my own conscience. The women I'd...known before weren't virgins."

"Incredible, isn't it," she murmured, "that I'd get pregnant the very first time?"

"That's what they say happens to good girls." He stroked her hair. "God, I'm sorry, honey," he said softly. "Sorry I wouldn't listen, sorry I didn't go after you. I started to. And before I could, Bruce moved out and fed me a bunch of lies...."

She lifted her head and looked up at him. "I never told him about us," she said honestly, holding his eyes. "And I certainly never accused you of...of fumbling."

"I should have known that, shouldn't I?" he asked, his voice deep. "After today, anyway."

She frowned slightly. "Why after today?"

He traced her mouth with his finger. "If you were the kind of woman who'd laugh at a man, you'd have done it today. But you didn't. Instead of making fun of me, you took my hand and showed me how to touch you."

She blushed and buried her face in his warm throat.

He laughed softly, enjoying that very feminine reaction to his blatant teasing. He tugged lightly on her hair, savoring its softness. "Men aren't born knowing how to arouse women," he said, gently mocking. "We have to learn. It was exciting, having you show me what you liked. That's never happened for me before."

"Never?" she asked without lifting her head.

"Never. Bruce fed you some bull, too, honey, or haven't you cottoned on to that by now?"

"About your sordid reputation and the harem you kept?" she asked, keeping her red cheeks hidden.

"That's about the size of it," he agreed. "I'm not a virgin, but I've never been much of a rounder. Men who look like I do don't score that often."

That brought her head up, wide green eyes searching his curiously. "What do you mean, men who look like you do? What's wrong with you?"

He cocked his head a little to one side, staring at her. "I'm ugly."

She smiled, completely without malice. "You're sexy, too," she murmured.

His eyebrows shot up. "Me?"

She dropped her eyes to his chest. "And arrogant," she continued. "Bad-tempered. Impatient..."

"You could have stopped at 'sexy,'" he said.

She shifted restlessly. "No, I couldn't," she said. "We don't want you to get conceited."

"Hip hurting?" he asked softly.

"Nagging a bit." She peeked up at him. "I'll be your best friend if you'll stop making me do those exercises."

"No deal. You're going to walk again even if I become your worst enemy. Here." He swung her up into his arms without warning and carried her back to bed.

She clung, drowning in the masculine scent of him, the feel of that powerful, lean body. "You're very strong," she murmured absently.

"I don't sit behind a desk and count my money. I work for what I've got." He put her down on the coverlet, and as he rose up, his eyes caressed the curves of her body like seeking hands.

She didn't try to cover herself, although part of one creamy breast was revealed by her disheveled gown. She let him look, glorying unashamed in the pleasure she saw in his silver-gray eyes.

"Have you ever let another man look at you like this?" he asked, his voice deep and faintly cutting.

"No," she said.

"Bruce wanted to, didn't he?" he asked, lifting his eyes to hers. "He wanted that and a hell of a lot more."

"He never got it," she replied, her eyes steady, intent. "I never felt that way about him. He was my friend, until he started wanting more than I could give him. I had no idea he was that obsessed with marrying me until the day after I left here the first time. He...he raved like a lunatic about the way you looked at me," she confided hesitantly. "I tried to tell him that you didn't even like me, but he wouldn't listen." She lowered her eyes. "I'm sorry, if that helps. I wouldn't have caused trouble between you for anything."

"Bruce and I had never been close. We were raised separately and he was six years younger. He always tried to compete with me. He had to have the fastest car, the most expensive clothes, the finest house." He shrugged. "I never cared about those things. I have money, but I'd do as well without it. I'd rather have a good horse and a day's work ahead of me than sit in some damned restaurant putting on airs for other people."

She searched his hard face. "I think I liked that about you most of all, even at first," she said. "You were never a snob. Bruce was."

"I know," he replied slowly.

"Why did he want to cause trouble?" she asked. "He knew you disliked me. Why tell a lot of lies?"

"Because he sensed that there was something under the dislike." He stared down at her. "He knew that I wanted you."

Her heart jumped. "I didn't. Not until that night." She lowered embarrassed eyes to the coverlet. "I'm sorry I disappointed you," she added hesitantly. "I didn't know much."

"You didn't disappoint me," he snapped angrily. "That was all bad temper and Bruce's lies!"

His vehemence startled her. She looked up into blazing silver eyes. "I didn't?" she asked.

"I think you were a hell of a lot more disappointed than I was." He watched her intently. "You got nothing out of it except pain and a baby that I cost you with my black temper."

She shook her head. "The baby wasn't meant to be," she said gently. And she meant it . . . now. Seeing his guilt had knocked the bitterness out of her once and for all. "You can't spend your whole life blaming yourself for it."

"Can't I?" he asked coldly.

"You'll get married someday," she said, hating the thought even as it was forming. "You'll have other children."

He took a cigarette from his pocket and lit it. "Will I? Sure, maybe I could advertise: 'Rich man with no looks seeking wife. . . .'"

"Don't," she said, grimacing.

"I told you, I'm realistic. No woman is ever going to want me—unless it's for my money. So why not lay it on the line at the outset?" he asked with a mocking smile.

"All right, if you're going to wallow in self-pity, maybe I will, too," she shot back, infuriated with him. "I'm scarred and crippled, and no longer a virgin. So maybe now that I'm independently wealthy, I could use the same kind of ad for myself!"

His face went hard. The cigarette poised in midair, inches away from his lips. "Those scars won't matter to any man who cares about you."

"And how about my scarlet past and my stiff leg?" she continued, sitting up straight. The bodice of her gown was slipping, but she was too angry to notice.

Ty wasn't. "How about your exquisite breasts?" he murmured, watching one that was all but exposed to his hungry gaze.

"Ty!" she gasped, sidetracked by the expression in his face.

"They are exquisite, too," he said softly. "You can't imagine what a hell of a time I'm having trying to stand here and smoke my cigarette. So would you mind pulling that up—" he nodded toward her bodice "—before I come down there and make a grab for you?"

She tugged the strap up again, coloring prettily for what seemed like the tenth time. "Do you really want to make a grab for me, the way I look?"

"Especially the way you look," he replied, lifting the cigarette to his faintly smiling mouth. "I still ache from having to leave you here in the first place. It's a damned good thing Grandy chose that particular time to tell me about the dog."

She glanced toward him and away. "Is it?"

"I'd say so," he replied, staring at her intently. "Considering that you're not on the Pill and I didn't have anything to use."

"I thought men were always prepared."

"Was I prepared the last time?" He laughed roughly. "My God, Erin, do you realize how small Ravine is? There's a lady clerk at the drugstore—Mrs. Blake, whom I've known since I was ten years old—and I can just imagine her expression if I walked up to her to buy something like that, when she knows I'm a bachelor and you're in the house with me."

Her lips parted. "Oh."

"Oh, indeed. No wonder there are so many un-planned pregnancies. Kids these days don't practice restraint, and most boys that age are too damned shy to walk into a drugstore and buy what they need. So they trust it all to luck." He took a long draw from his cigarette. "You and I aren't kids, but we know the consequences all too well now, don't we?"

"I didn't plan to... to do that with you," she faltered, averting her gaze.

"Neither did I. But we were both half-starved for each other, and completely alone, and we knew it. I should have protected you. I did try,'' he said softly. "But it was too much. It had been such a long time for me, and I'd wanted you until it was just short of obsession.''

That was shocking. And interesting. "A long time?'' she asked, looking up.

He smiled at her ruefully. "About two years, if you're curious; I told you I had hangups.''

She liked that. She even smiled a little shyly. "Well, I never had.''

"I noticed,'' he murmured.

She glanced up again, then down at her folded hands. "Have you . . . since?''

"I told you in the car. No. And I haven't wanted to.'' He finished the cigarette and crushed it out in the ashtray on the bedside table. "I don't want anyone else. I'd rather have the memory of you, that night, than the reality of any other woman in the world.''

She couldn't help it. Her eyes brimmed with tears that trickled onto her silky cheeks while she stared at him spellbound.

"Little watering pot,'' he chided. He pulled out a handkerchief and dabbed it clumsily at her eyes. "Stop that. The only way I could possibly comfort you wouldn't be sensible, with you in that damned little see-through gown.''

"Coward.'' She smiled at him through her tears.

"You bet, honey; in that respect, at least.'' He gave her the handkerchief and paused to pick up his gloves.

He stared at her with narrowed eyes while she blew her nose and wiped away the last of the tears. "Erin, what you said at the doctor's office—does the talk about you and me really bother you?"

She looked up, surprised. "Are people really talking?"

He sighed. "I'm afraid so. One of the men mentioned something he'd heard." He didn't tell her that the man had mentioned it himself, because he'd had one drink too many, or that Ty had planted a hard fist right in the middle of his face and fired him seconds later.

She shifted quietly on the bed. "Well, there's nothing to be done about it," she said after a minute. "I own half the property, as things stand. I can't leave without hurting a lot of people."

"There's one thing we could do," he said, staring at his dusty boots.

"What?"

He turned his boot and looked at the mud on the sole. "We've already agreed that I may grow old trying to find a woman who'll have me, what with my looks. And you don't seem too confident about getting a man. And neither of us has slept with anyone else since the night before you left." He glanced at her. "Maybe we could learn to get along, if we worked at it. And the will doesn't really leave us much choice. You'll be here for life."

She knew what he was going to say. She could refuse. It would be the sensible thing to do. But part of her was still powerfully attracted to him. She liked lying in his hard arms, being touched and kissed and held by him. She responded to his strength, his stubbornness. She'd never want anyone else. And although he didn't love her, he'd at least look after her; she knew that instinctively. Perhaps in time things would work out. There could be children....

She cocked her head and stared at him. "Would you want children?" she asked levelly.

"If you're asking me to give you a child to replace the one you lost, yes. I can do that. Not now," he added, studying her body. "You're not in any condition to carry one. But we can have children, if that's what you want."

It sounded as if he weren't all that enthusiastic about it. Could she have been wrong about him? Did he not want a family? Or did he want one so badly that he was just hiding his feelings, afraid of being hurt?

She fiddled with the coverlet, thinking.

"You're stuck here, thanks to your conscience," he reminded her. "You might as well have my name as well as half my ranch."

"Thanks," she said curtly. "What a sweet proposal of marriage!"

"Well, take it or leave it, then!" he replied hotly. "I'm not all that thrilled myself, but it's the only solution I see."

"I won't sleep with you!"

"Sleep in the damned barn, for all I care." His face was harder than rock, his eyes blazing.

Erin's lower lip trembled, and she tugged the covers up higher. How in the world had it come to this so suddenly?

"If you marry me, you'll do it in a church," she said doggedly. "I'm not getting married by any justice of the peace."

His eyebrows arched. "Did I ask you to?"

"And I don't want a social event, either. Just a small wedding." She looked at her slender, ringless hands. "And I don't want my mother there. She'd make a circus out of it."

He relaxed a little. "Okay."

"And I don't want to have to walk down the aisle dragging my leg behind me."

"After we've done those exercises for a few weeks, you won't be dragging it behind you," he told her. "You'll improve. But it's going to take time and effort and hard work. And no backsliding."

"Tyrant," she muttered. "All right, I'll do it, even if I curl up and die of pain."

"When?" he asked, his voice strangely husky, his eyes searching hers.

"When do you want to?" she asked warily.

"Next week." When she gasped, he added, "Well, that's how it has to be unless you want newspaper coverage. I'm newsworthy—homely face and all."

"You are not homely; will you please stop running yourself down?" she asked, exasperated.

"If you'll stop talking about your gimpy leg, I'll stop talking about my homely mug," he replied.

"Done."

"Want a diamond?" he asked.

"No. Just a plain gold band."

"Have it your own way." He turned and started out the door.

"That's it?" she queried, astonished. "That's all?"

"What else do you want?" he asked reasonably. "If I get down on my knees on that cold floor, there's a good chance I'll be stuck there until spring. And kissing you to seal the engagement wouldn't make much sense, either, with you lying there naked."

"I am not naked!"

"As good as," he replied. "So I'm doing the decent thing and getting out of here, like a thoughtful prospective bridegroom. Don't stay up too late. We want to get a good start on those exercises in the morning. Sleep tight, now." And he closed the door behind him.

She stared at the door for a moment, open-mouthed. What a proposal! What an ardent bridegroom! She only wished she had some priceless Ming vase or something to fling at the door. She lay back, and with a muffled curse, pulled the covers over her head.

Ty, meanwhile, was walking down the long hallway whistling softly, his face animated, full of life—and almost handsome. He grinned and then he laughed. It was going to be a long, hard road, but he'd taken the first step. He was going to make up to her for every horrible thing that had happened. He was going to spoil her rotten. He opened the door to his own room and went in. Sleep would be a long time coming, he knew.

But he didn't even care.

Chapter Seven

Erin had hoped that being engaged would change Ty. Not so. He was the same as before, right down to the purely domineering way he made her do the hated exercises and stood over her the whole while.

"Why don't you do them too?" she grumbled a few mornings later as he was drilling her.

"My hip isn't busted," he explained patiently. "A little higher, honey; you aren't stretching far enough."

He never used to use endearments, but now he was calling her "honey" every chance he got. She smiled a little at that telling change of character. Well, she conceded, perhaps he had changed a bit. He was more relaxed since she'd been at the ranch, more approachable. She studied him while she did the bicycle exercise and thought that he didn't even seem all that homely to her anymore. He was a striking man physically, and he had beautiful hands—long-fingered, lean and elegant, darkly tanned like the rest of him, with flat nails and a sprinkling of dark hair on the backs.

"Take a picture," he advised, catching her appraisal. "It'll scare off the crows."

"Shame on you," she chided. "I was just admiring your manly physique, not criticizing you."

"You're not bad yourself," he murmured, smiling faintly as he ran his eyes over her body. "That burgundy thing you're wearing looks good on you."

"Thank you," she said, surprised by the compliment. "It's called a leotard."

"What are you going to get married in?" he asked between sips of coffee.

"Well," she began, panting as she sat up and wiped her face with a towel, "I have a beige street-length dress—"

"The hell you say," he interrupted hotly.

She stared at him, uncomprehending. "What's the matter with you?"

"White, that's what," he returned shortly. He put the cup down and kneeled beside her. "White. No beige or green or gray. You get married in a white dress."

Her face colored. "I don't have the right anymore," she murmured.

"It was me," he said levelly, although his eyes were flashing. "I remember exactly what you looked like, and how new it was to you. The instant it happened, I was looking straight into your eyes. I even remember how it felt: white."

She swallowed. "White," she said slowly, shaken by the passion in his voice, his eyes.

"No man ever had a sweeter virgin," he breathed, looking at her mouth. "No man ever enjoyed an initiation as much as I enjoyed that one. There's never been anyone but me, and we both know it. In the eyes of God, that married us as surely as any minister will, and nobody's going to shame you out of your white wedding dress. Not even your own little puritan conscience."

She managed a smile. "You're a nice man sometimes."

"I haven't had much practice at being nice," he confessed, toying with the sleeve of her leotard. "I grew up pretty alone, and I've been that way most of my life. I never mixed well. I still don't."

He was so different in these rare moods. So approachable. She reached out hesitantly and touched the back of his hand, letting her fingers learn the hair-roughened skin, the long, elegant fingers.

"Nicotine stains," she murmured, seeing the yellow between his forefinger and his middle finger. "Why do you smoke so much?"

"I only do it when I'm strung out, living on my nerves," he said quietly, looking straight into her eyes. "You do that to me. Having you around, being near you."

She smiled. "I can't imagine anything or anyone making you nervous, least of all me."

"Think so? Look." He held out his hand, and she saw that it was trembling slightly.

Shocked, she looked up into his eyes and saw the flames there, burning steadily, consuming. Suddenly she understood. "Oh, Ty..." she breathed.

"That's why you shouldn't carouse around here in see-through gowns," he murmured, smiling at his own vulnerability. "I'm a case when I get close to you."

She searched his silvery eyes quietly. So it hadn't been easy for him, either. His conscience had hurt because of the way things had happened. The loss of the baby disturbed him, Bruce's death had hurt, was still hurting probably. He'd had his own share of grief and guilt, yet he'd come himself to bring her back to Staghorn, forced her to feel again, bullied her into caring about her health. And she'd given him nothing except a hard time. Bruce had done this to them, out of misplaced love and blazing jealousy... but it was time to let go of the past and take responsibility for the future. Their future. It was too late to dwell on what might have been if Bruce hadn't interfered.

"After we're married," she said softly, choosing her words with exquisite care and looking into his eyes the whole time, "I'll let you have me."

A visible shudder went through his strong body. "You don't realize what you're saying," he said.

"So far, you've done most of the giving," she replied. "You've lost Bruce and part of your inheritance and been stuck with me to boot. You've made me go on living when I wanted to die. I think it's time I gave you something."

His jaw tensed. He got to his feet and moved away. "That's something we can discuss another time."

"I've set you off again." She sighed. "Oh, Ty, won't you ever learn not to blow up every time I say something personal?"

"Sure," he returned, wheeling, "when you stop offering me charity. I don't want your body in return for a roof over your head."

"I didn't mean it like that!"

"I don't want you that way," he said shortly. "Not as some damned sacrifice."

She shook her head. "You are the most maddening man," she said. "Just when I think I'm beginning to understand you . . . Okay, have it your own way. I'll sleep in the barn with the rats."

"I don't have rats in the barn," he said absently.

"Why not?"

"My king snake lives in there. He eats them."

She swallowed. "I take back my offer to sleep in the barn."

"It's just an old king snake. He wouldn't hurt you."

"Fear of snakes runs in my family," she told him. "I think my great-grandfather was eaten by one. He was a war correspondent. He disappeared in the jungles of South America, and his skeleton was found years later, they said, lying inside the skeleton of a monstrous python."

"A grisly end, all right," he agreed. "But king snakes don't eat people."

"That's what you say." She grimaced as she moved. "Damn these exercises! They get worse every day."

"You'll work the kinks out in a week or so. It will get easier, believe me."

"Why do I have to keep this up?" she groaned. "I'll never be able to model again, especially if I'm married."

He stared at her. "Won't you? Why not?"

"You'd let me work?" she asked, surprised.

"You're a human being, not my unpaid slave," he replied. "I don't believe in shackling a woman to the stove and keeping her pregnant. You're free to do whatever you want, except sleep with other men."

"I wouldn't want to do that," she said.

He laughed shortly. "No, I guess not. It must have been a pretty big disappointment." He turned back toward the door, lighting another cigarette as he went.

She gaped at him until she realized what he'd meant. Without giving herself time to think, she reached behind the easy chair, picked up one of his boots, and hurled it after him. It hit the wall instead of him, but it got his attention.

He stared at it as if he'd just found a dead fish on the carpet. He picked it up, looked at it, and turned to face Erin.

"Did you throw a boot at me?"

"Of course I did."

"Did you mean to hit the wall?"

"No," she said calmly. "I was aiming for your head."

"You could use a little practice," he observed.

"Not really. As big as your feet are, I could aim at a wall and still hit you if I tried hard enough."

He glared at her. "I do not have big feet."

"Neither do ducks."

He came back toward her, holding the boot, and the look in his eyes wasn't all that friendly.

She scrambled to her feet, grimacing and hobbling as she tried to get behind a barrier, any barrier. "No, go away!" she cried. "I'm crippled!"

"Not yet," he muttered, "but it's a distinct possibility."

"Ty! You wouldn't hit me!"

"Wouldn't I?" He grabbed her roughly around the waist, lifting her. "Now how brave do you feel?" he asked.

She shifted in his tight hold. "Put me down and I'll tell you."

"Stop squirming or you'll get put down the hard way." He looked into her eyes from an unnerving proximity. "Were your eyes always that shade of green?"

"I guess so."

"They look like leaves in early spring," he murmured, "just after the dew glazes them."

"Yours are like silver when you get mad," she told him. "And your eyelashes are almost as long as mine."

His eyes left hers, traveling slowly down to her mouth and lingering there. "Even thin as a rail and half dead, you're beautiful."

"I'm not, but thank you for saying so." She felt his breath, and her body reacted violently to his nearness. "I like the way your mouth feels when you kiss me," she said, half under her breath. "It's very hard and a little rough, and..." She moaned under the warm crush of his lips, stiffening, arching up against his hard chest, her arms clasping his neck violently.

If he was rough, so was she. She loved the feel of his muscular body, the male scent of him. Her mouth opened to taste more of his, and she moaned again as he took full advantage of that vulnerability.

He began to tremble, and she felt a twinge of guilt for inciting him. He didn't want her this way, and she shouldn't have thrown him off balance. But it was exciting to know she had such power over him.

She forced her throbbing body to be still, and her mouth gentled under his. Her fingers stroked his cheek, his hair, soothing him, as her lips moved to his cheeks, his nose, his closed eyes, his eyebrows. He was still trembling, but he didn't move, he didn't protest. He let her do what she wanted; stood quietly and let her explore his rough features.

"I'm sorry," she whispered as her lips moved back to his and brushed them apologetically. "I can't help it. When you touch me, I go crazy."

"I guess that makes two of us," he said gruffly. His eyes opened and looked into hers. "You're pretty wild when we make love. I never dreamed you'd be so uninhibited with me."

"Neither did I," she told him. Her mouth touched his cheek, opening, caressing. "I want...to do so...many shocking things with you."

He bit her lower lip gently, feeling her go taut at the tiny caress. "I ache," he whispered.

"So do I." She moved her breasts against his chest and whimpered a little with suppressed passion.

"Erin, if we don't stop now, we may not be able to. I wasn't this worked up the night I took you."

She let her forehead rest on his broad shoulder. "Neither was I," she said unsteadily. "But we've only been kissing."

"Not quite." He nuzzled his cheek against hers. "Move your breasts against me like that again."

She did, feeling them swell and go hard, feeling his sudden rigidity. "I don't want to hurt you," she whispered.

"You can't imagine what a sweet hurt it is." He drew her against him as he let her slide to her feet and feel every inch of him on the way down. His legs trembled a little at her nearness. "A kind of throbbing ache..."

"I want you," she said huskily, closing her eyes as his hands slid down to her hips and urged her even nearer.

"I want you, too," he replied. "But we can't. Not like this. It's too big a risk."

She sighed. "I guess so."

"It isn't my body saying that," he added dryly. "Only my mind."

She laughed at that, and the tension between them eased a little. "Is that so?"

He drew in a steadying breath and moved her away enough to satisfy her modesty. "We're getting married Tuesday," he reminded her. "I guess we can survive until then."

"I guess." She studied a loose button on his shirt and thought that after they were married, she could take better care of him. Sew on buttons and iron his shirts and wash his clothes—such intimate little things that were suddenly of earthshaking importance. She could even sleep in his arms....

She flushed, and he saw it and smiled.

"What brought that on?" he teased.

"Nothing."

He kissed her forehead tenderly. "You can sleep in my bed if you want to, after we're married," he whispered.

She felt hot all over. "Can I?" she asked. Her voice sounded breathless, wildly excited. She felt that way, too.

"All the time," he said huskily. "I can watch you undress, and you can watch me. We can touch each other. We can make love."

She trembled helplessly. "In the light?" she asked, looking up.

"In the light," he whispered, his voice urgent, deep. "Did you talk to the doctor about the Pill?"

"Yes. I..." She cleared her throat. It was hard to talk about something so intimate. She looked at his shirt instead. "It has to be started at a particular time, which...which I did two days ago," she faltered.

He chuckled softly. "I'm a cattleman," he whispered at her ear. "I know all about cycles and ovulation and 'that time of the month.'"

"Oh." She went really scarlet then and couldn't have looked at him to save her soul.

"Erin, it's part of life." He tilted her chin up, forcing her eyes to meet his. "There's nothing in marriage that should be taboo for a man and woman to discuss. I want honesty more than anything. I'll never lie to you, and I'll expect the same courtesy. I don't want you to be afraid to talk to me about anything that disturbs you."

"I never had anyone to talk to about sex," she whispered as if it were some deep, dark secret. "My mother did it all the time, but she was too embarrassed to discuss it with me. Everything I learned was from gossiping with other girls and reading books."

He smoothed her hair. "And with me," he added quietly.

"And with you," she agreed. "It was so intimate...." She hesitated.

"Talk to me," he urged. "Don't bottle it up."

He made it so easy, so natural. She toyed with the loose button on his shirt. It was a nice shirt, a brown check, and it moved when he breathed. She could see the swell of his muscles and the dark shadow of hair underneath it. "I'm sorry I fought you at the last," she whispered.

"You didn't expect it to hurt that much."

She raised her eyes. "No. Nobody told me. I thought it would just be uncomfortable."

"It probably would have been, if I hadn't been so hungry for you," he told her. "Women take a lot of arousing. But my education in that department is sadly lacking. Knowing the mechanics is one thing; putting them into practice is another. Put simply," he murmured, searching her eyes, "I know how to have sex. But I don't know how to make love. There's one hell of a difference."

"You never felt...you never wanted to do that with other women?" she asked.

He smiled, shaking his head.

She smiled back shyly. "I'm glad."

He brushed her hair away from her collar. "Didn't you ever want a man to make love to you?"

"Yes," she said, touching his shirt pocket gently. "I wanted you to, from the first time I saw you. It frightened me a little, because you didn't even like me."

"Like hell I didn't," he said gently. "I wanted you desperately."

"But you were horrible to me!"

"Sure I was," he said. "I didn't think you'd look twice at a face like mine."

So that was it. It had all been defensive on his part, and, as his father had taught him, the best defense was a good offense. She searched his hard face. "Bruce said you hated me."

His eyes darkened. "I know. I read the letters. It wasn't true. He played on my ego for all he was worth." He took one of her hands in his and stared at it for a long moment. "He said you laughed at me. At the way I was with you."

She shook her head slowly, deliberately. "That was the biggest lie of all."

He touched her face with gentle, searching fingers. "I'm sorry that I hurt you," he said. "That was the last thing I wanted, despite what I said at the time."

She felt like a young girl again, all shyness and excitement. "It wasn't all that bad," she told him. "I liked . . . touching you."

He remembered her hands, slowly exploring, feeling the hard contours of his body, deliciously uninhibited. He began to tremble. "God!"

"Ty. . ." She looked up with tormented eyes.

"Come here," he said roughly, pulling her hard against him, wrapping her up in a bearish embrace. "Come close. They say it helps if you hold each other until the ache goes away."

She closed her eyes and felt the rigidity slowly draining out of both of them. She was reminded of a particular passage in a book about lovemaking she'd once read. If a woman wasn't satisfied, it had said, she could ease the ache by being held very hard. Somehow Ty had known this.

"Do you read books about sex?" she asked.

"Sure," he replied dryly. "Don't you?"

"Not a lot," she confessed. "I found out more by listening to some of my girlfriends."

"What wild lives they must lead."

"You wouldn't believe it!" And she told him some of their adventures, right down to the scandalous details.

"For a shy girl, you tell a good story," he said, laughing. "Feeling better now?"

"Uh-huh," she murmured. "Are you?"

"I guess I'll live." He let her go reluctantly, looking into the softness of her eyes, enjoying the vivid alertness of her face. "What a change," he remarked, "from the pale little ghost I found in that New York apartment."

"I was pretty down," she admitted. "Life wasn't offering much just then."

He took both her hands in his. "I'll make it up to you," he said. "All of it, every bit."

"Ty..."

"Soak in a hot tub for a while, now," he advised, letting her go. "I have some outside work to get through. Later, I'll ride into Ravine with you and we'll pick out a wedding ring."

"All right." She watched him leave, her eyes soft and caring. Things were changing so rapidly. And what had begun as a trial, a fearful readjustment, was fast becoming the greatest joy of her life. She felt all the pain and bitterness draining out of her, being replaced by a growing excitement and feeling of closeness.

If only she could believe that he really felt something for her, something more than pity and desire and a need to make restitution for what he'd done to her. It was so difficult to read him, even now. She didn't want pity or guilt from him. She thought about the tenderness of his hands, the hungry roughness of his mouth... She wanted him, that was undeniable. But she wanted something else as well. She wanted him to... need her. Yes. Need her. Because she... needed him. There was another word, too, a deeper word. But she was afraid to even think it. That would come later, perhaps, if things worked out.

She went back to the hated exercises for the first time without being told. She had to get back on her feet, she had to be whole again; because it was imperative that she show him she could stand alone. Then, if he still turned to her after that, without pity and without guilt... then there might be the hope of something deeper between them.

But until he saw her as a woman, and not some crippled songbird with a broken spirit, she could never be sure of him—or herself.

Chapter Eight

Ty and Erin were married in a quiet ceremony in the small Presbyterian church where the Wades had worshiped for two generations.

Erin wore a white street-length dress with long sleeves and a high neckline. She'd hoped that she wouldn't need her cane, but it was still difficult to walk without it.

Ty was wearing a well-tailored three-piece suit, and he looked debonair and worldly. He towered over Erin, even though she wore high heels, and she felt small and vulnerable standing next to him.

A handful of people witnessed the ceremony, including Ty's foreman, Stuart Grandy, Conchita and José, and a few neighbors. It only took a few minutes, and as Ty slid the small circle of gold onto her finger, he brushed his lips gently against her mouth in a kiss that was more promise than reality.

Erin felt tears burning her eyes, and she tried desperately not to cry. Ty seemed to realize that her emotions were in turmoil because he smiled at her and produced a handkerchief as well-wishers gathered around them.

"Well, somebody had to cry at my wedding," she said, dabbing her eyes, "and who better than me?"

"I'd cry, too, if I had to marry him," declared Red Davis, one of Ty's cowhands.

Ty glared at him. "There went your Christmas bonus."

Red grinned. He was only in his early twenties, and full of rowdy humor. "Think so? In that case, wait until tonight, boss."

"You set one foot on my homestead and I'll load my Winchester," Ty told him.

"Reverend Bill, did you hear what he just said?" Red called out to the tall, bespectacled minister. "He says he's going to shoot me!"

"I never!" Ty said, looking shocked.

Reverend Bill Gates chuckled as he joined them. "I heard why he said that, Red, and if you go onto his porch, I'll lend him some buckshot for his shotgun."

Red shook his head sorrowfully. "Shame on you."

Bill grinned. "Shame on you."

Ty took Erin's hand in his and braced himself for all the congratulations. She wondered if he found this as much of an ordeal as she did. She wasn't all that comfortable in public yet, with her scars still visible and her self-confidence shot to pieces. But she leaned on Ty instead of the cane and forced herself to smile.

Eventually, they returned to Staghorn for the reception. Conchita had taken care of all the details, and had even hired a caterer to help so that there would be plenty of food. It seemed to take forever for the guests to eat their fill, and by then Ty was into a heavy discussion with two of the neighboring ranchers about the growing number of oil fields in the area.

Erin felt guilty for being so irritable, but she was fuming long before the last piece of cake had been finished off. She went into the kitchen with Conchita and helped her wash dishes.

"Is not right," Conchita grumbled, glaring down at *la señora*. "On your wedding day, this is not the proper thing for you to be doing."

"That's right," Erin agreed. "So you wade in there and tell my new husband that."

"Not me," Conchita replied. "I like my job."

"You and I could take this terrific dishwashing routine on the stage," she told the housekeeper. "We'd make a fortune."

Conchita stared at her, round-eyed. "Perhaps it is the fever."

"I don't have a fever."

"No?" Conchita grinned, her teeth a flash of white in her dark face.

Erin flushed and grabbed at a dishtowel. "I'll dry."

"As you wish, *señora*."

Ty found them there half an hour later. He stopped in the doorway, watching. "What a hell of a way to spend your wedding day," he said shortly.

"No, it's not," Erin replied, smiling poisonously over her shoulder. "It's super. Conchita and I are going to take this great act on the stage. We'll win awards."

"I wouldn't buy a ticket."

"You're just jealous because nobody would pay to watch you and Mr. Hawes and Mr. Danson stand around and talk oil and cattle for two hours."

"So that's it," he murmured.

"Now you will get an insight into the true nature of woman," Conchita informed him, putting her dishtowel aside. "Go off and fight, and then you can make up properly. José is taking me in to town to shop for Christmas, so you will have the house all to yourselves."

They waited, glaring at each other in silence, until she'd left the kitchen.

"I don't want to make up with you," she told him furiously.

"So stay in here and pout," he replied. "I can always go work off my temper with the men."

"Good! Why don't you start a fight? Maybe I could sell tickets to that!"

He glared at her one last time, turned on his heel, grabbed his Stetson, slammed it onto his head, and stomped off toward the porch. The door crashed loudly behind him.

Erin flung a plate at the door. Unfortunately, it was one of those new unbreakable ones, and it only made a loud thud, not a satisfying shatter. She sighed and picked it up to wash it again. By the time she'd finished, tears were streaming down her cheeks.

Ty stayed away all day. Conchita and José came home to find Erin in her own room and Ty outside with his men. They stared at each other for a moment and then shook their heads as they went about their business.

By early evening, Erin had taken a bath and settled into her bed, two short novels by her side. At eight-thirty she unlocked the door to Conchita, who bustled in with a bowl of homemade soup and some hot coffee. Erin closed her ears to Conchita's well-meant grumbling and in the process forgot to relock the door behind the housekeeper. She ate the soup, drank the coffee, and finished the second novel, by which time she had a genuine headache and a throbbing hip. She felt thoroughly miserable. She wished she'd never met Ty in the first place; she was sure that she hated him. Somewhere along the way she drifted off to sleep, tears drying on her cheeks.

Ty came in about midnight, dirty and disheveled and half out of humor, and found her asleep in her own room. He glared at her sleeping form for a long moment before he closed the door again and went to his room to spend a cold, unsatisfying night by himself.

The next morning, Erin was up before breakfast, exercising by herself in the living room. She'd show him! She'd get better, then she'd leave him! She'd go back to work and make a fortune and have men running after her all over the place, and then he'd be sorry! The thought gave her fresh energy. She was going full steam when Ty walked into the room, smoking a cigarette.

"Good morning," he said.

"Good morning," she replied sweetly. "I hope you had a horrible night?"

"I did, thanks. How about you?"

"I hardly slept."

"You were sawing logs when I came home," he remarked.

"Oh, then you did finally come home?" she asked sarcastically. "How kind of you."

"You started it," he muttered.

"No, you did." She glared at him. "Ignoring me like that in front of everybody, letting me go off and wash dishes on my wedding day! How could you!"

He took a deep breath. "I've been a bachelor for thirty-four years, and I'll remind you that this is no conventional love match. We got married to keep gossip down, didn't we? Or is there a reason I don't know about?"

He was right. She stared at him blankly while she went over their relationship in her mind. Then she forced herself to compare that reality to the idyllic little fantasy of mutual love she'd created. Finally she lowered her eyes.

"I'm sorry," she said dully. "I had no right to get upset like that. We did get married to keep gossip down, after all."

He was sorry he'd opened his mouth when he saw the life drain out of her. All the lovely brightness, all the excitement that had given her such beauty yesterday…gone. He hadn't thought about it from her point of view. Women took things so seriously. His eyes narrowed as he watched her sitting there, slightly stooped, and it suddenly occurred to him that she might have expected him to behave like a . . . well, like a bridegroom. He'd been so busy trying not to frighten her that he'd obviously gone overboard. Now she thought he didn't want her, that he didn't care.

"Did you want me last night?" he asked gently.

"No," she said.

He knelt beside her and tilted her chin up, forcing her wounded eyes to meet his.

"Yes," she mumbled.

"Then why didn't you say so?" he asked.

"What did you expect me to do, walk up to you in the middle of a discussion on artificial insemination and tell you I wanted to make love? I'm sure your neighbors would have found that interesting."

He smiled faintly. "I guess they would have." He touched her hair, feeling its dampness. "I don't know much about being a husband. You'll have to bear with me until I get the hang of it."

She searched his eyes. "Maybe I'm just expecting more from you than you want to give. Things have never been normal for us. I've been so confused...."

"And so hurt." He grimaced. "And I seem to do more of it every day. Hurting you is the last thing I want."

"And pity is the last thing I want." She touched his hand where it rested on her shoulder. "I'm having some problems with this hip." Well, that's almost the truth, she told herself; it does ache. "It's made me irritable. I'm sorry I've made things difficult for you. I won't be troublesome anymore, I promise." She got to her feet, moving away from him, oblivious to the stunned look on his face. "What Conchita said yesterday reminded me that I haven't done any Christmas shopping, either. I don't relish walking around a lot, but I need to buy some things. Could you spare someone to drive me over to San Antonio?"

His face hardened. "I'll drive you myself," he said coldly. "When do you want to go?"

"Saturday would be fine."

"All right." He turned and left her without another word. She didn't let herself think about why. She wasn't going to beg for his attention; if he didn't care enough to give it, she'd learn to live without it. Somehow.

It was a long week, during which she and Ty met at the table and nowhere else. She found things to keep her busy, as did he, and they communicated only when it was absolutely necessary. Conchita just shook her head and mumbled, but she was too wary of Ty to come right out and say anything. His temper went from bad to worse. Erin could hear him out at the corral, giving people hell for everything from leaving gates open to breathing. She felt responsible, and she kept out of his way as much as she could. The marriage that had started out with such promise was turning into a fiasco.

Finally Saturday came, and Ty was ready, as promised, to escort Erin to San Antonio. He looked rich and important in his cream-colored dress Stetson and boots—and every inch the Texan in faded jeans and a denim jacket. Erin felt a little dowdy beside him in a simple gray jersey dress. She didn't have many clothes, but she wasn't going to spend money buying new ones. She still didn't feel entitled to her share of the ranch, despite the will and everything that had happened to her because of the Wades. She'd never forgotten what Ty had said in the car, how he'd accused her of wanting to live off him. She didn't realize that he hadn't actually meant what he'd said, so she'd taken the words at face value.

"Is there any particular place you'd like to go?" Ty asked politely as they reached the outskirts of the city.

"I don't care," she murmured, staring out the window at the sprawling metropolis. Despite the fact that a million or so people lived in San Antonio, it seemed nicely spread out except for right downtown near the Alamo Plaza. At least there were plenty of parking lots around, she thought.

"It's a big city," he said. "It would help if I knew what you wanted to shop for. Are you looking for new clothes?"

"Why? Do I look like I need some?" she asked, glaring at him.

"You wear that same dress every time we go out," he remarked. "It's wearing on my eyes."

"Then by all means, I'll buy another one," she said coldly.

"Go ahead, take it personally," he said, his eyes never leaving the road. "Better yet, why don't you sit down and cry? That would make me feel even worse than I already do."

She bit her lower lip hard as sidewalks and pedestrians blurred past the window of the Lincoln. "I haven't had money to spend on clothes."

He glanced at her angrily. "Do you know what Staghorn is worth at current market prices?" he demanded.

"I am not spending your money on clothes. I'll spend what I made modeling."

"For God's sake! What the—"

He broke off as a parking lot caught his attention, near the Alamo. He pulled into the last vacant spot and parked before he turned to her with blazing silver eyes.

"Now look here..." he began. Then he caught the glimmer of tears in her eyes, despite the fact that her face was averted. Instantly he calmed down. He reached for one of her hands, tightly clenched on her purse, and pried it loose. It was soft and slender and very cool. He touched her pulse and found it was racing wildly.

Erin jerked her hand away and glared at him.

"Could we go shopping, please?"

"Yes, I think it's about time we did," he murmured. "And I know the perfect spot for it."

He took her arm and escorted her down the street, into an elegant old hotel. She watched, wide-eyed, as he booked a room, then drew the manager off to one side and murmured something. A minute later, he took the key, signed the register, and led her into the elevator.

The room was old but elegant, done up in shades of green with all the modern furnishings coordinated to please the eye. And there was a huge king-size bed.

"What are we doing here?" she asked hesitantly.

He locked the door and laid the key on the dresser before he turned toward her, his eyes as deep and mysterious as a winter day. "I'll give you three guesses," he said, moving toward her.

Her breath caught in her throat. She couldn't move. He took her purse away from her and then proceeded to undress her.

"You and I need a lot of privacy." He removed the dress and her slip and laid them aside. "We haven't had it at the ranch. But we'll have it here."

She swallowed. "We're going to...to...?"

"Yes." He bent and put his mouth softly over hers, feeling it tremble. "There's nothing to be afraid of, Erin," he murmured. "I won't hurt you this time."

"But-b...it's daylight," she faltered.

"We have to get used to each other sometime," he said reasonably. "And the curtains are drawn. It isn't so much light, is it?"

His hands were behind her, feeling for the clasp of her bra. He found it and loosed it, then gently removed the wisp of lace and silk. His eyes adored her for several long moments before he bent and removed the last silken undergarment. She was a little self-conscious, especially about the scars; but he didn't seem to mind them, and after a minute she relaxed and let him lower her to the bed.

"Get under the covers," he said gently, as if he knew how difficult it was for her. "You don't have to watch me if you don't want to. We've got plenty of time to get used to the sight of each other."

There were rustling sounds as he undressed, and a minute later she felt him slide under the cool sheets beside her.

"Now," he whispered, moving above her so that he could look down into her eyes. "Now, here, our marriage begins."

She pushed at his chest until she felt the erotic combination of hard muscle and abrasive hair. Her hands were fascinated by it, by the pulsating feel of it.

He moved the cover down to her waist and looked at her breasts with warm, curious eyes. His hand reached out and touched her there, feeling her go hard, watching her.

Her own eyes followed his, and she saw his long fingers exploring her, discovering the textures, with exquisite tenderness. Her breath caught, because it was new and exciting to realize that he was her husband now, that all the old taboos had been lifted.

"We're married," he said as if reading her thoughts. "Will you try to remember that it's all right for us to do this now?"

"I'll try...." Her eyes were drawn to his broad, tanned chest. "You must strip to the waist when you work outside," she said curiously.

"I do."

"I look white compared to you."

He lifted himself above her, letting his narrow hips move completely over her flat belly, watching her face contract at this new intimacy.

"Now move the cover away," he said, arching over her, "and watch me."

She trembled all over at the soft command, obeying him without even thinking, caught up in a growing tide of erotic pleasure. Her eyes traveled the length of their bodies, to where he was as white as she was; then he moved over her, and she felt the strength of him in an embrace that seemed more intimate than anything they'd done before.

"Oh, Ty...!"

"Put those soft hands on my hips," he whispered, "and hold me to you."

She moaned as his mouth came down over hers, feeling him tense, feeling the weight and warmth and maleness of him settling against her. His tongue probed inside her mouth, and she opened her lips to give him access, feeling him tremble as she moved and lifted toward him.

"You're my woman, Erin," he murmured, his lips a breath away from hers. He caressed her hips, urging them upward, moving them against his. "You're my wife."

She shuddered at the exquisite sensations flowing through her. She reached up, trembling as her breasts brushed against his hard chest, feeling him shudder too, feeling the tide of hunger overwhelm him.

"Sweet," he groaned, nudging her legs apart. "God, you're sweet, you're so sweet, so sweet...!"

His mouth shuddered against hers. He felt her move, heard her moan, and all at once it was happening. His head seemed to explode with the helpless urgency of his body. He moved feverishly against her, over her, feeling her body accept him with only a small spasm of protest.

She clasped his neck with her arms and gasped a little, but before she could begin to feel anything, it was over. He could feel her disappointment and damned himself for his infernal impatience. He was still shuddering helplessly in the aftermath of their lovemaking, but there was no pleasure in it for him now, no satisfaction: Erin had felt nothing.

He lifted his head and looked down at her, seeing the suspicious brightness in her eyes even as she tried to smile.

"Don't do that," he said gruffly. "Don't pretend. Don't you think I know how it was for you? You didn't begin to feel anything; I didn't give you time."

"It's all right—"

"No, it's not all right." He drew in a harsh breath and smoothed the hair away from her flushed face. "Oh, God, honey, I'm sorry," he whispered, bending to her mouth, kissing it with aching tenderness. "I'm sorry. Erin, I don't know how...." He groaned, burying his face in her throat. "I don't know how!"

He lifted himself away from her and got to his feet, reaching into his discarded shirt for a cigarette. He went to the window and stood staring out the slightly opened curtain, smoking, silent.

She stared at him curiously, uncertain. "Ty?"

"I've only had a handful of women, Erin," he said after a moment. "It was always just sex, nothing more. Just a need I satisfied. But it wasn't necessary to give back the pleasure. So I never learned how. I thought it might come naturally, but I guess it doesn't." He took a long draw from the cigarette. "I guess it doesn't."

She ached for him. With his intense pride, a confession like that must have taken a lot of courage. She got to her feet slowly, favoring her sore hip, and went to him.

"I don't know how to say this," she began, keeping her eyes on his chest. "But I don't think experience is all that important, if two people have a...a mutual need to please each other. I'm glad you haven't cared about those other women, because that makes it special with you. Almost as if I were the first woman for you."

"You are the first woman—in every way that counts," he said.

She lifted her eyes. "Then...then...maybe..."

"Can you tell me?" He searched her eyes. "Or at least show me? I'll do anything you want, anything I can to make you feel pleasure." He touched her hair hesitantly. "I don't get much out of it when I know you aren't enjoying it."

Her lips turned up a little at the corners. "I can't look at you and show you," she confessed shyly.

"You won't have to."

He put out the cigarette and lifted her easily in his arms. "Maybe I can hold back this time, since I'm not so hungry," he said, looking at her with kindling desire. "What do you want me to do?"

She arched her back a little, feeling the magic, feeling her femininity blossoming under his ardent gaze. "You know," she whispered.

"Yes, I think I do." And he bent suddenly and opened his mouth over the peak of her soft breast.

She moaned, stiffening, her voice breaking as she caught the back of his head and held him there.

He tasted her, savored her, as he lowered her to the bed. Her hands guided him, showed him where to touch her, how to please her with his mouth and hands. When he reached the softness of her inner thighs, she shuddered and cried out.

He grew drunk on the sound of those soft little cries, but carefully controlled the pulsating fever of his own body as he tasted and kissed and nibbled at her soft, sweetly scented skin. When he kissed her mouth again at last, she was crying.

He eased over her, slowly this time, and felt her arching under him, felt her hands at the back of his thighs, guiding, showing him where she was the most vulnerable, teaching him the rhythm she needed.

"Sweet," he whispered, opening his eyes to look at her.

She was moaning now, her skin glistening, her hair damp. Her eyes were half closed, glazed, her lips swollen and parted. She gasped and tossed her head restlessly back and forth on the bed. Her eyes opened, wild and frightened, then closed again.

"Shhhh, baby. Shhh." He soothed her with his voice, smoothed back her hair with his hands, comforting her even as he kept up the easy rhythm. "It's all right. Let go for me. Let go. That's it. Don't pull away, don't move back. Lie still and let me have you. Let me have you now."

Suddenly she cried out and opened her eyes wide. Her face contorted, her hands stretched out to the brass bars of the headboard and gripped them until the knuckles whitened. She writhed under him, moaning frenziedly and thrashing this way and that. She began to beg him, whisper to him. Her hips moved with his, moved, moved, until his mind began to feel the pleasure building in his own body.

All at once, her hips ground up against his and held there; she shuddered uncontrollably and began to cry as her body went into spasm after spasm after sweet, hellish spasm.

"Open your eyes!" he groaned, clenching his teeth as it began to explode in him, too.

She did, looking up at him. He saw her eyes for an instant, and then her face blurred as he was hurled through time in an explosion of unbearable brilliance—light and color and rainbows and waterfalls... Then, at last, all was still.

He felt her under him what seemed like hours later, felt her sweaty warmth, her pulsing heartbeat, the tender trembling of her arms and legs, and the faint sound of weeping.

"Oh, God, I didn't hurt you, did I?" He touched her face with his hand, gentling her. "Erin, did I hurt you?"

"No." She kissed his neck, his throat; she clung to him, still trembling softly. "Oh, sweet heaven, I never dared dream... I... Oh, Ty, that was so scary!"

"What was?"

"I... I went wild, didn't I?" she murmured. "I didn't even know what I was saying or doing, I just started shaking and I couldn't stop, and then... then, it burst inside me like an explosion, and I felt as if I were going to die of the pleasure, that I couldn't bear it..."

"The little death." He smiled. "The French call it that. I felt it too, for the first time in my life."

"People could die of it, all right." She clasped her arms tightly around him. "Let me feel all your weight," she whispered. "Lie on me."

He trembled a little at the husky note in her voice. "Like this?" he asked, giving her his weight. "I might crush you."

"I'd like that." Her hands slid down his muscular body, finding his hips and pressing them down over hers. She began to move, to surge sinuously under him. "Ty, I'm sorry, I can't seem to help it," she whispered.

"It's all right, honey," he whispered back, sliding his hands under her hips. "I'm just as hot as you are. Here." He moved her legs, positioning her, and then he lifted his smoldering eyes to hers and watched as he took her. "Don't close your eyes," he said softly. "This time, I want to see it."

She trembled gently, holding him as he moved. "Again, so soon?"

"I might make the record books," he said wryly, then grimaced at the surge of pleasure. "God!"

She lifted against him. "Can I watch you, too?" she whispered shakily.

"Yes!" His breath was coming wildly now as her body danced with his, matching each sharp move, teaching him, learning from him, in a rhythm that was quick and hard and devastating.

"Ty...Ty!" she moaned.

"Feel it!" he cried. "Feel it. Let me watch you...!"

Her eyes widened, dilated. She shuddered, and then it was all sharp pleasure and vast explosive sweetness, and his eyes were there, seeing her, dilating, bursting with it. She made a sound, then heard him cry out even as she saw his face contort and redden, his teeth clench, his body tense. She felt him in every cell of her body and clung to him while the world swayed drunkenly around them. . . .

The ceiling came into sharp focus. She stared at it, trembling, her skin saturated with warmth and dampness and pleasure. She felt him shuddering over her, and her hands smoothed down the long, muscular line of his back.

"We'll kill each other doing this one day," he whispered.

"I don't care." She nuzzled her cheek against his. "You're wet all over."

"So are you." He lifted himself away from her and fell onto his back. "My God. I can't believe I felt that."

"Neither can I." She sat up slowly and looked at him, really looked at him, with eyes that revealed both awe and delight.

He opened his eyes lazily and smiled when he saw her expression. "No comment?"

She smiled back and shook her head. "How about, 'Wow'?"

He laughed. "I could second that." He stretched and groaned. "I think we broke my back." Suddenly he sat up. "For God's sake, your hip!"

"It's all right," she told him gently. "Just a little sore. The doctor did say I should exercise it." She blushed.

"I wonder if that was the kind of exercise he had in mind." He grinned. "Should we discuss it with him?"

She hit him. That, of course, led to a bout of enthusiastic wrestling, which she lost. She laughed up at him, delighting in their newfound intimacy.

"I'll remember next time," he said, tracing her eyebrows softly. "You won't have to show me again."

She colored more vividly. "You're incredible," she said breathlessly, and dropped her eyes to his chest.

"So are you." He bent and brushed her mouth with his. "And now," he said, "how would you like to go shopping?"

She smiled. "I guess I can lean on the cane, can't I?" She laughed. "I think I'm too weak to walk."

"Then I'll carry you." He lifted her out of bed and set her on her feet. He searched her eyes. "No more regrets?"

"No more." She pillowed her cheek on his warm, damp chest. "Was this just an impulse, or did you plan it?"

"An impulse," he said. "I couldn't take any more nights like the past several. Cold showers are rough on the system in winter." He tilted her chin up. "And you were pretty jittery. I had a feeling we shared the same problem. Too many hangups, too little privacy. So I thought I'd try it."

She reached up and bit his lower lip. "Can I sleep with you from now on?"

He chuckled. "I think you'd better. The hall's pretty cold at night. And sneaking down it would wear me out."

"We wouldn't want that," she murmured dryly.

"No. We sure wouldn't." He tugged her hair. "Let's get some clothes on. I still have book work to do when we finish in town."

"Spoilsport."

He pulled on his jeans, glancing over his shoulder at her. "The sooner I get done with the books, the sooner we can go to bed."

She made a grab for her slip. "Well, what are you piddling around there for?" she asked. "Hurry up!"

He laughed softly. For the first time, he had some hope for the future.

Erin, watching him, was entertaining some hope of her own. She felt deliciously weary and fulfilled, and she wondered at his patience and stamina. He had to be the handsomest man alive, she thought dreamily as she watched him dress. He was more man than she'd ever known, and it was all of heaven to be his wife. She smiled to herself. What a beautiful start for a marriage, she thought. It could only get better.

Chapter Nine

Erin walked through the stores with Ty in a kind of dazed pleasure. He held her arm possessively, as if he might be afraid of losing her, and she pressed close beside him, drowning in the newness of belonging.

He needed a new watchband, so they stopped in a jewelry store. And after Ty had picked out a band and mumbled something to the jeweler, who was going to put it on for him, the friendly clerk talked him into trying on a huge diamond ring. He put it on and eyed it without much enthusiasm. And Erin got an idea.

She hadn't thought what to get him for Christmas, and she wasn't really sure that he'd like a wedding ring or would even wear one. But she had several hundred dollars saved up. And now she knew that the ring he'd tried on would fit him. He didn't like that one, but she saw him gazing steadily at a gold band inset with a string of diamonds. When the jeweler called him to look at the watchband, Erin motioned to the store clerk, told him what she wanted, and watched him slyly remove the ring from the case and size it. Glancing warily at Ty, he held his forefinger and thumb in a circle shape, and Erin grinned. While Ty was busy she quickly wrote a check and told the clerk to put the ring in a jar of jewelry cleaner.

"What are you doing? I'm ready to go," Ty asked impatiently as the clerk came back with a small sack.

"I needed some jewelry cleaner," she said with a straight face. "I'm ready now. Thank you," she told the clerk.

"My pleasure, ma'am," he replied politely.

"What do you need to clean?" Ty asked. "All you wear is that wedding ring."

"When I can keep up with it." She sighed. "I lost it for a while this morning. I know I left it on the sink, but when I went to get it, it had disappeared. And a few minutes later, it was back." She glanced at his rigid features. "Maybe I'm losing my mind."

"Not likely," he said. "Maybe your eyes were playing tricks on you."

She shrugged. "Maybe."

She didn't see him exchanging a grin with the jeweler. Which was just as well.

He went with her through the clothing stores in the mall, watching curiously as she looked at price tags more than at the dresses and jeans and blouses.

"That isn't necessary, you know," he told her. "You don't have to watch prices anymore. You own half the ranch, for God's sake. I maintain credit in this particular department store. You can have anything you want."

She glanced at him and smiled. She knew he wouldn't begrudge her a dress or two—or three or four, if it came to that. But it was important to her to maintain her independence. And she still didn't feel entitled to any inheritance. She was almost sure that Bruce had involved her mainly to hurt Ty, not because he'd loved her or had wanted to help. She simply couldn't use that money with a clear conscience. And Ty didn't know that she'd just drained her account to buy his Christmas present.

"I don't really see anything I like," she said at last. "I just like window-shopping."

He searched her wide eyes. "Erin, you don't have many clothes...." he began slowly.

"I don't need many, not when I'm just hanging around the house, do I?" she said. "Anyway, I don't care about having a lot of things to wear anymore. The days when I looked good in them are gone."

He looked as if he wanted to say something, then he shrugged and let it go.

The last stop Erin wanted to make was at a Christmas-tree lot. "We have to," she pleaded. "I can't celebrate Christmas without a tree to decorate."

He studied her. "Conchita usually sets up a little manger scene...."

"I want a tree," she moaned.

He sighed loudly. "You'll put yourself in bed with all this walking," he muttered, noticing the way she was leaning on the cane. "It doesn't have to be gotten today, does it?"

"I want a tree," she persisted.

He pulled off the road next to the tree lot and cut the engine, shaking his head. "Women."

"Men," she replied.

He opened the door and got out, and she smiled to herself.

The tree she wanted was a white pine, gloriously shaped and green. It still had its root ball, too, so that it could be planted after the holiday season.

"Oh, for God's sake!" he burst out. "Do you mean I'm going to have to pot the damned thing and then go plant it the day after Christmas?"

"I can't kill a tree in cold blood."

He gaped at her. "You what?"

"I can't kill a tree in cold blood, just to put it in the house for a few days. It isn't natural."

"Neither is this." He glared at the tree and the smiling man who'd just taken his money.

"If you don't let me have this tree, I'll stand one of your horses in the living room and decorate it," she threatened.

He stared at the tree. He stared at her. He stared at the man.

"Go ahead, say it," she told him. "Come on. Bah, humbug..."

He turned on his heel, grasping the tree in one hand. "Let's go," he muttered.

"You don't have to help me decorate it, either," she said after he'd put it in the trunk, of the Lincoln and helped her into the passenger seat.

"Good."

"You'll get used to it," she said gently.

He glared at her as he started the car and put it in gear. "Don't hold your breath."

She slid over next to him and almost immediately felt his body respond to the nearness of hers. He glanced down and then slipped his arm around her, pulling her even closer.

"That's better." She sighed and pressed her head against his shoulder.

His lips touched her hair, her forehead. His breath quickened. She reached up and touched his face, his rough cheek, his lips. He looked down and almost ran off the road staring into those soft, warm green eyes.

She smiled to herself, savoring his closeness, the spicy smell of his after-shave. In all her life, she thought, she'd never been happier.

They parked in front of the house, but before she could move away, Ty bent his head and kissed her. It was different from any of the kisses they'd shared before. Softer. More tender. More a caress than a kiss.

"I think we'll put you on the very top," he whispered. "You're as pretty as any angel I've ever seen."

"You sweet old thing," she said, and reached up to kiss him back.

"I'm not that old." He grinned.

She knew what he was thinking, and her cheeks went hot. "Quit that," she said, scrambling out of the car.

"We're married," he reminded her. "It's okay if we sleep together."

"Keep reminding me," she murmured, and glanced up at him. "You make it all sinfully exciting."

He chuckled. "So do you, wildcat."

"I'm going to get a bucket for the tree," she said, turning.

"Let Red do it," he replied. "You get off that leg before you break it. You've done enough walking for one day."

"Yes, Your Highness," she muttered.

"What are you going to decorate it with?" he asked suddenly.

She grimaced. "I forgot. Well, maybe Conchita can think of something."

"Maybe," he said.

The minute she went inside, he found Red, told him what he wanted done with the tree and slipped him a twenty-dollar bill to go and buy decorations.

Red gaped up at his boss. "Buy what?"

"Decorations," Ty said shortly. "For the Christmas tree."

"Christmas tree?"

"You eat a parrot for breakfast or something?" Ty demanded. "She wants a tree. She wants it decorated. I got the tree, but I don't have any decorations. There's twenty dollars." Ty nodded toward the bill. "Go get her something to put on it!"

Red whistled and pulled his hat low over his eyes. "Talk about earthquakes."

"I'll quake your earth if you don't get going."

"Yes, sir."

He walked off, shaking his head and muttering.

Ty glared after him. "You'd think he'd never seen a damned Christmas tree," he mumbled to himself as he headed for the house.

"The *señor* is putting up a tree? Inside the house?"

"A Christmas tree," Erin told Conchita. "To decorate."

There was a long, breathless garble of Spanish. "Never before." She shook her head. "Never, never. No tree, no fuss, he say; never mind turkey and things. Christmas is only for other people. Now here he buys a tree. I tell you, this is not the same man for whom I work since he is a young man. This is a stranger, *señora*. He smiles, he laughs, he compliments me on breakfast...." She threw up her hands. "A miracle!"

She went off to tell José about it, leaving Erin standing, amused and ummoving, in the hall.

"I thought I told you to sit down," Ty said, tossing his hat onto the side table.

"Well, I—Ty!"

He jerked her off her feet cane and all, and carried her into the living room, where a fire crackled merrily in the hearth. "Can't have you hurting that hip, can I?" he murmured. "I have plans for it later."

"Oh, do you?" she said, smiling as he found her mouth and kissed it gently.

He dropped into an armchair next to the fireplace and wrapped her up against him.

"Conchita told me you don't usually have a Christmas tree," she said lazily as his lips brushed hers.

"We don't. Not since my father died. It depressed me."

"Did he like Christmas?" she asked, fascinated.

He leaned back against the armchair, letting her head fall naturally onto his shoulder. "Sure," he said, smiling at the memories. "He was like a big kid. I bought him an electric train set the year before he died, and he played with it by the hour. He told me once that they'd been so poor when he was a kid, all he'd ever gotten in his stocking was fruit and nuts. He'd never even had a store-bought toy."

"Poor old soul," she said gently. "Did they love him, at least?"

"I don't think they'd wanted him," he said. "They had to get married because he was on the way. They never forgave him for forcing them to the altar."

She studied his collar, thinking about the child she'd lost. Some of the brightness went out of her.

He traced her cheek. "Don't look back," he said as if he knew what she was thinking. "We can't change the past."

She sighed. "I guess not."

He studied her averted face. "I sent Red after some decorations for the tree."

"Oh, Ty! That was nice of you," she said, diverted.

"I just thought it would be a shame to stand a live tree up in the house with nothing on it," he said. "People would stare."

"That's true." She cuddled closer. "Do you suppose we could forget my exercises tonight?"

He shifted her on his lap. "No," he said with a smile, and kissed her.

"Tyson!" she muttered. "I've walked around half the day!"

"That's good, but it's not what the doctor ordered. You want to walk again, don't you? Properly, I mean?"

"Yes," she admitted, then grimaced. "All right. I'll do the horrible things."

"That's my girl."

The odd thing was that she felt like his girl. There was a tenderness between them now that she noticed in the simplest acts. At dinner that evening, he seated her at the table. He creamed her coffee. And when he wasn't doing things for her, he watched her, stared at her with the most curious expression. She felt protected and safer than ever before in her life.

"Did your mother even come to see about you?" he asked as they sat over a second cup of coffee.

She shook her head. "She and I have never been close, you know."

"Why didn't Bruce tell me about the wreck?" he wanted to know, his eyes narrow and piercing.

She hesitated. It was just one more thing that would hurt him, and she'd had enough of that.

"Why didn't he?" he persisted.

"Ty, he wasn't deliberately cruel," she said, choosing her words carefully. She touched the back of his hand where it rested beside his coffee cup. "He was possessive . . . just obsessed with me—I wish I'd realized it sooner, but I didn't. Maybe he was afraid to tell you; or just didn't think you'd care . . ."

His face closed up. He turned his hand over and touched her fingers lightly. "He knew I cared," he said. "After he told me that bull about your opinion of me as a lover, I stayed drunk for two days. José told him about that."

"Oh, Ty," she breathed.

"I got over it." He looked up, his face harder than ever. "But I hated you for a while. If he'd told me about the wreck then..." He searched her wide green eyes, the elfin face in its frame of lustrous black hair, and the anger seemed to drain out of him. "Oh, hell, I'd have been there like a shot, who am I kidding?" he muttered. "I'd have walked straight through hell to get to you if I'd known you'd been hurt and needed someone."

Yes, he would have, she thought. But he didn't add that he would have done the same for any hurt or sick person. She knew how generous he was when people were down on their luck. Conchita had told her things about him—things she'd never known before—about the good works he did anonymously.

Her hand closed around his. "They told me that I was calling for you when they brought me in. It was already too late to save the baby, but I felt so empty and alone and frightened," she recalled, studying his lean hand. She saw it contract jerkily around her fingers.

He stood up suddenly, moving away from the table. "I'd better get that paperwork done," he said in a harsh, haunted tone.

She could have bitten her tongue for what she'd said. It just put up more walls between them. He was retreating into his, right now; withdrawing from the pain of the past.

"Ty..." she began.

"You'd better decorate your damned tree," he said without looking at her. "You can do those exercises later."

She threw down her napkin and stood up. "I wasn't trying to get at you," she said desperately. "You take every single thing I say at face value."

He turned and looked at her, his eyes blazing. "Do I? And without reason? You haven't forgiven me for what happened. In your heart, you blame me for the condition you're in and for losing the baby. And maybe I blame myself, too. Bruce made mischief, but I believed him. So did you. Maybe neither of us is willing to go that last step—to trusting each other. I haven't had any more practice at trust than you have. So it might not be a bad idea to step back and take a look at things before we start making commitments we don't really feel."

Her mind was spinning. She'd never heard him make such a long speech, and she didn't understand what he was saying. Did he mean that he didn't want a commitment to her? Did he want her to get well so that she could go away and leave him?

She started to ask him, but he was already striding away, lighting another infernal cigarette. She stared after him blankly for a moment, then got slowly to her feet and dragged herself into the living room. All the buoyancy, the magic of the day, seemed to have vanished.

It was hard going, standing long enough to get the decorations on. Conchita helped her dress the magnificent tree, talking animatedly about other Christmases when the *grande señor* was still alive, about all the company they'd entertained and the lavish parties they'd given.

"Never any parties since then." Conchita sighed. "Señor Ty does not like people."

"Especially female people," Erin muttered darkly, glaring at the ornament in her hand.

"*Sí*, that is true," Conchita agreed, taking the phrase at face value. "It is because of his looks, I think. He is sensitive about them, and he thinks no woman could ever care for him because he is not, how you say, a magazine pinup." She smiled and shook her dark head. "How sad, because it is not how a man looks, but what he is, that attracts a woman. Señor Ty is *muy macho*—you know, like my José. He will always be the man in the house, and that is how it should be."

Erin could have said something about that, but she bit her lip. She was in enough trouble with him already.

Ty didn't say a word about her tree when he walked into the living room later that evening. She was in her leotard, working out; he sat and watched her and coached for a few minutes, but his heart wasn't really in it.

"Do I get to sleep with you tonight, or am I still in the doghouse?" she asked finally, brushing back her damp hair.

He just stared at her, as if he couldn't quite believe what he'd heard. In fact, he didn't. He'd been sure she wouldn't let him near her, and here she was making propositions. He pondered over it until he decided that women probably felt the same urges men did, especially when they'd had a taste of fulfillment. She could therefore want him physically without loving him. Which was a bitter realization, because he'd only just come to the conclusion that the physical part of it wasn't all he wanted anymore. Somewhere along the way, he'd awakened to other needs: emotional ones.

"Do you want to sleep with me?" he asked, searching her eyes. "Now that you've had a taste of it, you can't live without it; is that what you're saying?"

It was like a slap in the face. She didn't see his hurt pride or his own insecurity or the disappointment he felt at what he interpreted as a self-centered expression of physical need. She only heard cutting words that made her feel like a tramp.

"I guess I can just turn on the electric blanket instead," she said after a minute, her eyes averted. "I can live without sex, thanks."

He started to speak, closed his mouth, got up and stomped out of the room. Erin stared after him with tears in her eyes. She couldn't bear the change in him, and all because she'd been trying to tell him that she loved him. She did love him, she realized. Perhaps she always had. At first, it had been a challenge to catch his eye, to make him notice her. And then, at some point—she couldn't say when—it had become something deeper, stronger. During all those long months of physical torment and mental anguish, the thought of him had sustained her. She'd wanted him so badly then; had wanted to call him, to tell him. But Bruce had managed to convince her that Ty despised her, that he still wanted nothing to do with her, especially now that she was a cripple. So she'd withdrawn into her shell and told herself she hated Ty for causing what had happened to her. But she hadn't, not really. One look at him was enough to open her heart, and being around him, with him, near him, had reawakened all the old hungers. Yes, she loved him. But in trying to tell him so, nervously working up to it, she'd only alienated him. And now there didn't seem to be a chance in the world of healing the old wounds.

As the days passed, things went from bad to worse. Ty ignored her. Unfortunately, his men weren't so fortunate; his temper was hot enough to start fires, and even Conchita and José were beginning to feel the heat. The food wasn't seasoned enough, the coffee wasn't strong enough, his car wasn't being cleaned properly, the stairs had dust on them. Everything irritated him. And when he wasn't complaining, he was locked in his study with the books. He hadn't touched Erin since they'd gone into San Antonio. He didn't seem to want to anymore, and she felt neglected and unwelcome.

By Christmas week, Erin began to notice how much she'd changed since coming to Staghorn. She'd been doing her exercises faithfully, even though Ty no longer watched her, and she was making some progress. She could walk for the first time without the cane. Her scars were fading. Her face had regained most of its radiance, and she was gaining weight. She looked more and more like the model Bruce had first brought to Staghorn—and the prettier she got, the angrier Ty got.

He'd begun to see her the way she'd been: a beauty, a lovely fairy who could have had any man she wanted, anytime. And then he looked at himself in the mirror and knew that he didn't have a hope in hell of holding her. Once she was completely well, she'd leave, go back to the old life, and he'd be alone. Well, damn it, he told himself, he'd known that from the beginning, hadn't he? He'd set out to shock her back to life and get her on her feet again; to make up to her for what he'd cost her.

She was well on the road to recovery. But he couldn't bear to get too close to her. His heart was vulnerable. If he didn't watch out, she'd carry it off to New York with her. It shocked him, disturbed him, to realize how vulnerable he was. He didn't want to care about her. He wanted to be whole and independent. But she was sapping him. He'd seen himself that day in San Antonio—so drunk on her that he was like a pet instead of a man, fawning on her. He'd hated his weakness. He kept hearing his father tell him not to let any woman do that to him; to keep himself strong, in command. All his life he'd denied those hungers, and now they were bringing him to his knees.

Finally, one morning, he decided it was time to fight back, to confront Erin—and himself. He headed for the living room, where he knew she'd be doing her exercises, then stood in the doorway for a moment, watching her with narrowed eyes.

When Erin saw him, she got to her feet with a minimum of awkwardness and brushed back her hair. "Yes?" she asked politely. "Did you want something?" She felt as if she were talking to a stranger. He was unapproachable now, carefully girded in his emotional armor. The iron man all over again.

He lifted the smoking cigarette in his hand to his lips, staring at her with amused contempt, the way he'd looked at her in the early days. It embarrassed her.

"Not bad," he said. "You're getting your figure back."

"Don't make fun of me," she said, keeping her voice even as she shifted from one foot to the other. "I can't help the way I look."

"That makes two of us."

She perched on the arm of the overstuffed chair and looked at him. He was thinner and, there were new lines in his face. Suddenly she realized how little communication there had been between them recently.

"Something's wrong, isn't it?" she asked, startling him. "And not just between the two of us."

He drew on the cigarette and blew out a thin cloud of smoke. "Guessing?"

She shook her head. "You look worried."

"I'm having a few financial problems," he said after a moment. "Or should I say, *we're* having a few financial problems, Mrs. Wade?"

"How bad is it?" she asked.

"Bad enough." He sighed. "I invested heavily in a consignment of grain to feed my cattle this winter. The silos were owned by a corporation that defaulted, and the grain was confiscated. That set me back on feed so I had to take a loss by selling off cattle in a bad market. One investment balances another, you see," he explained. "One loss causes another. Kind of like dominoes. We may pull out, we may not. It's going to take some quick thinking and a lot of legal advice. At that, we may lose half of what we own."

She smiled gently. "Well, half isn't so bad, is it, considering the size of Staghorn?"

"Could you live with half a body?"

"I've been doing it, haven't I?"

And that's all it took to set him off again. Without another word, he wheeled and walked out of the room. She cursed under her breath. If just once he'd stand still and talk about things!

She couldn't remember ever having had such a miserable Christmas. She'd wrapped his present and put it in a huge box, wrapped that, and put it under the tree. And all the time, she worried about what he would think. Their marriage was in terrible shape, yet she'd bought him a very expensive wedding band. She'd thought about returning it, but her stubborn heart wouldn't let her. As long as there was a ghost of a chance that he might someday learn to care for her, she couldn't give up. And maybe he'd like the diamonds, even if he didn't like the symbolism of the ring. Besides, he could always hock it if he got desperate for money, she thought, and then was astonished at her own cynicism.

She was up and dressed early on Christmas morning. Ty was already sitting in the living room when she walked in, and he looked wonderful in tailored slacks and a neat striped shirt. His hair was clean and meticulously combed, his face shaven. Erin knew he'd done it for her sake, and she wanted to thank him—or at least smile at him—but there'd been too much tension between them lately; she felt awkward and uncomfortable just being around him.

"Merry Christmas," she said politely.

"Merry Christmas." Ty stood up as she approached, motioning her to sit down across from him. He noticed that she was walking without her cane, and without limping noticeably. The emerald-green dress she had on complemented her eyes, as did the soft, natural-looking makeup she had artfully applied. Her hair was brushed forward, curling softly and framing her elfin face. All in all, she looked refined and thoroughly lovely. "Very nice," he murmured. At her expression of surprise, he added hastily, "The tree, I mean."

Erin glanced at it, then looked underneath and was faintly surprised to see a gaily wrapped package beside those she already knew were for José and Conchita.

"You got me something, didn't you?" he asked shortly, glaring at her.

"Well, yes..."

"So I got you something."

It was a big box. Of course his was, too, but that was just camouflage. She wondered if he might have done the same thing, then shook her head. Too wild a coincidence, she told herself. She poured some coffee from the elegant silver service Conchita had set up, then selected a sweet roll and settled back in the overstuffed armchair.

"You're walking much better these days," he observed. He leaned back against the sofa with his coffee cup in hand.

"I've been working hard," she replied.

"Quite a change from those first few days here."

She moved her shoulders restlessly. "Yes. Quite a change."

He sipped his coffee quietly. "Want to give out the presents?"

"Okay." She got up, faltering a little as she knelt. She heard him behind her, calling to José and Conchita.

They came in, grinning, took their presents and gave small ones to Ty and Erin. Then everyone opened their gift boxes and exclaimed over the contents. Erin found a beautiful shawl that Conchita had hand-crocheted for her and Ty, a muffler. Conchita opened a set of handkerchiefs from Ty and a small silver box from Erin, and José got a tie and a wallet.

"*Muchas gracias.*" Conchita grinned. "Now is okay if we go over to my sister's house, just for a little while, until time to serve the dinner?"

"Sure," Ty told her. "Go ahead."

"We come back soon." She laughed. "Thank you for these," she added, clutching her presents, and José echoed her thanks. Then they left, closing the door behind them. And Erin and Ty were alone, completely alone, for the first time since the day they'd bought the tree.

Chapter Ten

Erin finished her coffee nervously, wishing that she and Ty could go back to the early days of her residence here and recapture the budding magic of being together. There seemed to be such an insurmountable barrier between them now. He was always on the defensive—perhaps out of his own guilt—and she couldn't reach him anymore.

He seemed to be nervous himself, if his chain-smoking was any indication of it. He moved restlessly to the tree, picked up her present and handed it to her.

"We might as well get this out of the way," he said gruffly, pausing to pick up the box with his own name on it.

Erin, sitting quietly with her present beside her on the sofa, felt really uncomfortable as she watched him open it. What was he going to think of the ring? Would he be angry? Would he be surprised?

He removed the wrapping and looked inside at the smaller box. Glancing curiously at her, he picked it up, slowly unwrapped it and then opened it.

His expression was one of numb shock, and Erin wanted to go through the floor.

She got up and knelt a little awkwardly beside him. "I'm sorry," she said, reaching for the box. "It was a stupid thing to do. I didn't mean—"

He caught her wrist. "Here," he said in an odd, gruff tone. "Put it on."

It took a moment for her to realize that he wanted her to put it on his finger. She fumbled it out of the box nervously and slid it onto his ring finger, relieved to find that it was a perfect fit.

He looked up then, his eyes strange and glittering, holding hers.

"You don't...mind?" she faltered.

He put his hands on either side of her face, searching her fascinated eyes, and bent over her. His mouth descended, pressing her lips softly apart, shocking her with the aching tenderness of his kiss.

Tears stung her eyes as she closed them. It had been so long since he'd touched her, since he'd kissed her. She caught her breath as he deliberately deepened the kiss, tilting her face at a sharper angle to give himself better access to her soft mouth.

She wanted to reach up, to hold him to her and savor the sweetness of being near him at last. But it was too soon; there had been so many misunderstandings between them, so much grief. She couldn't be sure he wasn't just trying to find some new way to torment her.

She pulled back gently and lowered her face.

He sensed her withdrawal, and the tenderness he was feeling for her clouded over with pain. She was building a wall of her own now, and thanks to his black temper, he wasn't going to get past it easily.

"Thank you," he said. He wanted to add that he wouldn't take the ring off until he died, that it would always remind him of her.

"You're welcome," she said shyly. "I . . . bought it the day we went to San Antonio."

He remembered that day all too well; it had haunted him ever since. His face went hard with bitter regret. "What did you buy it with?" he asked suddenly. "You wouldn't let me stake you."

She shifted a little, tugging at the skirt of her dress. "I . . . had a little money saved."

He looked down at the ring. Diamonds. Real ones, set in gold. "My God," he said under his breath. His eyes met hers and saw the embarrassment there. "This was expensive."

She only looked more uncomfortable.

He sighed as he looked at the box he had wrapped for her. It was nowhere near as expensive as her gift to him. He hadn't known how she'd feel about a ring now, so he'd taken back the ring he'd bought her before all the difficulties began and traded it for an emerald necklace—a very small emerald, with a few tiny diamonds, on a slender gold chain. It had reminded him of her—bright and delicate and beautiful.

"I wish I'd taken more trouble over yours," he said hesitantly.

"I'll like it," she assured him.

He handed her the package and she opened it, finding that he had indeed duplicated her camouflage. She opened the first box, then the second, and caught her breath at the sight of the exquisitely crafted necklace nestled in the velvet lining of the box.

"Oh, it's so lovely," she whispered, touching it. "It's the loveliest thing I've ever seen!"

She took it out gently, fingering it, her face bright with pleasure, and he forgave himself for not having gotten her something more expensive. She seemed to be genuinely pleased with it.

She laced it around her neck and secured it, lovingly touching the stone as she smiled. "Thank you," she said softly, her voice tender and husky, her face so beautiful that he wanted to take her in his arms and lower her to the carpet in a fever of passion.

Her eyes caught the flash of desire in his, and she hesitated about touching him. But in the end, her pleasure at his gift forced her forward. Shyly, she reached up and kissed the corner of his mouth, just faintly brushing it.

"Thank you so much, Ty," she whispered.

He stiffened at the touch of her lips, trying not to betray how vulnerable he felt when she came close. Her gentle rejection of him earlier had hurt. He didn't want to risk it a second time, so he didn't touch her. When her lips moved away, he just looked at her, noticing the heavy shadows under her green eyes, the paleness of her face. She was beautiful, but there was a haunting sadness about her, a sadness he felt responsible for. He felt responsible for a lot of things. His conscience had disturbed him for days, for weeks. She might forgive him someday, but he couldn't forgive himself. And his growing feeling for her had only made it worse, had only deepened his guilt. He'd struck out at her in pain, but she couldn't know that. And he was too proud to tell her.

"I'm glad you like it," he said, rising. He moved away from her, pacing restlessly.

"The financial situation," she said after a minute. "Is it any better?"

His broad shoulders lifted and fell as he felt for a cigarette and lit it. "Not appreciably."

She bit her lower lip, thinking. She was walking much better now. And the more she exercised, the better she got. Before long, she'd be walking easily. The facial scars were fading, too. She was a new woman already. And she had talent, and the contacts to go back into modeling. Perhaps she could make enough money to help him out.

She sat back down on the sofa. "I've been thinking," she said hesitantly, glancing at him. "I'm improving every day. In a little while, I might be well enough to go back to New York and get back on with my agency."

His back went ramrod stiff. So here it was—she was feeling her beauty again. She was missing the old life, and she wanted to leave. She was hungry for—how had she put it?—the bright lights and the excitement. And maybe for a man whose face didn't look like the side of a cliff. He laughed bitterly to himself. At least he had no illusions about her feelings for him. He hadn't fooled himself into thinking that just because she responded to him physically, she felt anything emotionally.

"If that's what you want, go ahead," he said carelessly. "It might be a good idea, after all."

She'd known he was going to say that. Even so, his saying it gave her a sinking feeling, and she struggled to speak normally. "I can't go immediately, of course. I'll need a little more time."

"Wait until spring, if you like." He sounded indifferent, but the silvery eyes she couldn't see were telling a different story.

"No, I won't need that long," she said quickly. "I'll just take another few weeks."

"Suit yourself." He took a long draw from his cigarette and studied the ring she'd put on his finger. He loved the feel of it, the symbolism of it. When she'd bought it, she must have felt something tender for him, at least. The memory of it would have to last him all his life, through all the years without her, without his love.

He thought about the child she'd lost, and his eyes darkened with pain. She'd felt alone, she said, and empty. And he remembered that, and ached to think of her with no one to look after her, to care for her. She'd been all by herself in that hospital, and he wondered . . .

He turned unexpectedly and saw her watching him. "You wanted to die, didn't you?" he asked gruffly.

She blinked. "What?"

"After the accident." He held the forgotten cigarette carelessly in one lean hand. "You wanted to die."

How had he known that? She hated discussing it. Every time they talked about it, he got worse, more distant, more unapproachable.

"I thought my life was over," she said slowly. "I suppose, for just a little while, I didn't care about living."

He examined her carefully, noticing the becoming weight gain, the silkiness of her hair, the brightness of her eyes. "I guess you damned me to hell every time you thought about me," he murmured.

"I wanted to call you," she confessed, flushing.

He didn't move. He didn't breathe. "You...what?"

"I wanted to call you. I almost did." She searched his narrow eyes quietly. "But Bruce convinced me that you had no use for me, that you wouldn't have spoken to me anyway," she said. Her eyes darkened with remembered pain.

"I would have come, though," he said.

She tried to smile. "I think I realized that before, but it was nice to hear it, all the same. It feels so terrible now. I hated you for all the wrong reasons, for things that Bruce was responsible for. But I believed him, you see."

"I guess you had enough reason not to question what Bruce told you," he replied, his voice deep. "I'd been unspeakably cruel to you."

She searched his face. He had such a poor opinion of himself; how could she tell him that she thought he was the sexiest man alive, and that she grew as shy as a schoolgirl every time she was near him?

"Why?" she asked gently. "Was it really just because you wanted me?"

"What other reason could there have been?" he countered brusquely, drawing away.

Once, she thought wistfully. Just once to shake him out of his brooding, to unsettle him. She wondered what he'd do if she peeled open her bodice and let him look at her.

He walked to the door, touched the doorknob and hesitated. "I've got a new colt in the barn," he said with his back to her. "Want to come look at him?"

The invitation was unexpected, and it thrilled her. She smiled shyly. "I'd like that, yes."

"You'll need a jacket. It's cold out today."

She followed him into the hall, forcing herself to take slow, easy steps and not to limp. She was proud of her progress, and it showed in the radiance of her elfin face, her big green eyes. She laughed as he held out a denim jacket to her. It was broad and long-sleeved and had to be one of his.

"That will swallow me," she protested.

"You don't seem to have a winter coat," he replied, hesitating uncharacteristically. "I couldn't find one in the closet a few days ago."

She smiled at him. "I used to have a full-length mink. I sold it, after the... after I... Oh, Ty, don't," she said, the smile fading at the look in his eyes. "Please don't. You said yourself that it was in the past, and it was. We can't go back."

"I wish we could," he said fervently. "I'd give anything to change it."

"Here," she said as she handed him the coat. "Put this enormous thing on for me, and I'll try not to trip over the hem."

He actually laughed, although it was quick and faint. "All right. Put your arms in."

It was cold outside, and a little misty, and the sky was as gray as Ty's eyes. He took her arm, propelling her toward the large, modern barn.

All his hands had the day off, and most of them were away from the ranch with near and distant kin, celebrating Christmas. Erin followed Ty into the cool interior and waited until he closed the door. Then she followed him down the long, neat corridor that separated rows of clean, straw-filled stalls, only a few of which were occupied.

"Don't you have many horses?" she asked curiously.

"We," he corrected "have quite a few. But we only bring the expectant mamas in here."

"Because of the cold?"

"That's it." He stopped at the next stall and turned her to the right. "There he is. Born last night."

He was an Arabian. Pure black, with the small head that denoted a purebred stallion, and so tiny. He walked on spindly legs that seemed too tiny to support him, and his proud mama licked and nuzzled him. As she watched, Erin marveled at the ability of an animal to show such tenderness.

"Most mares make good mothers," he said, smiling at the little one. "You won't know him in about a month, when he's got the freedom of the paddock and can toss his head and gallop. He'll be a different colt then."

She leaned back against the side of the stall, searching his dark face. "You love your animals, don't you?" she asked.

"It's easy to love animals," he replied, pinning her with his eyes. "They can't hurt you, except maybe physically if you abuse them or pen them in a corner."

"And people can."

"I learned that as a boy," he told her. "Anything different gets attacked, haven't you figured that out by now?"

"Were you so different?" she asked.

"Big feet, big ears, a face only a mother could have loved, and a black temper," he replied. "You tell me."

"I did notice the black temper," she murmured.

"When?" He laughed coldly. "You haven't come near me lately."

"How could I, when you've avoided me?" she replied, her eyes kindling. "You've done everything except ask me to leave."

"I can't do that," he said. "You're half owner. And my wife."

"In name only."

"Not since that day in San Antonio," he replied curtly, and the memory was in his eyes, like a fire burning.

"That's right," she agreed, deliberately misunderstanding him. "Not since. Not once." She let the denim jacket slide down her arms, oblivious to the shock in his eyes. Her hands went to the bodice of her dress and began to unfasten the buttons.

"What in hell are you doing?" he demanded. But his eyes were watching her hands, not her face.

"I've gained weight," she said. "I thought you might like to see for yourself."

Without questioning her own motives, her own hunger, she opened the last button and slowly peeled the dress down her arms. The material was medium-weight, so she hadn't bothered with a bra. Her breasts were high and full and firm, and she displayed them brazenly, her heart throbbing wildly in her chest.

"Erin . . ."

She liked the rapt expression, the appreciation that darkened and narrowed his eyes and quickened his breathing. She came close to him, quietly removing his coat while he watched her, disbelieving. Slowly she unbuttoned his shirt, exposing his broad, hair-matted chest to her exploring hands. She smiled in satisfaction as the thick, cushy hair tickled her palms.

"Oh, Ty. . ." She slid her arms under his shirt and around his waist, so that she could press her taut breasts against him.

"God," he groaned. He caught her shoulder and moved her abrasively against him so that he could feel her silky firm flesh and aroused peaks brushing against his muscular chest. She was so warm, so sweet.

His heart ran wild when her hands found him, bla-tantly caressed him in a place she'd never touched before. He almost went to his knees with the force of the passion she aroused.

She felt his hunger for her and moved closer, letting her thighs touch his, drowning in the remembered pleasure of flesh against burning flesh.

"Your skin is hot," he whispered roughly.

"So is yours." She arched backward so that she could see his face. Her own was flushed with hunger, her eyes fiercely passionate, her lips parted sensually. "I want you."

"Yes, I know," he said, his voice harsh and almost unrecognizable. "I want you just as much."

Her breath sounded ragged as it sighed out. "Here," she whispered. "Can...we?"

"I think we'll have to," he replied with bitter humor, shuddering a little with his own arousal. He bent and lifted her, pressing his mouth hungrily against one full, perfect breast and glorying in her passionate response.

She moaned sharply, opening her eyes as he lifted his head. She shuddered in his hard embrace, feeling his body absorb the shock of his steps as he carried her to the end stall, which was filled with clean hay.

"No one will come, will they?" she asked.

"No one will see us, or hear us." With one hand he jerked a clean piece of canvas off the wall to use as a cover over the soft but prickly hay. Then he lowered her to their makeshift bed and slowly peeled the dress down her hips, taking her lacy undergarments and hose with it in an undressing that was pure seduction. His lips followed the movement of his hands, and he used them both to drive her wild, nibbling hungrily at her soft hips, caressing her thighs slowly, rhythmically, until he felt her arch and shudder helplessly beneath him.

He touched her then, and she cried out, because it had been so long, and it was so sweet. His warm hands on her body made her forget the chill of the stable and the sting of the cold cloth against her back. She lifted toward those exquisite hands, begging for them, savoring the exquisite roughness of them on her soft flesh. He felt himself throbbing all over with pleasure as he gazed into her lazy, misty eyes and saw her need for him.

"Oh . . ." she moaned, hurting for him, so on fire with the pleasure he was giving her that she couldn't quite hold it all. She bit her lip, trying to keep quiet.

"Cry out if you feel it like that," he whispered, his voice rough with passion. "Let me hear you."

"I . . . ache," she whimpered, trembling as he rubbed tenderly at the sensitive peaks of her breasts.

"Not half as much as I'm going to make you ache now." He bit at her soft lips, teased them, rubbed at them, laughing sensuously when she reached up and caught his head and dragged his mouth down hard onto hers.

The kiss they shared was hotter and wilder than anything that had come before. She couldn't get enough of him. She was drowning, and only he could save her.

"Please, now," she heard herself whisper into his demanding mouth. "Please, Ty, please, please . . ."

"Shh," he whispered gently. "Shh. Just a minute. Just another minute."

He moved a little away and removed his clothing slowly, watching her, feeling her eyes on him. He had a good body at least—if not a good face—and he liked the way she looked at him with those lazy, hungry green eyes. She shifted on the cloth, her hips moving sinuously, her eyes promising heaven.

He eased down beside her, and she touched his hips, pulling, half pleading.

"Not yet." He touched her softly, watching her arch and moan. "Not just yet. I want to make you beg me this time," he whispered roughly. "I want to watch you cry."

"Please . . . !"

His mouth covered hers and his hands touched her in new, unfamiliar ways, and for minutes that stretched like exquisite torture, he taught her new ways to ache. She lost her ability to reason in the throes of the most unbearable pleasure she'd ever experienced.

Finally he eased her down onto the cloth and moved over her, his hands on her thighs, his chest crushing gently over her taut breasts. He looked at her as she opened her tormented eyes and breathed in helpless shudders, her nails digging into his flat hips in fierce pleading.

"Easy, now," he whispered, his own voice unsteady, husky with controlled passion. He moved a little and felt her jerk, and saw her eyes dilate frantically. "Easy," he persisted, watching her eyes as he overwhelmed her in a slow, tender rhythm that had the effect of dynamite on her overstretched nerves.

She began to cry at the exquisite tenderness, the slowness of his movements as he deepened his thrusts and his weight gradually began to settle over her. She felt abrasive hair, warm, hard muscle and the heavy, quick throb of his heart over hers.

He slid his hands under her head, gently cradling it, and then saw her face contorting. "Don't close your eyes, sweetheart," he whispered tenderly. "Let me look at you. That's it. Lift up. Lift. Lift ... Feel the rhythm. Feel it with me. Lift up ... God, Erin, you ... make me whole ... you make me ... sweet ... you're so ... sweet ... God, Erin, God!"

He arched above her, shuddering, shuddering, and she felt it and felt it; a gentle kind of anguish that was terrible in its sweet, slow intensity, like giant hands crushing her with a throbbing warmth that consumed everything in a maelstrom of sensation.

He was whispering something, and she was crying, sobbing, her arms clasped furiously around him, her body trembling softly under his.

She felt his hands smoothing her hair; soothing, comforting her. He kissed away her tears with tender lips that searched over her face in an agony of caring. "Sweet," he breathed shakily. "Like a tender avalanche, flinging me up into the sun, burning me alive!"

"I didn't know it could be like that," she whimpered, clinging closer, feeling him in every cell of her body as he lay over her. She bit him, bit his shoulder, his neck, with bites that were gentle and possessive.

"It can be again." He moved softly against her. "It can be . . . now."

She shuddered a little, moving with him. Her face curved into his throat this time, savoring the throb of his body against her own as he slowly increased the sweet rhythm.

His mouth slid over hers while they loved. When it happened the second time, it was like a crescendo of fireworks, tender and slow and long-drawn-out, so that she vibrated like a taut bowstring for a long, long time until she felt the echoing vibration of his strong male body over hers; until she heard him moan her name in sweet anguish, and shudder and finally collapse gently on her damp body.

His mouth moved warmly on hers. "If you hadn't taken precautions," he whispered unsteadily, "we'd have made a baby just then."

She clung closer, her eyes closed. "I know," she said softly. "Oh, Ty, we never loved like that . . . !"

"It was loving, wasn't it?" he murmured. "Because that wasn't sex. There was nothing lustful about it, about what we did together." His strong body shuddered. "Erin, I'm on fire for you."

"And I am, for you." She closed her eyes tightly and clung to him. "Ty, why are you punishing us both for what happened? Why can't I sleep with you? Why can't we have a real marriage?"

He nuzzled his face in the hollow of her warm shoulder. "Is that what you want?" he asked. "A real marriage? I thought you wanted your career back."

She bit her lip. Was this a good time to tell him what she really felt: that she never wanted to leave him? That more than anything she wanted to have his children and grow old with him?

She swallowed. "Ty...I could stop taking the pill," she said hesitantly. Her arms contracted as she felt him go rigid. "We could make another baby."

He almost stopped breathing. Was that what she really wanted? Was it guilt, or pity for him, or was she addicted to making love with him? Could she settle for him, when she might have her career back? He wanted to take what she was offering. He wanted it desperately. But he owed her a chance at the old life, to make sure that it didn't have an unbreakable hold on her. She had been crippled and hurt, and she had bitter memories. Would he be taking advantage of a momentary weakness—one she'd regret when she was completely well?

He lifted his dark head and looked into her questioning eyes. "Not yet," he said gently. "Not right now. We'll sleep together, if that's what you want. God knows, it's what I want; I walk around bent over because I need you so desperately. But no babies. And no commitments," he added. "First, you go back to New York for a few weeks and pick up the threads of your old life. Then, when you've had a good taste of it and I've got my financial mess straightened out, we'll make decisions."

She searched his eyes. Was that an offer or a hedge? Did he really want his freedom? Was it all only pity? If only she could read him. Even in passion, he held back.

"All right," she said after a minute. If this was all she could expect, perhaps it would be enough. He wanted her, and that could grow into something lasting.

She'd go back to New York. Then she'd come home and show him that his looks didn't matter to her, that she could see any number of handsome, sophisticated city men and still prefer him. She smiled slowly. She'd get him; she already had a hold on him—he just hadn't realized it yet. She felt new, whole, hopeful. Her face radiated with beauty.

"Look at you." he chided, letting his eyes slide down her body. "In the middle of winter..."

"Look at you, tall man." She smiled up at him.

"You seduced me," he accused softly, smiling back. "Taking off your dress, baring those pretty breasts... I couldn't have stopped to save my life."

"You stopped long enough to torment me out of my mind." She blushed with the memory of how she'd begged for his body.

He bent and nipped her lower lip tenderly. "You begged me. You can't imagine what that did for my ego, hearing you plead with me to take you. God, it was sweet!"

"My poor, battered pride..."

"You loved it, you little liar," he murmured gruffly, burning her mouth with his. "You laughed up at me while I was having you...!"

She moaned as his mouth opened to explore hers in a kiss that was as intimate as lovemaking, sweet and heady and hungry.

Suddenly he pressed his face into her throat and groaned. "I want to," he whispered, "but I can't; I'm so damned tired!"

She smiled against his hair. "I'm tired, too." She sighed, gloriously content, and closed her eyes. "Can I sleep in your arms tonight?"

A fine tremor went through the hands holding her. "My God, of course you can!"

She sighed again, relaxing, feeling the warm hardness of his body against hers. "I don't want to get up."

"I don't either. But we could have visitors in here, and I don't think we'd ever get over the embarrassment," he murmured, smiling. He dragged himself away from her and sat up, studying her lovely, relaxed body. "So beautiful," he said absently, tracing her hips, her long legs. "I could look at you forever and never get enough."

She smiled. "You're not bad yourself."

"That's the way I feel right now," he confessed, and laughed with pure pride. He tossed her dress and underthings to her. "Better get those on while I can still drag my eyes away."

"Flatterer," she said demurely while she struggled to get dressed, feeling the cold for the first time and shivering a little.

He was dressed before she was, so he helped her button up between kisses, then lifted her to her feet.

"Why the canvas?" she asked curiously, pulling straw out of her disheveled hair.

He reached down and picked up some hay, showing her the briars liberally mixed in with pieces of straw. "Hay isn't just hay," he mused. "It's briars and wild roses and weeds and such. Think about how that would feel on your bare back with my weight over you."

She blushed scarlet at his words, and he smiled almost affectionately and bent to brush a tender kiss against her forehead.

"I love watching you blush," he murmured. "I love knowing there's been no one except me."

She nuzzled her forehead against his warm mouth. "I like knowing that you haven't been to bed with half the women in the county, if we're making confessions," she replied. "I could have gone down on my knees when you told me that day in San Antonio that you'd never really made love before. It was heaven."

"Some women wouldn't have thought so."

She pulled back and looked up at him. "I'm your wife," she said gently.

His chest swelled with pride as he looked at her. "Yes," he said. "My wife. My woman."

She pressed warmly against him, savoring his strength and the new affection between them. If only it would last this time, she thought, closing her eyes on a prayer. If only it would last! She had him now.

Oh, Lord, she prayed silently, *please, please let me keep him this time. Let him love me. Just let him love me, and I'll have everything in the world that I'll ever need or want.*

Chapter Eleven

There was still a part of Ty that Erin couldn't reach. They made wonderful, satisfying love together, and at night she slept in his hard arms. But the closeness came only in bed; the rest of the time he was the cold, taciturn man she'd first known. He watched her, frowning, as if he were worried. She exercised and grew strong, and eventually the day came when she had to go to New York—not because she wanted to go, but because Ty still insisted she prove to herself that she was whole enough to work again. And she didn't dare wonder if he wasn't just tired of having her around, if the guilt had worn off at last.

He drove her to the airport, and she had to fight tears every step of the way. He carried her suitcase into the terminal and waited for her to check in. Then he escorted her to the concourse, waiting while she selected her seat.

After she'd finished, she turned to him, her eyes dark green, troubled. He didn't allow himself to read things into that look. She felt sorry for him, he decided. She was going back to the life she loved, and because he'd made that possible by shaking her out of her apathy, she felt grateful to him as well. But he didn't want pity or gratitude, or even the magic of her body burning against his in the darkness. He wanted her love. Just that.

She came close to him, realizing belatedly that ever since the morning in the barn, when she'd tempted him, she'd had to make all the moves physically. He'd lie beside her in bed at night and never touch her unless she showed him that she wanted him to. It was an odd kind of relationship. He gave her anything she asked for, from dresses and trinkets to lovemaking, but only if she asked for it.

"Will you miss me, at least?" she asked with a faint smile.

He returned her smile. "The bed will get pretty cold," he observed.

"I'll mail you a hot water bottle," she assured him.

He touched her cheek gently, searching her face. "If you ever need me, all you have to do is call. I'll be on the next plane."

She smiled at the possessive note in his voice. He did feel protective of her—there was no doubt on that score. "I'll remember," she promised. Then they were calling her flight, and she looked up at him fearfully, gnawing on her lip.

"It'll be all right," he said gently. "You're strong now. You'll do fine."

"Will I, really?" she asked, trying not to cry. She searched his eyes. "Kiss me goodbye, Ty," she whispered.

He bent his head, holding her by the shoulders, and brushed his lips softly against hers. "Be a good girl," he whispered.

"What else could I be, without you around?" She laughed brokenly. "Oh, Ty...!"

She threw her arms around his neck and dragged his mouth down over hers, oblivious to other passengers, to passersby. She held him and savored the warm, hard crush of his hungry mouth, and drifted and drifted and drifted...

He pulled back abruptly, his eyes flashing, his face taut with desire, and she had to catch her breath and her balance before she moved away.

"Call me when you check into the hotel," he said tersely. "I want to make sure you got there all right."

"I will." She looked at him one last time, already feeling alone. "Take care of yourself."

"You, too."

She couldn't say goodbye. The word was painful, even in thought. She forced a smile and turned toward the tunnel that led to the jet. She didn't look back.

It was a short but trying flight. She cried most of the way there. Her leg was better; she was walking comfortably these days. She felt and looked at the peak of health. But her heart was hurting. She wanted Ty. And now he seemed not to want her anymore.

When she got to the hotel and into a suite that he'd insisted she book, she called him. But it was a brief conversation. He seemed to be in a blazing rush—took just long enough to remind her to call if she needed him, and then excused himself and hung up.

She stared at the receiver, feeling dismissed. Deserted. She cried herself to sleep. The next morning she felt stronger, and furious at him for not rushing up to bring her back home, to tell her he couldn't live without her. Then she laughed at her own stupidity. Ty would never do that; he needed no one.

She went by her old agency and talked to the man who'd represented her before. He was amazed at how well and strong and recovered she looked, and he arranged immediately to have a new portfolio shot. A week later, she was working.

Days passed with dull regularity. The life she'd once found exciting and fascinating was now little more than drudgery to her. She kept thinking about the ranch and Ty. She missed the sound of cattle in the meadows. She missed the leisurely pace and the quiet of the country. She missed Conchita's merry prattle and the fresh flowers that had graced the tables each day. But most of all, she missed the feel of Ty's hard body in the darkness, the warmth of him when she cuddled close and felt his arm go around her, his chest firm and comforting under her cheek. She missed watching him around the ranch, hearing the deep, measured sound of his voice with its faint drawl, the sound of his boots as he came in to supper every night. She missed the rare smiles and rough hunger in his voice when he made love to her. She even missed those homely, uneven features. She wondered what he'd think if she wrote and told him that she thought he was the handsomest man alive? He'd probably burn the letter, thinking she was being sarcastic.

She drove herself relentlessly, working long hours every day until she was weary enough to sleep at night. Every few days she called home, but Ty always seemed to be in a hurry. He never talked, except to exchange comments about work and the weather. He didn't ask when she was coming back. He didn't even ask if she was coming back. He didn't seem to care one way or the other.

That was when she began to worry. Perhaps he'd decided that life was sweeter when he could be alone and not have to put up with a wife he didn't really want. Perhaps he felt that guilt and pity alone could not sustain a marriage. She began to brood over it, and once, right in the middle of a photographic session, tears stung her eyes at the thought of living without Ty. The photographer stopped shooting and sent out for coffee and a sweet roll, thinking she was hungry. She was—but not for food.

In the end, she stood it for a few weeks—until spring was just beginning to melt the snows and brighten the skies; until Ty's very indifference shook her from wounded pride to fury.

She took the first plane home one day, right after she'd finished a commercial; she looked and felt viciously angry. Enough, she told herself. She'd had enough of his practised indifference. If he wanted a divorce, she'd give him one, but he was going to have to come right out and say he did. She wasn't going to be ignored to death. And even while she was thinking it, something inside her was dying. She loved him more every day. The thought of doing without him for the rest of her life was killing her.

It had all begun the wrong way, for all the wrong reasons. But she no longer blamed him for her troubles. In a way, she blamed herself. She needn't have believed Bruce's lies. She could have gone to Ty with them from the very beginning and avoided all of it. And she could have made him listen that day, instead of meekly accepting his bad temper—which had probably been nothing more than wounded pride, because he'd believed Bruce, too. If she'd made him listen, perhaps he'd have taken her in his arms and asked her to marry him, and they'd have had their baby....

She shook herself. That was over. She couldn't change it. So now she had to go on— With him or without him. But she knew that going on without him would be a kind of death—a life without pleasure or warmth or love. There could never be another man; she loved him too much.

There was no one to meet her at the airport, because no one knew she was coming back. She rented a car and made the long drive to Ravine without stopping. She went straight through town and out to Staghorn, where she pulled up in front of the house, glancing around. Well, the Lincoln was there. He could be out, of course; he had roundup in early spring. But she had a feeling he was somewhere nearby.

She got out of the car and looked from the house to the corral. A number of the men were gathered around the corral, calling enthusiastically to somebody on a horse.

With glittering green eyes, she walked down to them. She knew instinctively who it was on that unbroken horse. And sure enough, when she got there, she saw her tall, lean husband giving the animal a run for its money. He was wearing denims, wide leather chaps, and the old worn Stetson that looked near retirement age. His face was animated, full of challenge and male pride, and the animal was tiring. It leaped and bucked while the cowhands yelled encouragement to the tall, relentless rider. Finally, the weary horse gave up and trotted around the corral, panting and sweat-lathered.

Ty swung gracefully out of the saddle, patting the animal gently before he handed it over to one of the men to groom and water. Erin watched him with her hands in the pockets of her skirt; it had been all too long since she'd seen him, and her eyes devoured him hungrily. He was so much a man. A Texan.

He turned unexpectedly and saw her, and froze in place. Before he had time to say anything, she lifted her chin pugnaciously.

"Well?" she asked, glaring at him. "You might at least say hello, even if I'm not welcome. And while we're on the subject, thanks for all the cards and letters and phone calls; I sure enjoyed them!"

He climbed over the corral fence and dropped gracefully to his feet to approach her, while behind him the men stared and punched each other—they loved a good fight.

"Welcome home, Mrs. Wade," Ty said with faint mockery, but his eyes were running over her like tender hands. It had been a long time, and she was beautiful, and he wanted her until it was a raging fever. But she was different, too: eye-catching and expensive-looking in a pretty red-and-white outfit. The long white sweater overlapped a full red crinkle-cloth skirt that swirled around her calves when she walked, and she'd belted it with a macramé tie. Her hair was longer now, over her shoulders, softly waving, and her face was exquisitely made up. She was the perfect model. His eyes narrowed as he wondered how many men had looked at her and wanted her. Had she wanted any of them? He could only imagine how he'd compare with those city men. His face went hard thinking about it. He was going to lose her—so what the hell; he might as well help her leave, convince her that she didn't need to feel sorry for him anymore. The guilt was mostly gone. He had a few twinges now and then, but he could live with himself now. He didn't need her pity.

"Hello, yourself," Erin replied curtly. He sure didn't look like a man who couldn't sleep at night for missing her.

"Did you come back to get your gear?" he asked, pausing long enough to light a cigarette.

"Maybe I did." She straightened. "I can see how welcome I am."

"What did you expect, a brass band?" he asked. "I got along my whole life without anybody in the house. It's pretty pleasant, if you want to know."

"Well, New York isn't bad, either," she retorted, stung. "I'm having a glorious time! I work every day, in fact, and I'm much in demand for parties and such."

"Found somebody else, have you?" he asked with apparent indifference. "I hope he's rich. You'll be expensive to keep."

"As if I ever cost you a dime, Tyson Radley Wade!" she shot back, raising her voice.

"Radley?" Red Davis drawled from the corral fence.

Ty whirled, silver eyes blazing. "Stuff it, Davis!" he growled.

Red saluted him, but he shut up all the same.

"That's it, yell at the poor man," Erin said scathingly. "Nobody around here is allowed an opinion except you!"

"You don't have to start yelling out secrets, do you?" Ty asked, scowling.

"Oh, was your middle name a secret?" she asked innocently, and looked past him at the cowboys. "Well, it's not anymore."

"Why don't you go pack your damned bag?"

She stomped her foot. "Can't wait to get rid of me, can you? Why did you bother to marry me in the first place?"

"Because I didn't want Ward Jessup digging holes in my pasture looking for oil!" he said coldly. "That was it, that was all of it. That, and a little pity. You sure as hell were a basket case when I found you!"

"And now, thanks to you, I have a wonderful future in store!" she replied angrily. "I love living alone! I have the time of my life walking around stages while middle-aged hippopotamus women try to imagine themselves in dresses that would barely fit around one of their legs! I love being ogled by male designers and hurried by dressers and pestered to death by photographers and harassed by perfectionist directors on commercials! It's great coming home to an empty apartment and spending my whole weekend watching roller derbies and championship wrestling!''

The cowboys were trying not to laugh. Ty was gaping at her. He'd never seen her like this.

She clenched her small hands at her sides, her elfin face red, her eyes sparkling dangerously. "I hate you, you big ugly cowboy!" she raged at him. "I'm tired of waiting for the phone to ring and haunting the mailbox for letters that never come! They've offered me a week in Saint-Tropez to shoot a swimsuit commercial, and I'm taking it! The director is French and tall and handsome and sexy, and he wants me, and I'm going!''

"Like hell you're going!" he burst out, throwing down the cigarette with a violent flick of his wrist. "You're not traipsing off to the south of France with any damned Frenchman!"

"Why not?" she demanded, her voice high-pitched. "You don't want me! I'm just a burden to you, just a cripple you're carrying around on your conscience!''

"Some cripple," he murmured, studying her.

"I wish I had a wooden leg, I'd kick you with it, you arrogant cattleman!''

He smiled slowly.

"My, my, aren't we wound up, though?"

"'Wound up'?" She backed away a step, eyes narrowing. "Wound up! I'll show you wound up...."

She picked up the nearest object—an empty bucket sitting by the fence—and hurled it at him. He ducked, so she grabbed a bridle off the corral and threw that, following it with a piece of loose wood.

The cowboys were chuckling behind Ty. He glared at them as he dodged the wood.

"Ship me off to the city, will you?" She pushed back a strand of sweaty hair, looking around for another missile. "Throw me out on my ear, give me over to the mercy of strangers. A fine way to treat your own wife!"

"You never wanted to be my wife," he said. "You married me to get even with me!"

"Sure I did!" she cried, grasping a horse collar. "To get even with you for ignoring me all the time, for baiting me, for killing me with your indifference. You big, stupid man, I love you so much!" Her voice broke as she flung the collar. "I've loved you from the first day I saw you, and you've given me nothing but hell!"

He didn't duck. The horse collar was heavy and it caught him in the chest, but he didn't even flinch. His eyes were wide and unblinking as he gaped at her, disbelieving. Had he heard right?

"It was never Bruce I wanted!" she practically screamed at him. "It was you! You, with your homely face and your big ears and your big feet and your mean temper! I cared so much . . . and you didn't even like me! I tried so hard to make you care, but you hated me!''

He'd heard right. And at that realization, something inside him burst and bubbled up like a spring. She was still raging, something about hating him because he was dumber than a cactus plant, but he didn't even hear her—he just started to walk toward her like someone in a trance.

She loved him. Yes, it was in her eyes, in her face, in everything about her. She'd reached a peak now, her voice broken and wounded, and she was going to leave him and go be a famous model. . . .

In midtorrent, he bent and lifted her in his hard arms and put his mouth over hers. He wasn't rough. He couldn't have been rough with her—not now. But he wasn't that gentle, either, because it had been so long and his mouth was hungry for the sweet softness of hers.

She mumbled something for a few seconds before her mouth opened and her arms crept around his neck, and he tasted tears on her lips as she kissed him back.

The cowboys were grinning and chuckling, but neither of them heard. He turned, walking with her in his arms toward the house, opening his eyes only to keep from tripping as he went up the steps and through the front door.

"Señora!" Conchita laughed as she opened the study door for Ty. "Welcome home."

"Umm-hmm," Erin murmured under the crush of Ty's mouth, waving languorously as he walked through the door and kicked it shut behind him with one booted foot. He started walking again, then suddenly wheeled and locked the door.

She felt the sofa cradle her back and the weight of Ty's body settle completely over her. Her eyes opened a little as his mouth lifted just long enough for her to take a breath.

"Ty..." she whispered.

"Are you blind and deaf and dumb?" he asked, his voice deep and harsh. "Look." He held up the hand that was wearing the ring she'd given him. "Does that tell you anything, little shrew, or do you want the words? I'll give them to you, but once I start saying them, I may not be able to stop."

She touched his mouth, feeling its rough warmth. "I wouldn't mind," she whispered, her eyes loving, exquisitely tender.

His hands cupped her face. "I love you, Erin," he said fiercely, looking intently into her eyes. "I loved you the day you left here, and I was hurting until I thought I'd die of it. I didn't realize it... and I listened to my ego instead of my heart and ran you away. Oh, God, I've loved you so much, and not ever believed that you could love me back. I've been cruel, because I was so damned afraid of losing you...!"

"Losing me," she repeated ironically. "As if you could. I adore you. I love all the nooks and crannies of this face." She touched his lean cheeks while his eyes closed and he shuddered and thanked God for the fact that love was blind. "I love all of you, with all of me. And there is no man on the face of this earth who is handsomer or sexier or more tender than you are. Oh, you sweet big dumb man, you," she said lovingly, drawing him down to her. "I'll love you until I die. Until you die. And forever afterward."

He crushed her up against him, burying his face in her throat, shuddering with the fulfillment of every dream he'd ever had. "Erin," he whispered.

The unashamed adoration in his tone made her tingle all over. She bit his ear gently and cupped his face in her hands, making him look at her.

"Ty," she said softly, searching his eyes, "I'm not taking the Pill."

"Aren't you?" he asked unsteadily. His hands found her macramé belt and loosened it. Then they eased the hem of the sweater up over the lacy little bra she was wearing.

"You could make me pregnant if we..." She hesitated, feeling oddly shy with him.

"What a hell of a turn-on," he whispered, biting tenderly at her lips. He lifted his head and looked right into her eyes. "Say it."

Her lips parted, trembling, because she knew what he wanted her to say. It was the right time, at last—for the healing balm for all the wounds they'd inflicted, for the ultimate expression of the love they felt for each other.

"Give me a baby, Ty," she whispered with aching tenderness. "This time, let's make it happen."

He searched her eyes for a long moment, then slowly bent his head. And it was a kind of tender loving that erased every other time, that healed all the wounds, opened all the doors. He held nothing back, and neither did she. And what they shared was so profound, so exquisitely sweet and fulfilling, that she cried for a long time when it was over—tears of pure ecstasy—lying in the arms of the man she loved most in all the world.

She looked up at his face, adoring it, pushing back his damp black hair with hands that trembled.

"I love you," he whispered.

"If I hadn't known already," she replied, "I'd know now. We never loved like that. Not even that day in the stall when you made me cry."

"I wasn't sure of you then," he said gently. "I wanted to see if I could make you tell me what you felt. But I couldn't."

"You couldn't read my mind," she murmured. "Inside, I was screaming it."

"So was I." He bent to her mouth and smiled as he kissed it. "Come home, Erin," he breathed. "I'm lonely."

"I'm lonely, too." She nuzzled her face against his chest and smiled again. "But I never will be again, and neither will you. I'll never leave you."

He didn't say anything. He didn't need to. His mouth brushed down upon hers, and the fires began to burn again. She reached up her arms and closed her eyes and kissed him back.

Epilogue

Ed Johnson checked his briefcase one last time before he knocked on the door at Staghorn. Conchita let him in, grinning from ear to ear.

"You look like the cat left all alone with the canary bird," he said. "What's going on?"

"*Señor*, you will have to see it to believe it," she assured him. "Such changes in this house in the past year! I am constantly amazed. Come. I will show you."

She led him to the doorway of the den, and he stopped there, staring. Tyson Wade was lying on his back on the carpet with a fat, laughing baby sitting on his flat stomach, and Ty was laughing with it.

He turned his head sideways as Ed entered the room. "Good morning."

As he spoke, a second baby crawled up from his other side and pulled at his hair, cooing.

"You're baby-sitting the twins?" Ed asked.

"Erin's upstairs," Ty told him. "But I change a mean diaper. Got the papers?"

"Right here," the attorney said, patting the briefcase. "You made a hell of an amazing recovery, you know. Last year about this time, you'd just escaped bankruptcy."

"I had a strong incentive." He grinned. "A pregnant wife can sure light a fire under a man. And twins put wood on it."

"How old are they now?" Ed asked, kneeling beside Ty to grasp a pudgy little hand and be cooed at.

"Just five months," Ty replied. "We sit and stare at them sometimes, trying to believe it."

Ed remembered the baby Erin had lost and smiled at the tiny miracles. "Twin blessings," he murmured.

"Thank God." Ty looked up at the older man and laughed. "If you'll hold up that contract, I'll try to sign it."

"No need," Erin said, smiling as she joined them. "I'll take the boys while you do the honors."

"There's just one thing," Ty told the attorney as Erin scooped up Jason and Matthew. "If Ward Jessup blows a gusher under just one of my cows..."

"He won't. And he promised to lease just what he needed. Amazing," he murmured, watching Ty scrawl his signature on the contract, "how the two of you finally sat down and ironed out your differences. That feud's been going on since you were barely out of your teens."

"Not so amazing," Ty said, glancing past his attorney at Erin, who was cuddling the babies on her lap and looking so beautiful that his breath caught. "No, not so amazing at all."

Ed followed his rapt gaze and smiled. Ty had changed, and so had his outlook. He wondered if Erin knew how great a difference she'd made in the taciturn rancher's life, just with her presence.

She looked up at that moment and met his curious gaze. And she grinned. Yes, he thought; she knew, all right.

He packed up the contracts and said his goodbyes. As he walked out the door, he looked back and saw Erin handing Ty one of the boys with a look of such love that he turned away, feeling as if he were trespassing. Outside, the air was sweet with the smells of summer. He drank in a deep breath of Texas air. Maybe there was something to that marriage business, he decided. He'd have to start looking around. Babies were pretty cute, and he wasn't getting any younger.

He got into his car. The windows were down, and just as he started the engine, he heard the sound of deep, vibrant laughter coming from the open windows of the house. Ed smiled to himself and drove down the winding driveway. Out by the fence, the prickly pear cacti were in full bloom. Sometimes, he thought, the ugliest plants put out the most beautiful flowers. He guessed there was a man back the road a piece who wouldn't argue with that statement one bit. And neither would the woman who'd put the bloom there.

*   *   *   *   *

Read more about Erin and Ty Wade in
UNLIKELY LOVER, a Silhouette Romance by
Diana Palmer available in December.
Don't miss it!

UNLIKELY LOVER

Chapter One

Ward Jessup went to the supper table rubbing his big hands together, his green eyes like dark emeralds in a face like a Roman's, perfectly sculpted under hair as thick and black as crow feathers. He was enormously tall, big and rangy looking, with an inborn elegance and grace that came from his British ancestors. But Ward himself was all-American. All Oklahoman, with a trace of Cherokee and a sprinkling of Irish that gave him his taciturn stubbornness and his cutting temper, respectively.

"You look mighty proud of yourself," Lillian huffed, bringing in platters of beef and potatoes and yeast rolls.

"Why shouldn't I?" he asked. "Things are going pretty well. Grandmother's leaving, did she tell you? She's going to stay with my sister. Lucky, lucky Belinda!"

Lillian lifted her eyes to the ceiling. "I must have pleased you, Lord, for all my prayers to be so suddenly answered," she said.

Ward chuckled as he reached for the platter of sliced roast beef. "I thought you two were great buddies."

"And we stay that way as long as I run fast, keep my mouth shut and pretend that I like cooking five meals at a time."

"She may come back."

"I'll quit," was the gruff reply. "She's only been here four months, and I'm ready to apply for that cookhouse job over at Wade's."

"You'd wind up in the house with Conchita, helping to look after the twins," he returned.

She grinned, just for an instant. Could have been a muscle spasm, he thought.

"I like kids." Lillian glared at him, brushing back wiry strands of gray hair that seemed to match her hatchet nose, long chin and beady little black eyes. "Why don't you get married and have some?" she added.

His thick eyebrows raised a little. They were perfect like his nose, even his mouth. He was handsome. He could have had a dozen women by crooking his finger, but he dated only occasionally, and he never brought women home. He never got serious, either. He hadn't since that Caroline person had almost led him to the altar, only to turn around at the last minute and marry his cousin Bud, thinking that, because Bud's last name was Jessup, he'd do as well as Ward. Besides, Bud was much easier to manage. The marriage had only lasted a few weeks, however, just until Bud had discovered that Caroline's main interest was in how much of his small inheritance she could spend on herself. He had divorced her, and she had come rushing back to Ward, all in tears. But somewhere along the way Ward had opened his eyes. He'd shown her the door, tears and all, and that was the last time he'd shown any warmth toward anything in skirts.

"What would I do with kids?" he asked. "Look what it's done to Tyson Wade, for God's sake. There he was, a contented bachelor making money hand over fist. He married that model and lost everything—"

"He got everything back, with interest," Lillian interrupted, "and you say one more word about Miss Erin and I'll scald you, so help me!"

He shrugged. "Well, she is pretty. Nice twins, too. They look a little like Ty."

"Poor old thing," Lillian said gently. "He was homely as sin and all alone and meaner than a tickled rattlesnake. And now here he's made his peace with you and even let you have those oil leases you've been after for ten years. Yes sir, love sure is a miracle," she added with a purely calculating look.

He shivered. "Talking about it gives me hives. Talk about something else." He was filling his plate and nibbling between comments.

Lillian folded her hands in front of her, hesitating, but only for an instant. "I've got a problem."

"I know. Grandmother."

"A bigger one."

He stopped eating and looked up. She did seem to be worried. He laid down his fork. "Well? What's the problem?"

She shifted from one foot to the other. "My brother's eldest girl, Marianne," she said. "Ben died last year, you remember."

"Yes. You went to his funeral. His wife died years earlier, didn't she?"

Lillian nodded. "Well, Marianne and her best friend, Beth, went shopping at one of those all-night department store sales. On their way out, as they crossed the parking lot, a man tried to attack them. It was terrible," she continued huskily. "Terrible! The girls were just sickened by the whole experience!" She lowered her voice just enough to sound dramatic. "It left deep scars. Deep emotional scars," she added meaningfully, watching to see how he was reacting. *So far, so good.*

He sat up straighter, listening. "Your niece will be all right, won't she?" he asked hesitantly.

"Yes. She's all right physically." She twisted her skirt. "But it's her state of mind that I'm worried about."

"Marianne..." He nodded, remembering a photograph he'd seen of Lillian's favorite niece. A vivid impression of long dark hair and soft blue eyes and an oval, vulnerable young face brought a momentary smile to his lips.

"She's no raving beauty, and frankly, she hasn't dated very much. Her father was one of those domineering types whose reputation kept the boys away from her when she lived at home. But now..." She sighed even more dramatically. "Poor little Mari." She glanced up. "She's been keeping the books for a big garage. Mostly men. She said it's gotten to the point that if a man comes close enough to open a door for her, she breaks out in a cold sweat. She needs to get away for a little while, out of the city, and get her life back together."

"Poor kid," he said, sincere yet cautious.

"She's almost twenty-two," Lillian said. "What's going to become of her?" she asked loudly, peeking out the corner of her eye at him.

He whistled softly. "Therapy would be her best bet."

"She won't talk to anyone," she said quickly, cocking her head to one side. "Now, I know how you feel about women. I don't even blame you. But I can't turn my back on my own niece." She straightened, playing her trump card. "Now, I'm fully prepared to give up my job and go to her—"

"Oh, for God's sake, you know me better than that after fifteen years," he returned curtly. "Send her an airline ticket."

"She's in Georgia—"

"So what?"

Lillian toyed with a pan of rolls. "Well, thanks. I'll make it up to you somehow," she said with a secretive grin.

"If you're feeling that generous, how about an apple pie?"

The older woman chuckled. "Thirty minutes," she said and dashed off to the kitchen like a woman half her age. She could have danced with glee. He'd fallen for it! Stage one was about to take off! *Forgive me, Mari,* she thought silently and began planning again.

Ward stared after her with confused emotions. He hoped that he'd made the right decision. Maybe he was just going soft in his old age. Maybe...

"My bed was more uncomfortable than a sheet filled with cacti," came a harsh, angry old voice from the doorway. He turned as his grandmother ambled in using her cane, broad as a beam and as formidable as a raiding party, all cold green eyes and sagging jowls and champagne-tinted hair that waved around her wide face.

"Why don't you sleep in the stable?" he asked her pleasantly. "Hay's comfortable."

She glared at him and waved her cane. "Shame on you, talking like that to a pitiful old woman!"

"I pity anyone who stands within striking distance of that cane," he assured her. "When do you leave for Galveston?"

"Can't wait to get rid of me, can you?" she demanded as she slid warily into a chair beside him.

"Oh, no," he assured her. "I'll miss you like the plague."

"You cowhand," she grumbled, glaring at him. "Just like your father. He was hell to live with, too."

"You sweet-tempered little woman," he taunted.

"I guess you get that wit from your father. And he got it from me," she confessed. She poured herself a cup of coffee. "I hope Belinda is easier to get along with than you and your saber-toothed housekeeper."

"I am not saber-toothed," Lillian assured her as she brought in more rolls.

"You are so," Mrs. Jessup replied curtly. "In my day we'd have lynched you on a mesquite tree for insubordination!"

"In your day you'd have been hanging beside me," Lillian snorted and walked out.

"Are you going to let her talk to me like that?" Mrs. Jessup demanded of her grandson.

"You surely don't want me to walk into that kitchen alone?" he asked her. "She keeps knives in there." He lowered his voice and leaned toward her. "And a sausage grinder. I've seen it with my own eyes."

Mrs. Jessup tried not to laugh, but she couldn't help herself. She hit at him affectionately. "Reprobate. Why do I put up with you?"

"You can't help yourself," he said with a chuckle. "Eat. You can't travel halfway across Texas on an empty stomach."

She put down her coffee cup. "Are you sure this night flight is a good idea?"

"It's less crowded. Besides, Belinda and her newest boyfriend are going to meet you at the airport," he said. "You'll be safe."

"I guess so." She stared at the platter of beef that was slowly being emptied. "Give me some of that before you gorge yourself!"

"It's my cow," he muttered, green eyes glittering.

"It descended from one of mine. Give it here!"

Ward sighed, defeated. Handing the platter to her with a resigned expression, he watched her beam with the tiny triumph. He had to humor her just a little occasionally. It kept her from getting too crotchety.

Later he drove her to the airport and put her on a plane. As he went back toward his ranch, he wondered about Marianne Raymond and how it was going to be with a young woman around the place getting in his hair. Of course, she was just twenty-two, much too young for him. He was thirty-five now, too old for that kind of child-woman. He shook his head. He only hoped that he'd done the right thing. If he hadn't, things were sure going to be complicated from now on.

At one time Lillian's incessant matchmaking had driven him nuts before he'd managed to stop her, though she still harped on his unnatural attitude toward marriage. If only she'd let him alone and stop mothering him! That was the trouble with people who'd worked for you almost half your life, he muttered to himself. They felt obliged to take care of you in spite of your own wishes.

He stared across the pastures at the oil rigs as he eased his elegant white Chrysler onto the highway near Ravine, Texas. His rigs. He'd come a long damned way from the old days spent working on those rigs. His father had dreamed of finding that one big well, but it was Ward who'd done it. He'd borrowed as much as he could and put everything on one big gamble with a friend. And his well had come in. He and the friend had equal shares in it, and they'd long since split up and gone in different directions. When it came to business, Ward Jessup could be ruthless and calculating. He had a shrewd mind and a hard heart, and some of his enemies had been heard to say that he'd foreclose on a starving widow if she owed him money.

That wasn't quite true, but it was close. He'd grown up poor, dirt poor, as his grandmother had good reason to remember. The family had been looked down on for a long time because of Ward's mother. She'd tired of her boring life on the ranch with her two children and had run off with a neighbor's husband, leaving the children for her stunned husband and mother-in-law to raise. Later she'd divorced Ward's father and remarried, but the children had never heard from her again. In a small community like Ravine the scandal had been hard to live down. Worse, just a little later, Ward's father had gone out into the south forty one autumn day with a rifle in his hand and hadn't come home again.

He hadn't left a note or even seemed depressed. They'd found him slumped beside his pickup truck, clutching a piece of ribbon that had belonged to his wife. Ward had never forgotten his father's death, had never forgiven his mother for causing it.

Later, when he'd fallen into Caroline's sweet trap, Ward Jessup had learned the final lesson. These days he had a reputation for breaking hearts, and it wasn't far from the mark. He had come to hate women. Every time he felt tempted to let his emotions show, he remembered his mother and Caroline. And day by day he became even more embittered.

He liked to remember Caroline's face when he'd told her he didn't want her anymore, that he could go on happily all by himself. She'd curled against him with her big black eyes so loving in that face like rice paper and her blond hair cascading like yellow silk down her back. But he'd seen past the beauty to the ugliness, and he never wanted to get that close to a woman again. He'd seen graphically how big a fool the most sensible man could become when a shrewd woman got hold of him. Nope, he told himself. Never again. He'd learned from his mistake. He wouldn't be that stupid a second time.

He pulled into the long driveway of Three Forks and smiled at the live oaks that lined it, thinking of all the history there was in this big, lusty spread of land. He might live and die without an heir, but he'd sure enjoy himself until that time came.

He wondered if Tyson Wade was regretting his decision to lease the pastureland so that Ward could look for the oil that he sensed was there. He and Ty had been enemies for so many years—almost since boyhood—although the reason for all the animosity had long been forgotten in the heat of the continuing battle over property lines, oil rigs and just about everything else.

Ty Wade had changed since his marriage. He'd mellowed, becoming a far cry from the renegade who'd just as soon have started a brawl as talk business. Amazing that a beautiful woman like Erin had agreed to marry the man in the first place. Ty was no pretty boy. In fact, to Ward Jessup, the man looked downright homely. But maybe he had hidden qualities.

Ward grinned at that thought. He wouldn't begrudge his old enemy a little happiness, not since he'd picked up those oil leases that he'd wanted so desperately. It was like a new beginning: making a peace treaty with Tyson Wade and getting his crotchety grandmother out of his hair and off the ranch without bloodshed. He chuckled aloud as he drove back to the house, and it wasn't until he heard the sound that he realized how rarely he laughed these days.

Chapter Two

Marianne Raymond didn't know what to expect when she landed at the San Antonio airport. She knew that Ravine was quite a distance away, and her Aunt Lillian had said that someone would meet her. But what if no one did? Her blue eyes curiously searched the interior of the airport. Aunt Lillian's plea for her to visit had been so unusual, so... odd. Poor old Mr. Jessup, she thought, shaking her head. Poor brave man. Dying of that incurable disease, and Aunt Lillian so determined to make his last days happy. Mari had been delighted to come, to help out. Her vacation was overdue, and the manager of the big garage where she kept the books and wrote the occasional letter had promised that they could do without her for a week or so. Mr. Jessup wanted young people around, he'd told Lillian. Some cheerful company and someone to help him write his memoirs. That would be right up Mari's alley. She'd actually done some feature articles for a local newspaper, and she had literary ambitions, too.

Someday Mari was going to be a novelist. She'd promised herself that. She wrote a portion of her book every night. The story involved a poor city girl who was assaulted by a vicious gang leader and had nightmares about her horrible assailant. She'd told Aunt Lillian the plot over the phone just recently, and the older woman had been delighted with it. Mari wondered about her aunt's sudden enthusiasm because Lillian had never been particularly interested in anything except getting her married off to any likely candidate who came along. After her father's death, especially. The only reason she'd agreed to come down to Ravine was because of poor old Mr. Jessup. At least she could be sure that Aunt Lillian wasn't trying to marry her off to him!

Mari pushed back her hair. It was short now, a twenties-style pageboy with bangs, and it emphasized the rosy oval of her face. She was wearing a simple dropped-waist dress in blue-and-white stripes and carrying only a roly-poly piece of luggage, which contained barely enough clothes to get her through one week.

A tall man attracted her interest, and despite the shyness she felt with most men, she studied him blatantly. He was as big as the side of a barn, tall with rippling muscles and bristling with backcountry masculinity. Wearing a gray suit, an open-necked white shirt and a pearly gray Stetson and boots, he looked big and mean and sexy. The angle of that hat over his black hair was as arrogant as the look on his deeply tanned face, as intimidating as that confident stride that made people get out of his way. He would have made the perfect hero for Mari's book. The strong, tender man who would lead her damaged heroine back to happiness again...

He didn't look at anyone except Mari, and after a few seconds she realized that he was coming toward her. She clutched the little carryall tightly as he stopped just in front of her, and in spite of her height she had to look up to see his eyes. They were green and cold. Ice-cold.

"Marianne Raymond," he said as if she'd damned well better be. He set her temper smoldering with that confident drawl.

She lifted her chin. "That's right," she replied just as quietly. "Are you from Three Forks Ranch?"

"I *am* Three Forks Ranch," he informed her, reaching for the carryall. "Let's go."

"Not one step," she said, refusing to release it and glaring at him. "Not one single step until you tell me who you are and where we're going."

His eyebrows lifted. They were straight and thick like the lashes over his green eyes. "I'm Ward Jessup," he said. "I'm taking you to your Aunt Lillian." He controlled his temper with a visible effort as he registered her shocked expression and reached for his wallet, flashing it open to reveal his driver's license. "Satisfied?" he drawled and then felt ashamed of himself when he knew why she had reason to be so cautious and nervous of him.

"Yes, thank you," she said. *That* was Ward Jessup? *That* was a dying man? Dazed, she let him take the carryall and followed him out of the airport.

He had a car—a big Chrysler with burgundy leather seats and controls that seemed to do everything, right up to speaking firmly to the passengers about fastening their seat belts.

"I've never seen such an animal," she commented absently as she fastened her seat belt, trying to be a little less hostile. He'd asked for it, but she had to remember the terrible condition that the poor man was in. She felt guilty about her bad manners.

"It's a honey," he remarked, starting the engine. "Have you eaten?"

"Yes, on the plane, thank you," she replied. She folded her hands in her lap and was quiet until they reached the straight open road. The meadows were alive with colorful wildflowers of orange and red and blue, and prickly pear cacti. Mari also noticed long stretches of land where there were no houses and few trees, but endless fences and cattle everywhere.

"I thought there was oil everywhere in Texas," she murmured, staring out at the landscape and the sparse houses.

"What do you think those big metal grasshoppers are?" he asked, glancing at her as he sped down the road.

She frowned. "Oil wells? But where are the big metal things that look like the Eiffel Tower?"

He laughed softly to himself. "My God. Eastern tenderfoot," he chided. "You put up a derrick when you're hunting oil, honey, you don't keep it on stripper wells. Those damned things cost money."

She smiled at him. "I'll bet you weren't born knowing that, either, Mr. Jessup," she said.

"I wasn't." He leaned back and settled his huge frame comfortably.

He sure does look healthy for a dying man, Mari thought absently.

"I worked on rigs for years before I ever owned one."

"That's very dangerous work, isn't it?" she asked conversationally.

"So they say."

She studied his very Roman profile, wondering if anyone had ever painted him. Then she realized that she was staring and turned her attention to the landscape. It was spring and the trees looked misshapen and gloriously soft feathered with leaves.

"What kind of trees are those, anyway?" she asked.

"Mesquite," he said. "It's all over the place at the ranch, but don't ever go grabbing at its fronds. It's got long thorns everywhere."

"Oh, we don't have mesquite in Georgia," she commented, clasping her purse.

"No, just peach trees and magnolia blossoms and dainty little cattle farms."

She glared at him. "In Atlanta we don't have dainty little cattle farms, but we do have a very sophisticated tourism business and quite a lot of foreign investors."

"Don't tangle with me, honey," he advised with a sharp glance. "I've had a hard morning, and I'm just not in the mood for verbal fencing."

"I gave up obeying adults when I became one," she replied.

His eyes swept over her dismissively. "You haven't. Not yet."

"I'll be twenty-two this month," she told him shortly.

"I was thirty-five last month," he replied without looking her way. "And, to me, you'd still be a kid if you were four years older."

"You poor, old, decrepit thing," she murmured under her breath. It was getting harder and harder to feel sorry for him.

"What an interesting houseguest you're going to make, Miss Raymond," he observed as he drove down the interstate. "I'll have to arrange some razor-blade soup to keep your tongue properly sharpened."

"I don't think I like you," she said shortly.

He glared back. "I don't like women," he replied and his voice was as cold as his eyes.

She wondered if he knew why she'd come and decided that Aunt Lillian had probably told him everything. She averted her face to the window and gnawed on her lower lip. She was being deliberately antagonistic, and her upbringing bristled at her lack of manners. He'd asked Lillian to bring her out to Texas; he'd even paid for her ticket. She was supposed to cheer him up, to help him write his memoirs, to make his last days happier. And here she was being rude and unkind and treating him like a bad-tempered old tyrant.

"I'm sorry," she said after a minute.

"What?"

"I'm sorry," she repeated, unable to look at him. "You let me come here, you bought my ticket, and all I've done since I got off the plane is be sarcastic to you. Aunt Lillian told me all about it, you know," she added enigmatically, ignoring the puzzled expression on his face. "I'll do everything I can to make you glad you've brought me here. I'll help you out in every way I can. Well," she amended, "in most ways. I'm not really very comfortable around men," she added with a shy smile.

He relaxed a little, although he didn't smile. His hand caressed the steering wheel as he drove. "That's not hard to understand," he said after a minute, and she guessed that her aunt had told him about her strict upbringing. "But I'm the last man on earth you'd have to worry about in that particular respect. My women know the score, and they aren't that prolific these days. I don't have any interest in girls your age. You're just a baby."

Annoying, unnerving, infuriating man, she thought uncharitably, surprised by his statement. She looked toward him hesitantly, her eyes quiet and steady on his dark face. "Well, I've never had any interest in bad-tempered old men with oil wells," she said with dry humor. "That ought to reassure you as well, Mr. Jessup, sir."

"Don't be cheeky," he murmured with an amused glance. "I'm not that old."

"I'll bet your joints creak," she said under her breath.

He laughed. "Only on cold mornings," he returned. He pulled into the road that led to Three Forks and slowed down long enough to turn and stare into her soft blue eyes. "Tell you what, kid, you be civil to me and I'll be civil to you, and we'll never let people guess what we really think of each other. Okay?"

"Okay," she returned, eager to humor him. Poor man!

His green eyes narrowed. "Pity, about your age and that experience," he commented, letting his gaze wander over her face. "You're uncommon. Like your aunt."

"My aunt is the reincarnation of General Patton," she said. She wondered what experience he meant. "She could win wars if they'd give her a uniform."

"I'll amen that," he said.

"Thanks for driving up to get me," she added. "I appreciate it."

"I didn't know how you'd feel about a strange cowboy," he said gently. "Although we don't know each other exactly, I knew that Lillian's surely mentioned me and figured you'd be a bit more comfortable."

"I was." She didn't tell him how Lillian had described him as Attila the Hun in denim and leather.

"Don't tell her we've been arguing," he said unexpectedly as he put the car back in gear and drove up to the house. "It'll upset her. She stammered around for a half hour and even threatened to quit before she got up the nerve to suggest your visit."

"Bless her old heart." Mari sighed, feeling touched. "She's quite a lady, my aunt. She really cares about people."

"Next to my grandmother, she's the only woman that I can tolerate under my roof."

"Is your grandmother here?" she asked as they reached a huge cedarwood house with acres of windows and balconies.

"She left last week, thank God," he said heavily. "One more day of her and I'd have left and so would Lillian. She's too much like me. We only get along for short stretches."

"I like your house," she remarked as he opened the door for her.

"I don't, but when the old one burned down, my sister was going with an architect who gave us a good bid." He glared at the house. "I thought he was a smart boy. He turned out to be one of those innovative New Wave builders who like to experiment. The damned bathrooms have sunken tubs and Jacuzzis, and there's an indoor stream... Oh, God, what a nightmare of a house if you sleepwalk! You could drown in the living room or be swept off into the river."

She couldn't help laughing. He sounded horrified. "Why didn't you stop him?" she asked.

"I was in Canada for several months," he returned. He didn't elaborate. This strange woman didn't need to know that he'd gone into the wilderness to heal after Caroline's betrayal and that he hadn't cared what replaced the old house after lightning had struck and set it afire during a storm.

"Well, it's not so bad," she began but was interrupted when Lillian exploded out of the house, arms outstretched. Mari ran into them, feeling safe for the first time in weeks.

"Oh, you look wonderful," Lillian said with a sigh. "How are you? How was the trip?"

"I'm fine, and it was very nice of Mr. Jessup to come and meet me," she said politely. She turned, nodding toward him. "Thanks again. I hope the trip didn't tire you too much?"

"What?" he asked blankly.

"I told Mari how hard you'd been working lately, boss," Lillian said quickly. "Come on, honey, let's go inside!"

"I'll bring the bag," Ward said curiously and followed them into the rustic but modern house.

Mari loved it. It was big and rambling and there was plenty of room everywhere. It was just the house for an outdoorsman, right down to the decks that overlooked the shade trees around the house.

"I think this place is perfect for Ward, but for heaven's sake, don't tell him that! And please don't let on that you know about his condition," Lillian added, her eyes wary. "You didn't say anything about it?" she asked, showing Mari through the ultramodern upstairs where her bedroom overlooked the big pool below and the flat landscape beyond, fenced and cross-fenced with milling cattle.

"Oh, no, Scout's honor," Mari said. "But how am I going to help him write his memoirs?"

"We'll work up to it in good time," Lillian assured her. "He, uh, didn't ask why you came?"

Mari sighed. "He seemed to think I'd asked to come. Odd man, he thought I was afraid of him. Me, afraid of men, isn't that a scream? Especially after what Beth and I did at that all-night department store."

"Don't ever tell him, please," Lillian pleaded. "It would . . . upset him. We mustn't do that," she added darkly. "It could be fatal!"

"I won't, truly I won't," Mari promised. "He sure is healthy looking for a dying man, isn't he?"

"Rugged," Lillian said. "Real rugged. He'd never let on that he was in pain."

"Poor brave man," Mari said with a sigh. "He's so tough."

Lillian grinned as she turned away.

"Did his sister like this house?" Mari asked later after she'd unpacked and was helping Lillian in the kitchen.

"Oh, yes," Lillian confided to her niece. "But the boss hates it!"

"Is his sister like him?" Mari asked.

"To look at, no. But in temperament, definitely," the older woman told her. "They're both high-strung and mean tempered."

"You mentioned that he had a male secretary," Mari reminded her as she rolled out a piecrust.

"Yes. David Meadows. He's young and very efficient, but he doesn't like being called a secretary." Lillian grinned. "He thinks he's an administrative assistant."

"I'll have to remember that."

"I don't know what the boss would do without him, either," Lillian continued as she finished quartering the apples for the pie. Another apple pie might soften him up a little, she was thinking. "David keeps everything running smoothly around here, from paying the accounts to answering the phone and scheduling appointments. The boss stays on the road most of the time, closing deals. The oil business is vast these days. Last week he was in Saudi Arabia. Next week he's off to South America."

"All that traveling must get tiresome," Mari said, her blue eyes curious. "Isn't it dangerous for him in his condition?"

For a moment Lillian looked hunted. Then she brightened. "Oh, no, the doctor says it's actually good for him. He takes it easy, and it keeps his mind off things. He never talks about it, though. He's a very private person."

"He seems terribly cold," Mari remarked thoughtfully.

"Camouflage," Lillian assured her. "He's warm and gentle and a prince of a man," she added. "A prince! Now, get this pie fixed, girl. You make the best pies I've ever tasted, even better than my own."

"Mama taught me," Mari said gently. "I really miss her sometimes. Especially in the autumn. We used to go up into the mountains to see the leaves. Dad was always too busy, but Mama and I were adventurous. It's been eight years since she died. And only one since Dad went. I'm glad I still have you."

Lillian tried not to look touched, but she was. "Get busy," she said gruffly, turning away. "It isn't good to look back."

That was true, Mari thought, keeping her own thoughts on the present instead of the past. She felt sad about Ward Jessup—even if he was a dreadful oilman. She'd heard her aunt talk about him for so many years that she felt as if she knew him already. If only she could make it through the week without making him angry or adding to his problems. She just wanted to help him, if he'd let her.

Mari was just going into the other room to call him when her attention was caught by the stream running through the room, lit by underwater colored lights. It was eerie and beautiful indoor "landscaping," with plants everywhere and literally a stream running through the middle of the living room, wide enough to swim in.

Not paying much attention to where she was going, Mari backed along the carpet, only half aware of footsteps, and suddenly collided with something warm and solid.

There was a terribly big splash and a furious curse. When she turned around, she felt herself go pale.

"Oh, Mr. Jessup, I'm sorry," she wailed, burying her cheeks in her hands.

He was very wet. Not only was he soaked, but there was a lily pad on top of his straight black hair that had been slicked down by all the water. He was standing, and though the water came to his chin, he looked very big and very angry. As he sputtered and blinked, Mari noticed that his green eyes were exactly the shade of the lily pad.

"Damn you..." he began as he moved toward the carpeted "shore" with a dangerous look on his dark face. At that moment nobody would have guessed that he was a dying man. As quick as lightning he was out of the water, dripping on the carpet. Suddenly Mari forgot his delicate condition and ran like hell.

"Aunt Lillian!"

Mari ran for the kitchen as fast as her slender legs could carry her, a blur in jeans and a white sweatshirt as she darted down the long hall toward the relative safety of the kitchen.

Behind her, soggy footsteps and curses followed closely.

"Aunt Lillian, help!" she cried as she dashed through the swing door.

She forgot that swing doors tend to swing back when forcibly opened by hysterical people. It slammed back into a tall, wet, cursing man. There was an ominous thud and the sound of shattering ceramic pieces.

Lillian looked at her niece in wide-eyed shock. "Oh, Mari," she said. Her ears told her more than she wanted to know as she stared at the horrified face of her niece. "Oh, Mari."

"I think Mr. Jessup may need a little help, Aunt Lillian," Mari began hesitantly.

"Prayer might be more beneficial at the moment, dear," Aunt Lillian murmured nervously. She wiped her hands on her printed apron and cautiously opened the swing door to peer into the dining room.

Ward Jessup was just sitting up among the ruins of his table setting, china shards surrounding him. His suit was wet, and there was a puddle of water under him as he tugged his enormous frame off the floor. His eyes were blazing in a face that had gone ruddy in anger. He held on to a chair and rose slowly, glaring at Lillian's half-hidden face with an expression that told her there was worse to come.

"She's really a nice girl, boss," Lillian began, "once you get to know her."

He brushed back his soaked hair with a lean, angry hand, and his chest rose and fell heavily. "I have a meeting just after supper," he said. "I sent the rest of my suits to the cleaner's this afternoon. This is the last suit I had. I didn't expect to go swimming in it."

"We could dry it and I could...press it," Lillian suggested halfheartedly, pretty sure that she couldn't do either.

"I could forget the whole damned thing, too," he said curtly. He glared at Lillian. "Nothing is going to make up for this, you know."

She swallowed. "How about a nice freshly baked apple pie with ice cream?"

He tilted his head to one side and pursed his lips. "Freshly baked?"

"Freshly baked."

"With ice cream?"

"That's right," she promised.

He shrugged his wet shoulders. "I'll think about it." He turned and sloshed off down the hall.

Lillian leaned back against the wall and stared at her transfixed niece. "Honey," she said gently, "would you like to tell me what happened?"

"I don't know," Mari burst out. "I went in to call him to the table, and I started looking at that beautiful artificial stream, and the next thing I knew, he'd fallen into it. I must have, well, backed into him."

"How you could miss a man his size is beyond me." Lillian shook her head and grabbed a broom and dustpan from the closet.

"I had my back to him, you know."

"I wouldn't ever do that again after this if I were you," the older woman advised. "If it wasn't for that apple pie, even I couldn't save you!"

"Yes, ma'am," Mari said apologetically. "Oh, Aunt Lillian, that poor, brave man." She sighed. "I hope he doesn't get a chill because of me. I'd never be able to live with myself!"

"There, there," Lillian assured her, "he's tough, you know. He'll be fine. For now, I mean," she added quickly.

Mari covered her face with her hands in mingled relief and suppressed amusement. Ward Jessup was quite a man. How sad that he had such little time left. She didn't think she'd ever forget the look on his face when he climbed out of the indoor stream, or the excited beat of her heart as she'd run from him. It was new to be chased by a man, even an ill one, and exhilarating to be uninhibited in one's company. She'd been shy with men all her life, but she didn't feel shy with Ward. She felt...*feminine*. And that was as new to her as the rapid beat of her heart.

Chapter Three

"I didn't mean to knock you into the pool," Mari told Ward the minute he entered the dining room.

He stopped in the doorway and stared at her from his great height. His hair was dry now, thick and straight against his broad forehead, and his wet clothes had been exchanged for dry jeans and a blue plaid shirt. His green eyes were a little less hostile than they had been minutes before.

"It isn't a pool," he informed her. "It's an indoor stream. And next time, Miss Raymond, I'd appreciate it if you'd watch where the hell you're going."

"Yes, sir," she said quickly.

"I told you not to let him put that stream in the living room," Lillian gloated.

He glared at her. "Keep talking and I'll give you an impromptu swimming lesson."

"Yes, boss." She turned on her heel and went back into the kitchen to fetch the rest of the food.

"I really am sorry," Mari murmured.

"So am I," he said unexpectedly, and his green eyes searched hers quietly. "I hope I didn't frighten you."

She glanced down at her shoes, nervous of the sensations that his level gaze prompted. "It's hard to be afraid of a man with a lily pad on his head."

"Stop that," he grumbled, jerking out a chair.

"You might consider putting up guardrails," she suggested dryly as she sat down across from him, her blue eyes twinkling with the first humor she'd felt in days.

"You'd better keep a life jacket handy," he returned.

She stuck her tongue out at him impulsively and watched his thick eyebrows arch.

He shook out his napkin with unnecessary force and laid it across his powerful thighs. "My God, you're living dangerously," he told her.

"I'm not afraid of you," she said smartly and meant it.

"That isn't what your Aunt Lillian says," he observed with narrowed eyes.

She stared at him blankly. "I beg your pardon?"

"She says you're afraid of men," he continued. He scowled at her puzzled expression. "Because of what happened to you and your friend," he prompted.

She blinked, wondering what her aunt had told him about that. After all, having your purse pinched by an overweight juvenile delinquent wasn't really enough to terrify most women. Especially when she and Beth had run the offender down, beaten the stuffing out of him, recovered the purse and sat on him until the police got there.

"You know, dear," Lillian blustered as she came through the door, shaking her head and smiling all at once. She looked as red as a beet, too. "The horrible experience you had!"

"Horrible?" Mari asked.

"Horrible!" Lillian cried. "We can't talk about it now!"

"We can't?" Mari parroted blankly.

"Not at the table. Not in front of the boss!" She jerked her head curtly toward him two or three times.

"Have you got a crick in your neck, Aunt Lillian?" her niece asked with some concern.

"No, dear, why do you ask? Here! Have some fried chicken and some mashed potatoes!" She shoved dishes toward her niece and began a monologue that only ended when it was time for dessert.

"I think something's wrong with Aunt Lillian," Mari confided to Ward the moment Lillian started back into the kitchen for the coffeepot.

"Yes, so do I," he replied. "She's been acting strangely for the past few days. Don't let on you know. We'll talk later."

She nodded, concerned. Lillian was back seconds later, almost as if she was afraid to leave them alone together. How strange.

"Well, I think I'll go up to bed," Mari said after she finished her coffee, glancing quickly at Aunt Lillian. "I'm very tired."

"Good idea," Ward said. "You get some rest."

"Yes," Lillian agreed warmly. "Good night, dear."

She bent to kiss her aunt. "See you in the morning, Aunt Lillian," she murmured and glanced at Ward. "Good night, Mr. Jessup."

"Good night, Miss Raymond," he said politely.

Mari went quietly upstairs and into her bedroom. She sat by the window and looked down at the empty swimming pool with its wooden privacy fence and the gently rolling, brush-laden landscape, where cattle moved lazily and a green haze heralded spring. Minutes later there was a stealthy knock at the door, and Ward Jessup came into the room, scowling.

"Want me to leave the door open?" he asked hesitantly.

She stared at him blankly. "Why? Are you afraid I might attack you?"

He stared back. "Well, after the experience you had, I thought..."

"What experience?" she asked politely.

"The man at the shopping center," he said, his green eyes level and frankly puzzled as he closed the door behind him.

"Are you afraid of me because of that?" she burst out. "I do realize you may be a little weak, Mr. Jessup, but I promise I won't hurt you!"

He gaped at her. "What?"

"You don't have to be afraid of me," she assured him. "I'm not really as bad as Aunt Lillian made me sound, I'm sure. And it's only a red belt, after all, not a black one. I only sat on him until the police came. I hardly even bruised him—".

"Whoa," he said curtly. He cocked his dark head and peered at her. "You sat on him?"

"Sure," she agreed, pushing her hair out of her eyes. "Didn't she tell you that Beth and I ran the little weasel down to get my purse back and beat the stuffing out of him? Overweight little juvenile delinquent, he was lucky I didn't skin him alive."

"You weren't attacked?" he persisted.

"Well, sort of." She shrugged. "He stole my purse. He couldn't have known I was a karate student."

"Oh, my God," he burst out. His eyes narrowed, his jaw tautened. "That lying old turkey!"

"How dare you call my aunt a turkey!" she returned hotly. "After all she's doing for you?"

"What, exactly, is she doing for me?"

"Well, bringing me here, to help you write your memoirs before...the end," she faltered. "She told me all about your incurable illness—"

"Incurable illness?" he bellowed.

"You're dying," she told him.

"Like hell I am," he said fiercely.

"You don't have to act brave and deny it," she replied hesitantly. "She told me that you wanted young people around to cheer you up. And somebody to help you write your memoirs. I'm going to be a novelist one day," she added. "I want to be a writer."

"Good. You can practice with your aunt's obituary," he muttered, glaring toward the door.

"You can't do that to a helpless old lady," she began.

"Watch me." He was heading for the door, his very stride frightening.

"Oh, no! You can't!" She ran after him, got in front of him and plastered herself against the door. "You'll have to go through me."

"Suits me, Joan of Arc," he grumbled, catching her by the waist. He lifted her clear off the floor until she was unnervingly at eye level with him. "You sweet little angel of mercy, you."

"Put me down or I'll...I'll put you down," she threatened.

He stared amusedly into her blue eyes under impossibly thick lashes. "Will you? Go ahead. Show me how you earned that red belt."

She tried. She used every trick her instructor had taught her, and all it accomplished was to leave her dangling from his powerful hands, panting into his mocking smile.

"Had enough?" she huffed.

"Not at all. Aren't you finished yet?" he asked politely.

She aimed one more kick, which he blocked effortlessly. She sagged in his powerful hold. Lord, he was strong! "Okay," she said, sighing wearily. "Now I'm finished."

"Next time," he told her as he put her back on her feet, leaving his hands tightly around her waist, "make sure your intended victim didn't take the same course of study. My belt is black. Tenth degree."

"Damn you!" she cursed sharply.

"And we'll have no more of that in this house," he said shortly, emphasizing the angry remark with a reproachful slap to her bottom, nodding as she gasped in outrage. "You've been working in that garage for too long already, if that's any example of what you're being taught."

"I'm not a child!" she retorted. "I'm an adult!"

"No, you aren't," he replied, jerking her against him with a mocking smile. "But maybe I can help you grow up a little."

He bent his head and found her lips with a single smooth motion, pressing her neck back against his muscular shoulder with the fierce possessiveness of his hard mouth.

Mari thought that in all her life nothing so unexpected had ever happened to her. His lips were warm and hard and insistent, forcing hers open so that he could put the tip of his tongue just under them, his breath tasting of coffee and mint, the strength of his big body overwhelming her with its hard warmth.

For an instant she tried to struggle, only to find herself enveloped in his arms, wrapped up against him so tightly that she could hardly breathe. And everywhere her face turned, his was there, his mouth provocative, sensuous, biting at hers, doing the most intimate things to it.

Her legs felt funny. They began to tremble as they came into sudden and shocking contact with his. Her heart raced. Her body began to ache with heat and odd longings. Her breath caught somewhere in her chest, and her breasts felt swollen. Because these new sensations frightened her, she tried to struggle. But he only held her tighter, not brutally but firmly, and went on kissing her.

His fingers were in her hair, tugging gently, strong and warm at her nape as they turned her face where he wanted it. His mouth pressed roughly against hers and opened softly, teaching hers. Eventually the drugging sweetness of it took the fight out of her. With a tiny sigh she began to relax.

"Open your mouth, Mari," he murmured in a deep, rough whisper, punctuating the command with a sensual brushing of his open lips against hers.

She obeyed him without hearing him, her body with a new heat, her hands searching over his arms to find hard muscle and warm strength through the fabric. She wanted to touch his skin, to experience every hard line of him. She wanted to open his shirt and touch his chest and see if the wiry softness she could feel through it was thick hair....

Her abandon shocked her back to reality. Her eyes opened and she tugged at his arms, only vaguely aware of the sudden, fierce hunger in his mouth just before he felt her resistance. He lifted his head, taking quick, short breaths, and by the time her eyes opened, he was back in control.

He was watching her, half amused, half mocking. He lifted his mouth, breathing through his nose, and let her move away.

"You little virgin," he accused in a tone that she didn't recognize. "You don't even know how to make love."

Her swollen lips could barely form words. She had to swallow and try twice to make herself heard. "That wasn't fair," she said finally.

"Why not?" he asked. "You tried to kick me, didn't you?"

"That isn't the way...a gentleman gets even," she said, still panting.

"I'm no gentleman," he assured her, smiling even with those cold green eyes. The smile grew colder as he realized how close he'd come to letting her knock him off balance physically. She was dangerous. Part of him wanted her off the property. But another part was hungry for more of that innocently ardent response he'd won from her. His own emotions confused him. "Haven't you realized yet why you're here, Georgia peach?" he asked mockingly. And when she shook her head, he continued, half amused. "Aunt Lillian is matchmaking. She wants you to marry me."

Mari's pupils dilated. "Marry you!"

His back stiffened. She didn't have to make it sound like the rack, did she? He glared down at her. "Well, plenty have wanted to, let me tell you," he muttered.

"Masochists," she shot back, humiliated by her aunt, his attitude and that unexpectedly ardent attack just minutes before. "Anyway," she said salvaging her pride, "Aunt Lillian would never—"

"She did." He studied her with a cold smile. "But I'm too old for you and too jaded. And I don't want to risk my heart again. So go home. Fast."

"It can't be fast enough to suit me. Honest," she told him huskily as she tried to catch her breath. "I don't want to wake up shackled to a man like you."

"How flattering of you."

"I want a partner, not a possessor," she said shakily. "I thought I knew something about men until just now. I don't know anything at all. And I'll be delighted to go back home and join a convent!"

"Was it that bad?" he taunted.

"You scare me, big man," she said and meant it. She backed away from him. "I'll stick to my own age group from now on, thanks. I'll bet you've forgotten more about making love than I'll ever learn."

He smiled slowly, surprised by her frankness. "I probably have. But you're pretty sweet all the same."

"Years too young for a renegade like you."

"I could be tempted," he murmured thoughtfully.

"I couldn't. You'd seduce me and leave me pregnant, and Aunt Lillian would quit, and I'd have to go away and invent a husband I didn't have, and our child would grow up never knowing his father..." she burst out.

His eyes widened. He actually chuckled. "My God, what an imagination."

"I told you I wanted to be a writer," she reminded him. "And now, since you're not dying, would you mind leaving me to pack? I think I can be out of here in ten minutes."

"She'll be heartbroken," he said unexpectedly.

"That's not my problem."

"She's your aunt. Of course it's your problem," he returned. "You can't possibly leave now. She'd—"

"Oh!"

The cry came from downstairs. They looked at each other and both dived for the door, opening it just in time to find Lillian on her back on the bottom step, groaning, one leg in an unnatural position.

Mari rushed down the stairs just behind Ward. "Oh, Aunt Lillian!" she wailed, staring at the strained old face with its pasty complexion. "How could you do this to me?"

"To you?" Lillian bit off, groaning again. "Child, it's my leg!"

"I was going to leave—" Mari began.

"Leave the dishes for you, no doubt." Ward jumped in with a warning glance in Mari's direction. "Isn't that right, Miss Raymond?" Fate was working for him as usual, he mused. Now he'd have a little time to find out just why this woman disturbed him so much. And to get her well out of his system, one way or another, before she left. He had to prove to himself that Mari wasn't capable of doing to him what Caroline had done. It was a matter of male pride.

Mari swallowed, wondering whether to go along with Ward. He did look pretty threatening. And huge. "Uh, that's right. The dishes. But I can do them!" she added brightly.

"It looks like...you may be doing them...for quite a while, if you...don't mind," Lillian panted between groans while Wade rushed to the telephone and dialed the emergency service number.

"You poor darling." Mari sighed, holding Lillian's wrinkled hand. "What happened?"

"I missed Ward and wondered if he might be . . . if you might be . . ." She cleared her throat and stared at Mari through layers of pain. "You didn't say anything to him?" she asked quickly. "About his . . . condition?"

Mari bit her tongue. *Forgive me for lying, Lord,* she thought. She crossed her fingers behind her. "Of course not," she assured her aunt with a blank smile. "He was just telling me about the ranch."

"Thank God." Lillian sank back. "My leg's broken, you know," she bit off. She glanced up as Ward rejoined them, scowling down at her. She forced a pitiful smile. "Well, boss, I guess you'll have to send for your grandmother," she said slyly.

He glared at her. "Like hell! I just got her off the place! Anyway, why should I?" he continued, bending to hold her other hand. "Your niece won't mind a little cooking, will she?" he added with a pointed glance at Mari.

Mari shifted restlessly. "Well, actually—"

"Of course she won't." Lillian grinned and then grimaced. "Will you, darling? You need to . . . recuperate." She chose her words carefully. "From your bad experience," she added, jerking her head toward Ward, her eyes pleading with her niece. "You know, at the shopping center?"

"Oh. That bad experience." Mari nodded, glancing at Ward and touching her lower lip where it was slightly swollen.

A corner of his mouth curved up and his eyes twinkled. "It wasn't that bad, was it?" he murmured.

"It was terrible!" Lillian broke in.

"You said it," Mari agreed blithely, her blue eyes accusing. "Besides, I thought you couldn't wait to push me out the door."

"You want her to leave?" Lillian wailed.

"No, I don't want her to leave," Ward said with suffering patience. He lifted his chin and stared down his straight nose at Mari, then smiled. "I've got plans for her," he added in a tone that was a threat in itself.

That was what bothered Mari. Now she was trapped by Lillian's lies and Ward's allegiance to his housekeeper. She wondered what on earth she was going to do, caught between the two of them, and she wondered why Ward Jessup wanted her to stay. He hated women most of the time, from what Lillian had divulged about him. He wasn't a marrying man, and he was a notorious womanizer. Surely he wouldn't try to seduce her. Would he?

She stared at him over Lillian's supine form with troubled eyes. He had an unscrupulous reputation. She wasn't so innocent that she hadn't recognized that evident hunger in his hard mouth just before she'd started fighting him.

But his green eyes mocked her, dared her, challenged her. She'd stay, he told himself. He'd coax her into it. Then he could find some way to make her show her true colors. He was betting there was a little of

Caroline's makeup in her, too. She was just another female despite her innocence. She was a woman, and all women were unscrupulous and calculating. If he could make her drop the disguise, if he could prove she was just like all the other she-cats, he could rid himself of his unexpected lust. Lust, of course, was all it was. He forgave Lillian for her fall. It was going to work right in with his plans. Yes, it was.

Chapter Four

Lillian was comfortably settled in a room in the small Ravine hospital. The doctor had ordered a series of tests—not because of her broken leg but because of her blood pressure reading taken in the emergency room.

"Will she be all right, do you think?" Mari asked Ward as they waited for the doctor to speak to them. For most of the evening they'd been sitting in this waiting room. Ward paced and drank black coffee while Mari just stared into space worriedly. Lillian was her last living relative. Without the older woman she'd be all alone.

"She's tough," Ward said noncommittally. He glared at his watch. "My God, I hate waiting! I almost wish I smoked so that I'd have something to help kill the time."

"You don't smoke?" Mari said with surprise.

"Never could stand the things," he muttered. "Clogging up my lungs with smoke never seemed sensible."

Her eyebrows lifted. "But you drink."

"Not to excess," he returned, glancing down at her. "I like whiskey and water once in a blue moon, and I'll take a drink of white wine. But I won't do it and drive." He grinned. "All those commercials got to me. Those crashing beer glasses stick in my mind."

She smiled back a little shyly. "I don't drink at all."

"I guess not, tenderfoot," he murmured. "You aren't old enough to need to."

"My dad used to say that it isn't the age, it's the mileage."

His eyebrows arched. "How much mileage do you have, lady?" he taunted. "You look and feel pretty green to me."

Her face colored furiously, and she hated that knowing look on his dark face. "Listen here, Mr. Jessup—"

"Mr. Jessup." His name was echoed by a young resident physician, who came walking up in a white coat holding a clipboard. He shook hands with Ward and nodded as he was introduced tersely to Mari.

"She'll be all right," he told the two brusquely. "But I'd like to keep her one more day and run some more tests. She's furious, but I think it's for the best. Her blood pressure was abnormally high when we admitted her and it still is. I think that she might have had a slight stroke and that it caused her fall.''

Mari had sudden horrible visions and went pale. ''Oh, no,'' she whispered.

''I said, I think,'' the young doctor emphasized and then smiled. ''She might have lost her balance for a number of reasons. That's why I want to run the tests. Even a minor ear infection or sinusitis could have caused it. I want to know for sure. But one thing's certain, and that's her attitude toward the high blood pressure medication she hasn't been taking.''

Ward and Mari exchanged puzzled glances. ''I wasn't aware that she had high blood pressure medication,'' Ward said.

''I guessed that,'' the young doctor said ruefully. ''She was diagnosed a few weeks ago by Dr. Bradley. She didn't even get the prescription filled.'' He sighed. ''She seems to look upon it as a death sentence, which is absurd. It's not, if she just takes care of herself.''

''She will from now on,'' Mari promised. ''If I have to roll the pills up in steak and trick them into her.''

The young resident grinned from ear to ear. ''You have pets?''

''I used to have a cat,'' Mari confided. ''And the only way I could get medicine into him was by tricking him. Short of rolling him up in a towel.''

Ward glared at her. "That's no way to treat a sick animal."

She lifted her thin eyebrows. "And how would you do it?"

"Force his mouth open and shove the pills down his throat, of course," he said matter-of-factly. "Before you say it," he added when her mouth opened, "try rolling a half-ton bull in a towel!"

The young doctor covered his mouth while Mari glared up at the taciturn oilman.

"I'll get the pills into her, regardless," Mari assured the doctor. She glanced at Ward Jessup. "And it won't be by having them forced down her throat like a half-ton bull!"

"When will you know something?" Ward asked.

"I'll have the tests by early afternoon, and I'll confer with Dr. Bradley. If you can be here about four o'clock, I'll have something to tell you," the young man said.

"Thank you, Doctor... ?"

"Jackson," he replied, smiling. "And don't worry too much," he told Mari. "She's a strong-willed woman. I'd bet on her."

They stopped by Lillian's room and found her half sedated, fuming and glaring as she sat propped up in bed.

"Outrageous!" Lillian burst out the minute they entered the room. "They won't give back my clothes.

They're making me spend the night in this icebox, and they won't feed me or give me a blanket!"

"Now, now." Mari laughed gently and bent to kiss the thin face. "You're going to be fine. They said so. They just want to run a few more tests. You'll be out of here in no time."

That reassured the older woman a little, but her beady black eyes went to Ward for reassurance. He wouldn't lie to her. Not him. "Am I all right?" she asked.

"You might have had a stroke," he said honestly, ignoring Mari's shocked glare. "They want to find out."

Lillian sighed. "I figured that. I sure did. Well," she said, brightening, "you two will have to get along without me for a day or so." That seemed to cheer her up, too. Her eyes twinkled at the thought of them alone together in the house.

Ward could read her mind. He wanted to wring her neck, too, but he couldn't hurt a sick lady. First he had to get her well.

"I'll take good care of baby sister, here," he said, nodding toward Mari, and grinned.

Lillian's face fell comically. "She's not that young," she faltered.

"Aunt Lillian!" Mari said, outraged. "Remember my horrible experience!"

"Oh, that." Lillian nibbled her lip. "Oh. That!" She cleared her throat, her eyes widened. "Well..."

"I'll help her get over it," Ward promised. He glanced down at Mari. "She's offered to help me get some of my adventures in the oil business down on paper. Wasn't that nice? And on her vacation, too," he added.

Lillian brightened. *Good.* They weren't talking about his "fatal illness" or her "brutal attack." With any luck they wouldn't stumble onto the truth until they were hooked on each other! She actually smiled. "Yes, how sweet of you, Mari!"

Although Mari felt like screaming, she smiled at her aunt. "Yes. Well, I thought it would give me something interesting to do. In between cooking and cleaning and such."

Lillian frowned. "I'm really sorry about this," she said, indicating her leg.

"Get well," Ward said shortly. "Don't be sorry. And one more thing. Whether or not this fall was caused by your blood pressure, you're taking those damned pills from now on. I'm going to ride herd on you like a fanatical ramrod on a trail drive. Got that?"

"Yes, sir, boss," Lillian said, pleased by his concern. She hadn't realized she mattered so much to anyone. Even Mari seemed worried. "I'll be fine. And I'll do what they tell me."

"Good for you," Ward replied. He cocked his head. "They said it could have been an ear infection or sinusitis, too. So don't go crazy worrying about a stroke. Did you black out before you went down?" he persisted.

Lillian sighed. "Not completely. I just got real dizzy."

He smiled "That's reassuring."

"I hope so. Now, you two go home," Lillian muttered. "Let me sleep. Whatever they gave me is beginning to work with a vengeance." She closed her eyes as they said their goodbyes, only to open them as they started to leave. "Mari, he likes his eggs scrambled with a little milk in them," she said. "And don't make the coffee too weak."

"I'll manage," Mari promised. "Just get well. You're all I have."

"I know." Lillian sighed as they closed the door behind them. "That's what worries me so."

But they didn't hear that troubled comment. Mari was fuming all the way to the car.

"You shouldn't have told her what the doctor said." She glowered at him as they drove out of the parking lot.

"You don't know her very well," he returned. He pulled into the traffic without blinking. Ravine had grown in the past few years, and the traffic was growing with it, but speeding cars didn't seem to bother him.

"She's my aunt. Of course I know her!"

"She isn't the kind of woman you nurse along," he shot back. "Any more than I'm that kind. I like the truth, even if it hurts, and so does she. You don't do people any favors by hiding it. You only make the impact worse when it comes out. God, I hate lies. There's nothing on earth I hate more."

He probably had a good reason for that attitude, but Mari wasn't going to pry into his privacy by asking.

At least now she understood Aunt Lillian's matchmaking frenzy. If the older woman had expected to die, she might also have worried about Mari's future. But to try to give Mari to a man like the one beside her was almost criminal! The very thought of being tied to that ex-drill rigger made her blanch. He frightened her in a way no other man ever had. It wasn't fear of brutality or even of rough behavior. It was fear of involvement, of being led on and dumped, the way Johnny Greenwood had teased her and taken her places, and then when she was drunk on loving him, he'd announced his engagement to someone else.

Ward Jessup wasn't the man for marriage, but he wouldn't mind amusing himself with a woman and then dropping her. He seemed to hate women, to be spoiling for revenge on the entire sex. She remembered him saying that he could only tolerate his grandmother and Lillian under his roof, and that said it all. She'd have to be very careful not to fall under his spell. Because he was just playing, and she didn't even know the first thing about his game.

She went to her room as soon as they were back at Three Forks, and although she hated her vulnerability, she actually locked her bedroom door. Not that he'd try anything, she assured herself. But, just in case, a little precaution wouldn't hurt.

The next morning she was awake at dawn. Rather than lie in bed and worry about Aunt Lillian, she got up, dressed in jeans and a yellow pullover and went to cook the beast's breakfast.

She did love this house, indoor waterway and all. It seemed to catch and scatter light so that the darkest corner was bright and cheery. The kitchen reflected the rest of the house. It was spacious and cheerful and contained every modern appliance known to man.

She started the coffee maker and fried bacon. By the time the aroma of coffee was filling the kitchen, she had biscuits in the oven and was setting the big, elegant dining room table.

"What the hell are you doing that for?" Ward Jessup asked from the doorway. "I don't mind eating in the kitchen."

She jumped, turning in time to see him shrug into a chambray shirt. His chest was...incredible. She couldn't help but stare. Despite her age and her exposure to men at the garage where she worked, she'd never in her life seen anything like Ward Jessup without his shirt. Talk about masculine perfection! His chest was as tanned as his face. Broad, rippling with muscle, tapering to his belt, it had a perfect wedge of dark, thick hair that made Mari's jaw drop.

"Close your mouth, honey, you'll catch flies that way," he said, then chuckled, torn between exasperation and honest flattery at her rapt and explicit stare.

She turned back to her table setting with trembling fingers, hating her youth and inexperience, hating the big man who was making fun ot it. "Excuse me. I'm not used to men . . . half dressed like that."

"Then you should have seen me ten minutes ago, sprout, before I got up. I sleep in the raw."

Now Mari was sure she was blushing. She pursed her lips as she put silverware at their places.

He came up behind her so that she could feel the heat of his big body and took her gently by the shoulders. "That wasn't fair, was it?" he murmured.

"No," she agreed, "considering what a beautiful breakfast I just fixed you."

His lips tugged into a smile. "Do I smell bacon?"

"And biscuits and an omelette and hash brown potatoes and hot coffee," she continued, glancing up at him.

"Then what are you standing here for?" he asked. "Feed me!"

She was rapidly becoming convinced that his appetite was the great love of his life. Food could stop his temper dead, keep him from teasing and prevent homicide, as that apple pie had done after she'd knocked him into the water. It was useful to have such a weapon, when dealing with such a formidable enemy, she thought as she went to put the platters on the table.

He ate without talking, and he didn't sit and read a newspaper, as her father always had done in her youth. She watched him curiously.

His eyebrows shot up. "Something bothering you?"

"Not really." She laughed self-consciously. "It's just that the only man I've ever had breakfast with was my father, and he read his paper all through it."

"I don't read at the table," he said. He finished his last mouthful of biscuit, washed it down with coffee and poured himself a second cup from the carafe. Then he sat back in his chair and stared straight into Mari's eyes. "Why does my chest disturb you?"

She tingled from her head to her toes at the unexpected question and felt a wave of heat wash over her. Some old lines about fighting fire with fire shot into her mind. "Because it's beautiful, in a purely masculine way," she blurted out.

He pondered that for a minute before he smiled into his coffee. "You don't lie well, do you?"

"I think it's a waste of time," she replied. She got to her feet. "If you're through, I'll clear the table."

She started to pick up his plate. His big hand, and it was enormously big, caught her wrist and swallowed it, staying her beside him.

"Have you ever touched a man, except to shake hands?" he asked quietly.

"I'm not a shrinking violet," she said, flustered. "I'm almost twenty-two years old, and I have been kissed a few times!"

"Not enough, and not by anyone who knew how." He pulled her closer, feeling her resistance, but he stopped short of dragging her down onto his lap. "Why are you afraid of me?"

"I am not!" she retorted.

His fingers on her wrist were softly caressing. She reacted to him in a way that shocked him. In all the years, with all the women, he'd never felt such response. She was innocent, despite her denials. He'd have bet an oil well on it.

"Calm down," he said softly, feeling so masculine that he could have swallowed a live rattler. He even smiled. "I won't hurt you."

She flushed even more and jerked away from him, but he was much too strong. "Please," she bit off. "Let me go. I don't know how to play this kind of game."

His thumb found her moist palm and rubbed it in a new and exciting way, tracing it softly, causing sensations that went far beyond her hand. "I stopped playing games a long time ago, and I never played them with virgins," he said quietly. "What are you afraid of, Mari?" He spoke her name softly, and she tingled like a schoolgirl.

"You hate women," she said in a voice barely above a whisper. She met his green eyes levelly. "I don't think there's any real feeling in you, any deep emotion. Sometimes you look at me as if you hate me."

He hadn't realized that. He stared down at their hands, hers so pale against his deeply tanned one. "I got burned once, didn't your aunt tell you?"

"I got burned once, too," she replied, "and I don't want to—"

"Again," he finished for her, looking up unexpectedly. "Neither do I."

"Then why don't you let go of my hand?" she asked breathlessly.

He drew it relentlessly to his hard mouth and brushed at it with soft, moist strokes that made her go hot all over. "Why don't you stop me?" he countered. He pried open her palm and touched his tongue to it, and she caught her breath and gasped.

He looked up, his eyes suddenly hotly green and acquisitive, and she felt the first tug of that steely hand on hers with a sense of fantasy. Her eyes were locked into his possessive gaze, her body throbbed with new longings, new curiosities.

"I'm going to teach you a few things you haven't learned," he said, his voice like velvet as he drew her relentlessly down toward him. "And I think it's going to be an explosive lesson for both of us. I feel like a volcano when I touch you . . ."

Her lips parted as her eyes dropped to his hard, hungry mouth. She could almost see it, feel it, the explosive desire that was going to go up like fireworks when he put his hard mouth on hers and began to touch her.

She almost cried out, the hunger was so formidable. Silence closed in on them. She could hear his breathing, she could feel her heartbeat shaking her. In slow motion she felt his hard thighs ripple as she was tugged down onto them, she felt the power and strength of his hands, smelled the rich fragrance of his cologne, stared into eyes that wanted her.

She parted her lips in breathless anticipation, aching for him. Just as his hand went to her shoulder, to draw her head down, the front door opened with a loud bang.

Chapter Five

"Good morning," a pleasant auburn-haired young man was saying before Mari was completely composed again. He seemed to notice nothing, equally oblivious to Mari's flushed face and Ward's uneven breathing.

"Good morning, David," Ward said in what he hoped was a normal voice. From the neck down he had an ache that made speech difficult. "Have some coffee before we start to work."

"No, thank you, sir," the young man said politely. "Actually, I came to ask for a little time off," he added with a sheepish grin. "You see...I've gotten married."

Ward gaped at him. His young secretary had always seemed such a levelheaded boy, with a head full of figures. As it turned out, the figures weren't always the numerical kind.

"Married?" Ward croaked.

"Well, sir, it was kind of a hurried-up thing," David said with a grin. "We eloped. She's such a sweet girl. I was afraid somebody else would snap her up. And I wondered, well, if I could just have a couple of weeks. If you could do without me? If you have to replace me, I'll understand," he added hesitantly.

"Go ahead," Ward muttered. "I'll manage." He shifted in the chair. "What would you like for a wedding present?"

David brightened immediately. "Two weeks off," came the amused reply.

"All right, you've got it. I'll hold your job for the time being. Now get out of here. You know weddings give me indigestion," he added for good measure and then spoiled the whole thing by smiling.

David shook his hand with almost pathetic eagerness. "Thank you, sir!"

"My pleasure. See you in two weeks."

"Yes, sir!" David grinned at Mari, to whom he hadn't even been introduced, and beat a path out the door before he could be called back. He knew his boss pretty well.

"That tears it," Ward grumbled. "What in hell will I do about the mail?"

She stared at him, stunned by his lack of feeling. "He just got married."

"So what?" he demanded. "Surely the only time he really needs to be with her is after dark."

"You male chauvinist!"

"What are you so keyed up about, honey?" he taunted irritably. "Frustrated because I couldn't finish what I started before he walked in on us?"

What good would it do to argue? she asked herself as she noisily loaded up the dirty plates and utensils and took them out to the kitchen without a single word.

He followed her a few minutes later, looking half out of humor and a little guilty.

Standing in the doorway he filled it with his big, tall frame. His hair looked rakish, falling over his broad forehead, and he was so handsome that she had to fight to keep from staring at him all over again.

"I've got to ride over and see about my rig on Tyson Wade's place," he said quietly. "Can you handle the phone?"

"Sure," she told him, walking over to the wall phone. "This is the receiver," she began, pointing to it, speaking in a monotone. "When it rings, you pick it up and talk right in here—"

"Oh, for God's sake," he burst out. "What I meant was that it rings all day long, with everything from stock options to social invitations to notices of board meetings!"

She pushed back her bangs. "I've worked in offices since I was eighteen," she told him.

He cocked his head. "Can you type?"

"How ever do you think I'll manage all the housekeeping and cooking as well as looking after your appointments and answering mail and waiting on Aunt Lillian all at once?" she demanded.

His eyebrows arched. "Well, if you aren't capable of it, I'll hire a cook and a maid and a nurse and a secretary..."

Mari could only imagine how her aunt would react to that. She glared at him. "And break Aunt Lillian's old heart by importing a lot of strangers to keep us apart?"

He laughed in spite of himself. "I guess it would," he confessed. His green eyes narrowed, and there was a light in them that disturbed her as he ran his gaze slowly over her slender body. "God forbid anything should keep us apart."

"Don't you have an oil well to check on?"

"Several, in fact," he agreed. He folded his arms. "But at the moment I'd rather look at you."

"And I'd rather you didn't," she said curtly, averting her eyes to the dishwater.

"I like the way you react to me, Mari," he said softly. "I like the way your body starts to tremble when I come close. If I'd started kissing you a few minute ago, we'd still be doing it. I don't even know if I could stop. And that being the case," he added, leveling with her, "I think you'd better practice ways to discourage me. Lillian won't be around much when she comes back until her leg heals. So you and I are going to get a bit of each other's company. I'd just as soon manage your little visit without showing you how good I am in bed."

His blatant speech shocked her. She turned, soapy hands poised over the sink, and stared at him. "Are you?" she asked without thinking.

He nodded slowly, holding her gaze, his face dead serious. "A man doesn't have to be emotionally involved to make love well. I've had years of practice. But it's never meant much, except physically. It never will. So you keep that in mind, sprout, okay?"

"Okay," she replied, all eyes.

His eyes narrowed at her expression. "Haven't you ever discussed these things with a man?"

"My parents didn't discuss things like that," she replied. "Most of the girls I've known had a distorted view of it because they did it with so many people. I... find the thought of it distasteful, somehow. Sleeping with someone, well, it's intimate, isn't it? Like using someone's toothbrush, only more so. I couldn't... just do that, without loving."

She sounded so hopelessly naive. He searched her face and realized with a start that he'd never made love to a virgin. Not one. Not ever. And the thought of touching her in all the ways that he'd touched other women produced a shocking reaction from his body—one he was grateful that she wouldn't recognize.

"What an unusual attitude," he said involuntarily.

"That isn't the word most people use," she replied, her eyes dull and lackluster. "Men avoid me like the plague, except to do typing and answer phones. I'm what's known as an oddball."

"Because you don't sleep around?" he asked, stunned.

"Exactly. Didn't you know that the pill has liberated women?" she explained. "They're allowed the same freedom as men. They can sleep around every night without any consequences. Of course, they sacrifice a few things along the way that the liberals don't mention. Things like that deep-seated guilt that all the permissive ideals in the world won't change."

He stared at her. "My God, you are a fanatic, aren't you?" he mused.

She smiled slowly. "How would you like marrying a woman and hearing all about her old lovers? Meeting them occasionally and wondering if you measured up? How would you like to have a pregnant wife and wonder if the baby was really yours? I mean, if she sleeps around before marriage, what's to keep her from doing it afterward? If promiscuity is okay, isn't adultery okay as well?"

Everything she was saying disturbed him. Caroline had slept around. Not only with him, but, as he'd later found out, with at least two of his business acquaintances. He frowned at the thought. Yes, he'd have wondered. And he'd only just realized it.

"But I'm just a prude," she announced dryly. "So don't mind me. I'll grow into happy spinsterhood and die with the reputation that Elizabeth I had."

"Unless you marry," he said involuntarily.

She laughed ruefully. "Men don't marry women they haven't slept with. Not these days." She turned back to the dishes, oblivious to the brief flash of pain that crossed the face of the man behind her. "I'm not into self-pity, but I do face facts," she continued calmly. "I'm not pretty, I'm just passable. I'm too thin, and I don't know how to flirt. And, as you yourself said, I'm a greenhorn when it comes to intimacy. All that adds up to happy spinsterhood." She gazed thoughtfully out the window over the sink. "I'll grow prize roses," she mused aloud. "Yes, that's what I'll do. And zinnias and crape myrtle and petunias and lantana and hibiscus."

He wasn't listening anymore. He was staring at the back of her head. Her hair was very dark and sleek, and he wished she'd left it long, the way it was in the photograph he'd seen. She wasn't a beauty, that was true. But she had a pretty good sense of humor, and she didn't take herself or anyone else too seriously. She had guts and she told the truth. Damn her.

He didn't like his attraction to her. He didn't like how she could make him tremble all over like a boy when he started to kiss her. He didn't want her knowing it, either. The whole point of this exercise was to *exorcise*. He had to get rid of this lunatic obsession he felt.

"I'm going," he said shortly, shouldering himself away from the doorjamb. "I'll be back by three-thirty to go to the hospital with you."

"I'll phone meanwhile," she said.

"Do what you please." He stormed off, leaving her curious and speechless. What an odd man. What a dangerous man.

She spent the rest of the day working herself into exhaustion so that she wouldn't dwell on what had happened at breakfast.

When they got to the hospital, Lillian was sitting on the side of her bed, dressed.

"It's about time," she began hotly. "Get me out of here! They've put on a cast and decided it was infected sinuses that made me fall. They've given me some tablets they say will lower my blood pressure, and if you don't spring me, I'll jump out a window!"

"With that?" Ward asked, nodding toward the heavy plaster walking cast on one of her legs.

"With that," she assured him. "Tell him I'm serious about this, Mari," she added.

Mari was trying not to laugh. "You look pretty serious."

"I can see that. Where's the doctor?"

"He'll be here any minute," Lillian began.

"I'll go find him," Ward returned, walking quickly out into the hall, moving lightly for a man his size.

"How's it going?" Lillian asked, all eyes.

"How's what going?" Mari asked with assumed innocence.

"You were alone all last night!" she hissed. "Did he try anything?"

Mari lifted her eyebrows and pursed her lips. "Well, he did try to call somebody on the phone, but he couldn't get them."

Lillian looked pained. "I mean, did he make a pass at you?"

"No," Mari lied. It was only a white lie, just enough to throw the bloodhound off the scent.

The older woman looked miserable. It didn't bode well that Ward was so irritable, either. Maybe her matched pair had been arguing. Lillian had to get out of here and do a little stage-managing before it was too late and her whole plan went down the tube!

Ward was back minutes later, looking as unapproachable as he had since he'd driven up to the house at three-thirty with a face like a thunderhead.

"I found him. He says you're okay, no stroke," he told Lillian. "You can leave. I've signed you out. Let's go."

"But we need a wheelchair . . ." Mari began.

He handed her Lillian's purse, lifted the elderly woman easily in his arms and carried her out the door, his set features daring anyone to question or stop him.

Back at Three Forks Lillian's room was on the ground floor, and despite all the protests she immediately returned to the kitchen and started supper.

"Do you want to go back to the hospital?" Ward demanded, hands on hips, glaring. "Get into bed!"

"I can cook with a broken leg," she returned hotly. "It isn't my hands that don't work, and I've never yet used my toes!"

He sighed angrily. "Mari can do that."

"Mari's answering your letters," he was pointedly reminded. "She can't do everything. And with David gone..."

"Damn David," he muttered darkly. "What a hell of a time to get married!"

Lillian glared at him until he muttered something rough under his breath and strode off toward his den.

Mari was inside the paneled room, working away at the computer. She was trying to erase a mistake and was going crazy deciphering the language of the computer he'd shown her. The word processing program was one of the most expensive and the most complicated. She couldn't even get it to backspace.

"I can't do anything with your aunt," he grumbled, slamming the door. "She's sitting on a stool making a pie."

"No wonder you can't do anything with her," she commented innocently. "Your stomach won't let you."

He glared at her. "How's it going?"

She sighed. "Don't you have a typewriter?"

"What year do you think this is?" he demanded. "What kind of equipment have you got at that garage where you work?"

"A manual typewriter," she said.

His head bent forward. "A what?"

"A manual type—"

"That's what I thought you said. My God!"

"Well, until they hired me, one of the men was doing all the office work. They thought the manual typewriter was the latest thing. It did beat handwriting all the work orders," she added sweetly.

"I work with modern equipment," he told her, gesturing toward the computer. "That's faster than even an electronic typewriter, and you can save what you do. I thought you knew how to use it."

"I know how to turn it on," she agreed brightly.

He moved behind her and peered over her shoulder. "Is that all you've done so far?"

"I've only been in here an hour," she reminded him. "It took me that long to discover what to stuff into the big slots."

"Diskettes," he said. "Program diskettes."

"Whatever. Anyway, this manual explains how to build a nuclear device, not how to use the word processing program," she said, pushing the booklet away. "Or it might as well. I don't understand a word of it. Could you show me how it works?" She looked up at him with eyes the color of a robin's egg.

He actually forgot what he was saying. She had a way of looking at him that made his blood thaw, like the sun beating down on an icy pond. He could imagine how a colt felt on a spring morning with the breeze stirring and juicy grass to eat and a big pasture to run in.

"Could you?" she prompted, lost in his green eyes.

His big hand touched the side of her face tentatively, his thumb moving over her mouth, exploring its soft texture, mussing her lipstick, sensitizing her lips until they parted on a caught breath.

"Could I what, Mari?" he asked in a tone that curled her toes inside her shoes.

Her head was much too far back. It gave him access to her mouth. She saw the intent in his narrowing eyes, in his taut stance. Her body ached for his touch. She looked up at him helplessly, his willing victim, wanting his mouth on hers with a passion that overwhelmed her.

He bent slowly, letting his gaze fall to her parted lips. She could smell the heady fragrance of his cologne now because he was so close. There was mint and coffee on his breath, and he had strong white teeth; she could see them where his chiseled lips parted in anticipation of possession. Her breasts throbbed, and she noticed a tingling, yearning sensation there.

"Your skin is hot," he whispered, tracing her cheek with his fingers as he tilted his face across hers and moved even closer. "I can feel it burning."

Her hands were on his arms now. She could feel the powerful muscles through the white shirt that he'd worn with a tie and jacket when they went to pick up Lillian. But the jacket and tie were gone, and the shirt was partially unbuttoned, and now the overwhelming sight of him filled Mari's world. Her short nails pressed into his skin, bending against those hard muscles as his lips brushed over hers.

"Bite me," he whispered huskily and then incited her to do it, teasing her mouth, teaching her.

She knew nothing, but she wanted so desperately to please him so that he wouldn't stop. This was magic, and she wanted more.

Her mouth opened and she nipped at his firm lower lip, nibbling it, feeling its softness. He laughed softly deep in his throat, and she felt his hand move from her cheek to her shoulder, down her arm to her waist. While he played with her mouth, his fingers splayed out and then moved up, and the thin fabric of her flowery shirtwaist dress was no barrier at all as he found her rib cage and began to tease it.

This was explosive. Mari trembled a little because she was catching fire. He hadn't been kidding when he told her he was a good lover. She hadn't dreamed of the kind of sensations that he was showing her. She hadn't realized how vulnerable she was. Her mind was telling her that it was a game, that he didn't mean it. He'd said so. But her body was enthralled by new feelings, new pleasures, and it wouldn't let her stop.

"Oh," she whispered unsteadily when his tongue began to taste the soft inner surface of her lips.

"Open my shirt," he whispered against her warm mouth. He drew her hands to the remaining buttons and coaxed them until they had the fabric away from him.

She put her hands against hard muscle and thick hair and gasped at the contact. She'd never touched a man this way, and he knew it and was excited by it.

He bit her lower lip with a slow, ardent pressure that was arousing. "Draw your nails down to my belt," he murmured against her parted mouth.

She did, amazed at the shudder of his big body, at the soft groan her caress produced. She drew away slightly so that she could see his face, could see the lazy, smoldering desire in his green eyes.

"I like it," he told her with a husky laugh.

She did it again, lowering her eyes this time to watch his muscles ripple with pleasure as she stroked them, to watch his flat stomach draw in even more with a caught breath. It was exciting to arouse him. It gave her a sense of her femininity that she'd never experienced.

Meanwhile, his hand was moving again, this time up her rib cage. Not blatant but subtle in its caress, teasing lightly, provocative. It reached the outer edges of her breast even as her nails were tenderly scoring him, and his fingers lifted to touch around her nipple.

She shuddered, looking up at him with the residue of virginal fear in her wide blue eyes. Her hand went to his hairy wrist and poised there while she tried to choose between pleasure and guilt.

"Have you ever done this before?" he asked, his lips against hers.

"No," she confessed.

Odd, how protective that made him feel. And how much a man. He brushed his lips gently over hers. "Lillian isn't fifty feet away," he whispered. "And we won't do anything horribly indiscreet. But I'm as excited by this as you are, and I don't want to stop just yet. I want to touch you and feel your reaction and let you feel mine. Mari," he murmured, tracing a path up her soft breast, "I've never been the first. Not in any way, even this. Let me teach you. I promise you, there's not the slightest danger. Not right now."

"Oh, but I shouldn't..." She was weakening and her voice betrayed her.

"Don't feel guilty," he whispered over her mouth. "This is love play. Women and men have indulged themselves this way since the beginning of time. I'm human. So are you. There's no shame in being hungry."

He made it sound natural. It was the seducer's basic weapon, but Mari was too outmatched to care. She arched toward his fingers because she couldn't help herself. That maddening tracing of his fingers was driving her to her limits. She wanted his hand to flatten on her body. She wanted him to touch her...there!

His teeth nibbled at her lower lip, catching it in a soft tug just as his fingers closed on an erect nipple and tightened gently.

She cried out. The sound would have penetrated the walls and door, but he caught it in his mouth and muffled it, half mad with unexpected arousal. Her cries and her trembling were driving him over the edge.

Somehow he had her on the sofa, flat on her back with his heavy body half covering her. Her dress was coming undone, she could feel the air on her bare skin, and her bra was all too loose, and his hand was... there.

She shuddered and her eyes opened, hazy with passion. Her mouth was swollen, her cheeks red, her upward gaze full of rapt wonder.

His big hand flattened over her soft breast, feeling the tip rub abrasively on his palm as he caressed her. His thumb circled it roughly, and she shuddered all over, her breath sighing out unsteadily like his own.

She wanted him to kiss her some more, but his eyes were on her dress now. He peeled it slowly away from the breast he was touching, moving her bra up so that he could see the pink and mauve contrast and that taut little nub. It was as if he'd never looked at a woman before. She was beautiful. Sweetly curving and high, and not too big or too little. Just right.

She felt as if she were watching from a distance. Her eyes wandered over his absorbed expression, seeing the veiled pleasure there, the wonder. If she was awed by him, so was he awed by her. He was touching her like some priceless treasure, taking his time, lovingly tracing every texture.

He took the nipple between his thumb and forefinger and felt its hardness. He looked up into her fascinated eyes. "If I put my mouth on you, you'll cry out again," he whispered softly. "And Lillian might mistake the sound and come hopping."

She was trembling. She wanted it. Her body arched sinuously. She reached up, shyly, and cupped his face, gently tugging at it.

"I won't...cry out," she whispered, biting her lower lip to make sure.

"Say 'taste me,'" he whispered back, searching her eyes.

She blushed feverishly and turned her face into his throat to hide her embarrassment.

"Virgin," he breathed, trembling himself with the newness of it. "Oh, God, I want to have you so much!"

She thought she knew what he meant, but just then he took her breast into his warm mouth, and she had to chew her lip almost through to keep from screaming at the incredible sensation.

Her hands released his face, and she clenched them over her head. Writhing helplessly, she was caught up in the throes of something so powerful that it stopped her breath in her throat. She twisted up toward him, her body shuddering, her breast on fire with the feel of his mouth.

With a rough groan he suddenly rolled away from her and sat up with his face in his hands, shuddering, bent over as if in agony.

She lay there without moving, shaking all over with reaction and frustration, too weak from desire to even cover herself.

After a minute he took a deep, steadying breath and looked down at her. If she expected mockery or amusement, she was surprised. Because he wasn't smiling.

His dark green eyes ran over her like hands, lingering on all the places where his mouth had been, devouring her. He drew the bra slowly back down and reached around her for the hooks, fastening them. Then he pulled the edges of her dress together and buttoned them. He didn't speak until he was through.

"Do you understand why I stopped?" he asked gently. Yes, there was that. There was tenderness in every line of his face, in his voice, in the fingers that brushed her cheek.

"Yes," she returned slowly. "I think so."

"I didn't frighten you?"

That seemed to matter very much. She felt suddenly old and venerable and deeply possessive. "No," she said.

He tugged gently on a strand of damp hair. "Did I please you?" he persisted and this time he smiled but without mockery.

"As if you couldn't tell," she murmured, lowering her face so that he couldn't see it.

"If we ever make love completely, it will have to be in a soundproof room," he said at her ear. "You'd scream the house down."

"Ward!" she groaned and buried her face in his chest.

"No." He shuddered, moving her away, and he looked pale all of a sudden.

Her eyes questioned his. All these feeling were very new to her.

He drew in a harsh breath, holding her hands in his. "Men are very easy to arouse," he told her without embarrassment. "When they get to fever pitch, it takes very little to fan the fire. Right now I'm beyond fever pitch," he mused with a faint laugh, "and if you touch me that way again, we're both going to be in a lot of trouble."

"Oh," she returned, searching his eyes. "Does it hurt?" she whispered softly.

"A little," he replied. He brushed back her hair. "How about you?"

"Wow." She laughed shakily. "I never dreamed that could happen to me."

He felt incredible. New. Reborn. He touched her face lightly as if he were dreaming. Bending over her, he took her mouth softly under his and kissed her. It was different from any other kiss in his life. When he let her go, he had to stand up or lay her down.

"You'd better get back to work," he said and gestured toward the computer. "And, no, I'm not going to try to teach you. My body won't let me that close without making impossible demands on both of us so you'll have to muddle through alone." He laughed angrily. "Damn it, are you a witch?"

She stood up, smoothing her dress and hair. "Actually, until about five minutes ago, I thought I was Lady Dracula."

"Now you know better, don't you?" He stood watching her, his mouth slightly swollen, his shirt open, his hands on his narrow hips. The sight of him still took her breath away.

She went quickly back to the computer and sat down, keeping her eyes on the screen. "I'll get these finished before supper, if I can," she promised.

He smiled to himself. It took him a minute to leave her, his mind grappling furiously with the conflict between his desire and his calculating mind that insisted she was only interested in what he had—his ranch, his oil, his money.

Women had never wanted him for himself; why should Mari be different? But why had she reacted with such sweet ardor unless she'd wanted him as desperately as he'd wanted her? That kind of fever was hard to fake. No, he thought. No, she'd wanted him.

But was she really that unmaterialistic? The only
women he'd let himself get close to were his mother
and Caroline, both of whom had been self-centered
opportunists. How could he trust this one? She bothered him terribly. He no longer felt any confidence in
his own judgment. He left the room scowling.

Chapter Six

Mari was so shaken by what had happened with Ward that she had eventually needed to escape from the den. She was afraid everything they'd done would show on her face, and Lillian had sharp eyes. She also wondered if Ward would tease her. That would be the last straw, to have a worldly man like that make fun of her for a physical reaction she couldn't help.

She needn't have worried. Ward was nowhere in sight, and Lillian was muttering furiously as she hobbled around the kitchen with a crutch under one arm.

"I wish you'd let me do that," Mari scolded. She picked up the plate of ham that Lillian was trying to take to the table and carried it in for her. "You shouldn't be trying to lift things, Aunt Lillian. You know what the doctor said.''

''Yes, but it's pretty hard asking people for help,'' the older woman said irritably. She glanced at Mari. ''He's gone.''

Mari tried to look innocent. ''He?''

''The boss. He decided to fly down to South America. Just like that.'' She snapped her fingers while Mari tried not to let her eyes reflect the shock she felt.

''He left tonight?'' Mari asked blankly. It didn't seem possible. She'd been talking with him—among other things—less than two hours ago.

''Yep. He sure did. Bag and baggage. Imagine, getting a flight out of here that quickly. He'll go on a commercial flight from San Antonio, you see.'' She added, ''Flew himself over to the airport, he did.''

Mari cleared her throat. ''You said a few days ago that he'd have to go to South America.''

''Yes. But I didn't expect him to leave in the middle of my first night back home,'' Lillian said hotly.

''He knows I'm here,'' she returned and impulsively hugged the older woman. ''I'll take care of you.''

Lillian sighed miserably. ''Nothing is working the way it was meant to,'' she grumbled. ''Nothing!''

Now was her chance to perfect her acting ability. ''Whatever do you mean, Aunt Lillian?'' she asked with a smile.

Lillian actually flushed. "Nothing. Not a thing. Here, set the table and help me get the food in here. There'll be a lot for just the two of us, seeing the boss and his appetite are missing, but we can freeze the rest, I suppose."

"Did you take your pill?" Mari asked.

Lillian glowered at her. Then she grinned. "Yep."

"Good for you," Mari returned. "Now I'll get to keep you for a lot longer."

Lillian started to speak, and then she just laughed. But her eyes were troubled when she hobbled back out to the kitchen.

Mari wandered around by herself during the next few days, when she wasn't helping Lillian, enjoying the spaciousness of the ranch and the feeling of being self-sufficient. It must have been very much like this a hundred years before, she thought as she gazed out at the level horizon, when bad men and cattlemen and refugees from the Confederacy had come through on the long trails that led north and south and west.

It was so quiet. Nothing like the noisy bustle of Atlanta. Mari felt at peace here, she felt safe. But she missed Ward in ways that she never would have expected. She'd only really known him for a matter of days, but even that made no difference to her confused emotions. She could close her eyes and feel his hard mouth, his hands holding her, touching her. It had been the most exquisite thing that she'd ever experienced, being in his arms that day. She wanted it again, so much.

But even wanting it, she realized how dangerous it was to let him that close a second time. He only wanted her, he'd admitted that. He didn't believe in marriage. Apparently, he'd had a rough time with a woman at some point in his life, and he'd been soured. Aunt Lillian had mentioned that his mother ran away with another man, leaving Ward and Belinda to be raised by their grandmother. So she couldn't really blame him for his attitude. But that didn't make her own emotions any easier to handle.

She found herself watching the driveway and looking out the window, waiting. When the phone rang, and it did constantly, she ran to answer it, sure that it would be him. But it never was. Five days passed, and despite the fact that she enjoyed Aunt Lillian's company, she was restless. It was almost the end of her vacation. She'd have to leave. What if she never saw him again before she had to go?

"Missing the boss?" Lillian asked one evening, eyeing her niece calculatingly over the chicken and stuffing the younger woman wasn't touching.

Mari actually jumped. "No. Of course not."

"Not even a little?"

Mari sighed as she toyed with a fresh roll. "Maybe a little."

Lillian smiled. "That's nice. Because he's just coming up the driveway."

Mari couldn't stop herself. She leaped up from the table and ran to the front door, threw it open and darted out onto the porch. She caught herself just before she dashed down the steps toward him. She hadn't realized until that moment just how deeply involved she already was. Boys had never paid her much attention. Surely it was just the newness of being touched and kissed. Wasn't it?

She held on to the porch railing, forcing herself not to take one more step.

He got out of the Chrysler, looking as out of humor as when he'd left, a flight bag slung over one shoulder. Striking in a deep-tan vested suit and creamy Stetson, he closed the door with a hard slam, turned and started for the steps. Then he spotted Mari and stood quite still, just looking.

She was wearing a gauzy sea-green blouse with beige slacks, and she looked young and very pretty and a little lonely. His heart shot up into his throat, and all the bad temper seeped out.

"Well, hello, little lady," he said, moving up the steps, and he was actually smiling.

"Hello." She forced herself to look calm. "Did you have a good trip?"

"I guess so."

He stopped just in front of her, and she could see new lines in his face, dark circles under his eyes. Had he been with some woman? Her eyes narrowed curiously.

"Do I look that bad?" he taunted.

"You look tired," she murmured.

"I am. I did two weeks' business in five days." He searched her big, soft blue eyes quietly. "Miss me?"

"I had lots to do," she hedged. "And the phone hasn't stopped."

"That's not surprising." He let the bag fall to the porch and took her face in his big hands, tilting it up to his curious green eyes. "Dark circles," he murmured, running his thumbs gently under her eyes. "You haven't slept, have you?"

"You look like you haven't, either," she returned. There was a note in her voice that surprised and secretly delighted him.

"I never mix business with women," he whispered lazily. "It's bad policy. I haven't been sleeping around with any of those gorgeous, dark-eyed Latins."

"Oh." She felt embarrassed and lowered her shocked eyes to his chest. "That's none of my business, after all," she began.

"Wouldn't you like it to be?" he asked softly. He leaned toward her, nuzzling her face so that she lifted it helplessly and met his quiet, steady gaze. "Or would you rather pretend that what we did the night I left meant nothing at all to you?"

"It meant nothing at all to you," she countered. "You even said so, that you..."

He stopped the soft tirade with his mouth. His arm reached across her back, pillowing her head, and his free hand spread on her throat, smoothing its silky softness as he ravished the warm sweetness of her parted lips. He was hungry, and he didn't lift his head for a long time, not until he felt her begin to tremble, not until he heard the soft gasp and felt the eager ardor of her young mouth.

He was breathing through his nose, heavily, and his eyes frightened her a little. "You haunted me, damn you," he said roughly, spearing his fingers into her thick dark hair. "In my sleep I heard you cry out..."

"Don't hurt me," she whispered shakily, her eyes pleading with him. "I'm not experienced enough, I'm not... old enough... to play adult games with men."

That stopped him, softened him. The harsh light went out of his eyes, and he searched her delicate features with growing protectiveness.

"I'll never hurt you," he whispered and meant it. He kissed her eyes closed. "Not that way or in bed. Oh, God, Mari, you make me ache like a teenager!"

Her nails bit into his arms as he started to lean toward her again, and just as his lips touched hers in the prelude to what would have become a violently passionate exchange, they heard the soft, heavy thud of Lillian's cast as she headed toward them.

"Cupid approaches," he muttered, a subtle tremor in the hands that gently put her away from him. "She'd die if she knew what she just interrupted."

Mari stared at him, a little frightened by her lack of resistance, by the blatant hunger that she'd felt.

"Passion shouldn't be frightening to you," he said gently as the thuds grew closer. "It's as natural as breathing."

She shifted, watching him lift his bag without moving his eyes from her. "It's very new," she whispered.

"Then it's new for both of us," he said just before Lillian opened the door. "Because I've never felt this with another woman. And if that shocks you, it should. It damned well shocks me. I thought I'd done it all."

"Welcome home, boss." Lillian beamed, holding the door back. "You look good. Doesn't he, Mari?" Flushed face on the girl, and the boss looked a little flustered. Good. Good. Things were progressing. Absence worked after all.

"I feel pretty good, too," he returned, putting an affectionate arm around Lillian. "Been behaving?"

"Yes, sir. Pills and all." Lillian glared at her niece. "It's pretty hard not to take pills when you're threatened with being rolled in a towel."

He laughed warmly, glancing over at Mari. "Good girl."

"I should get medals for this," Mari returned, her eyes searching his, searching his face, quiet and curious and puzzled.

He hugged Lillian. "No doubt. What's for dinner? I'm starved."

"Finally," Lillian said with a grin. "Things are back to normal. You should see all the food I've saved up."

"Don't just stand there, both of you, go fetch it," he said, looking starved. "I'll die if I don't eat soon!"

Lillian responded to his order, producing an abundance of hearty food. While Ward dug in, Mari watched him with pure admiration. She'd never seen a human being put it away with such pleasure. He didn't seem to gain an ounce, for all his appetite. But then he was on the run most of his life, which probably explained his trim but masculine build.

He finished the last of the dressing and sat back with a heavy sigh to sip his second cup of coffee while Lillian, despite offers of help and threats, pushed a trolley of dirty dishes out to the kitchen and dishwasher.

"She won't slow down," Mari said. "I've tried, but she won't let me take over. I called the doctor, but he said as long as she was taking her medicine and didn't overdo standing on that cast, she'd be okay. I do at least get her to sit down, and I help when she lets me."

"Good thing her room's on the ground floor," he remarked.

"Yes."

He studied her over the rim of his coffee cup, his eyes narrow and quiet and full of green flames. There was no amusement in them now, no mockery. Just frank, blatant desire.

She looked back because it was beyond her powers of resistance not to. He held her in thrall, his darkening eyes full of promised pleasure, exquisite physical delight. Her body recognized that look, even if her brain didn't, and began to respond in frightening ways.

"I should bring in the dessert," she said as she rose, panicked.

"I don't want dessert," he said deeply.

She thought she knew what he did want, and she almost said so, but she dropped back down into her chair and put more sugar in her already oversweet coffee.

"Keep that up, and you can take rust off with it." He nodded toward her efforts with the sugar bowl.

She flushed. "I like it sweet."

"Do you?" He reached over and stilled her hand, his fingers lightly caressing it. While he held her eyes, he took the spoon away from her and linked his fingers slowly with hers in a light, caressing pressure that made her want to scream with frustrated hunger.

She couldn't help it. Her fingers contracted, too, convulsively, and she looked at him with aching desire.

His face went hard. "Suppose we go over those phone messages?" he asked.

"All right."

They both knew it was only an excuse, a reason to be alone together in the den to make love. Because that was surely what was going to happen. Being apart and then experiencing this explosive togetherness had taken its toll on them. He stood up and drew her along with him, and she could feel the throbbing silence that grew as they walked down the hall.

"Don't you want dessert?" Lillian called after them but not very heartily. She was grinning too much.

"Not right now," Ward replied. He looked down at Mari as he opened the door to the den, and there were blazing fires in his steady, possessive eyes.

Mari felt her lips part as she looked up at him. She started past him, feeling the warmth of his big body, the strength and power of it, and smelling his spicy cologne. She could hardly wait to be alone with him.

Just as he started to follow her into the room, into the secret silence of it, the heady atmosphere was shattered by a loud knock at the front door.

He cursed under his breath, whirling with such unexpected violence that Mari felt sorry for whoever was out there.

He opened the door and glared out. "Well?" he demanded.

"Well, you invited me, didn't you?" came an equally curt reply in a voice as deep and authoritative as Ward's. "You called me from the airport and said come over and we'd work out that second lease. So here I am. Or did you forget?"

"No."

"Do you want to serve my coffee on the damned porch?"

Ward tried not to grin, but he couldn't help it. Honest to God, Ty Wade was just like him.

"Oh, hell, come in," he muttered, holding the door open.

A tall, whipcord-lean man entered the house, Stetson in hand. He was as homely as leftover bacon, and he had eyes so piercing and coldly gray that Mari almost backed away. And then he saw her and smiled, and his face changed.

"Marianne, this is my neighbor, Tyson Wade," Ward told her curtly.

Ty nodded without speaking, glancing past Mari to where Lillian was standing in her cast. "What did you do, kick him?" he asked Lillian, nodding toward Ward.

Lillian laughed. "Not quite. How are Erin and the twins?"

"Just beautiful, thanks," Ty said with a quiet smile.

"Give them my best," Lillian said. "Coffee?"

"Just make it, I'll come and get the tray," Ward said firmly.

Lillian grumbled off toward the kitchen while Mari searched for words.

"I think I'll turn in," she said to Ward. "If you still want me to help with the office work, I need to get some sleep so that I can start early."

Ward looked harder than usual. Mari couldn't know that seeing Ty and the change marriage had made in him had knocked every amorous thought right out of his head. Ty spelled commitment, and

Ward wanted none of it. So why in hell, he was asking himself, had he been coming on to a virgin?

"Sure," he told Mari. "You do that. If you don't mind, try to get your aunt into bed, too, could you? She's going to make a basket case of me if she doesn't start resting. Tell her that, too. Play on her conscience, girl."

Mari forced a smile. "I'll try. Nice to meet you, Mr. Wade," she told Ty and went after Lillian.

"Imagine, Tyson Wade in this very house," Lillian said with a sigh as she fixed a tray. "It's been a shock, seeing those two actually talk. They've been feuding as long as I've worked here. Then Mr. Wade got married and just look at him."

"He seems very much a family man," Mari commented.

"You should have seen him before." Lillian grinned. "He made the boss look like a pussycat."

"That bad?"

"That bad. Bad enough, in fact, to make the boss get rid of a half-wolf, half-shepherd dog he loved to death. It brought down some of Ty's cattle, and he came over here to 'discuss it' with the boss." She turned, grinning at her niece. "The very next day that dog was adopted into a good home. And the boss had to see his dentist. Tyson Wade was a mean man before Miss Erin came along. Ah, the wonder of true love." She gave Mari a sizing-up look and grinned even more when the younger woman blushed. "Well, let's get to the dishes, if you're determined to get in my way."

Mari was and she did, quickly shooing Lillian out. Then she disappeared herself before Ward came for the coffee tray. She'd had enough for one night.

Breakfast was an ordeal, Ward was cold all of a sudden, not the amorous, very interested man of the day before. Mari felt cold and empty and wondered what she'd done to make him look at her with those indifferent eyes. She was beginning to be glad that her vacation was almost over.

He followed her into the office and started opening mail. It had piled up in his absence, and he frowned over the amount waiting for him.

"Can you take dictation?" he asked Mari without looking up.

"Yes."

"Okay. Get a pad and pen out of the desk drawer and let's get started."

He began to dictate. The first letter was in response to a man who owed Ward money. The man had written Ward to explain that he'd had a bad month and would catch up on his payments as soon as he could. Instead of an understanding reply, Ward dictated a scorching demand for full payment that ended in a threatened lawsuit.

Mari started to speak, but the look he gave her was an ultimatum. She forced back the words and kept her silence.

Each letter was terse, precise and without the least bit of compassion. She began to get a picture of him that was disappointing and disillusioning. If there was any warmth in him, she couldn't find it in business. Perhaps that was why he was so wealthy. He put his own success above the problems of his creditors. So he had money. And apparently not much conscience. But Mari had one, and the side of him that she was seeing disturbed her greatly.

Finally Ward was finished dictating the letters, but just as she started to type them, the phone rang. Ward answered it, his face growing darker with every instant.

It was a competitor on the phone, accusing him of using underhanded methods to get the best of a business deal. He responded with language that should have caused the telephone company to remove his phone and burn it. Mari was the color of a boiled lobster when he finished and hung up.

"Something bothering you, honey?" he chided.

"You're ruthless," she said quietly.

"Hell, yes, I am," he returned without embarrassment. "I grew up the butt of every cruel tongue in town. I was that Jessup boy, the one whose mother was the easiest woman around and ran off with Mrs. Hurdy's husband. I was that poor kid down the road that never had a decent family except for his battle-ax of a grandmother." His green eyes glowed, and she wondered if he'd ever said these things to anyone else. "Success is a great equalizer, didn't you know? The same people who used to look down their noses at me now take off their hats and nod these days. I'm on everybody's guest list. I get recognized by local civic groups. I'm always being mentioned in the newspapers. Oh, I'm a big man these days, sprout." His face hardened. "But I wasn't always. Not until I had money. And how I get it doesn't bother me. Why should I be a good old boy in business? Nobody else is."

"Isn't Mr. Wade?" she fished.

"Mr. Wade," he informed her, "is now a family man, and he's missing his guts. His wife removed them, along with his manhood and his pride."

She stood. "What a terrible thing to say," she burst out. "How can you be so coldhearted? Don't you realize what you're doing to yourself? You're shriveling up into an old Scrooge, and you don't seem to realize it."

"I give to charity," he said arrogantly.

"For appearances and to get ahead," she replied hotly. "Not because you care. You don't, do you? You don't really care about one living soul."

His chin lifted and his eyes sparkled dangerously. "I care about my grandmother and my sister. And maybe Lillian."

"And nobody else," she said, hurt a bit by his admission that he didn't feel a thing for her.

"That's right," he said coldly. "Nobody else."

She stood there with her hands clenched at her sides, hurting in ways that she'd never expected she could. "You're a real prince, aren't you?" she asked.

"I'm a rich one, too," he returned, smiling slowly. "But if you had any ideas about taking advantage of that fact, you can forget them. I like my money's worth. And I'm not suited to wedding cake and rice."

When what he had said finally broke through the fog and she realized what he was accusing her of, she had to bite her tongue to keep from crying. So that was what he thought—that she was nothing but a gold digger, out to set herself up for life on his fortune.

"I know," she said with an icy look. "And that's good because most women who are looking for a husband want one who doesn't have to be plugged into a wall socket to warm up!"

"Get out of my office," he said shortly. "Since you're here to visit your aunt, go do it and keep the hell out of my way! When I want a sermon, I'll get it in church!"

"Any minister who got you into church would be canonized!" she told him bluntly and ran out of the room.

She didn't tell Lillian what had happened. Shortly thereafter Ward stormed out, slamming the door behind him. He didn't come back until well after bedtime. Mari hadn't gone back into the den, and by the time she crawled into bed, she was already planning how to tell Aunt Lillian that she'd have to return to Georgia.

It wouldn't be easy to leave. But now that she'd had a glimpse of the real man, the character under the veneer, she was sure that she was doing the right thing. Ward Jessup might be a rich man with a fat wallet. But he was ice-cold. If she had any sanity left, she'd get away from him before her addiction got so bad that she'd find excuses to stay just to look at him.

That remark about not caring for anyone except family had hurt terribly. She did understand why he was the way he was, but it didn't help her broken heart. She'd been learning to love him. And now she found that he had nothing at all to give. Not even warmth. It was the worst blow of all. Yes, she'd have to go home now. Aunt Lillian was coping beautifully, taking her medicine and even resting properly. At least Ward would take care of the older woman. He cared about *her*. He'd never care about Mari, and it was high time she faced facts.

Chapter Seven

Mari had a miserable day. She kept out of Ward's way, and she didn't go back into the den. Let him get a temporary secretary, she thought furiously, if he couldn't manage his dirty work alone. She wasn't going to do it for him.

"Talk about unarmed conflict," Lillian muttered as Mari went out the back door in a lightweight jacket and jeans.

"He started it," Mari said irritably. "Or didn't you know how he did business?"

Lillian's expression said that she did. "He's a hard man to understand sometimes," she said, her voice gentle, coaxing. "But you can't imagine the life he's had, Mari. People aren't cold without reason. Very often it's just a disguise.''

"His is flawless."

"So is yours," Lillian said with a warm smile. "Almost. But don't give up on him yet. He might surprise you."

"He won't have time. Have you forgotten that I have to go home in two more days?"

The older woman looked worried. "Yes, I know. I had hoped you might stay a little longer."

"You're feeling better," she returned. "And he doesn't want me here. Not anymore. I'm not even sure I'd stay if I was asked." She opened the door. "I'm going to look at the horses."

She walked out without another word, crestfallen and miserable. She stuck her hands in the pockets of her jacket and walked aimlessly along the fence until she came in sight of the barn.

There he was, sitting astride a huge chestnut-colored horse, his working clothes making him look even bigger than usual, his Stetson cocked over one eye. Watching her.

She stopped in her tracks, glaring at him. He urged the horse into a slow trot and reined in beside her, resting his crossed hands on the pommel. The leather creaked as he shifted in the saddle and pushed back his hat.

"Are we still speaking?" he asked, his tone half amused.

"Can someone run me to the bus station in the morning?" she asked, ignoring the question. "My vacation is up the day after tomorrow. I have to get back to Atlanta."

He stared at her for a long moment before he spoke. "How are you going to explain that decision to Lillian?" he asked, carefully choosing his words. "You're supposed to think I'm dying, aren't you? You're supposed to be helping me write my memoirs."

"I don't think my stomach is strong enough," she replied.

His green eyes glittered at her. "Stop that. I'm trying to make friends with you."

"I tried to make friends with a gerbil once," she commented. "I stuck my hand down into its cage to let it have a nice sniff, and it tried to eat my little finger."

"You're making this difficult," he grumbled, tilting his hat back over his eyes.

"No, you are," she corrected. "I'm doing my best to relieve you of my gold-digging, sermonizing presence."

He sighed heavily, searching her eyes. "I've never had to justify myself to anyone," he told her. "I've never wanted to." He studied the pommel as if he hadn't seen one before, examining it as he spoke. "I don't want you to go, Mari."

Her heart ran away. "Why not?"

He shrugged and smiled faintly. "Maybe I've gotten used to you." He looked up. "Besides, your aunt will never get over it if you leave right now. All her plans for us will be ruined."

"That's a foregone conclusion as far as I'm concerned," she said, her voice curt. She clenched her hands in her pockets. "I wouldn't have you on a stick, roasted."

He had to work to keep from grinning. "Wouldn't you?"

"I'm going home," she repeated.

He tilted his hat back again. "You don't have a job."

"I do so. I work at a garage!"

"Not anymore." He did grin this time. "I called them last week and told them that you had to quit to take care of your sick aunt and her 'dying' employer."

"You what!"

"It seemed like the thing to do at the time," he said conversationally. "They said they were real sorry, and it sure was lucky they'd just had a girl apply for a job that morning. I'll bet they hired her that very day."

She could hardly breathe through her fury. She felt as if her lungs were on fire. "You . . . you . . . !" She searched for some names she'd heard at the garage and began slinging them at him.

"Now, shame on you," he scolded, bending unexpectedly to drag her up to sit in the saddle in front of him. "Sit still!" he said roughly, controlling the excited horse with one hand on the reins while the other was on Mari.

"I hate you," she snapped.

He got the gelding under control and wheeled it, careful not to jerk the reins and unseat them both. The high-strung animal took gentle handling. "Care to prove that?" he asked.

She didn't ask what he meant. There was no time. She was too busy trying to hold on to the pommel. She hadn't realized how far off the ground that saddle was until she was sitting in it. Behind her, she felt the warm strength of his powerful body, and if she hadn't been so nervous, she might have felt the tense set of it in the saddle.

He rode into a small grove of oak and mesquite trees and dismounted. Before she knew it, she was out of the saddle and flat on her back in the lush spring grass with Ward's hard face above her.

"Now," he said gently, "suppose you show me how much you hate me?"

His dark head bent, and she reached up, unthinking, to catch his thick hair and push him away. But it only gave him an unexpected opening, and she caught her breath as his full weight came down over her body, crushing her into the leaves and grass.

"Better give in, honey, or you could sink down all the way to China," he commented wickedly. His hands were resting beside her head, and somehow he'd caught hers in them. He had her effectively pinned, without any effort at all, and was just short of gloating about it. He wasn't trying to spare her his formidable weight, either, and she could just barely breathe.

She panted, struggling, until she felt what her struggles were accomplishing and reluctantly subsided. She contented herself with glaring up at him from a face the color of pickled beets.

"Coward," he chided.

She was very still, barely breathing. His hands were squeezing hers, but with a caressing pressure not a brutal one. The look in his eyes was slowly changing from faint amusement to dark passion. If she hadn't recognized the look, his body would have told her as he began to move subtly over hers, sensually, with a practiced expertness that even her innocence recognized.

"Yes, that makes you tremble, doesn't it?" he breathed, watching her as his hips caressed hers.

"Of course...it does," she bit off. "I've never...felt this way with anyone else."

"Neither have I," he whispered, bending to brush his hard mouth over her soft one. "I told you that when I got home, and I meant it. Never like this, not with anyone..." His eyes closed, his heavy brows drawing together as he slowly fitted his mouth to hers.

She wanted to protest, but she couldn't move, let alone speak, and his mouth was making the most exquisite sensations in places far removed from her lips.

With a shaky little sigh she opened her mouth a little to taste his and felt him stiffen. She felt that same tautness in her legs, her arms, even in her stomach, sensations that she'd never experienced.

His hard fingers flexed, linking with hers caressingly, teasing as he explored her mouth first with his lips and then with the slightest probing of his tongue.

She hadn't been kissed that way before, and her eyes opened, puzzled.

He lifted his head a little, searching her face with green eyes that were dark and mysterious and as full of answers as her blue ones were full of questions.

"You can trust me this once," he whispered, sensing her apprehension in the smooth as silk young body that wouldn't give an inch to the dominance of his. "Even if I went half mad with wanting, I wouldn't risk trying to make love to you within sight of the barn."

He couldn't have been less convincing, but she did trust him. She searched his eyes, feeling the warm weight of him, smelling the leathery scent that clung to him, and she began to relax despite the unknown intimacy of the embrace.

"You've never felt a man this way, have you?" he asked quietly. "It's all right. You're old enough to leave chaste kisses and daydreams behind. This is the reality, little Mari," he whispered, shifting his hips as he looked down into her wide, awed eyes. "This is what it's really like when a man and a woman come

together in passion. It isn't neat and quiet and un-
complicated. It's hot and wild and complex.''

"Is it part of the rules to warn the victim?" she
asked in a husky whisper.

"It is when the victim is as innocent as you," he returned. "I don't want a virgin sacrifice, you see," he
added, bending again to her mouth. "I want a full-
blooded woman. A woman to match me."

At that moment she almost felt that she could. Her
body was throbbing, blazing with fire and fever, and
instead of shrinking from the proof of his desire for
her, she lifted her body up to his, gave him her mouth
and her soft sighs.

Ward felt the hunger in her slender body, and it
fostered an oddly protective impulse in him. He, who
was used to taking what he wanted without regret or
shame, hesitated.

His mouth gentled, slowed and became patiently
caressing. He found that she followed where he led,
quickly learning the tender lessons that he gave her
without words. He let go of her hands and felt them
go instinctively to his shirt, pressing over the hard,
warm muscles, searching. His heart pounded furiously against breasts whose softness he could feel under him. He wanted to strip off his shirt and give
himself to her young hands, he wanted to strip off her
own shirt and put his mouth on those tender breasts
and look at them and watch her blush. It was then that

he realized just how urgent the situation was becoming.

His body was taking over. He could feel himself grinding down against her, forcing her hips into intimate contact with his, he could feel his own taut movements. His mouth felt hot. Hers felt like velvet, feverish and swollen from the hungry probing of his own.

He lifted his head, surprised to find himself breathing in gasps, his arms trembling slightly as they held him poised over her. Her eyes were misty, half closed, her lips parted and moist, her body submissive. His.

She drew in a slow, lazy breath, looking up at him musingly, so hungry for him that she hadn't the strength to refuse him anything he wanted. From the neck down she was throbbing with sweet pulses, experiencing a pleasure that she'd never known before.

"No," he whispered roughly. "No. Not like this."

He rolled away from her, shuddering a little before he sat up and breathed roughly. He brushed back his hair with fingers that were almost steady but held a fine tremor.

Mari was just realizing what had happened, and she stared at him with slowly dawning comprehension. So that was what happened. That was why women didn't fight or protest. It wasn't out of fear of being overpowered. It was because of the sweet, tender pleasure that came from being held intimately, kissed and kissed until her mind got lost in her body's pleasure. He could have had her. But he stopped.

"Surprised?" He turned his head, staring down at her with dark green eyes that still held blatant traces of passion. "I told you I wouldn't take advantage, didn't I?"

"Yes. But I forgot."

"Fortunately for you I didn't." He got to his feet and stretched lazily, feeling as if he'd been beaten, but he wasn't letting her see that. He grinned down at her. "Men get good at pulling back. It comes from years of practice dating virgins," he added in a wicked whisper as he extended a hand to her.

She sat up, flushed, ignoring his outstretched hand as she scrambled to her feet. "I can't imagine that many of them were still virgins afterward," she muttered with a shy glance.

"Oh, some of them had great powers of resistance," he admitted. "Like you."

"Sure," she said shakily, pushing back her damp hair. "Some great resistance. If you hadn't stopped..."

"But I did," he interrupted. He picked up his hat from where he'd tossed it and studied the crown before he put it back on his head. "And for the time being you can forget going back to Georgia," he added with a level gaze. "Lillian needs you. Maybe I need you, too. You've given me a new perspective on things."

"I've butted in and made a spectacle of myself, you mean," she said, her eyes quietly curious on his hard, dark face.

"If I'd meant that, I'd have said it," he returned. "You're a breath of fresh air in my life, Mari. I was getting set in my wicked ways until you came along. Maybe you were right about my attitude toward money. So why don't you stay and reform me?"

"I can't imagine anyone brave enough to try," she said. She lifted her face. "And besides all that, how dare you cost me my job!"

"You can't work in a garage full of men anymore," he said blandly. "Remember your horrible nightmares about the assault?" he added. "Men make you nervous. Lillian said so."

"Those men wouldn't make anyone nervous. All they did was work on cars and go home to their wives," she informed him. "Not one of them was single."

"How sad for you. What wonderful luck that Lillian found me dying and sent for you." He grinned. "It isn't every girl who gets handed a single, handsome, rich bachelor on a platter."

"I am not a gold digger," she shot at him.

"Oh, hell, I know that," he said after a minute, studying her through narrowed eyes. "But I had to have some kind of defense, didn't I? You're a potent little package, honey. A fish on the hook does fight to the bitter end."

His words didn't make much sense to her, but Mari was a little dazed by everything that had happened. She just stared at him, puzzled.

"Never mind," he said, taking her hand. "Let's go back. I've got a few odds and ends to take care of before lunch. Do you like to ride?"

"I think so," she admitted.

"You can have your own horse next time," he promised. "But for now I think we'll walk back. I'm just about out of self-control, if you want the truth. I can't handle you at close proximity right now."

That was embarrassing and flattering, and she hid a smile. But he saw it and gathered her close to his side, leading the horse by the reins with one hand and holding her with the other. The conversation on the way back was general, but the feel of Ward's strong arm had Mari enthralled every step of the way.

He went off to make some business calls. Lillian took one look at Mari's face and began humming love songs. Mari, meanwhile, went up to her room to freshen up and took time to borrow one of the outside lines to call Atlanta. Her boss at the garage was delighted to hear from her and immediately burst into praise of her unselfishness to help that "poor dying man in Texas." How fortunate, he added brightly, that a young woman about Mari's age had just applied for a job the morning poor Mr. Jessup had called him. Everything had worked out just fine, hadn't it, and how did she like Texas?

She mumbled something about the weather being great for that time of year, thanked him and hung up. Poor Mr. Jessup, indeed!

Ward had to go out on business later in the day, and he wasn't back by supper time. Lillian and Mari ate alone, and after Mari had finished helping in the kitchen, she kissed her aunt good night and went upstairs. She was torn between disappointment and relief that Ward hadn't been home since that feverish interlude. It had been so sweet that she'd wanted it again and that could be dangerous. Each time it got harder to stop. Today she hadn't been able to do anything except follow where he led, and it was like some heady alcoholic beverage—she just couldn't get enough of him. She didn't really know what to do anymore. Her life seemed to be tangled up in complications.

She laid out a soft pink gown on the bed—a warm but revealing one with a low neckline—and fingered it lovingly. It had been an impulse purchase, something to cheer her up on a depressing Saturday when she had been alone. It was made of flannelette, but it was lacy and expensive, and she loved the way it felt and clung to the slender lines of her body.

She ran a bath in the big Jacuzzi and turned on the jets after filling the tub with fragrant soap that was provided, along with anything else a feminine guest might need, in the pretty blue-tiled bathroom. To Mari, who lived in a small efficiency apartment in Atlanta, it was really plush. She frowned as she stripped off her clothing and climbed into the smooth tub with its relaxing jets of water surging around her. The apartment rent was due in a week or so, and she hadn't paid it yet. She'd have to send a check. She also wished that she'd brought more clothes with her. She hadn't counted on being here for life, but it looked as if Ward wasn't in any hurry to let her go.

Too, there was Lillian, who was behaving herself only as long as her niece was around to make her. If Mari left, what would happen to the older woman? With Ward away on business so often, it was dangerous for Lillian to be left alone now. Perhaps Ward had considered that, and it was why he wanted Mari to stay. The real reason, anyway. He didn't seem to be dying of love for her, although his desire was apparent. He wanted her.

With all her turbulent thoughts and the humming sound of the Jacuzzi, she didn't hear the door to her room open or hear it close again. She didn't hear the soft footfalls on the carpet, or the soft sound that came from a particularly male voice as Ward saw her sitting up in the tub with her pretty pink breasts bare and glistening with soap and water.

She happened to glance up then and saw him. She couldn't move. His green eyes were steady and loving on the soft curves of her body, and with horror she felt the tips of her breasts harden under his intent scrutiny.

He shook his head when she started to lift her hands to them. "No," he said gently, moving toward her. "No, don't cover them, Mari."

She could hardly get her breath. Although she'd never let anyone see her like this in all her life, she couldn't stop him. Mari couldn't seem to move at all. He towered over her, still and somber, and as she watched, he began to roll up the sleeves of the white shirt that was open halfway down his chest. He'd long ago shed his jacket and tie, although he was still wearing dress boots and suit trousers. He looked expensive and very masculine and disturbing, and as he bent beside the tub, she caught the scent of luxurious cologne.

"You mustn't!" she began frantically.

But he picked up the big fluffy sponge she'd soaped and shook his head, smiling faintly. "Think of it as a service for a special, tired guest," he whispered amusedly, although his eyes were frankly possessive. "Lie back and enjoy it."

She started to protest again, but he didn't pay the least attention. One lean hand moved behind her neck to support her in the bubbling water while the other slowly, painstakingly, drew the sponge over every soft line and curve of her body.

She hadn't realized how many nerve endings she had, but he found every single one. In a silence that throbbed with new sensation, he bathed her, pausing now and again to put the sponge down and touch her, experience the softness of her skin with the added silkiness of soap and water making it vibrantly alive.

Her eyes were half closed, languorous, as his fingers brushed lightly over her small, high breasts and found every curve and hardness, every sensual contrast, every texture, as if she fascinated him.

She trembled a little when he turned off the Jacuzzi and let the water out of the tub, especially when he began to sponge away the last traces of soap, and her body was completely revealed to him.

He lifted his dark, quiet eyes to hers and searched them, finding apprehension, fear, awe and delight in their blue depths. "I've never bathed a woman before," he said softly. "Or bathed with one. In some ways I suppose I'm pretty old-fashioned."

She was breathing unsteadily. "I've never let anyone look at me before," she said in a hesitant tone.

"Yes. I know." He helped her out of the tub and removed a warmed towel from the rail. It was fluffy and pink, and warm against her skin as he slowly dried her from head to toe. This time she could feel his hands in a new way, and she clutched at his broad shoulders when he reached her hips and began to touch her flat stomach. She felt a rush of sensation that was new and shocking.

"Ward?" she whispered.

He knelt in front of her, discarding the towel and all pretense as he held her hips and pressed his mouth warmly against her stomach.

She cried out. It was a high-pitched, helpless cry, and it made his blood surge like a flood through his veins. His fingers flexed and his mouth drew over her stomach with agonizing slowness, moving up with relentless hunger to her soft, smooth breasts.

She held him there, held his hard, moist mouth over the tip of one, felt him take her inside, warming her. He touched her then in a way she'd never expected, and her breath drew in harshly and she shivered.

"Shhhh," he whispered at her breast. "It's all right. Don't fight me."

She couldn't have. She shuddered and trembled, crying as he made the most exquisite sensations felt in the nether reaches of her slender body. Her nails dug into him and she couldn't help it.

"Marianne," he whispered, shifting his mouth over hers. He stopped his delicate probing and lifted her in his arms. She felt the soft shock of his footsteps as he carried her to the bed, felt the mattress sink under their combined weights.

His mouth moved slowly back down her to her stomach, her thighs, and then she did fight him, fought the newness and the strangeness and the frank intimacy.

He lifted his head and slid back up to look at her shocked face. "All right," he said gently. "If you don't want it, I won't force you."

Her face was creamy pink now, fascinated. He looked down at her body, smoothing over it with a lean, very dark hand, savoring its soft vulnerability.

"This is so new," he whispered. "I never realized how soft a woman's body really was, how exquisitely formed. I could get drunk just on the sight of you."

She was trembling all over but not from the soft chill of the room. She felt reckless under his intense gaze.

He looked up into her eyes. "You aren't protected, are you?" he asked softly.

It took a minute for her to realize what he was asking, and it made the situation take on alarming, very adult implications. To him this was familiar territory. But Mari was a pioneer.

"No," she whispered unsteadily. "I'm not."

"It's just as well," he murmured, bending to her mouth. "I think... it might spoil things right now to force that kind of total intimacy on you." His hand smoothed tenderly over her breast as he probed at her trembling lips. "Don't you want to touch me like this?"

She did, but she couldn't say it. Her hands went slowly to his shirt and slid under it, finding the exciting abrasion of thick chest hair over warm muscle a heady combination. His mouth moved hungrily against hers at the first tentative touch, and one hand went between them to rip the fabric completely out of the way and give her total access.

His harsh breathing disturbed her, but she was intoxicated by the intimacy they were sharing. Impulsively she moved her hands and arched upward letting her breasts tease his chest, feeling the sudden acceleration of his heartbeat with wonder.

He poised over her, lifting his head. His eyes were dark with passion, his chest shuddering with it. "Do that again," he said roughly.

She did, on fire with hunger, wanting something more than the teasing, wanting him. She felt his chest tremble, and she looked down at his darkness against her paler flesh with a sense of wonder.

"Yes, look at it," he whispered, his voice harsh, shaken as he stared, too. "Look at the differences. Dark against light, muscle against softness. Your breasts are like bread and honey."

As he spoke, he eased down. His heavy body surged against hers as he fitted it over her bareness, and her pupils dilated helplessly at the warm ecstasy of his full weight over her.

"Give me your mouth now," he whispered, bending. "Let me feel you completely."

It was a kiss like nothing she'd ever imagined in her life. She held him tenderly, her hands smoothing his thick, dark hair, her body throbbing its whole length where she could feel the powerful muscles of his body taut and smooth.

He tasted of coffee, and there was a new tenderness in him, in the lips that delicately pushed at hers so that his tongue could enter the soft, sweet darkness of her mouth. She felt it touch hers, tangle with it, and she gave herself up to a sensation that was all mystery and delight.

His hands smoothed down her sides, her back, savoring the smooth suppleness of her skin. He ached like hell, and he could have cursed himself for causing this, for forgetting how naive she was. She wanted him and, God, he wanted her! But he could make her pregnant. And part of her would hate him forever if he forced this on her. It wasn't going to be good for her. She was so much a virgin . . .

His cheek slid against hers, and he rolled onto his side, holding her protectively to him, feeling her breasts crush softly against his chest.

"Hold me," he whispered. "Just hold me until we stop trembling."

"I want you," she whimpered, beyond thought, beyond pride. She bit his shoulder. "I want you."

"I know. But we can't." His cheek nuzzled hers, and his lips touched her tear-streaked face tenderly. He hadn't realized she was crying until then. He drew a breath. "Are you all right?" he asked softly.

"I ache," she sobbed.

"I could satisfy you," he whispered. "Without going all the way."

She sensed that. Her eyes searched his in wonder. "No," she said after a minute. "I won't do that to you." She touched his face, fascinated by the look the words produced. "I'm sorry. I should have said something a long time ago. I should have asked you to stop."

"But it was too sweet, wasn't it?" he asked, his voice quiet and deep as he touched her face with fingers that were possessive and gentle. "So sweet, like making love with every part of us. I've never in my life experienced anything like it. Not even sex was ever this good."

That shocked her, and her eyes mirrored it. "Not . . . even sex?"

He shook his head. "With you I think it would be lovemaking, not sex. I don't think you and I could accept something as coldly clinical as that."

She was so tempted. She wanted him desperately. Everybody did it these days, didn't they? Maybe she wouldn't get pregnant. She loved him. Loved him!

But he saw the uncertainty in her eyes and mistook it for fear. For God's sake, where was his brain, anyway? She was a virgin. Lillian was right downstairs. Was he crazy? He ignored the feverish hunger of his body and managed to smile reassuringly as he slowly drew away from her to sit up with a hard sigh.

"No more, honey," he said heavily and managed to laugh. "I'm too old for this kind of playing."

Playing? She stared at him helplessly as he forced his staggered brain to function and found her gown. He put her into it with a minimum of fuss and then lifted her long enough to turn down the covers. He put her under them, smoothing them over her breasts.

He couldn't tell her that his own vulnerability and weakness had shocked him. He hadn't planned this, he hadn't expected to be drawn into such a long, intimate loving. It had been loving, of a kind. He scowled, watching her, fascinated by her innocence, her helpless reaction to his touch. He'd come to her room, in fact, to tell her that he wanted to get on a friendly footing with her, to stop the intimacy that could all too easily overwhelm both of them. But the sight of her in that tub had wiped every sane thought right out of his mind. Now he looked at her and saw commitment and the loss of his precious freedom. He saw all the old wounds, the helplessness of his attraction to that tramp who'd taken him in.

With a rough curse he got to his feet, running an angry hand through his hair.

"You needn't look at me that way," she bit off, close to tears again but for a totally different reason. "As if I were a fallen woman. I didn't walk into your bathroom and start staring at you."

"I didn't mean for that to happen," he said curtly.

She softened a little at the confession. He looked as shaken as she felt. "It's all right," she replied, fumbling with the coverlet. "I didn't, either."

"I'm old enough to know better, though," he murmured, feeling venerable and protective as he stared down at her. He put his hands in his pockets with a long sigh. "I came up here to see if we might get on a different footing. A friendly footing, without all these physical complications." He laughed softly. "I suppose you noticed how well I succeeded."

"Yes," she murmured tongue in cheek. She recalled everything she'd let him do and went scarlet, dropping her embarrassed eyes.

"None of that," he chided. "You're a woman now, not a little girl. Nothing we did would make you pregnant."

"I know that!" she burst out, feverishly avoiding his mocking gaze.

"I just wanted to reassure you." He stretched lazily, very masculine with his shirt unbuttoned and his hair mussed. Very disturbing, watching her that way. "No one will ever know what we did in here," he added. "Just you and me. That makes it a very private thing, Mari."

"Yes." She glanced up and then down again. "I hope you don't think I do that with just anyone."

"I don't think that at all." He bent and brushed his lips gently over her forehead. "It's very exciting being the first," he whispered. "Even in this way."

Her face felt hot as she looked up into lazy, warm eyes. "I'm glad it was with you."

"Yes. So am I." He searched her eyes gently and started to lean toward her, but his survival instincts warned him against it. Instead, he stood up with a smile and went to the door. "Good night, honey. Sleep well."

"You, too."

He closed the door without looking back, and Mari stared at it for a long time before she drew a shuddering sigh and turned out the light.

Chapter Eight

Mari hardly slept. She felt his hands all through the night, along with a new and curious kind of frustration that wouldn't subside. Every time she thought about Ward, her body began to throb. These new feelings frightened her because they were so unexpected. She didn't know what to do. The urge to cut and run was very strong.

Lillian was hobbling around putting platters on the table for breakfast. She looked up, smiling, as Mari came into the room dressed in jeans and a pullover burgundy knit blouse.

"Good morning, glory," Lillian said brightly. "Isn't it a beautiful day?"

It was, in fact, but Lillian seemed to be overjoyed at something besides the great outdoors. "Yes," Mari returned. She glanced at the empty chair at the head of the table.

"He'll be back in a minute," the older woman said knowingly. "Looks like a storm cloud this morning, he does. All ruffled and absentminded. Been staring up that staircase ever since he came downstairs, too," she added wickedly.

Mari darted into the kitchen. "I'll help you get breakfast on the table," she said quickly, avoiding that amused gaze. At least Lillian was enjoying herself. Mari wasn't. She was afraid.

She and Lillian had started eating before Ward came back. He looked tired, but his face brightened when he spotted Mari. He smiled without really wanting to and tossed his hat onto a side table before he sprawled into a chair. His jeans were dusty and his blue checked shirt was a little disheveled.

"I've washed up," he told Lillian before she could open her mouth. "I had to help get a bull out of a ditch."

"How did he get into the ditch?" Mari asked curiously.

Ward grinned. "Trying to jump a fence to get to one of my young heifers. Amazing how love affects the mind, isn't it?"

Mari flushed. Lillian giggled. Ward leaned back in his chair, enjoying the view, watching Mari try to eat scrambled eggs with forced enjoyment.

"Don't you want something to eat, boss?" Lillian asked.

"I'm not really hungry," he said without realizing what he was giving away to the old woman, who beamed at him. "But I'll have some toast and coffee, I guess. Sleep well, Mari?" he asked as Lillian handed him the carafe.

Mari lifted her eyes. "Of course," she said, bluffing. "Did you?"

He shook his head, smiling faintly. "Not a wink."

She got lost in his green gaze and felt the force of it all the way to her toes. It took several seconds to drag her eyes down to her plate, and even then her heart ran wild.

Ward watched her with evident enjoyment, caught up in the newness of having a woman react that way to his teasing. Everything was new with Marianne. Just ordinary things, like sharing breakfast, took on new dimensions. He found that he liked looking at her. Especially now since he knew exactly what she looked like under her clothes. His eyes darkened in memory. God, how exquisite she was!

Mari felt his intent stare all through her body. She could have made a meal of him, too, with her eyes. He looked so good. For all his huge size he was lithe and graceful, and she loved the way he moved. He was as sensuous a man as she'd ever known, a very masculine presence with a disturbing effect on her senses. She didn't think her feet would ever touch the ground again. Just being near him set her on fire. She wanted to get up and touch him, put her mouth on his, feel his arms crushing her to every inch of that long, elegant body. Her fingers trembled on her fork, and she flushed with embarrassment when he noticed her nervousness.

"Come for a ride with me," Ward said suddenly.

She looked up at him. "Now?"

He shrugged. "Lillian can answer the phone. There's nothing pressing for today. Why not?"

"No reason at all," Lillian agreed quickly. "Go ahead. I'll handle the home front."

Mari submitted before she could begin to protest. Why pretend? She wanted to be alone with him, and he knew it. Her blue eyes searched his green ones longingly, everything plain and undisguised in her oval face. He felt explosive. Young. A boy again with a special girl.

He threw down his napkin and got to his feet, hoping his helpless urgency didn't show too much. "Let's go," he bit off.

Mari followed him. She barely heard Lillian's voice behind her saying something about having fun. Her eyes were on Ward's strong back, her body moving as if she were a sleepwalker. She was on fire for him. Whatever happened now happened. She loved him. If he wanted her, she wasn't going to stop him. He had to feel something for her, too. He had to care just a little!

He saddled two horses in stark silence, his hands deft and firm as he pulled cinches tight and checked bridles.

When he helped her into the saddle, his eyes were dark and possessive, his hand lingering when she was seated. "You look good on a horse, honey," he said quietly.

She looked down at him and smiled, feeling the warmth of his chest against her leg. "Do I?" she asked gently, her voice soft with longing.

"I want you, Marianne," he said half under his breath. "I've thought about nothing else all night. So go slow, will you? I want to talk today. Just talk. I want to get to know you."

That was flattering and a little surprising. Maybe even disappointing. But she had to keep it from showing so she kept smiling. "I'd like that," she said.

He didn't answer her. He felt the same hunger she did, but he was more adept at hiding his yearnings. He didn't want to frighten her off, not before he made a stab at establishing a relationship with her. He didn't know how she was going to react to what he had in mind, but he knew they couldn't go on like this. Things had to be settled—today. Business was going to suffer if he kept on mooning over that perfect young body. Physical attraction was a damnable inconvenience, he thought angrily. He'd thought he was too old to be this susceptible. Apparently he was more vulnerable than he'd ever realized.

He swung into the saddle and led the way down the long trail that ran around the ranch. His men were out working with the cattle, getting them moved to summer pasture, doing all the little things around the ranch that contributed to the huge cow-calf operation. Fixing machines. Planting feed. Cleaning out stalls. Checking supplies. Making lists of chores. It was a big task, running a ranch even this size, but Ty Wade's, which adjoined it, was huge by comparison. The oil business was Ward's main concern, but he did like the idea of running cattle, as his grandfather had done so many years before. Perhaps it got into a man's blood. Not that he minded sinking wells under his cattle. He had one or two on his own property, and Tyson Wade's spread was proving to be rich in the black gold. His instincts hadn't failed him there, and he was glad. Ty would never have let him live it down if he'd been wrong and the oil hadn't been there. As it was, the discovery on that leased land had saved Ty from some hard financial times. It had worked out well all the way around.

Mari glanced at him, curious about that satisfied look on his hard, dark face. She wondered what thoughts were giving him such pleasure.

He laughed out loud, staring ahead. "Those old instincts never seem to let me down," he murmured. "I think I could find oil with my nose."

"What?"

He looked over at her. "I was thinking about that oil I found on Ty Wade's place. It was a hell of a gamble, but it sure paid off."

So. It was business that made him feel so good, not her company. "Is business the only pleasure in your life?" she asked gently.

He shrugged. "The only lasting one, I guess." He stared toward the horizon. "There were some pretty hard times around here when I was a kid. Oh, we always had plenty of food, you know—that's one of the advantages of living on a ranch. But we didn't have much in the way of material things. Clothes were all secondhand, and I wore boots with holes in the soles for most of my childhood. That wasn't so bad, but I got ragged a lot about my mother."

She could imagine that he had. "I guess I was pretty lucky," she said. "My parents were good to me. We always got by."

He studied her quietly. "I'll bet you were a tomboy."

She laughed, delighted. "I was. I played sandlot baseball and climbed trees and played war. There was only one other girl on my street, and she and I had to be tough to survive with all the boys. They didn't pull

their punches just because we were girls. We had a
good time growing up all the same."

He fingered the reins as they rode along to the mu-
sical squeak of saddle leather. "I liked playing cowboys and Indians," he recalled. "Had my own horse."

"Which were you?"

He chuckled. "Mostly I was the Indian. I had a
Cherokee ancestor, they say."

"You're very dark," she agreed.

"Honey, that's sun, not inherited. I spent a lot of
time working rigs when I was younger, and I still help
out on occasion. The heat's easier stripped to the
waist."

She'd noticed how dark his skin was when he'd
stripped off his shirt the night before and let her touch
him. Her eyes went involuntarily to the hard muscles
of his torso and lingered there.

"You don't do much sunbathing, do you?" he
asked unexpectedly, and his eyes told her that he was
remembering how pale she was.

Her face colored. "No. There's no beach nearby,
and I live upstairs in an apartment building. I don't
have any place to sunbathe."

"It isn't good for the skin. Mine's like leather," he
commented. "Yours is silky soft...."

She urged her mount ahead, embarrassed because
she knew what he was seeing in his mind.

His mount fell into easy step beside her. "Don't be shy with me," he said gently. "There's nothing to be ashamed of."

"I guess I seem grass green to you," she commented.

"Sure you do," he replied and smiled. "I like it."

Her eyes went to the flat horizon beyond, to the scant trees and the long fence lines and the red coats of the cattle. "I never had many boyfriends," she told him, remembering. "My dad was very strict."

"What was he like?"

"Oh, very tall and stubborn. And terrific," she added. "I had great parents. I loved them both. Losing Mama was hard, but having both of them gone is really rough. I never missed having brothers or sisters until now."

"I suppose it makes you feel alone."

"I've felt that way for a long time," she said. "My father wasn't really an affectionate man, and he didn't like close ties. He thought it was important that I stand alone. Perhaps he was right. I got used to being by myself after Mama died."

He studied her averted features. "At least I had Grandmother and Belinda," he said. "Although with Grandmother it's been a fight all the way. She's too much like me."

She remembered him saying that the only women he cared about were those two. "What is your sister like?" she asked.

He grinned. "Like Grandmother and me. She's another hardheaded Jessup."

"Does she look like you?" she asked curiously.

"Not a lot. Same green eyes, but she's prettier, and we're built differently."

She glared at him. "I do realize that."

"No. She's small. Petite," he clarified. "I suppose I take after my father. He was a big man."

"An oilman?"

He nodded. "Always looking for that big strike." His eyes suddenly had a faraway look. "Right out there is where we found him, in that grove of trees." He gestured to the horizon. "Hell of a shock. There was hardly a mark on him. He looked like he was asleep."

"I'm sorry."

"It was a long time ago." He turned his horse, leaving her to follow where the trail led down to the river and a grove of trees. He dismounted, tying his horse to a small tree growing on a grassy knoll. He helped Mari down and tied hers nearby.

"Funny, I never thought of Texas being like this," she mused as she watched the shallow river run over the rocks and listened to its serene bubbling. "It's so bare except for occasional stands of timber. Along the streams, of course, there are more trees. But it's not at all what I expected. It's so...big."

"Georgia doesn't look like this?" he asked.

She watched him stretch out on the leaves under a big live oak tree, his body relaxed as he studied her. "Not a lot, no. We don't have mesquite trees," she said. "Although around Savannah we do have huge live oaks like these. Near Atlanta we have lots of dogwoods and maples and pines, but there's not so much open land. There are always trees on the horizon, except in south Georgia. I guess southwest Georgia is a lot like here. I've even seen prickly pear cactus growing there, and there are diamondback rattlers in that part of the state. I had a great-aunt there when I was a child. I still remember visiting her."

He drew up a knee and crossed his arms, leaning back against the tree. "Homesick yet?"

"Not really," she confessed shyly. "I always wanted to visit a real ranch. I guess I got my wish." She turned. "Do you think Aunt Lillian will be all right now?"

"Yes, I do." He laughed. "She's having a hell of a good time with us. You haven't told her that we know the truth about each other?"

"No," she said. "I didn't want to disappoint her. But we really ought to tell her."

"Not yet." He let his darkening eyes run down her body, and his blood began to run hot. "Come here."

She gnawed her lower lip. "I don't think that's a good idea," she began half convincingly.

"Like hell you don't," he returned. "You didn't sleep last night any more than I did, and I'll bet your heart is doing the same tango mine is."

It was, but she was apprehensive. Last night it had been so difficult to stop.

"You want me, Marianne," he said under his breath. "And God knows, I want you. We're alone. No prying eyes. No one to see or hear what we do together. Make love with me."

Her mind kept saying no. So why did her legs carry her to him? She couldn't hear reason through the wild slamming of her heart at her throat. She needed him like water in the desert, like warmth in the cold.

He opened his arms, and she went down into them. Coming home. Feeling his big body warm and close to hers, his arms protecting, his eyes possessive.

He rolled over, taking her with him until she was lying on her back under the shade of the big tree with its soft green leaves blowing in the warm breeze.

As she watched, his hand went to his shirt. He flicked open the buttons until his chest was bare, and then his hand went to the hem of her blouse. She caught his wrist, but it didn't even slow him down. He slid his hand under it and around to the back, easily undoing the catch of her bra.

"Why bother with that thing?" he whispered, sliding his hand around to tease the side of her breast. "It just gets in my way."

Her body trembled at the lazy brushing of his fingers. "Why can't I fight you?" she whispered huskily.

"Because what we give each other defies reason," he whispered. He looked down at her mouth as his fingers brushed closer and closer to the hard, aching tip of her breast. "Little virgin, you excite me beyond bearing, do you know that? I can feel what this does to you. Here..."

His forefinger touched the hard tip and she gasped, shuddering under him, her eyes huge and frightened.

"My God, you can't imagine what it does to me," he said curtly. "Feeling that and knowing that I'm causing it. Knowing how hungry you are for me. If I took you right now, you'd scream, Marianne. You'd writhe and cry out, and I wouldn't be able to hold back a damned thing because you've already got me so aroused I don't know where I am."

As he spoke, he moved, letting her feel the proof of the statement as his weight settled against her. His big hand smoothed up, cupping her warm breast, and his mouth opened, taking her lips with it in a silence that shattered her resistance.

Her body lifted toward him as he slid both hands under it, taking her breasts, savoring them with his warm, callused hands. His mouth was taking a wild toll of hers, crushing against her parted lips, tasting the sweetness of them in a blazing hunger.

Her hips shifted and he groaned huskily. Her eyes opened, looking curiously up into his.

"What you feel is getting worse by the minute," he whispered huskily. "If you start moving your hips, I'm going to lose control. Are you willing to take that risk?"

She almost was. Her body was crying out for fulfillment. She wanted his hands on all of her. She wanted his clothes out of the way so that she could touch his skin. She wanted to smooth her fingers down the hard muscles of his back and thighs and feel him in the most intimate embrace of all.

He groaned at the look in her eyes. His hand found hers, pulling it to his body, pressing it flat against him, letting her experience him.

She trembled and jerked away from that intimacy, and it brought him to his senses. He rolled over, bringing up his legs, covering his eyes with his forearms. He stiffened, groaning harshly.

"I'm sorry," she whispered, biting her lip. "Ward, I'm sorry!"

"Not your fault," he managed roughly. His teeth clenched. "God, it hurts!"

She sat up, helpless. She didn't know what to do, what to say. It must be horrible for him, and it was her fault, and she didn't know how to ease that obvious pain.

He jackknifed to a sitting position, bent over his drawn-up legs, breathing unsteadily. His hands were clenched together, and the knuckles went white. He shuddered and let out an uneven breath.

"I never realized . . . it hurt men like that," she faltered. "I'm so sorry!"

"I told you it's not your fault," he said curtly. He didn't look at her. He couldn't yet. His body was still in torment, but it was easing just a little. He sat quietly, waiting for the ache to go away. She was potent. He wondered if he was ever going to be able to stand up again. Damn his principles and damn hers!

"If I were modern and sophisticated . . ." she began angrily.

"That's what we're going to talk about in a minute," he said.

She stared at his downbent head, absently fumbling to close her bra and pull down her blouse. Together they were an explosive pair. She loved him beyond bearing. Did he, could he, feel the same way? Her heart flew up into the sun. Was he going to ask her to marry him?

She scrambled to her feet, feeling nervous and shy and on the edge of some monumental discovery. "What are we going to talk about?" she asked, her eyes bright, her smile shy and soft.

He looked up, catching his breath at the beauty in her face. "I want you."

"Yes, I know."

He smiled slowly. "I guess you do, honey," he said, reminding her of that forbidden touch that made her blush.

She lowered her eyes to the ground, watching an ant make its way across a twig. "Well?"

"We can't go on like this," he said, getting slowly to his feet. He stopped just in front of her, near the edge of the river. "You realize that, don't you?"

"Yes," she said miserably.

"And one of these days I'm going to go off my head. It could have happened just now. Men aren't too reliable when their bodies start getting that involved," he added quietly. "I'm just like any other man in passion. I want fulfillment."

She swallowed. This was it. She looked up. "So. What do you want to do about it?" she asked gently.

He stuck his hands into his pockets and searched her eyes with a weary sigh. "I'll set you up in an apartment for a start," he said, his voice reluctant but firm. "I'll open an expense account for you, give you whatever you need. Lillian can be told that you've got a job in the city. Not Ravine, obviously. Maybe in Victoria. That's not too far away for me to drive, and it's big enough that people won't be too curious."

She stared at him. "But it's so far from the ranch..." she began, wondering how they were going to stay married with that kind of arrangement.

"Far enough to keep people from making remarks," he said. "I don't want to expose you to gossip."

"Gossip?" She blinked. Wasn't he proposing?

"You know how I feel about my freedom," he said curtly. "I can't give that up. But you'll have a part of my life that I've never shared with anyone else. You'll never want for anything. And there won't be another woman. Not ever. Just you. I'll manage enough time to keep us both happy when we're together."

It was all becoming clear now. His hard face and his determined eyes gave her all the information she needed.

"You're asking me to be your mistress." She almost choked on the word, but she had to be sure.

He nodded, confirming her worst fears. "That's all I can give you, Marianne. That's all I have to give. Marriage isn't something I want. I've had a taste of commitment that left me half demented. I'll never risk it again."

"And you think that I can be satisfied with this kind of arrangement?" she asked in a ghost of her normal voice.

"You'll be satisfied, all right," he said, his voice sensual and low. "I'll satisfy you to the roots of your hair, little virgin."

"And . . . Aunt Lillian?"

He shifted uncomfortably. Somehow this was all leaving a bad taste in his mouth. It had seemed the right thing, the only thing, to do when he'd worked it out last night. But now it sounded and felt cheap.

"Lillian will never have to know," he said shortly.

"And what if I get pregnant?" she asked blatantly. "Nothing is foolproof."

He drew in a slow breath. Children. He hadn't realized that children might come of such a liaison. He studied her, wondering absently if they might have a son together. His body surged in a new and unexpected way. His reaction shocked him.

"Pregnant." He said the word aloud, savoring it.

"It does happen," she reminded him, going colder by the second. "Or hasn't the problem ever arisen before?" she added, wondering how many women had come and gone in his life.

"I've never been desperate enough to compromise a virgin before," he said quietly, searching her eyes. "I've never wanted anything the way I want you."

She pulled herself erect. "I'm sorry," she said stiffly. "Sorry that you think so little of me that you could make a proposition like that. I guess I've given you every reason to think I'd accept, and I'm sorry for that, too. I never realized how... how easy it would make me seem to you."

His face fell. He could feel his heart sinking. "Cheap?" he asked softly. "Marianne, that's the last thing I think of you!"

"Do tell?" She laughed through building tears. "I'll bet you've made that little speech until it's second nature to you! I'll bet you've even forgotten the names of the women you've had in your bed!''

His lips parted on a caught breath. This wasn't working out the way he'd envisioned. Nothing was going right. There were tears in her eyes, for God's sake.

"Marianne, don't..." he began, reaching for her.

"Don't you touch me, Ward Jessup," she sobbed, sidestepping. "I've made an awful fool of myself, and I guess you had every reason to ask me what you did, but I don't want to be any rich man's kept woman, thanks."

"Look here—" He started toward her again.

Instinctively her hands went out, and she pushed jerkily at his chest. Ordinarily it wouldn't have moved him. But the riverbank was slick, and his boots went out from under him. He went over backward with a horrible splash.

Mari didn't stay around to see how wet he was. She ran for her horse, fumbled for the reins from around the trunk of the tree and struggled into the saddle through a blur of tears.

Ward stood up, dripping wet, watching her ride away. He didn't think he'd ever in his life felt so miserable or so stupid. It had seemed like a good idea, that proposition. He didn't want marriage, he didn't. For God's sake, why did women have to have so much permanence? Why couldn't they just enjoy themselves like men did? Then he thought about Mari "enjoying" herself with another man, and his face went ruddy with bad temper. He didn't understand himself lately. But the sight of her riding away, almost certainly to a speedy departure from the ranch, made him feel hollow inside.

Mari rode home feeling just as hollow herself. She should have been flattered, she supposed, at such a generous offer. But she only felt cheap. Stupid, she told herself. You let him do whatever he wants and then get angry at him for making the obvious assumption. She hated herself for giving in, for giving him license to such intimacy. Her body had betrayed her, hungry for pleasure, and she'd lost her reason somewhere along the way. Now she was going to have to leave here. All because she hadn't been sensible. All because she loved him too much to deny herself the ecstasy of his lovemaking.

"You've got a lot to answer for," she told her body angrily. She could have died of shame. Now he'd be sure that she was an idiot.

What was she going to tell Lillian? Her heart sank. The older woman would be heartbroken. Mari closed her eyes, feeling the tears burn them. Why had she ever come here? It had begun so sweetly, only to end in such tragedy. Well, she'd made her bed. Now she'd have to try to lie in it. That wouldn't be much comfort in the lonely years ahead. Leaving Ward Jessup behind would hurt more than anything else ever had. She'd loved him too much, and now she was going to lose him because of it. Because he didn't want commitment and she did.

Perhaps she should have said yes, she thought miserably. Then she thought about how she'd feel, being kept, being used and then abandoned. No. It was better to never know him that way than to have a taste of him and lose him. It would only make things worse, and she'd never respect herself again. Oddly enough, she had a feeling that he wouldn't have respected her, either. Pride would get her through, she promised herself. Yes. She still had that, even if her heart was shattered. She lifted her face and dried the tears on her sleeve. She had to think up some good excuse to go back to Georgia. Something that would give Lillian a reason to think she'd be back, which would keep her on the mend. Her eyes narrowed in deep thought as she approached the ranch house.

Chapter Nine

Mari thought she had it down pat when she left her horse with one of the men at the stable and went into the house to tell Lillian she was leaving.

The older woman was sitting down in the living room, looking smug while she thumbed through a magazine.

Mari paused in the hall, took a deep breath and went into the room determinedly. "Well," she said brightly, "I've got a terrific assignment!"

"You've what?" Lillian asked, staring at her niece.

"Mr. Jessup is sending me to Atlanta to get some information on a distant relative of his," she continued, pretending for all she was worth. "You know, to go into his memoirs. It will give me a chance to see about my rent at the apartment and get some more clothes, too."

Lillian had stiffened, but she relaxed all at once with a smile. "Just for a few days, I guess?" she probed.

"That's right." Mari sighed, laying it on thick. "Isn't he just the nicest man? What a pity he's got so little time." She peeked at Lillian out of the corner of one eye. "There's not much sense in getting attached to a dying man, you know."

Lillian hadn't considered that. She gnawed her lip thoughtfully. "He's not a goner yet," she said. "He could get well." She warmed to her topic. "That's right. They could find a treatment that would work and save him!"

"That would be lovely. He's so macho, you know," Mari said with a forced smile.

"Isn't he, though? You two seem to be spending quite a lot of time together these days, too," she added. "Exchanging some very interesting looks as well."

Mari lowered her eyes demurely. "He's very handsome."

"You're very pretty." Lillian put the magazine aside. "When are you going to Atlanta?"

"This very afternoon!" Mari enthused. "I want to hurry and get back," she added.

Lillian fell for it, hook, line and sinker. "Is he going to let you fly there?" she asked.

"No, I'm, uh, taking the bus. Hate flying, you know. Just do it when I have to." Actually, she didn't have the price of a ticket, thanks to her lost job and small savings account. It would take all she had to pay her rent, and then she'd have to pray that she could find another job. Damn Ward Jessup!

"Bus?" Lillian began, giving her suspicious looks.

"He'll come after me, of course," she said. "We might drive back...."

The older woman brightened. Lots of opportunities if they had to stop overnight. Of course, they wouldn't do anything reckless. She knew Mari wouldn't.

"Do you need some help packing?" she asked Mari.

"No, thanks, dear, I can do it. And I'd better get busy!" She blew Aunt Lillian a kiss. "You'll be all right until I get back?" she added, hesitating.

"Of course," Lillian huffed. "I just have a broken leg. I'm taking those stupid pills."

"Good." Mari went upstairs and quickly threw things into her bag. She called the bus station to ask about an outgoing bus and was delighted to find that she had an hour to get to the station. She grabbed her bag and rushed back down the staircase just in time to watch a wet, angry, coldly polite Ward Jessup come in the front door.

"I told Aunt Lillian about the job, Mr. Jessup," she said, loud enough for Lillian to hear. "My goodness, what happened to you? You're all wet!"

Ward glared at her. "So I am, Miss Raymond," he returned. His gaze went to the bag in her hand. Well, he'd expected it, hadn't he? What did she think he'd do, propose marriage?

Mari went the rest of the way down the staircase, keeping her features calm when she felt like throwing herself at his wet boots and begging him to let her stay. She did have a little pride left. Anyway, he was the one who should be ashamed of himself, going around propositioning good girls.

"Boss, you'd better get into some dry clothes," Lillian fussed.

"I will in a minute." He glared at Mari. "When do you leave?"

"In an hour. Can you get somebody to run me to the bus station? After all, the research trip," she raised her voice, "was your idea."

"Tell Billy I said to drive you," he said curtly, and his eyes cut into hers.

"I'll do that," she replied, struggling to maintain her tattered pride. Her hands clutched the bag. "See you."

He didn't reply. Lillian was getting suspicious.

"Aren't you going to drive her?" Lillian asked him.

"He's soaking wet, poor thing," Mari reminded her. "You wouldn't want him to get worse."

"No, of course not!" Lillian said quickly. "But should you go alone, Mari, with your bad experience?"

"She's tough," Ward told his housekeeper, and his eyes were making furious statements in the privacy of the hallway. "She'll get by."

"You bet I will, big man," she assured him. "Better luck next time," she added under her breath. "Sorry I wasn't more . . . cooperative."

"Don't miss your bus, honey," he said in a tone as cold as snow.

She smiled prettily and went past him to kiss Lillian goodbye.

Lillian frowned as she returned the hug. "Are you sure nothing's wrong?"

"Not a thing," Mari said and smiled convincingly. "He's just trying not to show how hurt he is that I'm leaving," she added in a whisper.

"Oh," Lillian said, although she was feeling undercurrents.

"See you soon," Mari promised. She walked straight past Ward, who was quietly dripping on the hall carpet, his fists clenched by his side. "So long, boss," she drawled. "Don't catch cold, now."

"If I die of pneumonia, I hope your conscience hurts you," he muttered.

She turned at the doorway. "It's more likely that pneumonia would catch you and die. You're dripping on the carpet."

"It's my damned carpet. I'll drip on it if I please."

She searched his hard eyes, seeing nothing welcoming or tender there now. The lover of an hour ago

might never have been. "I'll give Georgia your re-
gards."

"Have you got enough money for a bus ticket?" he
asked.

She glared at him. "If I didn't have it," she said
under her breath, "I'd wait tables to get it! I don't
want your money!"

He was learning that the hard way. As he tried to
find the right words to smooth over the hurt, to stop
her until he could sort out his puzzling, disturbing new
feelings, she whirled and went out the door.

"She sure is in a temper." Lillian sighed as she
hobbled out of the living room and down the hall.
"Sure is going to be lonesome around here without
her." She stopped and turned, her eyes full of regret
and resignation. "I guess you know what I told her."

"I know," he said curtly. "Everything."

She shrugged. "I was getting older. She was alone.
I just wanted her to have somebody to care about her.
I'm sorry. I hope both of you can forgive me. I'll write
Mari and try to explain. No sense trying to talk to her
right now." She knew something had gone badly
wrong between them, and the boss didn't look any
more eager to discuss it than Mari had. "I hope you'll
forgive me."

"I already have."

She looked up with a wan smile. "She's not a bad
girl. You…will let her come back if I straighten things
out and stop trying to play cupid?"

He studied her quietly. "You heard what was said out here, didn't you?"

She stared at the floor. "I got ears that hear pins falling. I was all excited about it, I thought you two were . . . Well, it's not my business to arrange people's lives, and I've only just realized it. I'll mind my own business from now on." She looked up. "She'll be all right, won't she? Thanks to us, she doesn't even have a job now."

He was dying inside, and that thought didn't help one bit. He didn't want her to go, but he was going to have to let her.

"She'll be all right," he said, for his own benefit as well as Lillian's. Of course she'd be all right. She was tough. And it was for the best. He didn't want to get married.

What if she went back and married someone else? His heart skipped a beat and he scowled.

"Can she come back, at least to visit?" Lillian asked sadly.

"Of course she can!" he grumbled. "She's your niece."

Lillian managed a smile. "Thanks for letting her come. You could have fired me."

"Not on your life—I'd starve to death." He smiled halfheartedly. "I'd better change."

A truck started up, and they both looked toward the window as Mari went past sitting beside Billy in the ranch truck.

Ward's face hardened. He turned on his heel without a word and went up the staircase. Lillian sighed, watching him. Well, the jig was up and no harm done. Or was there? He did look frustrated. She turned and went toward the kitchen. Maybe things might work out better than she had expected. She hummed a little, remembering the explosive force of that argument she'd overheard. And then she smiled. Where there was smoke, there was fire, her daddy used to say.

A week later, back in Atlanta, Mari was just getting over bouts of crying. Her small savings account was enough to pay the rent for the next month, thank goodness. She had bought groceries and cleaned her apartment and done her best not to think about what had happened in Texas.

Getting a job was the big problem, and she haunted the unemployment office for secretarial positions. There just weren't any available, but when there was an opening for a beginning bank clerk, she jumped at it. She hated figures and adding numbers, but it wasn't a good time to be choosy. She reported for work at a big bank in downtown Atlanta, and began the tedious process of learning to use computers and balance accounts.

After Mari was settled in Aunt Lillian called to make sure she'd made it home all right.

"I'm sorry, girl," the older woman said gruffly. "I never meant to cause you any hurt. I just wanted someone to look after you when I was gone. Now that I know I'm going to live, of course, I can do it by myself.''

Mari was touched by her aunt's concern, even though she felt as if part of her had died. "I'll be okay," Mari promised brightly. "I'm sorry I had to leave so suddenly. I guess you figured out that we'd had a big argument."

"Hard to miss, the way you were going at each other before you left," Lillian said. "I knew the jig was up when he asked if you had the bus fare. He said you both knew I'd been spinning tales."

"We knew almost from the beginning," Mari said with a sigh. "We played along because we both think so much of you. But no more cupid, all right? You're much too tall to pass for the little guy, and you'd look pretty funny in a diaper carrying a bow and arrow."

Lillian actually laughed. "Guess I would, at that." She paused. "The boss left an hour ago for Hawaii. He said it was business, but he wasn't carrying any briefcase. He looked pretty torn up."

That would have been encouraging if Mari hadn't known him so well, but she didn't allow herself to feel hopeful. She wanted to tell Lillian just what the scalawag had offered to do, but she didn't want to crush all her aunt's illusions. He had been pretty good to Lillian, after all. He could afford to be. It was only eligible women he seemed to have it in for.

"He'll be back in form in no time," Mari told her aunt. "He'll proabably find some new woman to make passes at in Hawaii."

"He made a pass?" Lillian sounded almost girlish with glee.

Mari groaned, realizing what she'd given away. "Well, that was what you wanted, wasn't it?" she asked miserably. "You got your wish, but it wasn't commitment he had in mind."

"No man in his right mind ever wants to make a commitment," the other woman assured her. "They have to be led into it."

"I don't want to lead your boss anywhere except maybe into quicksand," Mari said darkly.

"You will come and see me again, won't you?" Lillian probed gently. "When you get over being mad at him?"

"Someday maybe."

"How about a job? Do you have any prospects yet?"

"Finally," Mari sighed. "I started working in the accounts department of a bank this morning."

"Good girl. I knew you'd bounce back quickly. I love you, Marianne."

Mari smiled in spite of herself. "I love you, too, Aunt Lillian. Take care of yourself. Please take your pills."

"I will, I promise. Good night."

Mari hung up and stared at the receiver. So the boss had gone to Hawaii. How nice for him. Balmy breezes, blooming flowers, beautiful women doing the hula. Well, he wouldn't be depressed for long or even missing the one that got away. Thank goodness she'd had sense enough to refuse his proposition. At least she still had her pride and her self-respect.

"And they'll keep you very warm on winter nights, too," Mari muttered to herself before she went to bed.

The bank job was interesting, at least, and she met some nice people. She liked Lindy and Marge, with whom she worked, and there was even a nice young assistant vice president named Larry, who was single and redheaded and just plain nice. She began to have coffee and sweet rolls with him in the mornings the second week she was at the bank. Little by little she was learning to live without the shadow of Ward Jessup.

Or she told herself she was. But the memory of him haunted her. She could close her eyes and feel the warm, hard crush of his mouth, the tantalizing seduction of his big hands. It had been so beautiful between them, so special. At no time in her life had she felt more secure or safe than she had with him. Despite his faults he was more man than she'd ever known. She found that love forgave a lot. She missed him terribly. Sometimes just seeing the back of a dark-headed tall man would be enough to make her heart jump. Or if she heard a deep masculine voice. Or if she saw Texas license plates on a car. She began to wonder if she was going to survive being away from him.

She called Lillian the third week, just to see how her aunt was getting along, she told herself. But it wasn't Lillian who answered the phone.

When she heard Ward's deep voice, her heart ran away. She hadn't realized how shattering it was going to be to talk to him. She'd assumed Lillian would answer.

"Hello?" he repeated impatiently.

Mari took a calming breath. "Is Aunt Lillian there, please?" she asked formally.

There was a long pause. She couldn't know that hearing her voice had made a similar impact on him.

"Hello, Mari," he said quietly. "Are you all right?"

"I'm very well, thank you. How is Aunt Lillian?"

"She's fine. It's her church social night. Billy ran her over there in the pickup. She'll be home around nine, I guess. Have you got a job?"

That was no business of his, especially seeing as how he'd caused her to lose the one she had in the first place. But hearing his voice had done something to her pride.

"Yes, I'm working at a bank," she told him, mentioning its name. "It's big and convenient to where I live. I work with nice people, and I'm making a better salary there than at the garage. You needn't worry about me."

"But I do," he said quietly. "I worry about you a lot. And I miss you," he added curtly, the words so harsh that they sounded quite involuntary.

She closed her eyes, gripping the receiver. "Do you?" she asked unsteadily, trying to laugh. "I can't imagine that."

"Someday soon I may work on making you imagine it," he said, his voice deep and slow and sensuous.

"I thought I'd told you already that I am not in the market for a big bank account and my own luxury apartment in Victoria, Texas," she returned, hating the unsteadiness that would tell him how much that hateful proposition had hurt her.

He said something rough under his breath. "Yes, I know that," he said gruffly. "I wish you were here. I wish we could talk. I made the biggest mistake of my life with you, Marianne. But I think it might help if you understood why."

Mistake. So now that was all he felt about those magical times they'd had. It had all been just a mistake. And he was sorry.

Tears burned her eyes, but she kept her voice steady. "There's no need to explain," she said gently. "I understand already. You told me how much you loved your freedom."

"It wasn't altogether just that," he returned. "You said Lillian had told you about what happened to me, about the woman I planned to marry."

"Yes."

He sighed heavily. "I suppose she and my mother colored my opinion of women more than I'd realized. I've seen women as nothing more than gold-digging opportunists for most of my adult life. I've used them that way. Anything physical came under the heading of permissible pleasure with me, and I paid for it like I paid for business deals. But until you came along, I never had a conscience. You got under my skin, honey. You're still there."

She imagined that he hadn't told anyone what he was telling her. And while it was flattering, it was disturbing, too. He was explaining why he'd made that "mistake" and was trying to get them back on a friendly footing. She remembered him saying the night he'd come to her room that he'd had that intention even then. It was like lighting a match to the paper of her hopes. An ending.

"Don't let me wear on your conscience, Ward," she said quietly. "You can't help the way you are. I'm a puritan. An old-fashioned prude. I won't change, either, even if the whole world does. So I guess I'll be like Aunt Lillian when I'm her age. Going to church socials and playing cupid for other women..." Her voice broke. "Listen, I have to go."

"No," he ground out. "Marianne, listen to me!"

"Goodbye, Ward."

She hung up before he could hear the tears that were falling hotly down her cheeks, before the break in her voice got worse. She went to bed without calling back. He'd tell Lillian she'd called, she knew, but she couldn't bear the risk that he might answer the phone again. Her heart was in tatters.

She went to work the next morning with her face still pale and her eyes bloodshot from the night before. She sat at her desk mechanically, answering the phone, going over new accounts, smiling at customers. Doing all the right things. But her mind was still on Ward and the sound of his voice and the memory of him that was eating her alive.

It would get better, wouldn't it? It had to! She couldn't go on like this, being haunted by a living ghost, so much in love that she could barely function as a human being. She'd never understood the idea of a couple being halves of the same whole until she met Ward. Now it made perfect sense because she felt as if part of her was missing.

When a long shadow fell across her desk just before lunchtime, she didn't even look up.

"I'll be with you in just a minute," she said with a forced smile as she finished listing a new account. And then she looked up and her body froze.

Ward stared down at her like a blind artist who could suddenly see again. His green eyes found every shadow, every line, every curve of her face in the stark, helpless silence that followed. Around them was the buzz of distant voices, the tap of fingers on keyboards, the ringing of telephones. And closer there was the rasp of Mari's hurried breathing, the thump of her heart shaking the silky pink blouse she was wearing with her gray skirt.

Ward was wearing a suit—a very elegant three-piece beige one that made him look even taller than he actually was. He had a creamy dress Stetson in one big hand, and his face looked thinner and drawn. His green eyes were as bloodshot as hers, as if he hadn't slept well. She thought as she studied him that he was the handsomest man she'd ever seen. If only he wasn't such a cold-blooded snake.

She stiffened defensively, remembering their last meeting. "Yes, sir?" she said with cold politeness. "May I help you?"

"Cut that out," he muttered. "I've had a long flight and no breakfast, and I feel like hell."

"I would like to point out that I work here," she informed him. "I have no time to socialize with old acquaintances. If you want to open an account, I'll be delighted to assist you. That's what I do here. I open accounts."

"I don't want to open an account," he said through his teeth.

"Then what do you want?" she asked.

"I came to take you home—where you belong." He searched her puzzled eyes. "Your boss will be sorry you have to leave, but he'll understand. You can come with me right now."

She blinked. Somewhere along the line she was sure that she'd missed something.

"I can what?" she asked.

"Come with me right now," he repeated. He turned the Stetson in his hands. "Don't you remember my condition? I'm dying, remember. I have something vaguely terminal, although medical science will triumph in plenty of time to save me."

"Huh?" she said blankly. None of this was getting through to her. She just stared at him.

"You're going to help me write my memoirs, remember?" he persisted.

"You aren't dying!" she burst out, coming to her senses at last.

"Shhhhh!" he said curtly, glancing stealthily around. "Somebody might hear you!"

"I can't quit! I just started working here the week before last!"

"You have to quit," he insisted. "If I go home without you, Lillian is going to starve me to death. She's getting her revenge in the kitchen. Small portions. Desserts without sugar. Diet foods." He shuddered. "I'm a shadow of my former self."

She glared at him. "Poor old thing," she said with poisonous sweetness.

He glared back. "I am not old. I'm just hitting my prime."

"That's nothing to do with me," she assured him. "I hope you didn't come all the way to Atlanta just to make this little scene!"

"I came to take you back with me," he replied. His eyes took on a determined hardness. "And, by God, I'm taking you back. If I have to pick you up bodily and carry you out of here in a fireman's lift."

Her heart jumped, but she didn't let him see how he was disturbing her. "I'll scream my head off," she said shortly.

"Good. Then everyone will think you're in pain, and I'll tell them I'm taking you to the hospital for emergency treatment." He glared at her. "Well?"

He had a stubborn streak that even outmatched her own. She weighed the possibilities. If he carried her out by force, she'd lose all credibility with her colleagues. If she fought him in front of everyone, Ward would get all the sympathy, and Mari would look like a heartless shrew. He had her over a barrel.

"Why?" she asked, her voice quiet and defeated. "Why not just let me stay here?"

He searched her eyes. "Your aunt misses you," he said gruffly.

"She could call me collect and talk to me," she replied. "There's no reason at all for me to go back to Texas and complicate my life and yours."

"My life is pretty boring right now, if you want to know the truth." He sighed, watching her. "I don't even enjoy foreclosing on people anymore. Besides all that, my cousin Bud's come to stay, and he's driving me out of my mind."

Cousin Bud was a familiar name. He was the one Ward's fiancée had wound up marrying for a brief time. She couldn't imagine Ward actually welcoming the man as a guest.

"I'm surprised that you let him," she confessed.

He stared at her. "So you know all about that, too?"

She flushed, dropping her eyes to the desk. "Aunt Lillian mentioned it."

He sighed heavily. "Well, he's family. My grandmother worships him. I couldn't say no without having her jump all over me—and maybe even rush home to defend him. She's having a good time at Belinda's. No reason to disturb her."

She knew about old Mrs. Jessup as well, and she almost smiled at his lack of enthusiasm for his grandmother's company.

"If you've already got one houseguest, you surely don't need another one."

He shrugged. "There's plenty of room. My secretary quit," he added, studying his hat. "I sure could use some help in the office. You could almost name your own salary."

"You forced me to leave Texas in the first place," she shot back, glaring up at him. "You did everything but put me on the bus! You propositioned me!"

His cheeks had a sudden flush, and he looked away. "You can't actually like this job," he said shortly. "You said you hated working with numbers."

"I like eating," she replied. "It's hard to eat when you aren't making money."

"You could come home with me and make money," he said. "You could live with your aunt and help me keep Cousin Bud from selling off cattle under my nose."

"Selling off cattle?"

His powerful shoulders rose and fell. "He owns ten percent of the ranch. I had a weak moment when he was eighteen and made him a graduation present of it. The thing is, I never know which ten percent he happens to be claiming at the moment. It seems to change quarterly." He brushed at a speck of dust on his hat. "Right now, he's sneaking around getting statistics on my purebred Santa Gertrudis bull."

"What could I do about Cousin Bud—*if* I went with you?" she asked reasonably.

"You could help me distract him," he said. "With you in the office, he couldn't very well get to any statistics. He couldn't find out where I keep that bull unless he found it on the computer. And you'd be watching the computer."

It was just an excuse, and she knew it. For reasons of his own it suited him to have her at the ranch. She didn't flatter herself that it was out of any abiding love. He probably did still want her, but perhaps it was more a case of wanting to appease Lillian. She frowned, thinking.

"Is my aunt all right?" she asked.

He nodded. "She's fine. I wouldn't lie to you about that. But she's lonesome. She hasn't been the same since you left." Neither had he, he thought, but he couldn't tell her. Not yet. She didn't trust him at all, and he couldn't really blame her.

She fiddled with a pencil, considering Ward's offer. She could tell him to go away and he would. And she'd never see him again. She could go on alone and take up the threads of her life. What a life it would be. What a long, lonely life.

"Come with me, Mari," he said softly. "This is no place for you."

She didn't look up. "I meant what I said before I left. If I come back, I don't...I don't want you to...to..."

He sighed gently. "I know, I know. You don't have to worry," he told her. "I won't proposition you. You have my word on that."

She shifted. "Then I'll go."

He forced back a smile. "Come on, then. I've got the tickets already."

She lifted her eyebrows. "Were you that confident?"

"Not confident at all," he replied. "But I figured I could always put my Stetson in one of the seats if you refused."

She did smile faintly at that. "I always heard that a real Texan puts his hat on the floor and his boots on the hat rack."

He lifted a tooled leather boot and studied it. "Yep," he said. "I guess I'd put my boots in the extra seat, at that. But I'd rather have you in it."

She got to her feet and put her work aside. "I need to see Mr. Blake, my boss."

"I'll wait." He wasn't budging.

After Mari had apologetically informed her boss of her departure, she picked up her purse, waved at her new friends and went quietly out the door with Ward. It felt odd, and she knew it was foolhardy. But she was too vulnerable still to refuse him. She only hoped that she could keep him from knowing just how vulnerable she was.

He drove her back to her apartment and then wandered around the living room while she packed.

His fingers brushed the spines of the thick volumes in her small bookcase. *"The Tudors of England,"* he murmured, "ancient Greece, Herodotus, Thucydides—quite a collection of history."

"I like history," she commented. "It's interesting reading about how other people lived in other times."

"Yes, I think so, too," he agreed. "I prefer Western history myself. I have a good collection of information on the Comanche and the cowboy period in south Texas, from the Civil War up to the 1880s."

She took her bag into the living room, watching the way he filled the room. He was so big. So masculine. He seemed to dwarf everything.

"We don't really know a lot about each other, do we?" he asked as she joined him. He turned, hands in his pockets, spreading the fabric of his trousers close against the powerful muscles of his legs.

"Getting to know women isn't one of your particular interests, from what I've heard," she returned quietly. "At least, not in any intellectual way."

"I explained why," he reminded her, and his green eyes searched her blue ones. "It isn't easy learning to trust people."

She nodded. "I suppose not." She wanted to ask him why he seemed to be so interested in where she lived, but she was too shy. "I'm packed."

He glanced toward her suitcase. "Enough for a little while?"

"Enough for a week or so," she said. "You didn't say how long I was to stay."

He sighed heavily. "That's something we'll leave for later. Right now I just want to go home." He looked around him. "It's like you," he said finally. "Bright. Cheerful, Very homey."

She hadn't felt bright and cheerful and homey in recent weeks. She'd felt depressed and miserable. But it fascinated her that her apartment told him so much.

"It doesn't have an indoor stream," she commented.

He smiled slowly. "No, it doesn't. Good thing. With my batting average so far, I guess I'd be in it by now, wouldn't I?"

She cleared her throat, feeling embarrassed. "I didn't mean to push you in the river."

"Didn't you? It seemed like it at the time." He searched her eyes quietly. "I meant what I said, Marianne. I won't make any more insulting propositions."

"I appreciate that. I'm just sorry that I gave you such a poor opinion of me," she added, admitting her own guilt. "I shouldn't have let things go on the way they did."

He moved closer, lifting his hands to her shoulders, lightly holding her in front of him. "What we did together was pretty special," he said hesitantly. "I couldn't have stopped it any more than you could. Let's try not to look back. That part of our relationship is over."

He sounded final, and she felt oddly hurt. She stared at his vest, watching the slow rise and fall of his chest.

"Yes," she murmured.

He looked down at her silky dark hair, smelled the soft floral scent that clung to her, and his heart began to throb. It had been so long since he'd held her, kissed her. He wanted to, desperately, but he'd just tied his own hands by promising not to start anything.

"Do you like kittens?" he asked unexpectedly.

Her eyes came up, brightly blue and interested. "Yes. Why?"

"We've got some," he said with a grin. "Lillian found an old mama cat squalling at the back door in a driving rain and couldn't help herself. The very next morning we had four little white kittens with eyes as blue as—" he searched hers with a disturbing intensity "—as yours."

"You let her keep the kittens?" she asked softly.

He shifted restlessly. "Well, it was raining," he muttered. "The poor little things would have drowned if I'd put them outside."

She wasn't buying that. Odd, how well she'd come to know him in the little time she'd spent on his ranch. "And...?" she prodded with raised eyebrows.

He almost smiled at the knowing look on her face. She knew him, warts and all, all right. "Cousin Bud's got one hell of an allergy to little kitties."

He was incorrigible. She burst out laughing. "Oh, you black-hearted fiend, you!" she groaned.

"I like little kitties," he said with mock indignation. "If he doesn't, he can leave, can't he? I mean, I don't lock him in at night or anything."

If love was knowing all about someone—the good things and the bad—and loving them just the same, then it sure did apply here, she mused silently. "Ward Jessup," she said, sighing, "you just won't leave Bud alone, will you?"

"Sure I will, if he'll go home and leave my bull alone," he returned. "My God, you don't know how hard I fought to get that critter into my breeding program. I outbid two of the richest Texans in cattle to get him!"

"And now Cousin Bud wants him. What for?" she asked.

"Beats me." He sighed. "Probably for his advertising agency."

She sat down on the sofa. "He wants your bull for an ad agency?" she asked dubiously.

His eyebrows rose while his brain began to grasp what she was thinking. "Ad agency...oh, no, hell, no, he isn't going to use the bull to pose for male underwear commercials! He wants to sell it to finance expanding his advertising agency!"

"Well, don't glare at me, it sounded like he wanted to make a male model out of it," she defended herself.

He sighed heavily. "Woman, you're going to be my undoing," he said. And probably she would if he let himself think too hard about just why he'd come all this way after her. But missing her was just part of the torturous process. Now he had to prove to himself that he could have her around and not go off his head anymore. He still wanted her for certain, but marriage wouldn't suit him any more than being his mistress would suit her. So they'd be...friends. Sure. Friends. Lillian would stop starving him. There. He had noble motives. He just had to get them cemented in his mind, that was all.

"Can't you just tell Cousin Bud to go home?" she asked curiously.

"I have!" he grumbled. "Lillian has, too. But every time we get him to the front door, he calls up my grandmother and she raises hell with Lillian and me for not offering him our hospitality."

"She must like him a lot," she mused.

"More than she likes me, I'm afraid," he returned. He whirled his Stetson in his hands. "I'll give you one of the kittens if you want it."

"Bribery," she said in a stage whisper and actually grinned.

He grinned back. She was pretty that way. "Sure it is," he said shamelessly. He glanced around her small apartment. "Will they let you keep a cat here?"

"I guess so. I haven't ever asked." So he was already planning for her to come back here, she thought miserably.

He shrugged. "You might not want to come back here, though," he said unexpectedly. He smiled slowly. "You might like working for me. I'm a good boss. You can have every Sunday off, and I'll only keep you at the computer until nine every night."

"You old slave driver!"

He didn't laugh as she'd expected him to. He just stared at her. "Am I old to you?" he asked softly as if it really mattered.

Watch it, girl, she warned herself. Take it easy, don't let the old devil fox you. "No," she said finally. "I don't think you're that old."

"To a kid like you I guess I seem that way," he persisted, searching her blue eyes with his darkening green ones.

She didn't like remembering how much older she felt because of his searching ardor. She dropped her eyes to the floor. "You said the past was over. That we'd forget it."

He shifted his booted feet. "I guess I did, honey," he agreed quietly. "Okay. If that's how you want it."

She looked up unexpectedly and found a strange, haunting look on his dark face. "It's an impasse, don't you think?" she asked him. "You don't want a wife, and I don't want an unattached temporary lover. So all that's really left is friendship."

He clutched the hat tighter. "You're making it sound cheap," he said in a faintly dangerous tone. He didn't like what she was saying.

"Isn't it?" she persisted, rising to her feet. He still towered over her, but it gave her a bit of an advantage. "You'd get all the benefits of married life with none of the responsibility. And what would I get, Ward? A little notoriety as the boss's mistress, and after you got tired of me, I'd be handed some expensive parting gift and left alone with my memories. No respectability, no self-respect, tons of guilt and loneliness. I think that's a pretty poor bargain."

"You little prude," he said curtly. "What do you know about grown-up problems, you with your spotless conscience? It's so easy, isn't it, all black and white. You tease a man with your body until he's crazy for it, you try to trap him into a marriage he doesn't want, you take whatever you can get and walk out the door. What does the man have out of all that?"

His attitude shocked her. She hadn't realized just how poisoned he was against the female sex until he made that bitter statement.

"Is that what she did to you?" she asked gently. "Did she tease you beyond endurance and then marry someone else because what you gave her wasn't enough?"

His face grew harder than she'd ever seen it. He'd never talked about it, but she was forcing his hand.

"Yes," he said curtly. "That's precisely what she did. And if I'd been fool enough to marry her, she'd have cut my throat emotionally and financially, and she wouldn't even have looked back to see if I was bleeding to death on her way to the bank!"

She moved closer to him, hating that hurt in his eyes, that disillusionment that had drawn his face muscles taut. "Shall I tell you what most women really want from marriage? They want the closeness of caring for one man all their lives. Looking after him, caring about him, doing little things for him, loving him... sharing good times and bad. A good marriage doesn't have a lot to do with money, from what I've seen. But mutual trust and caring about each other makes all the difference. Money can't buy those.''

He felt himself weakening and hated it. She was under his skin, all right, and it was getting worse all the time. He wanted her until he ached, and it didn't stop with his body. She stirred him inside, in ways no other woman ever had. Except Caroline. Caroline. Would he ever forget?

''Pretty words,'' he said bitterly, searching her eyes.

''Pretty ideals,'' she corrected. ''I still believe in those old virtues. And someday I'll find a man who believes in them, too.''

''In some graveyard, maybe.''

''You are so cynical!'' she accused, exasperated.

''I had good teachers,'' he retorted, slamming his Stetson down on his head to cock it arrogantly over one eye. ''Are you ready?''

''I'm ready,'' she muttered, sounding every bit as bad-tempered as he did.

He took her bag in one hand and opened the apartment door with the other. She followed him out, locked the door with a sigh and put the key in her purse. Her life was so unpredictable these days. Just like the man beside her.

The commercial flight seemed longer than it actually was. Mari had found a few magazines to read at the huge Atlanta Hartsfield International Airport, and it was a good thing that she had because Ward pulled his hat over his eyes and folded his arms and he hadn't said one word to her yet. The flight attendants were already serving their lunch, but Ward only glanced up, refusing food. Mari knew, as she nibbled at ham and cheese on a bun, that he had to be furious or sick. He never refused food for any other reason.

Mari was sorry that they'd quarreled. She shouldn't have been because, if he was angry, at least he wouldn't be making passes at her. But if he stayed angry, it was going to make working for him all that much harder, and she'd promised, God knew why, to do his secretarial work. Now she couldn't imagine what had possessed her to agree. At the time it had seemed a wonderful idea. Of course, she'd had some crazy idea that he'd cared a little in order to come all that way to get her. Now it was beginning to seem as if he hated himself for the very thought. Mari was miserable. She should have said no. Then she remembered that she had, and that, ultimately, she had little choice in the matter.

She sighed over her food, glancing at him under the hat. "Aren't you hungry?" she offered.

"If I was hungry, I'd be eating, wouldn't I?" he muttered indistinctly.

She shrugged. "Then go right ahead and starve if you want to. I couldn't care less."

He lifted the brim of the hat and glared at her. "Like hell you couldn't," he retorted. "You and your pristine little conscience would sting for months."

"Not on your account," she assured him as she finished the ham. "After all, you're starving yourself. I haven't done anything."

"You've ruined my appetite," he said curtly.

Her eyebrows arched. "How did I do that, pray tell? By mentioning the word marriage? Some people don't mind getting married. I expect to do it myself one of these days. You see, I don't have your blighted outlook. I think you get out of a relationship what you put into it."

His green eyes narrowed, glittering. "And just what would you plan to put into one?"

"Love, laughter and a lot of pillow talk," she said without hesitation. "I expect to be everything my husband will ever want, in and out of bed. So you just go right ahead and have affairs, Mr. Jessup, until you're too old to be capable of it, and then you can live alone and count your money. I'll let my grandchildren come and visit you from time to time."

He seemed to swell all over with indignation. "I can get married any time I want to," he said shortly. "Women hound me to death to marry them!"

Her mouth made a soft whistle. "Do tell? And here you are pushing forty and still single . . ."

"I'm pushing thirty-six, not forty!"

"What's the difference?" she asked reasonably.

He opened his mouth to answer, glared fiercely at her and then jerked his hat down over his eyes with a muttered curse. He didn't speak to her again until the plane landed in Texas.

"Are you going to ignore me the rest of the way?" Mari said finally when they were in the Chrysler just a few minutes outside of Ravine.

"I can't carry on a civilized conversation without having you blow up at me," he said gruffly.

"I thought it was the other way around." She picked a piece of lint off her sleeve. "You're the one doing all the growling, not me. I just said that I wanted to get married and have babies."

"Will you stop saying that?" He shifted angrily in the seat. "I'll get hives just thinking about it."

"I don't see why. They'll be my babies, not yours."

He was grinding his teeth together. He'd just realized something that he hadn't considered. Cousin Bud was young and personable and hungry to settle down. He'd take one look at this sweet innocent and be hanging by his heels, trying to marry her. Bud wasn't like Ward; he was carefree and his emotions were mostly on the surface. He didn't have scars from Caroline, and he wasn't afraid of love. In fact, he seemed to walk around in a perpetual state of it. And here was Ward, bringing him the perfect victim. The only woman Ward had ever wanted and hadn't got. Bud might be the one... Suddenly he slammed on the brakes.

"What!" Mari burst out, gasping as she grasped the dash. "What is it?"

"Just a rabbit," he muttered with a quick glance in her direction. "Sorry."

She stared at him. She hadn't seen any rabbit, and he sure was pale. What was wrong with him?

"Are you all right?" she asked cautiously, her voice soft with helpless concern.

It was the concern that got to him. He felt vulnerable with her. That evidence of her soft heart wound strands around him, binding him. He didn't want marriage or ties or babies! But when he looked at her, he felt such sweet longings, such exquisite pleasure. It had nothing to do with sex or carefree lust. It was... disturbing.

"Yes," he said quietly. "I'm all right."

A little farther down the road he suddenly pulled into a shallow farm road that was little more than ruts in the grass. It went beyond a closed fence, through a pasture, toward a distant grove of trees.

"My grandfather's place," he said as he turned off the engine. "My father was born out there, where you see those trees. It was a one-room shack in those days, and my grandmother once fought off a Comanche raiding party with an old Enfield rifle while my grandfather was up in Kansas on a trail drive."

He got out of the car and opened her door. "I know the owner," he said when she was standing beside him. "He doesn't mind if I come here. I like to see the old place sometimes."

He didn't ask if she wanted to. He just held out his big hand. Without hesitation she placed her slender one in it and felt tingly all over as his fingers closed warmly around it.

She felt small beside him as they walked. He opened and closed the gate, grinning at her curious stare.

"Any cattleman knows the value of a closed fence," he remarked as he grasped her hand once more and began to walk along the damp ruts. It had rained recently and there were still patches of mud. "In the old days a rancher might very well shoot a greenhorn who left a gate open and let his cattle get out."

"Were there really Indian raids around here?" she asked.

"Why, sure, honey," he said, smiling down at her. "Comanche, mostly, and there were Mexican bandidos who raided the area, too. Cattle rustling was big business back then. It still is in some areas. Except now they do it with big trucks, and in the old days they had to drive the herd out of the country or use a running iron."

She glanced up curiously. "What's a running iron?"

"A branding iron with a curved tip," he said. "It was used to alter brands so a man could claim another man's cattle. Here." He let go of her hand and found a stick and drew a couple of brands in the dirt, explaining how a running iron could be used to add an extra line or curve to an existing brand and change its shape entirely.

"That's fascinating!" she said.

"It's also illegal, but it happened quite a lot." He put the stick down and stuck his hands in his pockets, smiling as he looked around at feathery mesquite and live oak trees and open pasture. "God, it's pretty here," he said. "Peaceful, rustic... I never get tired of the land. I guess it's that damned Irish in my ancestry." He glanced down. "My grandmother, now, says it's British. But just between us, I don't think O'Mara is a British name, and that was my great-grandmother's maiden name."

"Maybe your grandmother doesn't like the Irish," she suggested.

"Probably not since she was jilted by a dashing Irishman in the war."

"Which war?" Mari asked cautiously.

"I'm afraid to ask," he said conspiratorially. "I'm not quite sure just how old she is. Nobody knows."

"How exciting," she said with a laugh.

He watched her with a faint smile, fascinated by the change in her when she was with him. That pale, quiet woman in the bank bore no resemblance to this bright, beautiful one. He scowled, watching her wander through the wooded area where the old ramshackle ranch house sagged under the weight of age and rotting timbers and rusting tin. She made everything new and exciting, and the way she seemed to light up when he was near puzzled him, excited him. He wondered if she might care about him. Love him...

She whirled suddenly, her face illuminated with surprised delight. "Ward, look!"

There were pink roses by the steps. A profusion of vines bore pink roses in tight little clusters, and their perfume was everywhere.

"Aren't they beautiful!" she enthused, bending to smell them. "What a heavenly aroma!"

"Legend has it that my father's grandmother, Mrs. O'Mara, brought those very roses from Calhoun County, Georgia, and nursed them like babies until they took hold here. She carried them across the frontier in a pot. In a Conestoga wagon, and saved them from fire, flood, swollen river crossings, robbers, Indians and curious little children. And they're still here. Like the land," he mused, staring around with eyes full of pride. "The land will be here longer than any of us and very little changed despite our meddling."

She smiled. "You sound just like a rancher."

He turned. "I am a rancher."

"Not an oilman?"

He shrugged. "I used to think oil was the most important thing in the world. Until I got plenty of it. Now I don't know what's the most important thing anymore. My whole life seems to be upside down lately." He stared straight at her. "I was a happy man until you came along."

"You were a vegetable until I came along," she replied matter-of-factly. "You thought robbing people was all right."

"Why, you little devil," he said in a husky undertone, and his eyes went a glittering green. "You little devil!"

She laughed because there was as much mischief as threat in that look. She started running across the meadow, a picture in her full gray skirt and pretty pink blouse, with her dark hair gleaming in the sun. He ran after her in time to catch the colorful glimmer of something moving just in front of her in the grass.

"Mari!" he called out, his voice deep and cutting and full of authority. "Stop!"

She did, with one foot in midair, because he sounded so final. She didn't look down. With her inborn terror of snakes, she knew instinctively what he was warning her about.

"Don't move, baby," he breathed, stopping himself just within reach of a fallen limb from one of the oaks. "Don't move, don't breathe. It's all right. Just stand perfectly still...."

He moved with lightning speed picking up a heavy branch and swinging his arm down, slamming. There was a feverish rattling, like bacon sizzling in a pan, and then only a bloody, writhing, coiling mass on the ground.

She was numb with unexpressed terror, her eyes huge at the thing on the ground that, only seconds ago, could have taken her life. She started to speak, to tell him how grateful she was, when he caught her up in his arms and brought his hard mouth down bruisingly on hers.

She couldn't breathe, couldn't move. He was hurting her, and she hardly noticed. His mouth was telling her things words couldn't. That he was afraid for her, that he was glad she was safe, that he'd take care of her. She let him tell her that way, glad of his strength. Her arms curled around his broad shoulders, and she sighed under his warm, hungry mouth, savoring its rough ardor.

"My God," he whispered unsteadily, his mouth poised over hers, his eyes dark in a face that was pale under its tan, his breath rough. "My God, one more step and it would have had you!"

"I'm all right, thanks to you." She managed to smile through the shaking relief, her fingers traced his rough cheek, his mouth. "Thank you."

He lifted her against his body, as rugged as any frontier man would have been, his face mirroring pride and masculinity. "Thank me, then," he whispered, opening his mouth as he bent to her lips. "Thank me..."

She did, so hungrily that he had to put her away from him or let her feel how easily she could arouse him. He held her by the waist, breathing unsteadily, watching her flushed face.

"We agreed that wouldn't happen again," he said.

She nodded, searching his eyes.

"But the circumstances were . . . unusual," he continued.

"Yes," she whispered, her eyes falling to his hard mouth with languorous remembered pleasure. "Unusual."

"Stop looking at me like that, or it won't end with kisses," he threatened huskily. "You felt what you were doing to me."

She averted her eyes and moved away. Sometimes she forgot how experienced he was until he made a remark like that and emphasized it. She had to remember that she was just another woman. He felt responsible for her, that was why he'd reacted like that to the snake. It wasn't anything personal.

"Well, thanks for saving me," she said, folding her arms over her breasts as she walked back to the car, and carefully she avoided looking at the dead snake as she went.

"Watch where you put your feet, will you?" he asked from behind her. "One scare like that is enough."

Scare for which one of us? she wanted to ask. But she was too drained to say it. Her mouth ached for his. She could hardly bear to remember that she'd inflicted this torment on herself by letting him bring her out here. How was she going to bear days or weeks of it, of being near him and being vulnerable and having no hope at all for a future that included him?

Chapter Ten

Ward was quiet the rest of the way to the ranch, but he kept watching Mari and the way he did it was exciting. Once he reached across the space between them and found her hand. He kept it close in his until traffic in Ravine forced him to let go, and Mari found her heart doing spins.

She didn't know how to handle this new approach. She couldn't quite trust him yet, and she wasn't altogether sure that he didn't have some ulterior motive for bringing her back. After all, he wasn't hampered by emotions as she was.

Lillian came quickly out to meet them, looking healthy and fit and with a healed leg.

"Look here," she called to Mari and danced a jig. "How's that for an improvement?" She laughed gaily.

"Terrific!" Mari agreed. She ran forward to embrace the older woman warmly. "It's good to see you again."

"He's been horrible," Lillian whispered while Ward was getting the bag out of the car. "Just horrible. He moped around for days after you left and wouldn't eat at all."

"He should have foreclosed on somebody, then," Mari said matter-of-factly. "That would have cheered him up."

Lillian literally cackled. "Shame on you," she said with a laugh.

"What's all the humor about?" Ward asked as he joined them, his expression tight and mocking.

"Your appetite," Mari volunteered tongue in cheek.

Lillian had turned to go back inside. Ward leaned down, holding Mari's eyes. "You know more about that than most women do, honey," he said in a seductive undertone. "And if you aren't careful, you may learn even more."

"Don't hold your breath," she told him, rushing away before she fell under the spell of his mocking ardor.

"Where's Bud?" Ward asked as they entered the hall.

"Did somebody call me?" came a laughing voice from the study.

The young man who came out to greet them was a total surprise for Mari. She'd been expecting Ward's cousin to be near his own age, but Bud was much younger. He was in his late twenties, at a guess, and lithe and lean and handsome. He had Ward's swarthy complexion, but his eyes were brown instead of green and his hair was lighter than his cousin's. He was a striking man, especially in the leather and denim he was wearing.

"Have you been sneaking around after my bull again?" Ward demanded.

"Now, Cousin," Bud said soothingly, "how would I find him in there?" He jerked his hand toward the study and shuddered. "It would take a team of secretaries a week just to find the desk!"

"Speaking of secretaries," Ward said, "this is my new one. Marianne Raymond, this is Bud Jessup. My cousin."

"Ah, the much-talked-about niece," Bud murmured, winking at Mari. "Hello, Georgia peach. You sure do your home state proud."

Ward didn't like Bud's flirting. His eyes told his cousin so, which only made Bud more determined than ever.

"Thank you," Mari was saying, all smiles. "It's nice to meet you at last."

"Same here," Bud said warmly, moving forward.

"Here, son," Ward said, tossing the bag at him. "You can put that in the guest room, if you don't mind. I'm sure Mari would like to see the study." Before anybody could say anything else, Ward had taken Mari by the arm and propelled her none too gently into the study.

He slammed the door behind them, bristling with masculine pride, and turned to glare at her. "He's not marrying material," he told her immediately, "so don't take him too seriously. He just likes to flirt."

"Maybe I do, too," she began hotly.

He shook his head, moving slowly toward her. "Not you, honey," he replied. "You aren't the flirting kind. You're no butterfly. You're a little house wren, all feathered indignation and quick eyes and nesting instinct."

"You think you know a lot about me, don't you?" She faltered on the last word because she was backing away from him and almost fell over a chair. He kept coming, looming over her with threatening eyes and sheer size.

"I know more than I ever expected to," he agreed, coming closer. "Stop running. We both know it's me you really want, not Bud."

She drew herself up, glaring at him. "You conceited..."

He moved quickly, scooping her up in his arms, holding her off the floor, his eyes wavering between amusement and ardor. "Go ahead, finish it," he taunted.

She could have if he hadn't been so close. His breath was minty and it brushed her lips when he breathed, warm and moist. He made her feel feminine and vulnerable, and when she looked at his hard mouth, she wanted to kiss it.

"Your office," she swallowed, "is a mess."

"So am I," he whispered huskily, searching her eyes. "So is my life. Oh, God, I missed you!"

That confession was her undoing. She looked up at him and couldn't look away, and her heart felt like a runaway engine. Her head fell back onto his shoulder, and she watched him lower his dark head.

"Open your mouth when I put mine over it," he breathed against her lips. "Taste me..."

Her breath caught. She was reaching up, she could already feel the first tentative brushing of his warm lips when a knock at the door made them both jump.

He lifted his head with a jerky motion. "What is it?" he growled.

Mari, trembling in his arms, heard a male voice reply, "Lillian's got coffee and cake in the dining room, Cousin! Why don't you come and have some refreshment?"

"I'd like to have him, fricasseed," Ward muttered under his breath as Bud's laughing voice became dimmer along with his footsteps.

"I'd like some coffee," she said hesitantly even though she was still shaking with frustrated reaction and her voice wobbled.

He looked down into her eyes. "No, you wouldn't," he said huskily. "You'd like me. And I'd like you, right there on that long sofa where we almost made love the first time. And if it hadn't been for my meddling, jealous cousin, that's where we'd be right now!"

He put her down abruptly and moved away. "Come on, we'll have coffee." He stopped at the door with his hand on the knob. "For now," he added softly. "But one day, Marianne, we'll have each other. Because one day neither one of us is going to be able to stop."

She couldn't look at him. She couldn't even manage a defiant stare. It was the truth. She'd been crazy to come here, but there was no one to blame but herself.

From that first meeting, Cousin Bud seemed determined to drive Ward absolutely crazy. He didn't leave Mari alone with the older man for a second if he could help it. He found excuse after excuse to come into the office when she was typing things for Ward, and if she ever had to find Ward to ask a question, Bud would find them before they said two words to each other. Mari wondered if it might just be mischief on Bud's part, but Ward treated the situation as if he had a rival.

That in itself was amazing. Ward seemed possessive now, frankly covetous whenever Mari was near him. He shared things with her. Things about the ranch, about his plans for it, the hard work that had gone into its success. When he came home late in the evening, it was to Mari that he went, seeking her out wherever she might be, to ask for coffee or a sandwich or a slice of cake. Lillian took this new attitude with open delight, glad to have her former position usurped when she saw the way he was looking at her puzzled niece.

Bud usually managed to weasel in, of course, but there eventually came a night when he had business out of town. Ward came in about eight o'clock, covered in dust and half-starved.

"I sure could use a couple of sandwiches, honey," he told Mari gently, pausing in the living room doorway. Lillian had gone to bed, and curled up on the sofa in her jeans and a yellow tank top, Mari was watching the credits roll after an entertainment special.

"Of course," she said eagerly and got up without bothering to look for her shoes.

He was even taller when she was barefoot, and he seemed amused by her lack of footwear.

"You look like a country girl," he remarked as she passed close by him, feeling the warmth of his big body.

"I feel like a country girl," she said with a pert smile. "Come on, big man, I'll feed you."

"How about some coffee to go with it?" he added as he followed her down the hall into the spacious kitchen.

"Easier done than said," she told him. She flicked the on switch of the small coffee machine, grinning at him when it started to perk. "I had it fixed and ready to start."

"Reading my mind already?" he teased. He pulled out a chair and sat down, sprawling with a huge stretch before he put his long legs out and rested his booted feet in another chair. "The days are getting longer, or I'm getting older," he said with a yawn. "I guess if I keep up this pace, before long you'll be pushing me around in a wheelchair."

"Not you," she said with loving amusement. "You're not the type to give up and get old before your time. You'll still be chasing women when you're eighty-five."

He sobered with amazing rapidity, his green eyes narrowing in his handsome face as he studied her graceful movements around the kitchen. "Suppose I told you that you're the only woman I'll want to chase when I'm eighty-five, Marianne?" he asked gently.

Her heart leaped, but she wasn't giving in to it that easily. He'd already come too close once and hurt her. She'd been deliberately keeping things light since she'd come back to the ranch, and she wasn't going to be trapped now.

She laughed. "Oh, I guess I'd be flattered."

"Only flattered?" he mused.

She finished making the sandwiches and put them down on the table. "By that time I expect to be a grandmother many times over,'' she informed him as she went back to pour the coffee. "And I think my husband might object."

He didn't like thinking about Marianne with a husband. His face darkened. He turned his attention to the sandwiches and began to eat.

"I have to go over to Ty Wade's place tomorrow," he murmured. "Want to come and meet Erin and the babies?"

She caught her breath. "Me? But won't I be in the way if you're going to talk business?"

He shook his head, holding her soft blue eyes. "You'll never be in my way, sweetheart," he said with something very much like tenderness in his deep voice. "Not ever."

She smiled at him. The way he was looking at her made her feel trembly all over. He was weaving subtle webs around her, but without the wild passion he'd shown her at the beginning of their turbulent relationship. This was new and different. While part of her was afraid to trust it, another part was hungry for it and for him.

"How about it?" he asked, forcing himself to go slow, not to rush her. He'd already had to face the fact that he wasn't going to be able to let her go. Now it was a question of making her see that he didn't have ulterior motives, and she was as hard to trust as he was.

"I'd like to meet Mrs. Wade," she said after a minute. "She sounds like quite a lady."

He laughed under his breath. "If you'd known Ty before she came along, you'd think she was quite a lady," he agreed with a grin. "It took one special woman to calm down that cougar. You'll see what I mean tomorrow."

The next afternoon Mari climbed into the Chrysler beside Ward for the trip over to the Wades' place. Ward was wearing slacks with a striped, open-necked green shirt, and she had on a pretty green pantsuit with a gaily striped sleeveless blouse. He'd grinned when he noticed that their stripes matched.

Erin Wade opened the door, a picture in a gaily flowing lavender caftan. She looked as if she smiled a lot, and she was obviously a beauty when she was made up, with her long black hair and pretty green eyes. But she wasn't wearing makeup. She looked like a country girl, clean and fresh.

"Hello!" she said enthusiastically. "I'm glad you brought her, Ward. Hello, I'm Erin, and you have to be Marianne. Come in and see my boys!"

"I'm glad to meet you, too." Marianne grinned. "I've heard legends about you already."

"Have you, really?" Erin laughed. She was beautiful even without makeup, Marianne thought, the kind of beauty that comes from deep within and makes even homely women bright and lovely when it shows. "Well, Ty and I got off to a bad start, but we've come a long way in very little time. I don't think he has many regrets about getting married. Not even with twin boys."

"I can just see him now, changing a diaper." Ward chuckled.

Erin's green eyes widened. "But you can," she said. "Follow me."

Sure enough, there he was, changing a diaper. It looked so touching, the big, tough rancher Marianne had met before bending over that tiny, smiling, kicking baby on the changing table in a bedroom decorated with teddy bear wallpaper and mobiles.

"Oh, hello, Jessup," he murmured, glancing over his shoulder as he put the last piece of adhesive in place around the baby's fat middle. "Matthew was wet, I was just changing him," he told Erin. He glanced toward a playpen, where another baby was standing on unsteady little fat legs with both chubby hands on the rail, biting delightedly on the plastic edging. "Jason's hungry, I think. He's been trying to eat the playpen for the past five minutes."

"He's teething," Erin said, leaning over to pick him up and cuddle him while he cooed and patted her shoulder and chanted, "Da, Da, Da, Da."

Ty grinned mockingly at his frowning wife. "She hates that," he told the guests. "Most babies say Mama first. Both of them call me instead of her."

"Don't gloat." Erin stuck her tongue out at him. "You just remember who got up with them last night and let you sleep."

He winked at her, with torrents of love pouring on her from his light eyes. Marianne glanced up at Ward and found him watching her with the oddest look on his face. His green eyes went slowly down to her flat stomach and back up again, and she blushed because she knew what he was thinking. *Exactly* what he was thinking. She could read it in the sudden flare of his eyes, in the set of his face. She went hot all over with the unexpected passion that boiled up so suddenly and had to turn away to get herself under control again.

"How about some coffee?" Erin asked them, handing Jason to his dad. "Ward, if you'll bring the playpen, the boys can come with us."

Ward, to his credit, tried to figure out how the device folded up, but he couldn't seem to fathom it. Ty chuckled. "Here, if Marianne will hold the boys, I'll do it."

"Surely!" She took them, cooing to them both, loving their little chubby smiling faces and the way they tried to feel every inch of her face and hair as she carried them into the living room.

"Oh, how sweet," she cooed, kissing fat cheeks and heads that had just a smattering of hair. The twins had light eyes like their father, but they were green.

"Thank God they both take after Erin and not me," Ty said with a sigh as he set up the playpen and took the boys from Marianne to put them back in.

"You're not that bad," Ward remarked, cocking his head. "I've seen uglier cactus plants, in fact."

Ty glared at him. "If you want that second damned lease, you'd better clean up your act, Jessup."

Ward grinned. "Can I help it if you go asking for insults?"

"Watch it," Ty muttered, turning back to help Erin with the coffee service.

The men talked business, and Marianne and Erin talked babies and clothes and fashion. It was the most enjoyable afternoon Marianne had spent in a long time and getting to cuddle the babies was a bonus. She was reluctant to leave.

"Ward, you'll have to bring her back to see me," Erin insisted. "I don't have much company, and I do love to talk clothes."

"I will," Ward promised. He shook hands with Ty, and they said their goodbyes. As they drove away, Ty had one lean arm around Erin, looking as if he were part of her.

"That marriage will outlast this ranch," she murmured, watching the landscape turn gray with a sudden shower. It seemed chilly in the car with that wetness beating on the hood and windshield. "They seem so happy."

"They are," he agreed. He glanced at her and slowly pulled the truck off onto one of the farm roads, pulling up under a huge live oak tree before cutting the engine. "Would you like to guess why I stopped?" he asked, his voice slow and tender as he looked at her. "Or do you know?"

Chapter Eleven

No, Marianne thought, she didn't really have to wonder why he'd parked the car. His face gave her the answer. So did the heavy, quick rise and fall of his chest under the green-striped shirt. He looked so handsome that she could hardly take her eyes off him, and the sheer arrogance in his narrowed eyes was intimidating.

But she wasn't sure she wanted a sweet interlude with him. Her defenses were weak enough already. Suppose he insisted? Could she resist him if she let herself fall in that heady trap?

"I don't think this is a good idea," she began as he unfastened his seat belt and then hers.

"Don't you?" he asked. "Even after the way you went scarlet when I stared at your waistline in the twins' room? You knew what I was thinking, Marianne," he whispered, reaching for her. "You knew."

He lifted her across him, finding her mouth even as he eased her down against his arm with her head at the window. Outside rain was streaming down the glass, making a quick tattoo on the hood and the roof, as driving as the passion that began to take over Mari's blood.

He bit at her soft lips, tender little nips that made her want him. His big hand smoothed over her blouse, under it, finding the softness of her breast in its silky casing.

"Lie still," he whispered when her body jerked under that gentle probing. "It's been a long time since we've enjoyed each other like this. Too long."

He kissed her wide eyes shut and found the catch that bared her to his warm, hard fingers. She couldn't let this happen, she kept telling herself. It was just a game to him, he didn't mean it. Any minute now he was going to let that seat down and turn her in his arms....

With a wounded cry she pulled out of his arms so suddenly that he was startled into releasing her. She fumbled the door open, deaf to his sharp exclamation, and ran out into the rain.

The long grass beat against her slacks as she ran, not really sure why she was running or where she was trying to go. Seconds later it didn't matter because he'd caught her and dragged her down onto the ground in the wet grass with him.

"Never run from a hunter," he breathed roughly, turning her under him as he found her mouth with his. The rain beat down on them, drenching them, making their bodies as supple as silk-covered saplings, binding them as if there had been no fabric at all in the way.

It was new and exciting to lie like this, to kiss like this, feeling the warm, twisting motions of Ward's big body against hers, their clothes wet and their skin sensitive.

"We might as well have no clothes on at all," he breathed into her open, welcoming mouth, his voice husky with passion. "I can feel you. All of you."

His hands were sliding down her body now, exploring, experiencing her through the wet thinness of fabric, and it was like feeling his hands on her skin.

She moaned as she slid her own hands against his hard-muscled back, his chest, his hips. She didn't understand what was happening, how this passion had crept up on her. But she was lost now, helpless. He could do anything he liked, and she couldn't stop him. She was on fire despite the drenching rain, reaching up toward him, sliding her wet body against his in the silence of the meadow with the rain slicking their hair as it slicked their skin.

He eased his full weight onto her, devouring her mouth with his. His hands smoothed under her back, sensuously pressing her up against him.

Her body throbbed, burned, with the expertness of his movements. Yes, he knew what to do and how to do it. He knew... too much!

"Tell me to stop," he challenged under his breath, probing her lips with his tongue. "Tell me to let you go. I dare you."

"I can't," she whimpered, and her eyes stung with tears as she clung to his broad, wet shoulders. "I want you. Oh, I want you!"

His lips were all over her face. Tender, seeking, gentling, his breath catching in his throat at her devastating submission. He was trembling all over with the force of this new sensation. He wanted to protect her. Devour her. Warm her. Hold her until he died, just like this.

His big hands framed her face as he touched it softly with his lips. "I want to give you a baby," he whispered shakily. "That's what you saw in my face at Wade's, and it made you go red all over. You saw, didn't you?"

"Yes," she whispered back, her body trembling.

He searched her wide eyes, his own blazing with hunger. "I could take you, Marianne," he said very quietly. "Right here. Right now. I could have you, and no one would see us or hear us."

She swallowed, closing her eyes. Defeated. She knew that. She could feel how capable he was of it, and her body trembled under his fierce arousal. She wanted him, too. She loved him more than her honor.

"Yes," she whispered, so softly that he could barely hear.

He didn't move. He seemed to stop breathing. She opened her eyes and saw his face above her, filled with such frank exultation that she blinked incomprehensibly.

"Baby," he breathed softly, bending. He kissed her with such aching tenderness that her eyes stung, tasting her lips, smoothing his lips over her cheeks, her forehead, her nose, her eyes. "Baby, sweet, sweet baby. You taste of roses and gardenias, and I could lie here doing this for all my life."

That didn't sound like uncontrollable passion. It didn't even sound like lust. She reached up and touched his face, his chin.

He kissed the palm of her hand, smiling down at her through wildly exciting shudders. "Do you know how wet you are?" he said with a gentle smile, glancing down at her blouse, which was plastered against breasts that no longer had the shelter of a bra.

"So are you," she replied unsteadily and managed to smile back. What good was pride now when she'd offered herself to him?

He touched her taut nipples through the cloth. "No more embarrassment?" he asked quietly.

"You know what I look like," she whispered.

"Yes." He opened her blouse, no longer interested in the rain that had slowed to a sprinkle, and his eyes feasted on her soft skin before he bent and tasted it warmly with his mouth.

Mari lifted softly toward his lips, savoring their sweet touch, so much a part of him that nothing seemed wrong anymore.

"You're so sweet," he whispered. He drew his cheek across her breasts, his eyes closed, savoring her. "For the rest of my life, I'll never touch another woman like this. I'll never lie with another woman, taste another woman, want another woman."

That was how she felt, too, about other men. She closed her eyes, smoothing his wet hair as he brushed his mouth over her pulsating, trembling body. She loved him so much. If this was all he could give her, it would be enough. Fidelity would do. She couldn't leave him again.

"I'll never want another man," she replied quietly.

He laid his cool cheek against her and sighed, holding her as she held him, with the wind blowing softly and the rain coming down like droplets of silk over them.

Then he moved away, gently rearranging her disheveled clothing. He brushed back her damp hair, kissed her tenderly one last time and carried her in his arms back to the car with her face pressed wetly into his warm throat.

"The car," she faltered. "We'll get the seats wet."

"Hush, baby," he whispered, brushing a kiss against her soft mouth as he put her into the passenger seat and fastened her seat belt. "It doesn't matter. Nothing matters now."

He got in beside her, found her warm hand and linked her fingers with his. He managed to start the car and drive it all the way home with one free hand.

Lillian took one look at them, and her eyebrows shot up.

"Not one word," Ward cautioned as he led Marianne inside. "Not one single word."

Lillian sighed. "Well, at least now you're getting wet together," she murmured with a smile as she wandered back toward the kitchen. "I guess that's better than mildewing alone."

Marianne smiled gently at Ward and went upstairs to change her clothing. He disappeared a few minutes later after an urgent telephone call and drove off by himself with only a wink and a smile for Mari. She walked around in a daze, dodging Lillian's hushed questions, waiting for him to come home. But when bedtime came, he still wasn't back.

Mari went up to her room and paced the floor, worrying, wondering what to do. She couldn't leave, not after this afternoon. He wanted her and she wanted him. Maybe he couldn't offer her marriage, but she'd just settle for what he could give her. He had to care a little. And she loved him enough for both of them.

Why hadn't he gone ahead, she wondered, when he had the chance this afternoon? Why had he stopped? Was he just giving her time to make up her mind, to be sure she could accept him this way? That had to be it. Well, it was now or never.

She put on her one seductive gown, a pretty white one with lots of lace and long elegant sleeves. She brushed out her dark hair until it was smooth and silky and dabbed on perfume. Then, looking in the mirror, she stared into her troubled blue eyes and assured herself that she was doing the right thing.

An hour later she heard Ward drive up. He came up the stairs, pausing at her door. Seconds later he started away, but Mari was already on her feet. She opened the door breathlessly and looked up at him.

He was wearing a dark pair of slacks with a patterned gray shirt open at the throat. His creamy dress Stetson was held in one hand. The other worried his hair. He stared at Mari with eyes that devoured her.

"Dangerous, baby, wearing something like that in front of me," he said softly and smiled.

She swallowed her pride. "I want you," she whispered shakily.

He smiled down at her. "I know. I want you, too."

She opened the door a little wider, her hands unsteady.

He cocked an eyebrow. "Is that an invitation to be seduced?"

She swallowed again. "I don't think I quite know how to seduce you. So I think you'll have to seduce me."

His smile widened. "What about precautions, little temptress?"

She blushed to her toes. She hadn't expected resistance. "Well," she began, peeking up at him, "can't you take care of that?"

His white teeth showed under his lips. "No."

Her blush deepened. "Oh."

He tossed his hat onto the hall table and went inside the room, gently closing the door behind him. "Now, come here." He drew her in front of him, holding her by both shoulders, his face gentle and almost loving. "What do you think I want, Marianne?"

"You've made what you want pretty obvious," she replied sadly.

"What you think I want," he corrected. His eyes went over her like hands, enjoying the exciting glimpses of her silky skin that he was getting through the gossamer-thin fabric of her gown. "And you're right about that. I could make a banquet of you in bed. But not tonight."

She turned her head a bit, looking up at him. "Are you too tired?" she asked innocently.

He grinned. "Nope."

None of this was getting through to her. "I don't understand," she said softly.

"Yes, I gathered that." He reached into his pocket and drew out a box. It was black and velvety and small. He opened it and handed it to her.

The ring was a diamond. A big, beautiful diamond in a setting with lots of little diamonds in rows encircling the large stone. Beside it was a smaller, thinner matching diamond band.

"It's an engagement ring," he explained. "It goes on the third finger of your left hand, and at the wedding I'll put the smaller one on your finger beside it."

She was hearing things. Surely she was! But the ring looked real. She couldn't stop staring at it.

"You don't want to get married," she told him patiently, her eyes big and soft. "You hate ties. You hate women. They're all deceitful and greedy."

He traced a slow, sensuous pattern down her silky cheek, smiling softly. "I want to get married," he said. "I want you to share your life with me."

It was the way he put it. She burst into tears. They rolled down her cheeks in a torrent, a sob broke from her throat. He became a big, handsome blur.

"Now, now," he murmured gently. He bent to kiss the tears away. "It's all right."

"You want to marry me?" she whispered unsteadily.

"Yes," he said, smiling.

"Really?"

"Really." He brushed back her hair, his green eyes possessive on her oval face. "I'd be a fool to let go of a woman who loves me as much as you do."

She froze in place. Was he fishing? Was he guessing? Did he know? If he did, how?

"You told me this afternoon," he said gently, pulling her to him. "You offered yourself to me with no strings. You'd never make an offer like that to a man you didn't love desperately. I knew it. And that's why I stopped. It would have been cheap, somehow, to have our first time on the ground without doing things properly."

"But... but..." she began, trying to find the right words.

"But how do I feel?" he probed softly, touching her lips with a faintly unsteady index finger. "Don't you know?"

His eyes were telling her. His whole face was telling her. But despite her rising excitement, she had to have it all. The words, too.

"Please tell me," she whispered.

He framed her face and lifted it to his darkening eyes, to his firm, hungry mouth. "I love you, Marianne," he breathed against her mouth as he took it. "And this is how much..."

It took him a long time to show her how much. When he was through, they were lying on the bed with her gown down to her waist, and he looked as if he were going to die trying to stop himself from going the whole way. Fortunately, or unfortunately, Lillian had guessed what was going on and was trying to knock the door down.

"It's bedtime, boss," she called loudly. "It's late. She's a growing girl. Needs her sleep!"

"Oh, no, that's not what I need at all," Marianne said with such tender frustration that Ward laughed through his own shuddering need.

"Okay, aunt-to-be," he called back. "Give me a minute to say good-night and I'll be right out."

"You're getting married?" Lillian shouted gleefully.

"That's about the size of it," he answered, smiling down at Mari. "Aren't you just overjoyed with your meddling now?"

"Overjoyed doesn't cover it," Lillian agreed. "Now, speaking as your future aunt-in-law, come out of there! Or wait until supper tomorrow night and see if you get fed! We're going to do this thing right!"

"I was just about to do this thing right," he whispered to Mari, his eyes softly mocking. "Wasn't I?"

"Yes." She laughed. "But we can't admit that."

"We can't?" He sighed. "I guess not."

He got up reluctantly, rebuttoning the shirt that her darting fingers had opened over a chest that was aching for her hands. "Pretty thing," he murmured, watching her pull the gown up again.

"You're pretty, too, so there," she teased.

"Are you coming out, or am I coming in?" Lillian was sounding militant.

Ward glowered at the door. "Can't I even have a minute to say good-night?"

"You've been saying good-night for thirty minutes already, and that's enough," she informed him. "I'm counting! One, two, three . . ."

She was counting loudly. Ward sighed at Mari. "Good night, baby," he said reluctantly.

She blew him a kiss. "Good night, my darling."

He took one last look and opened the door on ". . . Fourteen!"

Mari laid back against the pillows, listening to the pleasant murmur of voices outside the door as she stared at her ring.

"Congratulations and good night, dear!" Aunt Lillian called.

"Good night and thank you!" Mari called back.

"Oh, you're very welcome!" Ward piped in.

"Get out of here," Lillian muttered, pushing him down the hall.

Alone in her room Mari was trying to convince herself that she wasn't dreaming. It was the hardest thing she'd ever done. He was hers. They were going to be married. They were going to live together and love each other and have children together. She closed her eyes reluctantly, tingling all over with the first stirrings of possession.

Chapter Twelve

The next morning Mari was sure it had all been a beautiful dream until she looked at the ring on her finger. When she went down to breakfast, she found a new, different Ward waiting for her.

He went to her without hesitation, bending to brush a tender kiss against her smiling lips.

"It was real after all," he murmured, his green eyes approving her cool blue knit sundress. "I thought I might have dreamed it."

"So did I," she confessed. Her hands smoothed hesitantly over the hard, warm muscles of his chest. It felt wonderful to be able to do that, to feel so much a part of him that it no longer was forbidden to touch him, to look at him too long. "Are you really mine now?" she murmured aloud.

"Until I die," he promised, bringing her close against him. He sighed into her hair, rocking her against the powerful muscles of his body. "I never thought this would happen. I didn't think I'd ever be able to love or trust a woman again after Caroline. And then you came along, pushing me into indoor streams, backing me into corners about my business sense, haunting me with your soft innocence. You got under my skin that first night. I've spent the rest of the time trying to convince myself that I was still free when I knew all along that I was hopelessly in love with you."

She burrowed closer, tingling all over at that sweet, possessive note in his deep voice. "I was so miserable in Atlanta," she confessed. "I missed you every single day. I tried to get used to being alone."

"I shouldn't have propositioned you," he said with a sigh, lifting his head to search her eyes with his. "But I still thought I could stop short of a commitment. God knows how I'd have coped with the conscience I didn't even have until you came along. Every time Ty Wade was mentioned, I got my back up, thinking how he'd changed." He touched her face with wonder in his whole look. "And now I know how and why, and I think he must have felt this way with his Erin when he realized what he felt for her."

She sighed softly, loving him with her eyes. "I know I felt like part of me was missing when I left here. It didn't get any better, either."

"Why do you think I came after you?" he murmured dryly. "I couldn't stand it here without you. Not that I admitted that to myself in any great rush. Not until that rattler almost got you, and I had to face it. If anything had happened to you, I wouldn't have wanted to live," he added on a deep, husky note that tugged at her heart.

"I feel that way, too," she whispered, searching his eyes. "Can we really get married?"

"Yes," he whispered back, bending his head down. "And live together and sleep together and raise a family together..."

Her lips opened for him, welcoming and warm, just for a few seconds before Lillian came in with breakfast and knowing grins. Ward glowered at her.

"All your fault," he told her. "I could have gone on for years living like a timber wolf but for you."

"No need to thank me," she said with a big smile. "You're welcome."

She vanished back into the kitchen, laughing, as Ward led Mari to the table, shaking his head with an exasperated chuckle.

The wedding was a week later, and old Mrs. Jessup and Belinda had come home just for the occasion. They sat on either side of Lillian, who was beaming.

"Nice girl," Belinda whispered. "She'll make a new man of him."

"I think she has already." Old Mrs. Jessup grinned. "Spirited little thing. I like her, too."

"I always did," Lillian said smugly. "Good thing I saw the shape he was getting in and brought her out here. I knew they'd be good for each other."

"It isn't nice to gloat," Belinda reminded her.

"Amen," Mrs. Jessup harrumphed. "Don't I seem to remember that you introduced that Caroline creature to him in the first place?"

Lillian was horrified. "That wasn't me! That was Belinda!"

Mrs. Jessup's eyes widened as she glared past Lillian at the restless young woman on the other side. "Did you?"

"It was an accident," Belinda muttered. "I meant to introduce her to Bob Whitman, to get even for jilting me. Ward kind of got in the way. I never meant for her to go after my poor brother."

"It's all in the past now anyway," Lillian said, making peace. "He's got the right girl, now. Everything will be fine."

"Yes." Old Mrs. Jessup sighed, glancing past Lillian again. "If only Belinda would settle down. She goes from boyfriend to boyfriend, but she never seems to get serious."

Lillian pursed her lips, following the older woman's gaze to Belinda, who was sighing over Mari's wedding gown as she walked down the aisle accompanied by the organ music. She'd have to see what she could do....

The wedding ceremony was short and beautiful. Mari thought she'd never seen a man as handsome as her Ward, and when the minister pronounced them husband and wife, she cried softly until Ward kissed away the tears.

Lillian, not Belinda, caught the wedding bouquet and blushed like a schoolgirl when everyone giggled. The guests threw rice and waved them off, and Mari caught a glimpse of tall, slender Ty Wade with his Erin just on the fringe of the guests.

"Alone at last." Ward grinned, glancing at her.

"I thought they'd never leave," she agreed with a wistful sigh. "Where are we going? I didn't even ask."

"Tahiti," he said with a slow smile. "I booked tickets the day after you said yes. We're flying out of San Antonio early tomorrow morning."

"What about tonight?" she asked curiously and flushed at the look on his face.

"Let me worry about tonight," he murmured softly.

He held her hand as he drove, and an hour later he drove up to a huge, expensive hotel in the city.

He'd reserved the bridal suite, and it was the most incredible sight Mari had ever seen. The bed was huge, dominating the bedroom. She stood in the doorway just staring at it while Ward paid the bellhop and locked the door.

"It's huge," she whispered.

"And strategically placed, did you notice?" he murmured with a laugh, suddenly lifting her clear of the floor in her neat white linen traveling suit.

"Yes, I did notice," she said huskily, clinging to him. "You looked so handsome."

"You looked so lovely." He bent to her mouth and started walking. "I love you to distraction, did I tell you?"

"Several times."

"I hope you won't mind hearing it again frequently for the next hour or so," he murmured against her eager mouth and laid her gently down on the bed.

Mari had expected ardor and passion, and she had experienced a tiny measure of apprehension. But he made it so natural, so easy. She relaxed even as he began to undress her, his hands and mouth so deeply imprinted on her memory that she accepted them without the faintest protest.

"This is familiar territory for us, isn't it?" he breathed as he moved back beside her after stripping off his own clothing. "Up to this point, at least," he added at her rapt, faintly shocked visual exploration of him. "But you know how it feels to have my eyes and my hands and my mouth on you. You know that I won't hurt you. That there's nothing to be afraid of."

She looked back up into his eyes. "I couldn't be afraid of you."

"I won't lose control right away," he promised, bending slowly to her mouth. "Give yourself to me now, Mari. Remember how it was on the ground, with the rain soaking us, and give yourself to me the way you offered then.''

She felt all over again the pelting rain, the sweetness of his hands, the wild fever of his mouth claiming hers in the silence of the meadow. She reached up to him, suddenly on fire with the unaccustomed removal of all barriers, physical and moral, and she gave herself with an abandon that frankly startled him.

''Shhh,'' she whispered when he tried to draw back at the last minute, to make it gentle, to keep from hurting her. But she reached up to his hips and softly drew them down again, lifting, and a tiny gasp was the only sound she made as she coaxed his mouth back to hers. ''Now,'' she breathed into his devouring lips. ''Now, now...''

''Mari,'' he groaned. His body surged against hers, his arms became painfully strong, his hands biting into her hips, his mouth trembling as his body trembled. He was part of her. She was part of him. Locking together, loving, linking...

''Mari!''

She went with him on a journey as exquisitely sweet as it was incredibly intimate, yielding to his strength, letting him guide her, letting him teach her. She used muscles she hadn't realized she possessed, she whispered things to him that would shock her later. She wound herself around him and lost all her inhibitions in a wild, fierce joining that ripped the veil of mystery from the sweetest expression of shared love. Even the first time it was still a kind of pleasure that she hadn't known existed.

She stretched lazily, contentedly, and snuggled close to him under the lightweight sheet, nuzzling against his matted chest with a face radiant with fulfillment.

"I love you," he said softly as if the words still awed him. He smoothed her hair tenderly. "I always will."

"I love you just as much." She smoothed her hand over his chest. "Cousin Bud wasn't at the wedding." She frowned. Her mind had been curiously absent for a week. She lifted up. "Ward, Bud hasn't been at the house!"

"Not for a week," he agreed complacently, grinning. "Not since that day I took you to see Ty and Erin."

"But this is horrible! I didn't notice!"

"That's all right, sweetheart, I don't mind," he said, drawing her back down.

"Where is he?"

"Oh, I sent him on a little trip," he murmured at her temple. "I told him that bull he wanted was out to stud at a cattle ranch in Montana, and he went up there looking."

"Looking?" she frowned.

"Well, honey, I didn't exactly tell him which ranch it was on. Just the state. There are a lot of ranches in Montana."

"You devil!" she accused, digging him in the ribs.

He pulled her over him, smiling from ear to ear. "All's fair, don't they say? Cousin Bud always did cramp my style.'' He coaxed her mouth down to his and kissed it softly. ''I didn't want him on my case until I had you safely married to me.''

''You couldn't have been jealous?''

''I've always been jealous,'' he confessed, tugging a strand of her hair playfully. ''You were mine. I didn't want him trying to cut me out. Don't worry, he'll figure it out eventually.''

''I shouldn't ask,'' she mumbled. ''Figure what out?''

''That the bull is still on my ranch, just where I had him all along.''

''What are you going to tell Cousin Bud?''

''That I misplaced him,'' he said easily. ''Don't worry, he'll believe me. After all, he didn't think I was serious about you, either, and look how I fooled him!''

She would have said something else, but he was already rolling her over on the big bed and kissing the breath out of her. So she just closed her eyes and kissed him back. Outside it was raining softly, and Mari thought she'd never heard a sweeter sound.

* * * * *

NORA ROBERTS

Love has a language all its own, and for centuries, flowers have symbolized love's finest expression. Discover the language of flowers—and love—in this romantic collection of 48 favorite books by bestselling author Nora Roberts.

Two titles are available each month at your favorite retail outlet.

In August, look for:

Tempting Fate, **Volume #13**
From this Day, **Volume #14**

In September, look for:

All the Possibilities, **Volume #15**
The Heart's Victory, **Volume #16**

THE LANGUAGE of LOVE

Collect all 48 titles
and become fluent in

Silhouette®